IVAN NEJ—*He was the only man Stalin could trust, an evil genius recalled from exile to settle an old debt—with Anna Ragosina, the devil in angel skin, at his side.*

PRINCE PETER BORODIN—*No price was too great to bring down Stalin: his family, his honor, his life.*

DIANA HAYMAN—*The headstrong heiress would meet her match in Paris—and test her mettle in the lower depths of Moscow's infamous Lubianka prison.*

ROBERT LOUNG—*The unwitting tool of Prince Peter, he would be the irresistible lure to lead Diana into a death trap in the name of love.*

FORTUNE AND FURY

By Leslie Arlen
from Jove

THE BORODINS

BOOK I: LOVE AND HONOR
BOOK II: WAR AND PASSION
BOOK III: FATE AND DREAMS
BOOK IV: HOPE AND GLORY
BOOK V: RAGE AND DESIRE
BOOK VI: FORTUNE AND FURY

THE BORODINS

BOOK VI

FORTUNE and FURY

LESLIE ARLEN

A JOVE BOOK

FORTUNE AND FURY

A Jove book/published by arrangement with
the author

PRINTING HISTORY
Jove edition/August 1984

For information address: The Berkley Publishing Group,
200 Madison Avenue, New York, N.Y. 10016

ISBN: 0-515-07869-7

Jove books are published by The Berkley Publishing Group,
200 Madison Avenue, New York, N.Y. 10016.

PRINTED IN THE UNITED STATES OF AMERICA

FORTUNE and FURY

Chapter 1

THE DEPARTURE LOUNGE AT IDLEWILD INTERNATIONAL AIRport was crowded; SAS Flight Number 912, bound for Gander, Prestwick, and Copenhagen, for connections to Moscow, was about to board. Few of the passengers would go on to the Soviet Union, for in early 1952 the Cold War was at its peak. A great deal had happened in the six years since the United States and its allies Russia, Great Britain, France, and the Republic of China had jointly claimed victory over the Fascist powers of Nazi Germany and Imperial Japan. In those six years, China had also turned to Communism, while Soviet Russia and its satellites had closed ranks in aggressive opposition to the wayward freedoms permitted by the democracies, to project an ironclad national discipline that rejected all notions of individual rights as against those of the state. And for them all, even states' rights were interpreted by one man, Party Chairman Joseph Stalin.

Those Americans who wished to investigate the socialist dictatorship of Russia, and the far fewer numbers who managed to obtain visas to do so, knew they were regarded by their fellows either as intrepid explorers or possible traitors.

But even the Russian passengers were agitated. They could feel the tension among the flight attendants and the clerks, and the departure had already been delayed half an hour without explanations. But now at last something was happening. A group of topcoated and slouch-hatted men hurried into the lounge, nodded to the clerks, and marched to the four-engined aircraft without waiting for a summons.

As soon as the late arrivals were aboard, the flight was called. But by this time a newspaper reporter, who had been sleepily slurping his coffee in a far corner near the loading door, had put down his cup, staring after the crowd, and then flipped open a pocket photo album. It contained a dozen head shots, one of each of the top twelve Soviet diplomats stationed in the United States, but the reporter did not have to look beyond the first. It was that of a man with softly rounded features and a quiet smile, graying hair, and a slightly tired expression, but a face which at the same time projected an easy, confident authority, reflected in the way he had boarded the aircraft, which had clearly been kept waiting for him.

The reporter ran for the telephone booth in the corridor and dialed the main office of Hayman Newspapers Incorporated. "Front desk," he said. "Get this: Veteran Soviet Commissar Michael Nikolaievich Nej, Russian ambassador to the United Nations, tonight boarded SAS Flight 912 for Copenhagen and Moscow. Read that back."

He listened. "Sure, I know there was no prior notice of his leaving the country," he said. "That's what's important, don't you think? Someone spotted the embassy limo leaving Manhattan, so they sent me out here to see. No, his wife and daughter weren't along. Mr. Hayman will probably want to see that item, first thing tomorrow."

"Hm," remarked George Hayman, Jr., leaning back in his chair and gazing at the sheet of paper he held in his hand. It was one of a number that awaited him on his desk every morning. Geoıge Hayman, Jr., had inherited his habits, as he had inherited his vast newspaper empire, from his father. He even looked like his father, his face long and serious, his brown eyes pensive; his height, two inches over six feet, was equally inherited from his mother's Borodin ancestors. Only forty, the son of a multimillionaire, and already the acknowledged head of the greatest publishing empire in the United States—and that meant the world—he revealed no outward signs that he was also the son of a Russian princess, the great-grandson of the premier prince in all Russia. Indeed, he chose to forget these things as far as possible, as his family's history was so intimately bound up in the horrific events that had attended the downfall of the Romanovs, the end of the tsars. But Russia—having, since the decline of Great Britain and France and the defeat of Germany and Japan, become the only possible rival to the United States for world supremacy, and having recently exploded its own atomic bomb to declare that it *was* the military equal even of America—had to remain of prime interest to him. So if he was content, as his father had been, to leave the day-to-day running of the newspapers to his very competent editors, he also continued his father's habit of having the daily news items placed on his desk in two piles, one for the rest of the world and one for Russia. And like his father, he invariably read the Russian pile first.

Besides, Michael Nej, to George Hayman, Jr., was far more than a veteran Communist leader—*the* veteran Communist leader, in fact, as his friendship with Lenin dated back even before Stalin's—who was also Soviet ambassador to the United Nations, and who happened to be behaving rather oddly. Even more important, in the unthinkable upheaval of that far-off revolution, when the highest had had to turn to the lowest merely for survival, Michael had become, briefly, the lover of George Junior's own mother, Princess Ilona. Out of that tempestuous affair had been born George's older half-brother John, who had been raised as a Hayman. Michael Nej was a name no Hayman could see without stopping to think.

He looked up. "I think you'd better get the old man for me, Frances," he told his secretary.

"I have him on the line, Mr. Hayman." The young woman had been with Hayman Newspapers Incorporated for several years.

"Morning, Dad," George junior said. "Didn't get you out of bed, I hope."

"No, but you got me off the third tee," his father replied. George Hayman, Sr., might be in his seventies, but his voice was as crisp as ever—and, his son reflected ruefully, so were his drive, and his criticism of the running of the newspapers he had never actually relinquished control of, despite his official retirement.

"Thought you'd like to know that Michael Nej left the country last night, in one hell of a hurry, for Moscow."

"By himself?" George senior asked.

"If you're asking whether Catherine and Nona went with him, the answer is no."

"Well, well," George Hayman remarked. "You'd better keep your eye on that."

"You don't suppose it could be something to do with Gregory?" George junior asked.

"No." George Hayman's voice was flat. He did not like to be reminded of his Russian nephew, to whom he had extended the hand of hospitality when he had supposed the young man was genuinely seeking political asylum with his American cousins, and who had seduced George's own daughter before turning out to be a Russian spy. "Gregory Nej has been in Sing Sing for two years now, George. To the Russians he's old hat. If Michael has been recalled suddenly to Moscow, it's because something big is being planned, or has already happened."

"Well, it beats me," George junior said. "Apart from this continuing quarrel between the Soviets and Tito, everything seems quiet over there."

"Keep an eye on it," George said again. "Let me know as soon as you learn anything. And don't repeat any of this to your mother. Or John, come to think of it. Let's keep everything quiet over here, too, until we *have* to stir it up."

"Crowds. Always crowds," Michael Nej remarked as he disembarked at Moscow. "How they stare!"

"Because they are curious," suggested his secretary, an earnest young man named Gogol. "They're interested in the comings and goings of the great."

Michael grimaced. "And would any of those people believe I have no idea why I am here, Vladimir Vladimirovich? Ah, well, since I *am* here, you might as well send my wife a telegram to say I have arrived safely. She is very upset about this entire business."

"Are *you* worried about this business, comrade commissar?" Gogol inquired.

Michael glanced at him. Obviously, if he had been recalled because of some error, and thus was to suffer disgrace and possible exile to Siberia, the huge tentacles of the KGB would also seek to encompass his secretary as well as his family. Gogol had some reason to be anxious. Yet not enough. Michael

Nej was well aware of his position in the Party. As the only remaining associate of Lenin from the old pre-1914 days, he was unique; not only had he proved his ability to survive, but he had proved, time and again, his usefulness to Stalin. That usefulness, he knew, was at least partly because of his friendship with the American publisher George Hayman, a friendship begun nearly fifty years ago, in 1904, when Hayman had ridden into Port Arthur as a war correspondent to observe the Russian garrison during their final months under siege before surrendering to the Japanese. Hayman, as a wealthy American, had become a friend of the princely Borodin family—and, because of his republican inclinations, of the Borodin servants as well. Out of that strange meeting had come the great love affair between George Hayman and Ilona Borodina, which had spanned continents and caused almost as much diplomatic activity as a war. And out of *that* romance, when Ilona, passionate and strong-willed, had imagined herself robbed of the man she loved and doomed to marriage to a man she loathed, had come the strange secondary love affair between the princess and the valet, as Michael had then been. Between them they had produced a son, and caused more havoc than either had intended or supposed possible. And yet, even after Ilona had managed to regain her George, and had fled with him to wealth and security in America, the friendship of both Hayman and his wife toward Michael Nej had remained. It had even survived the destruction of Ilona's family home of Starogan by another Borodin ex-servant, Michael's younger brother Ivan, as it had survived the growth of the Soviet regime into its present monolith, a growth that had carried both Michael Nej and his brother—if temporarily, in Ivan's case—into the hallways of the great.

Thus his appointment as permanent ambassador at the United Nations had been inevitable; of all the senior members of the Politburo, he knew the most about Americans and America. But Michael had taken office at almost the moment his nephew Gregory—Ivan's son by Ilona's sister Tatiana Borodina—had been denounced and arrested as a spy. But by then Gregory's associates, headed by the infamous Anna Ragosina, had already achieved their objective of securing the atomic secrets. And he, Michael, had known nothing of the plot that had finally turned the Haymans against him. This he regretted. He had supposed that when he, his wife Catherine and his daughter

Nona had become settled in New York, they would see a great deal of the Haymans, and even more of John, his son by Ilona. What the Haymans saw as Gregory's treachery had spoiled that; John had become too much of an American to forgive. In the last two years Michael had not spoken to any member of the family. But this had not reduced his effectiveness as a Russian ambassador.

He had also been absent from the Security Council when the United States had put through its momentous resolution to oppose Communist aggression in Korea. Thus he had been unable to veto the measure, and the Americans and their allies had been able to put on an impressive show of force and unity. But that war had become bogged down in snow and ice and negotiation, and Stalin had never seemed very upset about the Americans becoming so involved in so remote a part of the world. Now it was two years since the outbreak of the Korean War. Since then everything had been going according to plan, apart from the continuing wrangle with Tito's Yugoslavia. So this recall . . . he frowned as Vyacheslav Molotov came toward him across the VIP lounge, smiling his cold smile, hand outstretched. As commissar for foreign affairs, Molotov was technically Michael's superior, although every commissar in Russia knew that Michael Nej acknowledged only Stalin himself as that.

"Michael Nikolaievich," Molotov said, kissing him upon each cheek in turn, "I am glad to see you. By God, I am glad to see you." He continued to hold Michael's arm, and hurried him toward the exit. "We must hurry. There is no time to lose."

"My things—"

"Will follow on later. We must hurry." He ushered Michael out to the black limousine waiting for them, engine running.

Michael sank into the leather upholstery with a sigh. At least he had not been greeted by any of Lavrenti Beria's KGB men. The crisis, if there was a crisis, apparently did not affect him personally. "Perhaps you will tell me what has happened."

Molotov sighed. "It is the catastrophe we have all feared for so long, Michael Nikolaievich. Joseph Vissarionovich has had a heart attack."

Michael's head turned, sharply, and Molotov's teeth gleamed in the gloom of the car. "It *was* a heart attack, Michael Nikolaievich. He has recovered, but is still in bed. But it is serious enough. We must never forget that Joseph Vissarionovich is seventy-three years old. I know he is a giant among men, but by the laws of nature he cannot be expected to continue too much longer. Yet he has never designated a successor."

"Neither did Lenin," Michael observed.

"Agreed, and we all remember the chaos after *his* death. In any event, Lenin was taken by surprise, so to speak. Who could have expected such a man to die in his early fifties? Joseph Vissarionovich has had ample time to indicate who he would expect to follow him as Party secretary. And he has not done so."

"Do you not suppose he is willing to leave that decision to the Party?" Michael inquired.

Molotov smiled again, indulgently. It was naïveté of this order that had always kept Michael Nej from real power. "The matter has been taxing us all, Michael," he said.

"Us?"

"Ah . . . well, Lavrenti Beria and myself."

Two of the triumvirate who were the pillars on which Stalin's power rested, Michael thought. But unlikely partners. Molotov was, like himself, a dyed-in-the-wool revolutionary. If, *un*like himself, he had never engaged in any important assassinations, he had yet been one of the Party gangsters in the old days before the First World War, robbing trains and banks to provide funds for Lenin's use. Beria was a comparatively recent arrival at the top. And Beria was head of the KGB, the secret police. A most powerful man.

But the operative word was *triumvirate*. "And so you sent for me," he said softly.

"Ah . . . as a matter of fact, no," Molotov said.

Michael's eyebrows rose.

"We certainly intended to keep you informed," Molotov added hastily. "Letters for you are on their way to New York. But of course, you will not be there to receive them."

"Quite," Michael said coldly. "These letters were to acquaint me with your decisions?"

"To ask your advice, Michael Nikolaievich," Molotov protested. "We felt that to bring you back would be to lend the whole business an air of crisis, and we did not wish that. However, as you *are* here—"

"The affair already has an air of crisis," Michael told him.

"I can assure you of that. But if you did not send for me, Vyacheslav Mikhailovich, who did?"

"Why, Joseph Vissarionovich himself, Michael. He wished you brought back just as soon as it could be arranged."

The room was dark, the curtains drawn. Only a single lamp glowed in the corner. Doctors and nurses, as well as several Politburo members, filled the room, but now Stalin waved his hand. "Leave us alone," he said. "It is Commissar Nej I wish to see. You too, Vyacheslav Mikhailovich. Leave us alone."

Glances were exchanged, throats were cleared. But no one in this room was prepared to argue with Joseph Stalin. Slowly the crowd filed out, and the door was closed. Michael stood by the bedside and gazed down at his master.

It was difficult to imagine that anything so serious as a heart attack had actually happened to this man, but that was partly because it was difficult to imagine anything *ever* happening to this man. His close-cropped hair was mostly gray now, but it had never been truly dark; his moustache was entirely white, but its thickness continued to hide his upper lip and effectively disguise his expression, leaving his face, as always, a genial mask for the thoughts and plans that roamed behind those somber eyes. His large, rounded features had not changed, either, in the three years since Michael had last seen him. His cheeks were pale, but no more than that. And his voice was as strong as ever. "Michael," he said, when the door had finally closed and they were alone. "Michael Nikolaievich. If you knew how good it is to see you!"

"It is good to see *you,* Joseph," Michael said. "After being told—"

"What they have tried to do to me?"

Michael frowned. "But . . . it was a heart attack, wasn't it? Vyacheslav Mikhailovich—"

"Molotov is a fool," Stalin said, without heat. "Oh, he is a faithful man, I think. But he is still a fool. I was poisoned."

Michael pulled up a chair and sat down. He also knew better than ever to argue with this man. Besides, he knew that what Stalin said was certainly possible. "But who would do such a thing, Joseph?"

"Who would you say, Michael?"

"Well, not Molotov, surely."

"I do not think so," Stalin agreed.

"Well, then . . . Malenkov? Khrushchev? I really don't see . . ."

"What either of them could hope to achieve without eliminating yourself and Molotov and Beria as well? You are entirely correct. So we dismiss them. But you have not yet mentioned Lavrenti Pavlovich." Stalin's voice was softer than ever.

"Beria? But . . . my God!"

"Exactly," Stalin agreed. "The head of my own secret police."

"You have proof of this?"

"Unfortunately, no. That proof must, however, be secured. But obviously we must be careful. Beria *is* the head of the KGB. I know the fault is mine, but I have so little time to take care of all the internal affairs of this great country, and Beria is certainly efficient . . ." He sighed. "Well, the long and the short of it is that he operates virtually a state within a state. One never knows who is a member of the KGB and who is not, and thus who is working for Beria and who is not."

Michael Nej nodded. "I have long felt that the KGB was growing too powerful."

"Yes," Stalin said, a trifle wearily. If Michael had a fault, it was his tendency to say I told you so. "This is a situation which must be corrected as soon as possible. But first Beria must be dealt with. This is why I have sent for you, Michael Nikolaievich." He smiled. "I can be certain that you, at least, do not work for Beria."

"I am rather the forgotten man of the revolution," Michael said, without bitterness.

"You underrate yourself," Stalin said. "Besides, I need you to reinstate the only man who can possibly deal with Beria, without tearing this country apart."

Michael's head came up. "Ivan? You want to recall *Ivan?"*

"I see no alternative."

"But . . . Joseph Vissarionovich, allow me to protest most strongly against such a step."

"Against the reinstatement of your own brother?"

"About the reinstatement of a man whose very name is associated with, well . . ."

"The purges of the thirties," Stalin said reflectively. "He did what had to be done. Ivan will always do that. Therein lies his value."

"Your image . . ."

"I would rather be alive and worrying about my image than dead with Beria running the country," Stalin pointed out. "I think you would prefer that also, Michael. To Beria, you are a forgotten man."

Michael got up, paced the room. "Joseph Vissarionovich, it seems almost certain, for what I have been able to learn, that Ivan ordered the murder of Tatiana Borodina . . ."

"Perhaps," Stalin said, mildly, "he did what he had to do."

Michael was still talking. "His own wife. And probably the greatest dancer Russia has ever produced. And—" Stalin's words penetrated his brain, and he stopped, frowning, as a monstrous suspicion crossed his mind: whatever Ivan had done during the purges of the thirties, had been at Stalin's command . . .

Stalin continued to smile. "He is in Tomsk," he said. "I sent him there."

"Exactly," Michael said, determined to argue to the last and try to decide just *what* he'd been told later. "You sent him to Tomsk, Joseph Vissarionovich, not only because of his crimes, but because he was clearly not the man he had once been. Do you suppose that four years in Tomsk will have restored him?"

"I think they may well have done that," Stalin said. "But the fact is, Michael Nikolaievich, I am not merely seeking to recall Ivan. Wherever he goes, there also will go Anna Ragosina."

"You . . ." Michael sat down again. "You would consider using that vampire again?"

"I think she is perhaps the only person in the world of whom Beria is truly afraid. I think her presence in Moscow, in Lubianka, may well provoke him to an overt act."

"Do you really suppose he will be afraid of her now? Did you not send her to Tomsk as Ivan's *assistant,* after she had had him placed under arrest and 'interrogated' him herself? Do you have any idea what it is like to be interrogated by Anna Ragosina?"

Stalin's smile widened. "I'm afraid not. Do you?"

"No, but . . . Joseph Vissarionovich, I must beg of you to leave the bitch where she is. Anyway, Ivan will have destroyed her, long ago."

Stalin shook his head. "My information is that this has not happened. Anyway, that is what I wish you to find out."

"Me?"

"Why else do you think I brought you all the way from New York?" Stalin asked. Suddenly he sat up, his voice incisive. "We must fight Beria. We will overthrow him by surrounding him with *our* people, Michael Nikolaievich. People who are utterly loyal to us. I know Lavrenti Pavlovich very well. When he imagines himself being surrounded, he will lose his nerve and make an overt move. Once he does that, we have him. Provided we have the right people in the right places. You will go to Tomsk and see Ivan, and see Anna Ragosina. I give you carte blanche. Find out what they are like, after four years of exile. If you think they *are* broken, return here alone. If you feel they are still as good as they once were, you will have letters from me authorizing you to reinstate Ivan as deputy commissar for internal security, and Anna Ragosina as a colonel in the KGB. You will then instruct them to return to Moscow as rapidly as possible."

"Will not Beria object?"

"He may well do so. And then he may well betray himself. Either way, he can do nothing about it. Ivan made a mistake, and has been punished for it. That punishment is now completed, and he is entitled to resume his career. So is Anna Ragosina. Do not forget that a very large number of the operatives in the KGB were personally loyal to Ivan before his disgrace, and that an equally large number were personally trained by Ragosina. I understand that she is a difficult woman to forget, once one has . . . known her."

"She is—" Michael waved his hand "—a virago, spawned by the pit of hell," he finished, flushing at his own lapse into melodrama.

"On the contrary," Stalin said, "she was spawned, almost literally, by your brother. He took her out of school, because he wanted a bedwarmer after Tatiana left him. He made her what she is today. She is worth an army, all on her own. Fetch them back for me, Michael Nikolaievich. I can send no one else, because no one else is capable of considering them objectively, and because Ivan will suspect that his recall is a trap, if it comes from anyone but you. Fetch them back. And then come back yourself. I will arrange a replacement for you in New York. We will form ranks, Michael Nikolaievich, against this canker in our midst. And with care and fortune, we will bring him down."

* * *

Michael Nej had not been east of the Urals since 1918. It was not a journey he had hoped to make again. The railway line to Tomsk passed through Sverdlovsk, a city originally named by the Great Catherine after herself, Ekaterinburg, but renamed after the revolution, because Ekaterinburg had possessed too many memories even for Lenin. It was to Ekaterinburg that Michael had gone in 1918, in his pocket an order for the execution of Tsar Nicholas II and all his family. Michael did not regret this action for a moment. To him then, and now, the tsar and his women had been bloodsucking leeches who deserved only death. But on that journey he had been reunited with Ilona Borodina Hayman, and with Judith Stein, both unluckily caught up in the tragedy of the Romanovs. Ilona, the woman who had left him, and Judith, who was destined to leave him. To return to Sverdlovsk could only bring an unwelcome mixture of nightmares and dreams.

"Were you ever exiled to Siberia during the bad days?" inquired the secretary, Gogol, observing his employer's mood of reflection.

"No," Michael said.

"But were you not arrested by the Okhrana after the murder of Prime Minister Stolypin?"

"Indeed I was," Michael agreed. "But as I happened to be guilty, I was sentenced to death, not exile."

"And you escaped," Gogol said admiringly.

"Yes." Michael saw no reason to remind the young man that his escape had been engineered by George Hayman. His trouble was that he owed too many debts, not all of which were reconcilable with his present august position. He even owed his brother Ivan a debt, and that was certainly not a debt of gratitude. But he also owed Joseph Stalin a debt, perhaps more than one. And Stalin's was the star he had chosen to follow, out of all the stars that had blazed, briefly, in the chaos following Lenin's death. Reluctantly at first, and often with revulsion, but with an always growing conviction that here was the man, perhaps the *only* man, to make the revolution work.

That conviction had become almost hero worship after the Great Patriotic War, when Stalin's will alone had stood between Russia and defeat. But at what cost? Perhaps he had never truly evaluated that. Michael had always recognized his master as an utterly ruthless man and had respected him for it. Now the conviction was growing in him that Stalin had ordered Tatiana Borodina's execution, had merely commanded that it be made to look like an accident, and had given the task to Ivan to carry out, sure that Ivan hated the wife who had deserted him.

Yet the idea was repellent. Of all the Russians who had adored Tattie Borodina and all she stood for, Stalin had seemed to adore her most. Like everyone else he had been fascinated as much by the uninhibited eroticism of her dancing as by the equally uninhibited ebullience of her personality. But who could tell what had happened to Tattie during the war? She had spent four years behind the German lines, ostensibly fighting with the partisans, but . . . for such an international figure, collaborating with the Nazis, for instance, would have been simple. And Tattie, for all her apparent acceptance of Communism, was nevertheless the sister of Peter Borodin, the erstwhile Prince of Starogan, and still a determined and vehement opponent of Bolshevism. And Tattie's sister was Ilona Hayman, the wife of an American millionaire.

Who could tell what Stalin might have discovered about her that had made her death necessary?

It was a nightmarish thought, because Michael had loved Tattie, in almost a brotherly fashion, himself. But Stalin dealt in nightmares. They were a part of the perpetual Russian subconscious, which he had learned how to manipulate. So now he had commanded Michael to resurrect two other creatures of nightmare, for the good of the state. And Michael had never questioned what Stalin thought was best for the state. Having become a follower of Lenin because he *had* questioned the tsarist regime, he had understood that the only essential for a successful revolutionary politician was to *know* that whatever he did, no matter how horrible or distasteful, was for the good of the revolution. So, perhaps the revolution in Russia was thirty-five years in the past. *That* revolution would undoubtedly be supplanted by another, should Beria replace Stalin as dictator. And that first revolution was the one to which *he* owed his loyalty. If Ivan and Anna Ragosina could prevent such a catastrophe, then who was he to feel distaste about employing them?

Assuming Ivan and Anna were still employable. Their time in Tomsk must have been a nightmare. From Sverdlovsk, in the foothills of the Ural Mountains, the train plunged to a totally level, monotonous plain. Here was taiga country, a thousand miles of pine forest, unrelieved by even the shallowest hill, broken only by stretches of even more dreary marshland. Spring was coming, so the temperature was almost bearable; in the summer, it would rise to a hundred and fifteen in the shade; in the winter, it would plunge to a steady minus fifty or lower. Tomsk itself lay down a branch line. Here, for the last two years, the two most feared personalities in Russia had languished, because they had either failed or annoyed Stalin. Michael wondered what he would find.

"Michael?" Ivan Nej nearly knocked over his swivel chair as he rose to his feet. "Michael Nikolaievich?" His gaze drifted past his brother, to Gogol, as a rabbit might look at a snake.

Ivan Nej was younger than his brother, was in fact sixty-three years old. He had a long, hooked nose and a protruding chin. With his spectacles and his drooping moustache he also contrived to remind Michael, somewhat, of Lev Trotsky. The comparison was an insult to Trotsky, of course. Michael, a Stalinist to the backbone, had played his part in Trotsky's downfall; but even then he had recognized that the downfall was necessary simply because Trotsky was more intellectually brilliant, and more Communistically ambitious, than any of the other men left, at Lenin's untimely death, to jostle for the supreme power. Ivan was a bootblack with the instincts of a thug, who had, by the upheaval of the revolution, been allowed to develop those instincts until they had taken over his entire personality. But he had always been afraid. This disgusting characteristic, allied to his nearly omnipotent power as Stalin's private hatchetman, had made him a totally contemptible object, to those who had been safe enough to regard him as such—and a total monster to those who had found themselves in one of his prison cells. Today Ivan's fear was very near the surface.

"Michael," he said again. "Michael Nikolaievich." He hurried round his desk to embrace his brother, and looked at Gogol again, obviously concluding that the mild-mannered secretary was at least an executioner. "I . . . I do not understand."

"That I should come to visit you?" Michael asked, sitting down and crossing his knees, carelessly, while he surveyed the tiny, airless office, in what was a tiny, airless building. In a graceless provincial town situated on an endless Siberian plain.

Ivan's last empire, he thought—four assistants and eight secretaries, ten million mosquitos, and incalculable boredom. "Oh, meet Vladimir Vladimirovich Gogol, my secretary," Michael said.

Ivan did not offer to shake hands; that might be the signal for his immediate demise. He nodded, and forced a ghastly facsimile of a smile. "From New York?" he asked anxiously.

"From Tiflis," Michael said.

Ivan stared, and sat down. The news that Gogol was a Georgian, like Stalin himself, was not reassuring.

"I have never been to Tomsk before," Michael remarked. "Is there much activity here?"

"Ah . . . we have a university," Ivan said. "The oldest university in Siberia. And a teacher's college. And a great deal of good timber."

"I meant, have *you* had much to do these past few years?" Michael asked.

"Ah . . ." Ivan's fingers twined together. "Black-marketeers, principally. That is a serious crime, you know, Michael. It carries the death sentence. And then, university students . . . there are always a few who wish to change the world. But we find them out. Oh, we find them out. Ah . . . you are here on holiday?" Again he looked at Gogol, and sweat trickled down his neck and into his already soiled collar. This, Michael thought, is the man Stalin seeks to pit against steely-eyed Lavrenti Beria, urban and intelligent.

"Yes," he said, and smiled. "I am on holiday in Siberia, Ivan Nikolaievich. I have always wanted a holiday in Siberia. Doesn't everyone? But I am glad to have seen you again. To be able to reassure myself that you are well and prospering. Yes, indeed. I am staying at the hotel. Perhaps you would dine with me." And then, he thought, I can take the next train back to Moscow and tell Joseph Vissarionovich that he must look elsewhere for help.

"That would be very pleasant," Ivan said. "Oh, that would be very pleasant indeed."

"Eight o'clock," Michael said, and stood up. But he had been given a task to carry out, and he never failed to complete an assignment. "I understand that Anna Ragosina is here in Tomsk with you."

"Ah, yes," Ivan said. "Where I go, there goes Anna Ragosina." His smile ws crooked.

"I do not think I have ever met her," Michael said, "although I have heard a great deal about her. I should like to meet Anna Ragosina, Ivan Nikolaievich."

Ivan nodded. "I will bring her to the hotel."

"Where is she now?"

"Ah . . . she is working. Anna is always working."

"I should like to see her working," Michael said. "Will you not take me to her now?"

Ivan himself drove the old United States Army Jeep away from the town and into the pine forest. "We have no proper facilities here," he explained. "Anna is indefatigable; I do not know what I would do without her. But in our small offices . . . When she wishes really to come to grips with a matter, she goes into the woods."

He spoke, Michael thought, with a strange mixture of near-reverence and contempt. Certainly not what he would have expected. But then, he had no idea *what* to expect. What *could* he expect to find, considering what he had found in Ivan?

"What was *that?"* cried Gogol, seated in the back seat beside Ivan's aide.

"Ah, Anna is at work," Ivan said, and stopped the Jeep. They were many miles from the town now, and the sky was almost shut out by the pine trees towering above the rough dirt track. Through them the terrifying scream had echoed.

"Madame Ragosina made that sound?" Michael asked.

"No, no," Ivan said. "That would have been the man she is with. She must be somewhere over there."

In the trees to their right a woman had appeared—a girl, rather, plump and blond, wearing a uniform and staring at them through binoculars. "Anna's assistant," Ivan explained, and beckoned her.

The girl came toward them. "Is there something wrong, comrade commissar?"

"No, no," Ivan said. "I have here a senior commissar from Moscow, who most urgently wishes to speak with Madame Ragosina."

The girl hesitated, looking at Michael, and then at Gogol. "Madame Ragosina is very busy," she said. "She does not like to be interrupted when she is working." Ivan might as well have been a clerk making a nuisance of himself.

"I will see her *now,*" Michael said.

The girl hesitated again, biting her lip in indecision.

"Stay here, all of you," Michael said, and stepped past her to walk through the trees, wondering why his heart was pounding. He was about to come face to face with a walking horror who masqueraded under the name of woman . . . A twig cracked, and he half-turned, his hand instinctively dropping toward his pocket.

"You had better have a very good reason, comrade, for being here." The voice was soft, liquid music playing about his ears. "Because if you do not, I will kill you."

He had the strangest wish to raise his hands, and kept them at his side with an effort. "I am Commissar Michael Nikolaievich Nej," he said, also requiring an effort to keep his voice even. "I am here on a mission from Premier Stalin. To see you, Madame Ragosina."

There was a moment's silence before she said, "Then I have made a mistake, no doubt, comrade commissar. Have you identification?"

Michael turned toward her slowly. A middle-aged virago, he thought. He gazed first of all at the most perfectly formed face he had ever seen, calm, flawlessly chiseled features, straight nose, pointed chin, perhaps slightly thin mouth, but magnificent deep black eyes, pale complexion, the whole framed in a cascade of raven hair that fell to either side from the exact center parting; although she wore the uniform of a colonel in the KGB, she was bareheaded. She made him think of superbly executed paintings he had seen of a Madonna. She might have been any age from fifteen to thirty. Forty was impossible. Her figure was trim rather than voluptuous; she was only a couple of inches taller than five feet, and her heavy uniform suppressed all but the essential curves at breast and thigh. Her legs were concealed in boots beneath her skirt. Michael did not doubt they would be as magnificent as the rest of her.

"*You* are Anna Ragosina?" he asked, disgusted with himself for the inanity of the question.

"You are Michael Nikolaievich Nej?" she answered, in faintly mocking tones. "Indeed you must be, for you are obviously John Hayman's father. I worked and fought with your son for four years, comrade commissar. He was a very brave man."

"And more recently?"

Her eyes became bottomless black pools of angry hatred. "He became my enemy," she said. *"Our* enemy, comrade commissar. The enemy of Soviet Russia." She smiled. "But a man is not *entirely* responsible for his son. I am pleased to make your acquaintance, comrade commissar." She made to hold out her hand, discovered she still held her revolver, and holstered it without embarrassment. "I have heard a great deal about you, comrade."

"As I have heard of you," he said. "Now I would see what you are doing."

Like her assistant, Anna Ragosina hesitated, and then shrugged. "As you wish." She turned away, and he caught a faint whiff of perfume. That surprised him. Yet was she a beautiful woman, and should she not be aware of that beauty? He watched the ripple of her straight black hair as she moved, the slight sway of the hips, the trace of damp sweat at her armpits and in the middle of her back. He thought she might have a strain of Tartar blood in her ancestry. His own wife, Catherine, had a great deal of Tartar blood. But Catherine had never been beautiful.

On the other hand, Catherine had never been a monster. He must keep reminding himself of that fact—if he needed reminding: Anna Ragosina had reached a small clearing, and there stopped. "He is a black-marketeer," she said.

Michael stared at the man. He had been stripped to his shoes and socks, and tied to a log of wood, on his back. He was not very old, appeared to be healthy and well built, and did not *look* harmed in any way; his naked body seemed a bit redder than normal, but that might be because of the blood pumping furiously through his arteries, for he was twisting and writhing against the rough wood as if he were on fire. He made a noise, too, and was obviously trying to make a much *greater* noise, to repeat the scream they had first heard—but his mouth had been crammed with a white linen handkerchief, and he could only utter a high-pitched moan.

"What have you done to him?" Michael asked flatly.

"I use pepper," Anna explained. "It is my own system. Red pepper, comrade commissar. It is very effective. The pain it can cause is quite unbearable."

"How do you know?" Michael asked, trying to keep his

breathing under control. "Have you ever felt it?"

She glanced at him in surprise. "Why, no, comrade commissar. But I have observed its effects often enough. Actually . . ." She smiled, and looked even younger. "I did feel it once. When I was still at the orphanage, I quarreled with some other girls, and they . . . held me and touched me with pepper while I slept. It is . . . almost unbearable. But it leaves no trace, unless it is used carelessly. Carelessly used, it can kill. In addition to the pain, you see, comrade commissar, where the part of the body is exceptionally tender, it induces great swelling, which can sometimes take days to subside. Days when the natural functions cannot take place."

Michael stood beside her and looked down on the tortured body. "And this man?"

"Oh, he will live to be executed. It is a long time since I have killed anybody by mistake."

"His crime?" His brain seemed to have gone blank.

"I told you, comrade commissar, he is a black-marketeer. One of a ring, but the foolish fellow will not give me the names of his accomplices. Not yet. He will, eventually." She reached down and pulled the man's ear playfully. "You know you will, Igor Igorovich. But be stubborn. I am in no hurry." She stooped, and picked up the cut pepper where she had left it on the ground. "I will demonstrate to you, comrade commissar. I think the last application may just be wearing off."

"I do not want a demonstration," Michael said. She *was* a monster, everything he had been led to expect. Except for the beauty. That had been suggested, but he had not believed it possible in such a creature. But he still could not be sure she was truly what Stalin was looking for. It is very easy to be efficiently destructive and heartlessly ruthless when one's victim is lying tied to a log at one's feet, just as in those circumstances it is also easy to be impressively fearless. And her only reason for existence lay in the uses her efficiency and ruthlessness and fearlessness could be put to by her superiors. Lacking such uses, it was a crime that such a creature should be allowed to draw a single breath of air, or eat a morsel of food that might feed someone else. It was his business to discover if she was everything she seemed, if she could successfully oppose Lavrenti Beria. "Leave me," he said.

Anna Ragosina frowned.

"Leave me alone with this man," Michael repeated. "I wish to ask him a question." He turned and pointed. "Go and stand over there, by those trees." The place he had indicated was about fifty yards away. "Stand there, with your back to me, until I call you."

Anna hesitated, still frowning, lips slightly parted. But he was one of the most powerful men in Russia. She nodded, turned, and walked away, then stood gazing into the forest, her head rigidly straight.

Michael gazed after her for some seconds, and then stooped beside the man, holding his breath against the stench of pain-sweat and fear-sweat. "Listen to me," he said. "I am going to remove your gag. But you must not cry out, or make a sound. Understand this. If you do make a sound, I will give you back to Anna Ragosina."

The man stared at him. But definitely the pain was subsiding. Michael pulled the handkerchief from his mouth, nose wrinkling as he discerned, despite the time it had been in place, that the handkerchief still contained wisps of her perfume. The man gasped in relief.

"Do you hate Comrade Ragosina?" Michael asked.

The man stared at him.

"Do you know who I am, Igor Igorovich?" Michael asked. "I am Commissar Michael Nej. You have heard of me, comrade. I know that you have committed a crime against the people of Russia, and that you deserve to face a firing squad. But I would like to give you a chance to live, at least until your next crime. Would you like that chance, comrade?"

The man inhaled harshly.

Michael smiled. "And to avenge yourself. I am going to release you, and I am going to provide you with a weapon. I wish you to kill Comrade Ragosina for me. If you do that, I will set you free. Do you understand me?"

The man stared at him for several more seconds, then he nodded. But he was frowning. He was too confused to be effective.

"She has been condemned to death," Michael explained. "And I am her appointed executioner. But I would rather have her die this way. Remember that she is a very dangerous woman. You will have to be fast, and accurate. Do you understand me?"

"Yes," the man said. "I understand you, comrade commissar." He licked his lips.

"Good," Michael said. He drew his pistol, placed it on the grass six feet away from the log, then took his pocket knife and cut the man free. "Now," he said, and knelt behind the log.

Igor Igorovich sat up, hesitated, and then lunged forward. His hands closed on the gun.

"Anna!" Michael shouted. "Behind you!"

Igor straightened, the pistol held in his hand. There were five explosions, so rapidly one on top of the other that they sounded almost simultaneous. Michael stood up, stepped over the log, and looked down at Igor Igorovich. The man lay on his side, blood flowing from his suddenly pale body, the pistol drooping from his hand. Michael stooped, picked the gun up, and examined it. Igor had fired once. And now he could see there were four bullet wounds in the shattered chest.

He straightened again, looked down the barrel of Anna Ragosina's revolver. "I have two bullets left, *comrade,*" she said.

Michael smiled at her. "Then why do you not reload?"

Anna frowned at him, half turned her head to listen to the shouts of Ivan and Gogol and the others as they ran through the wood. "You wanted me to kill him?"

"If he could not kill you first," Michael agreed.

Anna slowly walked toward him.

"I have need of you," Michael said, "if you are as good as they say."

"And now you know that I am." She stood in front of him, holstered the revolver. She also smiled. "I always knew they would send for me," she said. "They could not keep *me* locked away here forever. What is it you wish done, comrade commissar?" She looked down at Igor; she was not even breathing hard. "Who else do you wish killed?"

Michael found that his heart was settling down. He was, after all, going to turn this monster loose, with incalculable results for Russia. She would have to be controlled with some kind of a bridle. "I will tell you what I want done," he said, "in due course. But you will be operating with my brother. And under his command, as before. Do you understand this?"

Anna Ragosina gazed at him, and then smiled. "Of course,

comrade commissar. That will be a pleasure." She turned away from him, walked a few steps, and then looked over her shoulder, almost coyly. "Now that I know he has a brother who is even more ruthless than I, it *will* be a pleasure."

"I cannot believe it," Ivan Nej said, leaning back on the cushions in his first-class private compartment, and stretching his legs. He stared at Anna Ragosina; Michael had already returned to Moscow, and they were alone. "I just cannot believe it. I will tell you something, Anna Petrovna. When they sent me to Tomsk I assumed it was for life. When my brother came to me last week, I thought he had been sent to execute me."

"What nonsense!" Anna said contemptuously. "How could they execute me? Or even you? We are too valuable, as Stalin has found out."

"Beria," Ivan muttered. "Yes. Bringing down Beria will be a pleasure. But so many things are going to be a pleasure. I have dreamed so many dreams, these last four years . . ."

Anna looked out of the window. That was all he was truly capable of, nowadays: dreams. Once he had been a fearsome figure. The mere mention of his name had reduced people to gibbering wrecks. She could still remember that day, at the orphanage in Moscow, when she had been summoned to the director's office because Commissioner Ivan Nej had wished to see her. Only sixteen years old, she had known instinctively that something terrible was about to happen to her.

Well, she supposed that in the eyes of most people something terrible *had* happened: she had become Anna Ragosina. Once she had dreamed only of avenging the murder of her parents by men wearing the very uniform she now displayed. Soon she had accepted that was mere fantasy. But she had found a very acceptable substitute. If she could not be avenged on such creatures, she would join them, and dominate them, and through them be avenged on all the world. She hated all the world, anyway.

In time, she had come to hate this man more than anyone else. He had dominated her youth, and nauseated her even as he had terrified her. Then, when following his own selfish lusting after Ilona Hayman, the American millionairess, he had endangered his own career, he had sacrificed her without hesitation, had her sent to a labor camp for five years. Years in which she had realized she had never previously understood the *meaning* of the word hate. Yet as the Great Patriotic War against the Germans had loomed ever closer, she had had to be brought back, to triumph, fame, and a model as a Heroine of the Soviet Union. She had been standing alongside John Hayman the day she had received that medal, because he had also been honored for his deeds with the partisans. Following that there had been nothing but triumph, culminating in her appointment to command the North American station. Only she, Stalin had known, could obtain the atomic formulas that would give Soviet Russia military equality with the United States.

She had succeeded in all that—and then had come face to face with John Hayman again, and seen her organization ripped apart, herself disgraced. And as a punishment, she had been returned to Ivan. She would admit, if only to herself, that when she had heard that sentence she had all but despaired. Yet, having survived so much, she had not contemplated suicide, had braced herself for whatever hell Ivan might have waiting for her . . . and had found herself belonging to a broken wreck of a man. She had nearly completed *his* destruction, had considered the pleasure of doing that. And had thought better of it. She had learned, over twenty bitter years, that a woman could accomplish little, in her peculiar profession, without the backing of a man. If she had ever made a personal mistake, it had been that she had never taken the trouble to secure such backing, for herself alone, because she had not realized the importance of it. Thus her instincts had told her that she would only emerge once again from obscurity into fame and power, with the assistance of a man. And, for now at least, that man had to be Ivan Nej, simply because there was no one else available in Tomsk. And also because he had a brother who was still a power in the land. And because he had once had a reputation.

It had simply been a matter of patience. Patience to carry out her duties to the best of her ability, and patience to win Ivan back to utter subservience. That had given her no difficulty. She knew more of what men wanted than any other woman in the world; she had spent too much of her time inducing both pain and ecstasy, and exploring, with clinical detachment, that gray world that lies between, which so many men find attractive. Ivan had assumed—as nowadays he assumed of every arrival from Moscow, even of his own brother—that she had been sent to execute him. When he had discovered that she was again to be his assistant, she had watched his eyes become opaque, as he had started to wonder what he could do, what he *dared* do, to avenge himself for the humiliation she had inflicted on him when she had arrested him. And he had been lost when she had smiled and said, "So now you have me, Ivan Nikolaievich, groveling before you. Why do you not shave *me,* and beat me, and then mount me, and make me scream with pain?"

There had been no problems with Ivan after that. She had even enjoyed herself, because that gray never-never world of pain-induced ecstasy or ecstasy-induced pain was as fascinating to herself as to anyone; besides, she reasoned, if she did not, from time to time, experience just a little pain, how could she know what she was doing for others? And now, only two years later, her reasoning, her logical approach, had been proved as accurate as in the past. Ivan's brother had come, to reclaim her; he would not have come for Ivan alone. Come to reclaim her for greatness, and power. Beria was nothing. She knew him well, knew he was afraid of her—when she had briefly worked with him and had slept with him, he had been so nervous he had failed—and she knew, too, that he was more to be despised than feared. The important thing was that *Stalin* had realized he needed her. The future was all hers. This time she would make no mistakes.

"Gregory," Ivan said. "Now I can do something about Gregory."

Anna turned her head to regard him as she might have regarded a lizard. "That foolish boy?" she asked.

"He is my son," Ivan said with dignity. "My only son."

Which was not true, of course. Ivan had had children by his first wife. But they had been allowed to disappear—he did not wish to remember his first wife, the daughter of a village schoolmaster. Gregory was his son by Tatiana Borodina, and the last living memory of the wife he had murdered because he could never possess her.

"He is a traitor to the Soviet Union," Anna said evenly.

"That cannot be so. He is serving a sentence in an American jail for spying."

"Because he is an idiot. But he is still a traitor. It was his treachery, his falling in love with that Hayman woman, that caused my arrest. I hope he rots."

Ivan shook his head. "He made mistakes. He was too young for the assignment. I admit it freely. I would have advised against it. But *you* chose him, in my absence."

Anna looked out the window again. She did not enjoy being reminded of her mistakes.

"Now we must get him back," Ivan said. "It should not be difficult."

Anna's head turned again, sharply. "It will be impossible," she said. "Premier Stalin himself attempted to set up an exchange—out of some feeling of loyalty to the memory of Tatiana, I suppose—and the Americans were not interested. You do not understand how strongly they feel about him. They took him in, believing he was a genuine defector. All America supposed he was genuine, and because they are an incurably romantic nation, they warmed to his handsome looks and his air of innocence. And then they discovered that he had seduced his own cousin and was a spy. He must be the most-hated man in America. They will never let him go. Besides—" Her lip curled contemptuously. "—they think he is important. They think he is almost as important as me. They told us we had no one worth exchanging him for."

Ivan regarded her for several seconds, then seemed to lose interest in the conversation. Instead he felt in his pocket, and took out a piece of what appeared to be cardboard, which he began to study.

Anna's frown deepened. She did not like for Ivan to have secrets from her. "What is that?"

"A photograph."

Anna got up and sat beside him, then gazed at the family group.

"Michael gave it to me," Ivan said. "Do they not make a handsome picture?"

Anna stared at the faces, the expressions, so insufferably confident and arrogant, the clothes, so unthinkably expensive and worn so casually, the dogs in the foreground and the house in the background, the cars to either side, the jewels on the fingers and at the necks and ears of the women. "The Haymans," she said, her voice almost harsh.

"Relatives of mine," Ivan said mildly. "At least by marriage. Relatives of Gregory's. And important people. I do not believe there are any more important people in the United States than the Haymans. Presidents may come and go, but the Haymans, with their money and their power and their newspapers, which control Wall Street and public opinion, are there forever. That must be very comforting, and very important, to the Americans."

"Or nauseating," Anna commented. "It is a crime against humanity for one family to have so much, while others . . ." She was searching for Felicity Hayman, Gregory's mistress, the woman she had once shot, and regrettably, not killed; but Felicity was not in the picture. Instead she stared at John Hayman, standing next to his mother, and smiling at her. "They will go the way of all flesh, Ivan Nikolaievich," she said. "They are best forgotten."

"Is she not beautiful?" Ivan asked, again as if she had not spoken. "That one."

Anna peered at the girl in the very center of the group. Perhaps twenty years old, she estimated. She frowned. She was looking at an exquisitely beautiful woman in embryo, diminutive and small-boned, with delicate features, superbly etched by some immortal artist, and hair as straight and black as Anna's own.

"Who is she?" she sneered. "One of your precious Rachel Stein's grandchildren?"

"She is a Hayman," Ivan said.

"Nonsense," Anna declared. "With that coloring?"

"She takes after her mother," Ivan pointed out, "the wife of George Hayman, Jr. This girl, Diana, is their only child. Do you understand what that means, Anna Petrovna?"

"No," Anna said, in utter boredom. Ivan should know better than to still be indulging in his adolescent fantasies. "You will have to tell me."

"Simply that this little girl will one day be the most powerful woman in America, because she will own Hayman Newspapers Incorporated. And she is therefore already the most valuable thing the Haymans possess."

"And you dream of possessing her? One day you will have to grow up, Ivan Nikolaievich. Do not forget that we are returning to Moscow to carry out a very important assignment. For Premier Stalin."

Ivan continued to gaze at the photograph. "That will not be difficult," he said. "Not so difficult as you say getting Gregory back is going to be. But that will not be difficult either, Anna Petrovna." He raised his head and smiled at her as he replaced the photograph in his pocket. "If the Americans do not feel we possess anyone of sufficient importance to exchange for Gregory—well, then . . . we shall just have to *obtain* someone of sufficient importance. Shall we not?"

Chapter 2

SUNDAY LUNCH AT COLD SPRING HARBOR WAS A HAYMAN institution. As important, George Hayman thought with some satisfaction, to the younger members of the family as to Ilona and himself. They lived such busy, diverse lives that these get-togethers were the only opportunity they had of meeting their brothers and sisters, uncles and aunts and cousins, in a totally informal and relaxed atmosphere. Here, whatever their functions in the great world outside, they were all Haymans.

He smiled down the table. He had never intended to become a patriarch. His youth had been spent adventuring. As a war correspondent for his father's paper, the Boston *People*, he had pursued conflict after conflict, starting as a soldier in Cuba in 1898, then riding with the Boers in South Africa two years later, and finally with the Russians in Manchuria in 1904. There he had fallen in love, and there he had, without knowing it, set his feet on the patriarchal ladder.

Nowadays, he told himself, he must even look like a patriarch. He was seventy-five years old, and although he retained most of his hair, there was no trace of black left amid the bushy white, while his big, friendly features were overlaid with masses of wrinkles. He did not suppose he was quite six foot two any longer, either, although maybe the shrinkage could be put down to stooping over too many long putts. He was aware of aches and pains in various parts of his body where there had never been pains before, and of a necessity to be just a little careful of how much he ate and drank. But his heart and brain were as good as ever. In fact, if they had not been so good, he would not be suffering so acutely from the greatest curse of old age, boredom. He supposed he was better off than most. If he had reluctantly relinquished the presidency of the huge newspaper empire he had built upon his father's modest start, he left no one at Hayman Newspapers Incorporated in any doubt that he was still very much around. He never interfered, but he was fond of suggesting—and he was still majority shareholder. Ilona sometimes did some suggesting herself, that this was unfair to George junior. But George had no doubt that George junior, and all the thousand other employees of the company, welcomed his ideas.

Anyway, he reflected, how could a man be bored with such a family to gather around him every Sunday?

He could look first of all at two of his three children, for he counted John Hayman, Ilona's son by Michael Nej, as his own. John was forty-four now, and unquestionably part of the Hayman clan. If he had stepped aside from family affairs, that had been inevitable. John had known his talents were not those of presiding over a publishing company, and he was reluctant to give the slightest indication of wishing to muscle in on George junior's inheritance. For a while after his remarkable exploits in the war against Nazi Germany, he had seemed lost. George was happy to have been able to steer him into a profession where his talents *could* be used to the utmost. He was even happier that it should be a secret only *they* in the family shared; everyone else, even John's wife Natasha, supposed John was what he pretended to be, an advertising executive.

George junior was very obviously his father's son, big and expansive, wide-featured and fun-loving, but one of the sharpest brains and most astute businessmen George had ever encountered. The two men understood each other perfectly. When the younger Haymans had arrived, George had looked at his son with raised eyebrows, and George junior had shrugged. So there was nothing concrete out of Russia yet. Michael Nej had returned to New York in March; in the two months since then, all had seemed normal.

Felicity's chair was empty. Today was visiting day at Sing Sing. Idle to remind himself, or Ilona, that Felicity's chair had seldom been occupied for a Sunday lunch, even before Gregory Nej had come to America. Hers had been an unhappy life, despite her beauty and her intelligence and her wealth. For Felicity, they could only hope, and pray. And he, personally, could only attempt to give her what happiness he could. It was George who had secured her permission to visit her cousin once a week in prison. No one had approved, least of all the family; Felicity's regular journeys along the Hudson River to Ossining were a constant source of copy to every reporter or news photographer short of a story—and who happened to work for a paper *not* part of the Hayman chain. But it was Felicity's only source of happiness.

He could take more pride in his daughters-in-law. Natasha he had always adored. With her dark red hair and lean body, she was as far removed from golden, voluptuous Tattie Borodina as anyone could be; in her talents, and the fact that she had been Tattie's prize pupil and had eventually replaced her mentor as principal dancer, she was a constant reminder of the glory that had once dominated the stages of Europe. And she was a young woman of rare courage, too. At John's side she had fought in the war in the Pripet Marshes, had learned how to kill as she had learned how to suffer—and how merely to survive. And yet now she dangled a cigarette from a most elegant hand, as she happily sipped her after-lunch brandy. Her English, though, was still coated with the Russian accent she had found it so difficult to discard.

George junior's wife, Elizabeth, was also as different as anyone could be from the Hayman-Borodin mold. Short and slim, black-haired and brown-eyed, she was a bundle of nervous energy, waved her hand constantly as she spoke, seemed to draw pictures in the air to supplement the pictures she drew with words, left them constantly reminded of the pictures she painted so brilliantly with her brush, the skills that had made her one of New York's most sought-after portrait painters. She sat next to Ilona, and chattered away, while Ilona smiled her wise, slightly melancholy smile, and listened. The friendship of these two women, who had begun by loathing each other—Elizabeth Dodge finding it difficult to discover any substance, or what she would call substance, in a Russian princess who had abandoned all for love; and Ilona, as a Russian princess, finding it impossible to believe that a young woman who habitually drew nude men and women could possibly make a good wife for her son—George found one of his greatest pleasures. But everything to do with Ilona was a pleasure. With her long silver hair upswept—she had never cut it short, because Russian princesses did not cut their hair—in the calm repose of her magnificent features and the relaxed attitudes of her still magnificent body, in the simple luxury of her jewelry and her dress, she was without question the most elegant woman in the room.

Surprisingly, and sadly, they had between them been granted only three grandchildren. Nor did there seem any immediate prospect of more. Alexander, John and Natasha's eldest, was ten years old, while his sister Olga was only two, and occupied a highchair discreetly removed from the main dining table. But Natasha was forty-one and would probably not have another child. She had married John late, because of the commitments of her dancing career. George junior and Elizabeth had apparently never desired more than one child, and would certainly not now have another.

But at least, he reflected, that child was Diana.

"I wish to talk to you about Diana," Ilona said.

Elizabeth lit a fresh cigarette. She had known this was coming, the moment luncheon was finished and Ilona had ushered the entire family outdoors to play croquet, while suggesting that she and Elizabeth have another cup of coffee. But then, she had known this was coming before she ever left New York this morning to drive out here.

"I do feel it is quite unseemly, and *wrong*, for a young girl like that to go off to Europe on her own," Ilona said.

Elizabeth sighed, and prepared for battle. She did not doubt the certainty of victory. She understood how Ilona's mind worked, in logical straight lines. Therefore she also understood that her mother-in-law had to be met by logical answers, one for each point as it was raised. "She is not going on her own," she replied.

"Janice Corliss," Ilona remarked deprecatingly. "I don't even know the girl. Do you?"

"Yes, and I've met her parents. I like them. I'll arrange for Janice to come out here to meet you, if you like."

"I would appreciate that," Ilona said. "But these people, they aren't really, well . . ."

"Millionaires? No, but Janice has been Di's best friend for years. They have a lot in common—art, a desire to see the world—"

"To see the world. My God! Two young girls."

"Mother," Elizabeth said patiently. "Diana is nearly twenty years old."

"And that is not young?"

"I was in Paris when I was twenty," Elizabeth said reflectively. "And you were married, Mother, before *you* were twenty."

Ilona shot her a glance. Married to Sergei Roditchev, as everyone knew. Married because she had already had an affair, with George Hayman, and must marry quickly or face total ostracism. She decided to change tactics. "Anyway," she said. "This art business—well, it's an absurdity."

"Art is not at all an absurdity," Elizabeth declared, at last beginning to bridle.

"I don't mean in itself, my dear," Ilona said soothingly. "I meant for Diana. Her future is in newspapers, not in art."

"Perhaps she hopes to make newspapers into an art form," Elizabeth said, smiling. "I'm sorry, Mother, but this isn't 1905, and Diana is not a Russian princess. She is a very healthy, extroverted, American girl."

"Exactly," Ilona said triumphantly. "Is she sufficiently acquainted with the facts of *life*, Beth? In this day and age . . . and she is such a beautiful girl—"

"I can assure you that Diana is *fully* acquainted with the facts of life," Elizabeth said, a trifle grimly. "Sometimes I suspect she knows more about them than I do."

Ilona, of course, had no idea what she had just been told. "But is she aware that she is the *principal* heiress to the Hayman fortune?" she demanded. "That is what is really important. I mean, suppose she were to be kidnapped or something?"

Elizabeth arched her eyebrows. "I should think that is extremely unlikely, Mother. There has been no publicity about this trip; no one outside the family even knows she is going. And Diana has never played the heiress. Except for this new automobile of hers, one would almost think she was a pauper. She has never appeared in a single gossip column. I'll bet you could stop anyone on the street and ask them who Diana Hayman was, and they'd say, Diana *who?* Oh, sure, we know she's vulnerable, and is going to get more and more vulnerable with every year. We've discussed it time and again, George and I. But we are both determined not to make Di live a false life, just because she will one day own Hayman Newspapers. She has a right to live just like anyone else. I think a year to study art in London and Paris is a good idea. And I think I can truthfully say Diana knows how to take care of herself." Through the window she watched her daughter bringing off a perfect Chinese roquet, to send her Uncle John's ball plunging into the rhododendrons bordering the croquet lawn. "She's not quite the delicate little flower she seems to be."

"Excited about your trip?" George Hayman asked his granddaughter.

"I guess so." The game of croquet was over, and Diana sat beside her grandfather in one of the deck chairs under the sycamore trees. She knew how much he enjoyed her company.

"But you're not sure," he remarked.

"Sure I'm sure." She glanced at him, and gave one of her enchanting half-smiles. "Maybe I just don't want to build anything too big."

"Very wise." He leaned back. There were so many things he felt he should say to this girl. So many things he *wanted* to say. But he never actually said any of them. Nor, he suspected, did either Elizabeth or George junior.

He had never met anyone quite so self-contained. Perhaps even secretive, except that one hesitated to use such a derogatory term of so lovely and open-hearted a girl. And she *was* open-hearted. She had a tremendous sense of fun, which bridged far more years than she possessed; she would get down on the floor to play lead soldiers with little Alex or build bricks with Olga, and five minutes later would be gravely discussing the last session of the United Nations with himself and her father. She appeared to possess few of the vices of youth; she did not smoke and she drank very little, and if she had recently indulged herself in a Ferrari, there had been no reports of great speeding. Of course, with a girl like Diana, there were always young men around, but she seemed to view them all somewhat coolly.

Yet there was absolutely no means of knowing what was actually going on inside her head. Her blue eyes were like magnificently cut sapphires, the more sparkling because of the darkness of her hair, but they were also, if not as hard as sapphires, certainly as impenetrable. Of course, presumably at nineteen she had no secrets to keep—but he had an idea that all those handsome young executives who were anticipating the day when the boss was going to be a beautiful woman were going to get a bit of a shock. "Will you be looking up your Great-Uncle Peter?" he asked.

"Do I have to?"

"I don't think you have to do anything in this world you don't want to, Di. I just thought you might be curious."

"Well, maybe I am," she said. "Maybe I shall. I haven't made up my mind. Do you think that's wrong of me?"

"What, exactly?"

"Well . . . not to care all that much about the prince. About the whole Russian setup."

"I think that's eminently sensible of you," George remarked. "Although I suspect your grandmother would be disappointed to hear you say so. Has she never talked to you about the old days?"

"You mean about Starogan, and the serfs, and the thousands of acres of wheat . . ."

"They weren't serfs anymore," George interrupted, quietly. "Not in Ilona's time."

"Oh, they *were,* Grandpa. They might have been emancipated, officially, but they were still serfs. Anyway, that's history. Sure, when I'm Grandma's age, I hope to have a lot of memories to look back on. And I love to hear her talking about it. But it's as if she were reading *The Cherry Orchard* aloud, or *War and Peace,* or one of those. *I* can't ever live like that."

"And you can also hope, and pray, that you are never overtaken by quite such catastrophe as she was, either," George said.

Diana gazed at him. "Yes," she said. "That's true. That's why we're here, and not in Russia, isn't it, Grandpa?" Then she smiled. It was as if a million light bulbs had suddenly been illuminated behind her eyes and her mouth. She looked past him at the French doors leading to the drawing room. "Here's Aunt Felicity."

Diana, George remembered, being basically a romantic, had always been a supporter of Felicity and her strange, sad love affair with a cousin who was seven years younger than herself, and who was also a Russian spy. For the rest of them, all hastily turning toward the door from the house, Felicity Hayman appeared almost as a changeling.

Not physically. Felicity was a true Borodin, tall and voluptuously built; even at thirty-nine she moved with an athletic grace, and it would not be difficult to imagine her accompanying her aunt Tattie on one of those whirling, erotic dances of hers, skirts flying, mouth laughing, hair whipping to and fro. Save that Filly's mouth rarely smiled, and her hair was worn short these days. And where Tattie and Ilona had always looked at the world, and the people in it, with a vaguely surprised expression, as if wondering what all this vulgarity was doing impinging on *their* consciousness, Felicity looked from face to face defiantly, like a hunted animal prepared at any moment to turn at bay.

"Filly!" George junior kissed her on the cheek. "You've missed lunch, as usual."

"I had a sandwich," she said, her voice somewhat breathless. "Don't let me interrupt your game."

"We've finished," Diana said, hurrying up to embrace her. "You *are* going to come to lunch next week, though, aren't you Aunt Filly? It'll be my last for a year. I mean, here."

"Then perhaps I shall," Felicity said. She looked from face to face, nostrils dilating as she gazed at her half-brother—whose blundering interference she blamed for the collapse of her world—and turned to face her mother and Elizabeth, who had just emerged from the house. "Gregory sends you his regards," she said. "To all of you." She went inside, and up to her room.

"John Hayman. Come in, Hayman, and sit down." Allen Dulles was no less tall than his more famous brother, but projected a less acerbic image. "Ed Hoover's been telling me a lot about you."

"Not all of it good, I imagine." John Hayman cautiously lowered himself into the chair before the mahogany desk. It was not that he suffered from an inferiority complex. That was impossible for someone brought up as a Hayman, and very conscious that the Princess Ilona Borodina was his mother—even if he could never forget that Michael Nej was his father, and that he was a bastard. But, because of that background, he expected no one to take him at face value, everyone to wish to put him to some use, and that certainly included this man; Allen Dulles was his boss now. After the war old George had inveigled him into the FBI, mainly so that John's knowledge of Russia and Russians could be used to screen would-be immigrants into the United States. Thanks to that knowledge, he had been able to recognize Anna Ragosina and bring her house of spies crashing to the ground, but his relationship with J. Edgar Hoover had always been an uneasy one. Again, because of his background, John found it difficult to accept rules as anything more important than guidelines, and Hoover liked rules. Thus, following his triumph with Anna Ragosina, it had been Hoover himself who had suggested that he should transfer to this new organization, the Central Intelligence Agency, which, as the head of the FBI had wryly remarked, "makes up its rules as it goes along." In the two years he had been here, occupied at his old job of sifting through the files on Russian immigrants, John had seen little evidence of either making or breaking rules. But this was the first time he had been summoned to the office of the deputy director.

"Smoke?" Dulles asked.

John shook his head.

"We should've met before," Dulles said, leaning back in his chair. "I mean, you have to be the hottest potato in this entire outfit. Have you any idea what the great American public would have to say if they knew this organization was employing the son of one of Stalin's righthand men?"

John did not reply. Since Dulles *was* employing him, he supposed the question was rhetorical.

"It's not likely to happen," Dulles went on, "simply because nobody knows we exist, yet. They will find out eventually, of course. But we plan to keep things as they are for the time being. You've been with us two years. You know what our aims are." He paused.

"To combat the enemies, and further the policies, of the United States by all the means in our power," John said. "And nine times out of ten, we'll be eyeball to eyeball with the Reds."

"Which means you might one day be called upon to do something specifically intended to harm your old man. How do you feel about that?"

"I've made my choice," John said. "Don't get me wrong. I can't say I love my father. I don't know him well enough for that. But I respect him as a man who I believe is doing what he genuinely thinks is best for Russia. I don't happen to agree with him. So I figure that leaves me free to do what I genuinely think is best for Russia too, which is to oppose Communism."

Dulles gazed at him. "That's a pretty well-considered answer," he said at last. "And you certainly come highly recommended. Now tell me about your stepfather."

"George thinks I'm still working for the FBI," John said. "He knows about that. He got me in."

Dulles nodded. "He carries a lot of clout. I want you to keep him thinking that."

John sighed, regretfully. He, too, had enjoyed sharing so big a secret with George.

"What about the rest of your family?"

"They've accepted the cover, that I work with an advertising agency." John grinned. "It's a good cover. I even do some advertising work."

"That's the way a cover should be. So real it *is* real. What about your wife?"

"I don't enjoy lying to her," John said.

"But she accepts it too? That's good. That's how it has to be. Right?"

"Right."

"And your sister?"

John raised his eyebrows.

"You were involved in her boyfriend's arrest," Dulles reminded him.

"I was around, and I was responsible," John said. "Not involved, so far as she knows. The firm handled it very well. Seems I came across that photograph of Anna Ragosina in a friend's apartment, recognized her as the top KGB operative I had fought with during the war, and felt obliged to go to the FBI. Felicity hates my guts for that, though. She'd hate me even more, I guess, if she knew I ws only doing my job. But she doesn't."

Dulles gazed at him a moment longer, then tapped a file on his desk. "I want you to do some traveling."

John waited.

"We've heard indirectly, from your uncle, Peter Borodin," Dulles said. "You know about his activities?"

"Yes," John said, his brain starting to tick faster.

"Well, he's still at it, dreaming of bringing down the Reds." Dulles gave a quick smile. "Don't we all? Now he wants to communicate with the state department. Says he has information which could be of great value. He's probably looking for financing for another of his crazy projects. But you never know. I want you to go to England and find out what he *does* want, and what he has to say."

"Are you aware, Mr. Dulles, that my Uncle Peter is a nut?" John asked.

"I'd agree he has a phobia."

"You can say that again," John agreed. "You have to understand how his brain works. He was prince of Starogan. Unless he'd been born a Romanov he couldn't possibly have started life any higher. Then he had it all ripped away by the Bolsheviks. He hates them as . . . hell, as Torquemada must have hated the heretics. Or vice versa. He really isn't sane when it comes to Soviet Russia."

"That doesn't mean he may not have found out something worth knowing. He has agents all over the place, apparently. I wish I knew where his financing comes from."

"From Russian émigrés who feel as he does," John said. "There are still a lot of them around. And most of them look to the prince of Starogan as their natural leader."

"So talk to him," Dulles persisted. "There's something big happening over there right now. Or maybe it's already happened. From all the comings and goings at the Kremlin, it could be a major shake-up in the Soviet hierarchy. Rumor even has it old Joe may be on the way out. If that's the case, we want to know about it before anybody else. And it's just possible that's the information your uncle wants to sell. The point is, you know him and his phobia. Better than any other agent I could send, you'll know whether he does have something or is spouting hot air."

John sighed. "I have to tell you, Mr. Dulles, that I once worked for my uncle. That was when . . . well, I was brought up to believe that I was the son of my mother's first husband, Prince Roditchev."

"I remember the name. Wasn't he head of the tsar's secret police?"

"Right," John said. "A total monster. Anyway, I thought I was his son and heir—he was murdered when the Reds took over, you see—and I guess when I was a kid I wanted to avenge his death and get back my inheritance just as badly as Uncle Peter. So I was one of his agents for a while."

Dulles nodded. "It's in your file. Weren't you even arrested by the NKVD once? By your friend Ragosina?"

"That's right," John said.

"And your real father got you out. You've had a romantic life, Hayman. And it's just those incidents in your past that make you so valuable to us."

"What I am trying to say, sir, is that Uncle Peter and I quarreled when I discovered my true father. We haven't spoken to each other since. For me suddenly to turn up, twenty years later . . . he's bound to be suspicious of me."

"Not if you have a good reason. If you were having a vacation in England, wouldn't you pay him a call?"

"Maybe. But if I *was* vacationing in England, I'd have Natasha and the kids with me." He waited expectantly.

Dulles shook his head. "Too risky. It would be better if you went over on business for your advertising firm. But isn't your niece going over there in a week or two, on some sort of a grand tour?"

John frowned. "How the devil did you know that?"

Dulles tapped his nose. "It's my business to know everything. Or try to. If you happened to be in London on business—advertising business—at the same time as Diana Hayman, wouldn't you take her along to meet her great-uncle? I think you should."

"It would be involving Diana with a total lunatic. I'm not sure I can consider that."

"Consider it," Dulles said. "You'll be there. What harm can come to her with you breathing down her neck? *Tell* her he's a nut. Convince her. And she only has to meet him once. So you can get in and hear what he has to say."

"As what? Or who?"

"The state department will give you a personal letter, as an advertising executive, asking you to act as their unofficial agent in this matter. The FBI and the CIA don't come into it at all."

"You've figured it all out."

"We try."

"And if I say that I don't like it one little bit? Involving my own family isn't what I had in mind when I joined this outfit."

"I'd say you *have* joined this outfit, Hayman. And we—you—have a job to do. A job the end-product of which is making this world, this America, safe from Communism, remember. That means a safer place for your niece as well. So get to it." He grinned, and held out his hand. "And have a good trip."

"You're going to Europe? Are you really?" Ilona cried, giving her eldest son a hug. "Oh, John, that's wonderful news. I am so pleased. Have you told Diana yet?"

"As a matter of fact, no," John confessed. "Do you think she'll mind very much?"

"Why should she?" Ilona demanded.

"She'll be as mad as a wet hen," George said, smiling.

"Yes," John agreed. "I suspect you may be right. We'll just have to convince her that it *is* pure coincidence that I'll be traveling with her."

"She'll be delighted," Ilona asserted, decisively. "To be shown around London by her handsome uncle? What more could any girl ask?"

"Well," John said doubtfully, "don't forget that I *am* going over on business for the firm. But if she wants to be taken anywhere while I'm there..." He hesitated. "I thought I might look up Uncle Peter, since I'm going to be over there anyway."

"Oh, would you, John?" Ilona cried. "I'd be so grateful. I do write to him, you know, from time to time. But he never replies. I don't know what he's doing, and..."

"I have no doubt at all he's doing the same things he's always been doing," George said. "Plotting and scheming."

"Oh, I know he's crazy," Ilona agreed. "But to think of him, all alone over there... he *is* my only brother, you know. I'd be so very grateful if you'd pay him a visit, John. I'm sure he'd like to see the children, as well."

"I'm not taking the children," John explained. "Or Natasha. This is a business trip, Mother. You must get that through your head. Since Di is going to be on the same boat and I'll be in London at the same time, I'll keep an eye on her. But I *am* going to work. I did think though, that if I was going to pay a call on Uncle Peter, she might like to come along."

"Oh, I think that would be marvelous," Ilona exclaimed. "I'm sure she would like that very much."

"Yes," George observed dryly. He accompanied John out to the car. "Something up?" he inquired.

"Not really," John said. "A routine matter."

George studied him, and John knew his ears were red. "So it's none of my business," George said. "Although, you know, I almost had a feeling that Peter might be up to his old tricks. Then I decided he couldn't be, or you wouldn't risk involving Diana. Knowing how that scoundrel enjoys using his own family."

"Right," John agreed, attempting what he hoped was a reassuring smile.

"Anyway," George went on, "I'll be seeing Hoover when I'm in Washington next week."

"And he won't know a thing," John said, praying that would indeed be so. But his smile was sad as he got into the Studebaker and started the engine. He reflected that he must be the loneliest man in the world, now. Or maybe all CIA agents were lonely men.

And there was at least one other person as lonely as himself, he thought, pulling the car to the side of the road to catch up with a walking figure. "Can I give you a lift?"

Felicity did not turn her head. "I enjoy walking."

"You must," he agreed, thinking of the five cars in the Hayman garages behind him. "Felicity . . . couldn't we make up?" He drove beside her in low gear.

"Make up what?" She still did not turn her head, but she was suddenly short of breath, and her cheeks were flushed.

"Filly," he said, pulling in front of her this time, and opening his door. "I did what I had to do. For everyone's sake. For America's sake."

She stared at him.

"Okay," he said. "So we're all a bunch of lousy capitalists and you'd far rather live in Russia. Look, Felicity, I never had Gregory arrested, you know. He gave himself up, because of you. Because Anna Ragosina had shot you. He behaved in a very noble and courageous fashion. Everyone acknowledges that. But the fact is, he was spying against us, after having been accepted as a Russian defector, after having applied for U.S. citizenship. Whether you approve of us or not, he did break our laws."

"And now he's being punished for it," Felicity said. "Aren't you satisfied?"

"I want to be friends with you, Felicity. You're my sister, remember? My only sister."

"I suppose Mother has been at you," she said. "She thinks I should stop going to visit Gregory. She says it's a scandal. Do you think I give a damn if it's causing a scandal? He's locked up in Sing Sing, a man of thirty-two, just caged, day after day after day, while we're all free out here. Doing what? Making money? Playing croquet? Printing newspapers? Advertising junk? It makes me sick."

John sighed. "I feel sorry for the guy, really I do. But there is nothing either you or I can do about it now."

"Yes, there is," she said fiercely. "We can show the world that we think it's wrong. I can, anyway."

"So you're going to visit him every Sunday for the rest of your life, is that it?" John demanded, beginning to get angry himself.

"Until he's released, yes."

"And when do you suppose that will be?"

"He thinks he may get out after ten years. That's only eight years from now."

"Great balls of fire," John cried. "Eight *years?* You'll be damned near fifty, Felicity. And when he *is* released, what's going to happen then? He'll be deported back to Russia."

"Then I'll go with him."

"You'll do *what?*"

"If that's what's going to happen," Felicity said, "then that's what's going to happen. But wherever he goes, and whatever happens, I *am* going to go with him. *Nobody* is going to stop me. So why don't you drive off about your very important business and leave me to walk in peace?"

"Don't keep supper for me, Mother," Diana Hayman said. "I'll have a hamburger with Janice."

"After art class," Elizabeth remarked.

"That's right." Diana peered into the hall mirror of the Fifth Avenue penthouse and adjusted a wayward eyebrow with a dampened finger. She wore a white turtleneck sweater and pale blue slacks, loafers with bobby socks, and her hair was caught back in a pony tail. And she managed, in that inelegant state, to look absurdly beautiful.

"Di—" Elizabeth bit her lip.

"Yes, Mother?" Diana turned to look at her.

Elizabeth sighed. She was always intending to have a serious chat with her daughter, whenever there happened to be an appropriate time. The trouble was, there was never an appropriate time. Diana had only to look at her with that devastating gaze of hers, and serious chats became an impossible embarrassment.

They gave the world a tremendous impression of understanding each other—without any understanding at all, at least on Elizabeth's part. She could understand that obviously Diana had never got over that disastrous love affair of two years before. Richard Malling had been a boy of good family, lots of money, and even though they were both rather young, still she and George had been all in favor of the engagement, as had the Mallings. And then had come the afternoon when she returned early from a sitting, opened Diana's bedroom door without thinking, and found them in bed together. Elizabeth had been far less shocked than she had pretended to be. As a young artist in Greenwich Village, she had lost her virginity in far less acceptable circumstances. She had confessed as much to George when he had proposed, and it had made no difference to him at all. Besides, this *was* the boy Diana was going to marry. Nor had the girl seemed the least upset. And yet, two weeks later she had announced that she would not be seeing Richard again. And that was that. Elizabeth had almost begged her, using old-fashioned phrases such as "But you've given yourself to him," without making the slightest impression. She blamed herself, of course. Appearances aside, her interruption *had* obviously, deeply embarrassed them both, and no doubt caused a quarrel. Yet if such a thing *could* happen—well, obviously Richard was not the man for Di to marry. That she could accept.

What was so disturbing was that since that day Diana had never had another boyfriend. Or a girlfriend, save for Janice Corliss. Of course she had hundreds of dates, and appeared to flirt as much as anyone. But she had never brought another boy home, and she had seldom gone out with one more than once or twice. It was as if that *coitus interruptus* had put her off men, in a serious way, forever. Elizabeth had even discussed the matter with George. "Don't you think a good psychiatrist might be an idea? I mean, I don't want her to go to bed with every boy who asks her out. I don't *want* her to go to bed with *anybody*, until she's married. But I want her to *want* to, if you follow me. And she doesn't seem to."

"So she's choosy," George had pointed out, in that remarkably relaxed manner of his which sometimes nearly drove *her* to a psychiatrist. "You must be the most extraordinary mother in America. Most of them worry about their daughters *ever* getting into bed with a man. I won't have Di going to a shrink. That idea is absolutely out."

He didn't seem to understand, and she didn't really know how to put it to him, that she suspected there might be some kind of psychological bloc in Diana's mind. These things did happen; she had seen evidence of them during her youth in Greenwich Village. And while Diana came across as the most sane and sensible of young women, there was no use denying the fact that she *did* have Russian ancestry; it was impossible to say what strange hang-ups or phobias might have come lurking down the generations. Elizabeth had never met Tatiana Borodina, for instance, but from all accounts she appeared to have been most eccentric. While that remarkable old man, Uncle Peter, whom everyone carelessly described as nuts . . .

But what should she do? It was impossible even to consider forcing any solutions on Diana, because Diana was simply not to be forced. In little more than a year she would be twenty-one, and would come into her trust fund and an income of half a million dollars a year. She would then be a full adult—with only one friend. Since the day Elizabeth had glanced through Diana's portfolio and found it filled with nude studies of Janice Corliss, the possibilities that had occurred to her at two o'clock on every sleepless morning were hardly to be considered, and quite impossible to discuss with George. Thus she had jumped at Diana's desire to spend a year studying art in Europe, had written letters to friends making sure that the girl would be looked after and entertained, and would meet all the eligible young men in Britain and France. And then she had discovered to her consternation that Janice was going too. Of course everyone had been delighted; as Ilona had said, one does not allow a nineteen-year-old girl to go abroad by herself. When Edna Corliss had said how splendid it was, because the two girls would be able to share an apartment and be company for each other, she could only suppose that Edna had never looked through Janice's portfolio.

But she had had to appear as delighted as anyone. Her imagination simply could not cope with Ilona's reactions should she confess her real fears, even if it *had* meant almost having a quarrel with the dear old lady. But she couldn't discuss her fears with *anyone*.

And least of all, Diana.

So she said, "I was wondering if you were too upset about your Uncle John traveling with you."

"I'll tell you that when I come back," Diana said. "He's a sweetie, so having him along will probably be fun. But if I thought anyone was sending him as a chaperon . . ." She gazed at her mother.

"No one is," Elizabeth said hastily. "It *is* a business trip."

"Well, then—" Diana kissed her mother on the cheek. "See you." The door banged, and a moment later Elizabeth heard the whirr of the elevator, which would take Diana down to the basement garage and her Ferrari. She returned to the drawing room and gazed out the window, thoughtfully tapping her teeth with a pencil. John Hayman, she thought. He had experienced so much, encountered so much in his life, it was possible he might just take her seriously, without either being shocked or pooh-poohing the entire idea. And obviously he was a man Diana liked, and might even accept advice from.

She picked up the telephone.

Chapter 3

THE FERRARI EASED UP TO THE STREET CORNER WHERE JANICE Corliss waited. "Sorry I'm late," Diana said. "Mother got to talking."

Janice slipped into the passenger seat. She was several inches taller than Diana, and had a voluptuous figure to set off her short, curly yellow hair. She was a pretty girl, but had long resigned herself to playing second fiddle to her friend, and not only on account of wealth and position—no man who happened to glance at Diana ever looked beyond her. "About the trip?" she asked.

"Not exactly. We'll talk about it later." The car moved smoothly away from the curb.

Janice sighed. "I think you're crazy. Don't you ever use the telephone?"

Diana slowly drove through Central Park. "You know I can't do that, Jan."

"Oh, sure. When you break up with a guy you have to look him straight in the eye. And what happens then? He starts to play with your tits, and next thing you know you're on your back with your legs in the air, waiting to be screwed."

Diana emerged from the park and entered a side street, found a parking space, pulled in, switched off the engine, and regarded the young men who were regarding *her* from across the street; neither Ferraris nor Diana Hayman were common in this neighborhood. "Not this time," she said. "That's where you come in."

"I'd do you more good by bringing you off right here," Janice said.

Diana's head turned. "Would you like to?"

"What?"

Diana shrugged. "That's what Mother thinks we do, all the time."

"You're kidding!"

"She thinks we're lesbians, believe it or not."

"Oh, really, Di . . ."

"Fact. I think it's because you pose for me more than anybody else. She keeps making up her mind to talk to me about it, like tonight. Only she can't do it, because she's afraid I'll just say, yes, we are. And sometimes, you know, I wonder if that isn't the answer." She opened her door and got out. "Ten minutes," she said. "Not a second longer. And if those guys get fresh, there's a police whistle in the glove compartment. Ten minutes."

She crossed the street before Janice could protest further, smiled at the onlookers. "Hi," she said. "You'll get wet, standing there, when it starts to rain."

They stared at her. Her total self-confidence left them collectively speechless, for the moment. She had already reached the sports shop before one of them remembered to wolf-whistle.

In the doorway she hesitated, biting her lip. If those characters only *knew* . . . She pushed the door, stepped inside as a buzzer sounded at the back of the shop. "Hi," she said as the proprietor emerged from the office. "I'm looking for tennis socks, size five, white with red tops."

"You just made it," he said. "I'm about to close." And did so, shutting the door and dropping the blind, before turning back to catch her arm as she started inspecting the sock stand. "I thought you were never coming."

As Janice had predicted, she was in his arms. Nearly. But she got her hands on his chest and pushed him away. He was big and young and tough-looking and had a thrusting jaw . . . but he did not resist her. He loved her too much.

"What's wrong, Di?"

Diana sighed. She had done this so often in the past two

years that she could not understand why each time was as difficult as the last. Maybe because she never believed each time could *be* the last. Was she a nympho? She didn't think so. She was overresponsive, physically. It was as if she lacked that extra layer of unawareness that most people seemed to have. She was turned on all the time. Her problem was that she wanted to share it, all the time, so playing with herself had never brought more than temporary satisfaction. But what she really wanted was to *love*, and be loved. The second wasn't difficult; most men fell in love with her at first sight. And she had always figured that among all those loving men, there had to be *one* she could love back. That was where the trouble started. When a man *touched* her, sparks flew. She *belonged*. For five minutes. And then . . . The cycle had begun with Richard Malling. They had met, he had naturally been attracted to her, she had been equally attracted to him, they had started petting, and bingo. She had gone wild. Poor Richard. He had been very reluctant to go all the way, even when she provided all the necessary equipment. Even if pregnancy was no longer a risk, he had felt it was somehow wrong. When Mother had caught them at it he had been terrified. She had had to reassure him that Mother had never mentioned the matter and never would, certainly to his parents. But by then the cycle had already started. She had found herself thinking, but what am I *doing?* So he turns me on. So what? There's got to be more to it than that. And there *was* nothing more. She didn't even like him, not anything about him, all that much—not the clothes he wore or his scent or his conversation or his sense of humor.

No one had been able to understand her breaking off that desirable engagement, Mother least of all, while Diana had determined to replace it with another, just as quickly as it could be done. She wanted men to make love to her. But she wanted to be able to love them back. She just couldn't make up her mind which had to come first, and the lovemaking always seemed to do that. Suddenly she had been desperate—perhaps, she decided, she was incapable of love. She could confide in Jan, because Jan gave a good pretense of understanding, without, perhaps, *really* understanding at all. Jan certainly thought she was well on the way to becoming a nympho, but had willingly accepted the watchdog role, though not all that successfully. Diana's desperation had taken her through nine men in two years. Nine *affairs*. Logic and common sense kept telling her that since she was only nineteen, she had all the time in the world to find someone to love even if she stopped looking, but all the while she knew that she would never stop looking.

For the last three men she had stepped down a social class. For this one, two social classes. That had been a deliberate act of policy; maybe the men of the top drawer—her own drawer—had something about them that repelled her. So now there was Ben. She had met him playing tennis; he was a good tennis player, and a terrific lover. But she had become just as rapidly bored and repelled by *his* personality and habits and clothes as she had been by all the others.

Ben had, in fact, been the last straw. She had known that she had to get out of New York, out of the United States. She had to draw breath, and think. Mother had been for the idea, totally misunderstanding the situation. She had been less enthusiastic when she had learned that Janice was going too. The poor dear couldn't get it through her head that Janice was a very *necessary* watchdog.

She faced him. "I came to say good-bye."

"Good-bye?" He looked totally bewildered.

"I'm going away for a while."

"Away?" He was aghast. "Away where?"

"Canada," she told him, looking him in the eye. She knew there was a very good chance that he would shut up his shop and follow her.

"You never told me."

"I am telling you now, Ben," she explained.

He reached for her, held her wrists, drew her close to him. "But why?"

"Because . . . because I have to," she said. "Ben . . . please let me go."

"Your mother is sending you away, isn't she?" he demanded, holding her closer. "She's found out about us, and wants to break it up. Diana . . . oh, Diana . . ." He was kissing her now, crushing her against him while his fingers roamed under her sweater to find her naked flesh, sliding up to find and hold her breasts and then her shoulders, before slipping down her back, driving inside even the tightness of the pants to hold her buttocks. "Oh, Diana . . . Why don't we get married? The hell with your mother, and your inheritance—with the whole damn thing. Marry me! *I'll* take you to Canada, if you like. We'll honeymoon at Niagara. Anything you want, Di. Anything!"

Waves of sensation were racing through her, as usual. As usual, her eyes had closed and she knew nothing but sensation, mounting passion and ecstasy, the certainty that she was going to say yes, that nothing mattered except this man's touch . . .

The buzzer sounded.

"For Christ's sake," Ben growled, but his fingers were dragging away. "In there," he whispered, pointing at the office before turning away.

Diana retreated against the counter, taking deep breaths, and watched him open the door. "For Christ's sake," he said again. "What do *you* want?"

"If we don't leave now, we're going to be late," Janice said, and stepped past him, to find Diana hastily pulling down her sweater. "Have you said your piece?"

"What piece?" Ben demanded. "That she's going away? I won't let her. I—"

Janice looked at Diana. "This was your idea," she reminded her friend. "I belong to the phone-call brigade."

Ben looked from one to the other. "What *is* this?"

Diana took a long breath and left the support of the counter. "I came here to say good-bye, Ben," she said. "Mother isn't sending me away. I'm going of my own accord. I won't be seeing you again."

"You—" He stared at her. "You're not serious."

"I *am* serious, Ben." She stood beside Janice.

"But . . . why? We love each other. We—"

"We don't love each other, Ben. I don't love *you,* anyway. I liked making love to you for a while. Now I don't anymore. I'm sorry, Ben, but there it is."

He stared at her, and Janice opened the shop door.

Diana stepped through, almost ran down the pavement, tumbled into the seat of the Ferrari, and gunned the engine. Janice jumped in beside her, and they roared into the night.

"Do you think," Diana said, "that I'm the biggest cockteaser there ever was?"

"No," Janice said. "I can't honestly describe you as a cockteaser. But if I ever saw my brother taking you out I'd brain you with a hammer." She smiled, and squeezed Diana's hand.

"He's only fourteen, so stop worrying. By the time he's old enough to afford you, someone will have taken you *apart*."

"It's actually . . . my God, nearly forty years since I last saw Starogan." John Hayman made conversation with some desperation, as he walked between the two girls along the first-class promenade deck of the *Queen Mary,* watching the occasional whitecaps breaking in the June moonlight. If anyone had told him that he would be in a constant state of embarrassment at having to entertain two extraordinarily lovely young women for four days he would have laughed out loud. Yet this was proving ten times as difficult as he had thought it would be. That was because of his lunch with Elizabeth, of course. Yet the fact was there; he was afraid to stop talking. "It really is just a haze to me," he went on. "I remember space. Miles and miles of space. Not just outside. Outside one could ride for miles and miles and never leave Borodin land. But inside as well. You know, we think the house at Cold Spring Harbor, for instance, is pretty spacious. But we have no idea. The entire ground floor at Cold Spring Harbor could have been cut out of the drawing room at Starogan and never been missed. And servants! Wherever you turned, whatever you wanted to do, there was a servant at your side to keep you from having to make any effort."

"It sounds marvelous," Janice said. "Just marvelous. You know, I've read about places like that, but I don't think I believed they really exist."

Surely, he thought, Elizabeth had imagined the whole thing. The two girls were the best of friends, and undoubtedly very close. But if they were lovers, then they must have been lovers for a very long time. There was a complete absence of the glances, the deliberately accidental touches, the secret smiles, that new lovers could not resist.

He would have enjoyed the voyage much more had Janice not been here at all, he thought a little resentfully. So perhaps he wanted to shock her a little when he said, "On the other hand, we mustn't ever forget that those same servants were the ones who dragged Mother's sister-in-law around by her hair before cutting off her breasts and throwing her on a trash heap to bleed to death. That was Princess Irina."

"God!" Janice said. "You know, that is even more incredible, that such things happen."

What would this girl say if she knew one iota of the things *he* had experienced during the war? John reflected. Young German soldiers, still living, briefly, after Anna Ragosina had finished castrating them? Or his cousin Svetlana, Gregory Nej's sister, a crumpled bloodied mess after the Gestapo had got through with *her?* But there was a limit to the pleasure gleaned from shocking people.

"They did things like that because they were serfs, who suddenly got fed up with being treated like dirt." Diana stopped walking and leaned on the rail. John and Janice followed her example. Diana, John was coming to realize, traveled through life like a queen, never questioning that all others would fall into place beside her. He realized he had never really known her before; at Sunday lunches at Cold Spring Harbor her impact had always been diluted by the other strong personalities in his family.

In which he was the true changeling. But he couldn't just let her stamp him into the dust. "There were no serfs when I was there," he said.

"You know, that's just what Grandpa said. A serf is a serf is a serf, Uncle John, whether he's restricted by law or by debt. Human beings weren't meant to be serfs. They resent it. And after enduring it for a certain length of time, they do something about it."

"You're starting to sound like your Aunt Felicity, or my own father, for that matter. Let's hope you never experience recently emancipated serfs at first hand."

She smiled. "I'm sure I would hate to be dragged around by my hair and then have my breasts cut off. One or the other perhaps—but both?" She kissed him on the cheek. "Believe me, I can understand that Great-Uncle Peter may have had good reason for going nuts. I do believe I'm quite looking forward to meeting him."

"Ah," John murmured. He had broached the subject of Peter on the very first day at breakfast, because he had felt it his duty to do so. It was certainly not a part of the instructions he had received from Elizabeth, which had been to make sure that Diana met as many handsome—"but nice, really nice"—young men as possible. He did not suppose there would be any handsome, and nice, young men to be found in the vicinity of a seventy-two-year-old raving lunatic. But since he had to *be* met, the sooner it was done the better.

"Is he really nuts?" Janice said.

"Paranoid," Diana explained. "He wants to get his estates back, like Starogan. Isn't that it, Uncle John?"

"I don't think it is, anymore," John said. "He did want to get Starogan back, in the beginning, when it still seemed possible. Now . . . I think he just hates everything Communist. I really don't want either of you to take *anything* he says at all seriously. I think you should promise me that you won't."

"I promise you not to take anything about this entire trip seriously, Uncle John," Diana said, very seriously. "I'm here to relax. Just relax. And I think that's already happening. Tomorrow's the big dance, isn't it, since we dock the day after?"

"That's right."

"Then I think an early night is indicated. Coming, Jan?"

She blew her uncle a kiss, and went toward the ladder, Janice obediently following. They did everything together. And it was no use reminding himself that they had separate cabins, for the cabins were opposite each other.

What was far more disturbing was that they had been at sea three days now, and Diana had shown not the slightest interest in all the many young men, from officers to passengers, who had shown a great deal of interest in her.

What a hell of a mess to have to sort out, for a CIA operative in the midst of a difficult mission. Well, he thought, Peter will *have* to be tackled right away, so that I can concentrate on Diana for a day or two.

"You're Diana, of course," announced Prince Peter Borodin of Starogan, seizing Janice's hands and pulling her into his arms.

Janice gave a terrified squeal as she virtually disappeared. Peter Borodin had put on a great deal of weight, and looked like an enormous white-haired bear.

"No, no, Uncle Peter," John said. *"This* is Diana."

"This?" Peter Borodin seemed to have some difficulty in locating her. *"Your* child, you mean?"

"I am the daughter of George and Elizabeth Hayman, Uncle Peter," Diana said evenly. "And if you continue to pretend that you don't know that, I shall leave."

Peter Borodin stared at her with his mouth open.

"The young woman you are currently smothering is my

friend, Janice Corliss," Diana explained. "Now, would you like to kiss *me?*"

"Bless my soul," Peter Borodin remarked. "Bless my soul." He glanced at John, who shrugged, while hastily suppressing a grin. Cautiously Peter Borodin, having released Janice, embraced Diana. "Of course, I can see that you *are* a Borodin," he said. "It's in your eyes. But the rest of you . . . your mother must be an Indian."

"My mother is an American," Diana said. "And you can't get any better than that. What are all those pins for?" She was deciding she did not like her great-uncle very much, after all. Certainly, if it was going to come to a matter of putting the other down, she had no intention of being beaten. Now she disengaged herself from him to look at an enormous map of Europe and Russia which was placed on the study wall, and covered with multicolored pins.

"My theater of operations," Peter explained pompously. "The center of the war against Communism."

"Then what do the pins stand for?"

"Well . . ." He put his arm around her shoulder. "The red pins represent the present whereabouts of the twenty most important Russian leaders, based on the latest available information. You'll observe that most of them are accumulated in Moscow. But not all. And some . . ." He pointed. "These two, for example, you'll see are on the railway line proceeding west from Tomsk. Anna Ragosina and Ivan Nej." He waited expectantly.

"Are they so important?" Diana asked.

Peter gazed at John, eyebrows arched.

John shrugged again; suddenly he was enjoying himself enormously. "I don't think Diana ever read the memoirs I wrote for the paper," he explained.

"Good heavens," Prince Peter commented. "They are very old enemies of your family, my dear. Now, my agents have reported to me that they left Tomsk, traveling west, oh, three months ago. That was after a meeting with Michael Nej—your father, John—went to Tomsk to see them. Now, we presume they were going to Moscow. But nobody has yet reported seeing them there. So it would appear to be a secret move. But that they should have left Tomsk at all is interesting, wouldn't you say?"

"Why?" Diana asked.

Peter turned to John again. "Wouldn't *you* say?"

"I suppose I would. It means that Father has managed to have Ivan reinstated, I guess. Blood is supposed to be thicker than water. Or an awareness of crimes. And wherever Ivan goes, there goes Anna Ragosina."

"And all of that does not interest you?"

"I told you, it does. But I doubt it interests Diana."

"That man—" Peter pointed at the pin as if it had life, while his big Borodin features glowed with a mixture of whiskey and indignation. "—Murdered your aunt. He murdered my wife. He murdered my mother. He murdered my *grand*mother."

"Then he can't be any spring chicken," Diana observed. She had decided she would have to be cruel to be kind, or the evening would degenerate into a maudlin family history. "And these light-colored pins?"

Peter had removed his arm from around her shoulder. "They are other international leaders of importance," he said stiffly. "And the white-headed pins, of course, are my people."

Diana peered at the map. "Some of them are inside Russia."

"Naturally."

"Do the Russians know this?"

"Naturally not," Peter said, scathingly.

"But . . . you have this map sitting up here, with all their locations on it, for anyone to bust in and look at?"

"Bust in?" Peter inquired. "No one enters here, unless he or she is a member of my organization or an utterly trustworthy friend. Or relative." He frowned at her, as if wondering if she could possibly be included in the last category. Then he smiled. "But come. I have some young people for you to meet." He marched in front of them to the double doors, and threw them open.

"You're right," Diana whispered to her uncle. "He *is* a nut. A complete nut. But . . . there *is* something a little noble about him, too."

John squeezed her hand. "Just remember that most of the people you meet will fall into the same category—without, perhaps, the nobility."

To John's considerable surprise, there was quite a party going on in the living room, and equally to his surprise, the guests seemed to range in age from the very young to the middle-aged. Diana was equally surprised but obviously pleased when Peter ushered them into the larger room.

"My niece," Peter Borodin said to the group assembled there, airily waving his hand. "And her friend. And my nephew, John Hayman. You've all heard of John Hayman, of course. He used to work with us, back in the twenties, before . . ." He eyed John speculatively. "Before he went astray. Introduce yourselves, girls. John come over here and meet Roger Corby. He's my chief-of-staff."

"Now wait a moment," John said. "You mean all these people work for you?"

"I wouldn't say *for* me. They work *with* me, for the common good."

"You mean they are all Russian émigrés?"

"Good heavens, no. The only Russian émigrés here tonight are you and me. And Diana, of course."

John decided against arguing the point. He was too interested.

"These people are mostly English. One or two French. I have recruited them all very carefully. Or rather, we have, eh, Roger?"

"You can say that again." Corby shook hands. "I *have* heard a lot about you, Mr. Hayman, and I read your memoirs. I was with the Royal Marine Commandos. I guess we both had a busy war."

"And John is here on official business," Peter boomed. "It will be almost like old times."

John looked left and right in alarm. "That is supposed to be confidential, Uncle Peter."

"Everything here is confidential. We shall have to have a long talk. You'll stay to dinner?"

"What about the girls?"

Peter Borodin turned his head to look across the room at where Diana and Janice were completely surrounded by interested young men. "I imagine they'll find *somewhere* to eat," he remarked. "And even someone to eat with."

"My name is Robert Loung," the young man said. "And you are . . . ?"

Diana studied him. He was much taller than herself, without matching the men of her family in height. He was young, in his middle twenties, she estimated, a trifle too heavily muscled at his shoulders, which suggested some sort of vigorous athletics such as football, and aquiline in feature—not quite a hatchet face, but very strong. His eyes were blue, like her own, his hair similarly dark and wavy. He had a wide smile, which he was currently employing, and good teeth. His voice sounded like that of a BBC newscaster, which probably meant he had been to one of those peculiar English establishments known as a public school, despite the fact that it was exclusively private.

She found him distinctly attractive. "I'm Diana Hayman," he said, and allowed him to squeeze her hand.

"You're the old boy's niece."

"Grandniece."

"Well, I am absolutely delighted to meet you. Grandniece . . ." He composed an artificial frown of bewilderment. "That must mean your grandmother is Ilona Borodina. The princess."

"I know her as Ilona Hayman."

"Forgive me. But Prince Peter lectures us about the Russian aristocracy quite often. He doesn't often remind us of the names they've accumulated over the years. Are you going to be in London long?"

"A few weeks." She finished her drink. She had taken it from a tray offered her by another young man, and had no idea what it was she had drunk.

"Another?" asked Robert Loung.

"Why not? What is it, incidentally?"

"Port and lemon."

"What did you say?"

"Port wine and lemonade."

She peered into the glass. "At seven in the evening?" But, she reflected, this port could hardly be anything even faintly resembling her grandfather's 1928 Cockburn, lovingly produced at the end of the evening meal.

"Where are you staying, if I'm not being bold?"

"You're not. I'm staying at the Savoy Hotel. Do you know it?"

"The . . ." He gave a gulp. "You must be very wealthy, Miss Hayman."

Could it be possible that he had never heard of Hayman Newspapers? She gazed past him at Janice, who was doing all sorts of tricks with her eyebrows. Because she had promised, absolutely promised, not even to look twice at anything in pants for the whole six months.

And also, not to let on who she really was. That was to save them the trouble of dumping the inevitable hangers-on.

"My mother is Elizabeth Dodge," she explained.

Robert Loung waited.

"The artist," Diana explained.

"Oh, of course."

"You've never heard of her, have you?"

"Well . . . I'm not very up on modern art."

"I," Diana said crushingly, "am an art student."

"Oh. I should have guessed. Perhaps you could tell me about it. And about your mother. Over dinner. I'm afraid I can't rise to the Savoy Grill, but I know a neat little trattoria . . . or maybe you don't eat spaghetti."

"I adore spaghetti," Diana said. "But you'll have to ask my friend as well."

Robert Loung looked left and right. "I think we could find a fourth," he said.

"Then I'll come. If you promise to tell me why you work for an old creep like Great-Uncle Peter."

His face stiffened. "Prince Peter is a great man," he said. "One of the few who really recognize the threat posed by international Communism. By Soviet Russia in particular."

"You mean you *believe* that?"

"Of course I do. We all do, or we wouldn't be here at all."

He was so naïve. But charming, nonetheless. And she could tell he was simply a mass of rippling muscles, while there was something more . . . a certain innate toughness about him, for all his exquisite manners, which suggested he might be able to hold his own in a fight. So she had no intention of fighting him. But it also suggested that he might be a delicious companion in bed.

"Well, I'm waiting to hear all about it," she said. "And I'll tell you a secret: we're only staying at the hotel for a couple of nights, until our apartment is ready. Our flat, right? We're moving in on Thursday." She looked past him again, at Janice, and did some eyebrow waggling of her own.

"You need your head examined," Janice Corliss remarked icily. "And some other parts of you as well."

Dinner was over, and they had escaped to the ladies' room.

At least Janice, who had not enjoyed herself at all, had escaped. Diana had been rather reluctantly dragged away.

"He really is very nice," she protested. "I've never met an Englishman before, or at least not one my own age. Just visitors that Mother and Dad entertained."

"And you don't suppose he's like all the others?" Janice demanded. "He's after your body and then your money. Come to think of it, I may have the order wrong."

"Oh, come now," Diana said. "He doesn't even know who I am."

"That is the oldest dodge in the world," Janice pointed out. "Of course he knows who you are. Your great-uncle must have told him. Which means from the very start that he's a liar. And he's a man. And you promised—" She bit her lip, because the door had opened to admit another female diner.

"They said they were calling a taxi," Diana said, and hurried off.

"It's waiting for us." Robert held her hand as they left the restaurant. "What are you doing tomorrow?"

"Well . . ." She sat beside him in the back of the cab, Janice and her date pressed against them to reduce them to a huddle in the corner; his arm was around her shoulders and his hand flopped dangerously close to her right breast. She knew he wouldn't touch, because he was too much of a gentleman, but just having it there . . . "We only landed yesterday. We haven't really decided on anything. We don't have to check in at art school for weeks and weeks."

"Let me take you somewhere. The Tower. A boat trip down to Greenwich. The zoo. A walk in the park. Any park. Hyde, Regent, Green—you name it."

"Well . . ." The cab turned a corner and his fingers touched her, accidentally; they were immediately lifted away. "Maybe you'd better call me tomorrow morning."

"I'll do that. Early. Eight o'clock? Or is that too early?"

The cab was turning down the little cul-de-sac that led to the hotel, and his fingers brushed her again. Now she understood that the first time hadn't been an accident after all. But it was done so delicately it was sending shivers up and down her spine. "I'm always up by eight," she said.

"We'll spend the day together." His mouth was against her ear, his other hand was resting on her thigh, and she was trembling like gelatin. "Do you suppose you could get rid of your friend?" he whispered.

"I . . . I'll think about it," she whispered back, and turned her head, and was kissed on the mouth. Their tongues touched, and again it almost seemed an accident. She had never met anyone quite so forward, yet so gentle at the same time. On the other hand, as she had told Janice, she had never met an Englishman of her own age before at all; she had always heard they were very slow. So, how to explain that kiss?

The door opened, and she almost fell out. "I beg your pardon, miss," the doorman said.

"It's quite all right, really." She gave Robert a hasty smile, and plunged through the revolving doors. She hurried across the lobby to stare at the telex tapes as they rolled through the wall machine, while Janice went to get their room key.

"I saw that," Janice said at her elbow, having retrieved the key. "You are impossible."

"Janice . . . I think I'm in love."

"Oh, Jesus Christ!" Janice said. "Let's go up."

They faced each other in the elevator. "I am," Diana said. "He's so . . . so . . ."

"He wears pants," Janice said cruelly.

They walked along the corridor.

"It can't do any harm," Diana explained. "He's going to take me to the Tower of London tomorrow. And then for a boat ride on the river. And then—"

"Doesn't he have a job?"

"He works for Uncle Peter."

"Which makes him highly suspicious right there. And when he's finished showing you around London, he'll escort you back to his apartment and screw you," Janice said, unlocking the door to their suite.

"No, he won't," Diana said. "No, no, no, no."

Janice followed her inside and relocked the door. "You really believe that?"

Diana sat down, hands drooping between her knees. "I don't *want* that, Jan." Which was, of course, a lie. "Really and truly. It's just that . . . he's so nice."

Janice stood before her. "If you go out with that man tomorrow, Diana, I am catching the next boat back to New York, because I can't do you any good if you won't listen to me."

Diana sighed. "Oh . . . I guess you're right. But I can't stay here."

"We'll tell the desk not to accept any calls, that's all."

"What I mean is, I can't stay here in London." She picked up the telephone. "This is Diana Hayman. Would you book me two seats on the next boat train to Paris, please?"

"Ah . . . the boat train leaves Victoria at eight-fifteen tomorrow morning, Miss Hayman."

"That'll be fine."

"And . . ." The woman at the desk was obviously checking. "You have a booking with us for tomorrow night."

"Cancel it," Diana told her. "Oh, I'll pay for it. But I won't be here. Just get me on that boat to Calais." She hung up.

"But—" Janice was scandalized. "What about your Uncle John?"

"What about him? He's not my chaperon, you know. He just happens to be around."

"Yes, but . . . there's the apartment, too. The flat, as you've been calling it all evening."

"It's the English word," Diana explained. "We'll cancel that too, from Paris. I told you, I can't stay here."

Peter Borodin poured brandies, offered cigars, which both Roger Corby and John Hayman accepted, took one himself, and sat down with a sigh of relief in an overstuffed armchair. Only the three of them remained, but the room smelled of good tobacco and good whiskey, and now of good brandy as well. "What do you think of them?"

"They seem like a good bunch," John said.

"Good," Peter said thoughtfully. "They are that. And devoted to me. To the cause." He raised his glass. "To the downfall of Stalin and all his crew!"

John drank. He was here to listen and learn. And not to worry about Diana, at least for tonight. He *was* working, after all.

"So you're with the state department now," Peter remarked. "That is good. Very good."

"I am *not* with the state department, Uncle Peter," John said. "I am in advertising. I hope the letter I gave you explained that." He had, of course, read the letter, but he didn't want Peter to know that.

"But you're acting for them," Corby said.

"That's right. Reluctantly, I may say. But they felt that any other person—one of their own people, for instance—might not be able to evaluate as accurately what you have to offer us."

"What I have to offer you," Peter Borodin said thoughtfully. "Would you agree that I have been right from the very beginning, John? About the Soviets?"

"Well . . ."

"Of course, I have been. In 1918, everyone thought it was a private civil war. I said then, the Reds *must* be crushed, before they can consolidate. I offered to do the job. I had the men. All we needed was the munitions, the arms, and the money. I appealed to the British and the French, and most of all the Americans. And they said, We can't interfere, our people are tired of fighting, and they don't like the tsars anyway. This after the tsar had given his life for them! So we lost that round. And the Soviets grew and grew, as I had prophesied they would, like some mythical monster, feeding upon itself.

"But at last their revolution went sour, again as I had known it must, and so in 1938 I approached Roosevelt, and told him it was the time to crush them once and for all. They had torn themselves apart with those purges in 1937, their army was a shambles. He told me I was mad. So I went to Hitler. Well, maybe that was a mistake. I never knew he was going to take on the entire world. If he'd invaded only Russia . . . Anyway, the fact is, he *still* would have won, would've wiped the Soviets off the face of the earth, if you Americans hadn't started pouring munitions and arms and money into Stalin's hip pocket. The support you refused General Denikin and me twenty years before.

"Then there was another chance in forty-six. Again, I told Truman the facts. You had the atomic bomb. They didn't. Then was the time to send the whole bunch of them to perdition. He wouldn't do it. So what are we faced with now? Russia also has atomic weapons. And let me tell you something, Johnnie. When Stalin decides he has the drop on you, *he* isn't going to be reluctant to use it."

"I guess our business is to make sure Russia never does have the drop on us, Uncle Peter." John wondered if he was wasting his time; he had heard all this rhetoric too often before.

"But I don't think the state department is about to recommend to the president that he start blowing people off the face of the earth just because we don't happen to agree with their system of government. I'm here to listen. We want to know what you have to tell us, and what you think it's worth. It has something to do with all these strange movements inside the Soviet Union, right?"

Peter Borodin stared at him in total mystification.

"Uncle Peter," John said gently, "as I understand it, you wrote the state department, indicating that you had some very valuable information to sell. Believe me, they're interested. Interested enough to contact me and ask me if I'd come to see you. But they're not going to put up any money until they know what they're buying."

Roger Corby gave a brief laugh. "You people!" he said. "You Americans! You reduce everything to money. You worry about who is going where, and when. Oh, certainly there has been considerable movement within the Soviet Union during these last few months. You know your father is to leave the United Nations?"

"No," John said. "I didn't know that."

"Well, he is. He is returning to an unspecified post in Moscow. As, apparently, are Ivan Nej and Anna Ragosina. That can mean only one thing. That Stalin is planning a new purge, a new tightening of his grip on the country."

"Could be," John said. "But that's not exactly earth-shattering news, I'm afraid. I suppose it was bound to happen sometime."

"So I wish to offer your government a proposition," Peter Borodin said.

"Oh, yes?" John said wearily.

Peter got up and paced the study floor, watched admiringly by Corby. "I don't suppose I can expect much cooperation from Truman," he remarked. "But is it true he has announced he will not run for president again?"

"He has said so."

"So who will succeed him?"

John shrugged. "The Democratic front-runner is Adlai Stevenson."

"Hm," Peter said. "I don't know him. What if the Republicans were to get in?"

"It's a possibility. I have no idea who they'll nominate."

"What about Eisenhower? He resigned his command here in Europe six weeks ago. To do what, do you suppose? The papers over here are convinced it is to run for the presidency."

"That's also a possibility. But a remote one. The American people haven't elected a professional soldier as president in this century, unless you call Teddy Roosevelt a professional soldier."

"Is it not possible that the American people might be just a little more aware of what is needed than their so-called intellectuals?"

"I said it was possible."

"But unlikely. Well, then, I suppose the best thing we can do is deal with Truman. Better the devil you know, eh? Anyway, I cannot afford to wait any longer. I am seventy years old. Do you know, I am nearly as old as Stalin himself? And I have never felt better in my life." He stared at John. "What does that tell us?"

"That maybe good cigars and good whiskey *are* the secret of longevity, after all."

Peter Borodin waved his hand impatiently. "It tells us that Stalin may also feel better than ever in his life. He apparently had a siege of illness this spring, but in his recent photographs he again looks in the best of health. That tells us that we may have to endure him for perhaps another ten years."

"I think Soviet Russia is going to be around a whole hell of a lot longer than that," John remarked.

"Nonsense. Without Stalin that whole pack of cards will just fall apart. Providing it is given a good push."

"That's one theory. We'll just have to wait and see."

Peter gave him another long stare, then resumed pacing again. "I have devoted my entire life to the downfall of Bolshevism and all its emanations, and in particular to the monster Stalin. Were I to die tomorrow, I would have to be written off as a total failure. Is that not so?"

"Well . . ."

"Through no fault of my own," Peter went on. "Simply because I have never been able to persuade anyone to back me up, to follow my ideas. Anyone with the power to be effective, that is. When Lenin died, I knew that was our opportunity. I knew there would be several years of internecine fighting among his successors. We could have swept them away like so many crumbs from a table. But nobody was interested. Well, I am determined that my life is not going to *be* a failure."

John frowned at him, and glanced at Corby. But Corby was rapt as he listened to his chief.

"I could live another ten, fifteen years," Peter declared. "I probably shall. But to what purpose, I ask myself, if I can never persuade your government to act? And yours is the only government that *can* act, now, to bring that pack of butchers to justice. Thus *I* have decided to act, unilaterally, in the hope that the United States government may then find itself *obliged* to follow my example."

"What are you talking about?"

"But I still hope to gain the maximum effect from my action," Peter went on, ignoring the interruption, "and therefore I am offering the United States government this opportunity to know what I shall do, or at least in general what I intend, and therefore to be ready to act, the moment the signal is given."

John put down his brandy—he wished he hadn't drunk so much of it—and stubbed out his cigar as he sat up. "Just what do you mean, act unilaterally? Are you thinking of mounting some kind of White Russian invasion, all over again? That's crazy!"

Peter smiled and sat down again. His face was suddenly relaxed as he seemed to be seeing a vision. "A White invasion. Yes, that would be something. We would need ten million men. But one or two men may go where a million cannot."

John reached for his glass and took another sip. He needed it now. *"You?"*

"Of course. I have always led, never followed."

"And you really think the Russians would let you in?"

"I think so, yes. I have devised a means by which they will welcome me with open arms. Not suspecting my purpose, of course."

"And once you're in—supposing they do go for whatever crazy scheme you're dreaming of—you'll declare war on them, will you?"

"You think in such childish ways, John. Once I am in, the time will come, sooner rather than later, when I shall succeed in having an interview with Stalin. When that happens, I shall kill him. Now then, will the United States government be prepared to *act,* the moment that happens?"

Chapter 4

FOR SEVERAL SECONDS JOHN COULD ONLY STARE AT HIS UNCLE in horror. Then he said, "You can't be serious."

"I assure you, Mr. Hayman, that Prince Peter is very serious indeed," Corby said.

"And you . . . you go along with this idea?"

"It is the prince's idea," Corby said, smugly and contentedly.

"Now, really, Uncle Peter—"

"Really, what?" Peter inquired. "What are your objections? That I will certainly die? I am a front-line soldier. I have always been a front-line soldier, content to die for tsar and country should it ever become necessary. It now appears that my life is all I have left to offer. Why should I shrink back now? Do you suppose I am afraid of death? I am merely afraid of being useless. And that, pray God, I shall never be."

John took a long breath. He did not doubt that his uncle was deadly serious; all he knew about the man would confirm it. To Peter Borodin, all problems in life were simple ones, calling for equally simple solutions. To choose life, or death, was no more difficult than any other problem. Other people's lives and deaths were no more relevant than the question of whether or not to cross the road. If one intended to get to the other side, one crossed the road. And whoever died on that crossing, whatever accidents or catastrophes happened because of that simple decision, that was for fate to take care of.

"I will of course report what you have said to the state department," he said.

"Soon," Peter told him. "Very soon. All our plans are laid, and we are ready to go. We shall not delay much longer."

John looked at Corby, who nodded enthusiastically.

"And are you planning to accompany Prince Peter on this suicide mission?" he asked.

Corby flushed.

"Of course not," Peter Borodin said. "Roger is my chief-of-staff. I need him to stay here, to take over the organization."

"I see," John said. "Well, I shall return to Washington and report, just as fast as I can get there. But I must warn you that I am certain the United States government will have nothing whatsoever to do with your scheme. It's absurd and it's criminal."

"You mean that *you* will not recommend my proposal."

"Recommend it? My God!" John stood up. "It is not my place to recommend or not. My job is simply to report, as fully as I can. You will have to outline to me how you mean to get inside Russia, and be accepted by them."

Peter gave a cold smile. "Do you take me for a fool? Don't you suppose I know that if you persuade the state department not to back me, you'll recommend they inform the Russians of my plans? You always had the smell of a traitor about you."

John glared at him. "And don't you suppose I still might?"

"I will give you the telephone number of the Soviet embassy," Peter said. "Use it, if you *dare.*" His smile widened. "And become a traitor to all *mankind.*"

John hesitated, biting his lip. Then he turned and left the room.

"I know he is your nephew, Prince Peter," Corby said. "But don't you think I should go after him, and—"

"Get yourself hanged for murder?" Peter inquired.

"I am as prepared to die for the movement as anyone, sir," Corby said with dignity. "Suppose he *were* to go to the Russian embassy?"

"He won't," Peter said, pouring himself another brandy, and as an afterthought refilling Corby's glass as well. "John

Hayman is a totally confused man. Well, he has reason to be, with such a tangled background. But he's not really a traitor. He hates Communism as much as any of us. He's just confused about how it should be dealt with. Actually . . ." He sat down and crossed his knees, lit a fresh cigar. "I'm surprised at the state department sending him, of all people, when it must be aware of the differences we have had in the past, the skepticism with which Johnnie has always regarded most of my plans. I suppose that shows they have also made up their minds to be skeptical. Mind you, it's a great pity he *wouldn't* listen. Had we been able to convince him, and through him perhaps George Hayman and his son . . . They are two of the most powerful men in America, you know, Roger. Presidents may come and go, but the Hayman newspapers go on forever. And they're certainly interested in the Russian scene, because of Ilona. The support they would be able to engender for our plans . . . But those are dreams, and we are past the stage for that. I don't really suppose *any* of them would listen to us.

"The Americans, like the British and the French before them, keep looking at the world through *their* eyes. That is to say, the eyes of people who regard themselves as being the acme of man's progress, the personification of the human spirit, of the *Christian* spirit. The poor fools are quite incapable of understanding that their civilization, their Christianity, influences only a minute portion of the population of this earth. They know as well as you or I that the Soviets abolished Christianity in 1918. They know as well as you or I that when Britain and France were already making some pretensions to civilization and moral and ethical judgments, Russia was still ruled by the Khans of the Golden Horde, who acknowledged no god and no ethics whatsoever. I know these things, Roger. We are talking of my own ancestors. Now, it so happened that a few families, encouraged by Peter the Great, such as the Romanovs themselves, the Menshikovs, the Borodins, imbibed and accepted western culture, and sought to translate it for the Russian people as a whole. They failed. Let us be honest about this. They failed because they exaggerated the extent of their success. They were overthrown by sheer primeval force.

"Russia will never be ruled by any but primeval force, because it is at heart a Tartar state still, a direct descendant of the empires of Tamerlane and Genghis Khan. We are only talking of four hundred and fifty years since Timur, you know. Fifteen generations. That is not a long time. These dark men thrown up by the revolution have not changed all that much from their ancestors roaming the steppes. Everything a Russian leader says or does is directed to the good of the Russian state—that is, himself. You declare black is white, and if it suits him to agree with you, he will swear black is white. You *prove* white is white, and if it does not suit him to agree with you, or more, it suits him to *disagree* with you, he will produce proof that you are wrong. Yet the British and the French, and now the Americans, have always tried to deal with them as they might with each other. Christian ethics! How they must laugh in the Kremlin when the Americans talk piously of agreements and treaties and understandings and trust and mutual respect. Those are all just words, counters on the board, to Stalin, as they were to the Tartars. The Tartars respected only two things: naked force, and the power of life and death. It sickens me and fills me with despair. But we must never let that turn us away from our purpose.

"I can do our cause no more good now. I am too old, and I am being forgotten. I can only decide the most useful way in which I can die. I have made that decision, and I shall not change my mind. All that remains is the details, and that must be sorted out as quickly as possible, as I intend to act right away."

"You fear state department intervention?"

"There is certainly a possibility they may contact the British and ask them to keep an eye on me. Perhaps even impound my passport. No, no, we have no time to delay. But I *must* have an aide. Believe me, Roger, I would far rather do this entirely on my own. I have no desire to take any of our fine young men to death with me. But I know my limitations. The Russians will certainly treat me with suspicion, in the beginning. I shall be watched and searched and hounded for weeks, until they either believe in what I have to say or dismiss me as a harmless crank. My weapons must be smuggled into the country by a totally trustworthy aide. Even more important, I need him at my side when I see Stalin, just in case I am not strong enough to complete the task. Age is a terrible thing, Roger. Now, recommend."

"Well . . ." Corby stroked his chin. "The pick of the bunch is young Loung."

"I hoped you'd say that. I agree with you. I have never seen such a quick or accurate shot. And such courage, too."

"Mind you," Corby went on, "I'm not saying it is going to be easy for us to persuade a young man like Robert, however enthusiastic he may be for the cause, to commit virtual suicide. Because that's what you'll be asking him to do."

"Yes." Peter stroked his chin in turn. "It may be necessary to use a certain amount of subterfuge."

Corby frowned. "Won't that be rather . . . well, treacherous, where a man's life is at stake?"

Peter stared at him. "What is a life? What are several lives, where so much *else* is at stake? Am I not planning to sacrifice quite a few lives, including my own, to get the Russians first to believe in me, and then to destroy them? Don't talk to me about a single life, Roger, when *millions* may be at stake."

"Oh, quite," Corby muttered, abashed.

"So have Loung here to see me, tomorrow afternoon," Peter said. "We should start things moving right away. Tomorrow afternoon, Roger. Have him here."

John Hayman lay on his back in his hotel bed, hands clasped beneath his head, and stared at the ceiling. *He* was not staying at the Savoy, and as it was a warm night and there was no air conditioning, he had his windows open, allowing the unending growl of London traffic to seep up to his room. But he did not suppose it was the noise keeping him awake.

Was Peter Borodin serious? *Could* he be? It was impossible to persuade himself otherwise, however utterly crazy the scheme might appear. Peter had always dealt in grand gestures, nearly all of which had gone desperately awry. He had once, John remembered ruefully, kidnapped his own sister, the famous dancer Tatiana Borodina, simply because she had left Russia on tour and he wanted to stop her from going back. *John* had been persuaded to become involved in that, he recalled, even more ruefully, because at that time *he* had been one of those admiring young men who hung on Peter Borodin's every word.

But, remembering that fiasco and the several other fiascos since, was there anything to worry about? Would Peter ever be allowed near Stalin? Certainly never with a weapon on his person. So . . .

But Peter must know that as well as anyone did. He might be crazy, but he was not totally unable to analyze a situation.

So just what was he meaning to do? Strangle the man with his bare hands? That was absurd. Yet he was meaning to do something . . . Or was this just the opening ploy in an elaborate negotiation? But Peter himself had ruled out the possibility of negotiation.

Well, then, would the Russians even let him into the country? Peter Borodin was a name every Russian commissar, and probably every Russian policeman and border guard and immigration officer as well, knew as well as his own. He was a traitor and an enemy of the Soviet state, to be arrested and taken straight to Lubianka Prison. Yet he appeared to think that all he had to do was say, "I'm ready to come home," and they would clap their hands for joy.

Well, no doubt they would, but not to grant him an interview with Stalin.

Again, these all had to be facts of which Peter was aware. And yet he remained confident. Therefore he must have, or must believe he had, something to offer the Russians in exchange for the right to return to his homeland. What could that be? With Peter, even the most desperately sinister act could not be ruled out, if he could convince himself it was for the good of the cause. So, would he offer to betray his group, all the White Russian émigrés who were supporting him with money, enabling him to live so comfortably in London without a penny of personal income? Combine that with the propaganda value of having Prince Peter Borodin of Starogan seeing the light, realizing that Soviet Communism was the only hope of the world, and Stalin might find reason to let Peter in. And the organization in London would be left like a snake lacking its head, faintly wriggling, its members waiting to be eliminated by KGB gunmen. All those eager young men who had been at Peter's house tonight, two of whom had escorted Diana and Janice off to dinner.

Diana and Janice! It was broad daylight outside his window, but that didn't mean a lot in London, in June. He looked at his watch; it was seven-thirty in the morning. He had not slept a wink. But Diana was undoubtedly still sleeping at the Savoy, dead to the world.

He got out of bed and paced the floor. Betrayal of the group was one possibility. It was a tragic one, but not something he personally could prevent. But it was only *one* possibility. Because it was equally possible that Peter had actually got hold of some information that *could* be vital to the Soviets. He did have a wide network of agents and informants, a lot of them in England, as he had observed last night. Therefore it was possible he had learned of some strategic British plan . . . But he also must have agents in the United States.

The fact was that Peter Borodin was preparing something not only sinister but possibly highly dangerous as well. Then there was the personal factor. Michael Nej had apparently been recalled to Moscow by Stalin's order. He was certainly Stalin's most trusted associate. Who could say he would not be standing beside Stalin when Peter attempted his assassination, assuming he got that far? *Could* Michael Nej be one of Peter's targets? That might be one reason why Peter was not going to reveal his plans to John.

There could be no question that Peter Borodin had to be stopped. John was very tempted to go to Scotland Yard. But he was not a private citizen. He was a CIA operative on a mission, and had to remember that. But certainly he had no business wasting time in London; this was something Allen Dulles should know about right away. But where did that leave Diana? Well, he was *not* her watchdog. That he was here at all was pure coincidence. On the other hand, Elizabeth had begged him to keep an eye on the girl. He suspected she would rather see Diana back in New York than left on her own within a day of arriving in London.

Well, she would just have to change her plans. He telephoned the desk. "This is urgent," he said. "Will you get me three seats on the first available plane to New York?"

"Yes, sir," the clerk said. "There is actually a flight at ten this morning, arriving at Idlewild, at six this evening, local time. Shall I see if there are seats still available?"

"That would be great," John said. "Now, get me the Savoy Hotel." He drummed his fingers on the table as he waited. "Miss Hayman," he told the girl. "It is her uncle. Wake her up if you have to. It's urgent."

"Ah . . . I'm afraid Miss Hayman has checked out, sir."

"Checked out?"

"Not ten minutes ago, sir."

"But . . . to go where?"

"I don't think I can reveal that, sir."

"Goddamn it," John shouted, "I'm her uncle. Her chaperon. Where has she gone?"

"Well . . . She and Miss Corliss caught the boat train to Paris. It reaches Dover at ten o'clock."

"To Paris. She and Miss Corliss. Thank you." He replaced the receiver, and stared at the wall. What the hell was the little devil up to now? Paris? Deliberately dumping him?

The telephone jangled. "Mr. Hayman? We *are* fortunate, sir. There do happen to be three seats available on this morning's flight. I have reserved them in your name. The tickets will be waiting for you at the airport. But you must pick them up by nine-thirty."

John hesitated. Presumably he could have Diana stopped at Dover, by making a lot of telephone calls or even hiring a car and rushing down there himself. Either alternative would mean missing his flight. And whatever highjinks Diana and Janice were up to, they certainly weren't risking anyone's lives, including their own. Elizabeth would just have to send over another chaperon.

"That's great," he said. "But I'll only need one seat, after all."

"Ah, Robert." Peter Borodin beamed at the young man. "Come in, come in, and sit down. Close the door, will you, Roger?" His beam changed to a slight frown as he surveyed the smiling face of the young man in front of him. "You're looking uncommonly cheerful this morning."

"Yes, sir, Prince Peter. I would like to take a week off, with your permission."

"A week off? What ever for?"

"To go to Paris."

"Paris? My dear boy . . ." Peter's frown deepened. "What do you have to do in Paris?"

"Find Diana. Your grandniece, sir. She went over this morning. I only found out after she'd already left."

"My grandniece? Off to Paris? Well, well! But why should that interest you?"

Robert blushed. "I . . . well . . . I'm in love with her, sir."

"You . . ." Peter leaned back in his chair, and looked over at Corby, who gave a bewildered shrug. "How long have you known her?"

"Since last night, sir."

"And you're in love with her."

"Yes, sir, I am. I really am. I haven't slept a wink thinking about her. I think she's the most marvelous girl I ever met."

"And one of the wealthiest young women you're ever likely to meet, either, eh?"

It was Robert's turn to frown. "Is she, sir? I didn't know that. I know her mother is some sort of artist, and she's your grandniece, but . . ." He paused, his embarrassment growing. Everyone knew that Peter Borodin lived on the charity of his fellow émigrés.

"Not all my family has had the resolution to fight on," Peter said grimly. "My sister settled for wealth. Her son is Diana's father, and the president of Hayman Newspapers Incorporated."

"Good God," Robert said.

"Nor does *she* appear to have fallen in love with you, at first sight," Peter pointed out. "Scuttling off to Paris . . ."

"I rather thought she did—well, take to me," Robert said. "It was her friend who didn't like me. I'm sure she is responsible for their leaving so suddenly. I thought if I could go after them—"

"And do what, when you find them? *If* you find them?"

"Oh, I'll find them. I know the train they were catching. And two such pretty girls . . . I'll find them, Prince Peter. And when I do, well—I'm going to ask her to marry me."

"You *what?*"

"Well . . ." Robert looked utterly abashed. "I know she's your niece, sir, and I'm a nobody. I had absolutely no idea her people were well off. Of course, if you feel that I have no business . . ." He gazed at the prince.

Peter gazed back at him just as searchingly, while Corby began to frown. He had seen that expression on Peter Borodin's face before.

"Wasn't your father a brigadier?" Peter asked suddenly.

"Ah . . . no, sir. He was a major in the Royal Army Service Corps. He was dismissed, you remember, for—"

"Yes, yes, yes," Peter said. "But I'm sure he would have *become* a brigadier, given a few more years, had it not been for that unfortunate business with the black-market German binoculars. Anyway, you cannot possibly blame yourself for that. Nor can you possibly go through life belittling yourself because of your father's mistakes. That is no way to climb the ladder of success. No indeed. And I can tell you that, on Mr. Corby's recommendation, I have already selected you to climb that ladder." He beamed.

Robert glanced at Corby in astonishment. He found no clue in Corby's obvious discomfort.

"So I personally cannot think of a single man in the whole world I would rather have as my grandniece's husband. No, I cannot. I think you should go to Paris, Robert. With my blessing. Stay for as long as you wish. Tell Mr. Corby what funds you will need. Diana will expect to be well entertained. And don't forget to tell her that your father was a brigadier. All's fair in love and war, eh? The important thing is to get her to say yes."

"Why, sir . . . well, it's most awfully decent of you," Robert said. "I don't know what to say."

"Then listen, instead." Peter suddenly leaned across his desk. "It will not be easy. I am talking not about Diana, but about her family. It is very possible that she may reciprocate your . . . passion, but feel unable to accept your proposal, because she will know that her family will suspect you are nothing but a fortune hunter. That *is* what they will feel, I can tell you that. And you must not forget that Diana is not yet twenty-one. She probably has no legal right to marry without their consent. In any case they would threaten to disown her."

"Oh, we can wait for their consent," Robert said. "I wasn't planning an elopement."

"My dear boy, you *must* plan an elopement," Peter cried. "Let us suppose that Diana accepts you without hesitation, and tells her parents what she proposes to do. They will refuse her permission, almost certainly. She may then swear her undying love for you, but they will make sure you and she do not see each other for a year—a year in which they will surround her with the most eligible men in America, until she falls in love with one of them. But let us even suppose they say yes. I can tell you they are the most two-faced people on the face of the earth. I know. One of them is my own sister. They may well say yes, just to prevent a fight, and *then* start working on her, making her life a misery, until she breaks the engagement."

Robert gazed at him in consternation.

"This," Peter announced grandly, "is where I come in. I am, after all, still the head of the family. No one can deny that. Now listen to me, Robert. Go to Paris, find Diana, woo her, and win her. As soon as you have done that, telephone me at our French address. I shall come across in a few days and wait there, just to be on hand. You will not tell Diana this, of course. My appearance will seem to be a coincidence. Telephone me even if she refuses you. I will still appear, and talk her into accepting you. Then we will arrange a quiet little wedding, following which you and she will conveniently disappear for several weeks on your honeymoon. I know the very place, where no one will think of looking for you. While you are away, I will contact the family and inform them of what has happened, tell them that the marriage has my blessing, and get them to agree too. Besides, since you will have been married for some time when they finally catch up with you, there will not be very much they can do about it, anyway. What do you think of that?"

"Why . . . I'm quite amazed that you would go to this much trouble." Robert's tone was a mixture of pleasure and bewilderment.

"No trouble at all," Peter said benevolently. "For one of my brightest young men and my own favorite niece. I cannot remember when I have received happier news." He got up, came around the desk, and embraced the young man. "I am absolutely delighted. Now, off you go with Mr. Corby, who will give you whatever funds you may need. Have the time of your life. And win Diana." He smiled. "And then telephone me. I shall be waiting."

"I'm afraid I do not understand, Prince Peter." Corby's manner was stiff as he reentered the study and closed the door.

Peter smiled at him. "Has Loung left?"

"Oh, indeed. Like a dog with two tails. I believe he means to cross by tomorrow morning's boat. But—"

"We have set the ball rolling, Roger. Now everything should fall into place."

"But . . ." Corby sat down. "You were going to use Loung—"

"I *am* using Loung. In such a way that, no matter what the future may hold for him, he will at least have some happy days to look back upon. I think that is very nice. In fact, things could not have turned out better. Now I feel sure of ultimate success."

"I don't understand, sir."

"What were we talking about last night, Roger?" Peter asked him. "Was it not about how much we would benefit by involving the Haymans in our plans? Well, there is more than one way to involve them."

Corby stared at him. "You mean . . . through that girl?"

"Young Loung will woo and wed Diana. It will then, as I told him, be necessary for them to honeymoon somewhere they cannot be reached, while I deal with Diana's family. That means they must go somewhere no one would dream of looking. Why not Russia?"

"Oh, my God," Corby said. "But—"

"I know it will not be easy," Peter said. "But it is merely a matter of working out details. Only details. It came to me in a flash while Loung was telling me about his absurd love at first sight. The wedding will take place in Paris. Therefore the operation will start from Paris. This is better and better. I will leave for Paris in a few days, but you will secure me tickets to . . . Gothenburg, as if I were going to Stockholm. Then I will simply take the ferry for Calais. This means that even if John Hayman does persuade the state department into agitating the foreign office, they won't know where to find me. Now, as to the young couple . . ."

"Visas," Corby muttered.

"I told you I have thought it out. Isn't young Evans still on the embassy staff over there?"

"A most useful placement," Corby said, still shaking his head, incredulous.

"Well, get on to Evans right away. By courier. It would be best if I were not involved here. Tell Evans we wish applications made immediately for Russian visas for Robert and Diana. Give him all their particulars, but tell him we will not be able to let him have the passports for a week or so. He has that female contact inside the Russian embassy, hasn't he? He can fix it up with her for the applications to go through, so that when the passports are produced, he can shoot them along and have the visas affixed within twenty-four hours."

"I suppose that can be arranged," Corby said doubtfully. "I still don't see—"

"Then I wish you to go out and buy me the two most

expensive leather suitcases you can find. Have them embossed, in gold leaf—one R.L. and the other D.L. And bring them back here."

"Suitcases?"

"My wedding present to the happy couple," Peter told him. "Once we get the suitcases here it will be the simplest matter in the world to . . . prepare them, eh? Neither Robert nor Russian customs will have any idea what they really contain. Then you see, Robert and Diana will depart to Russia on their honeymoon. The day they leave, I will approach the Russian embassy in Paris and negotiate the sale of my information. I know there will be little time, but if I do not manage to gain entry into Russia quickly enough, you will have to get hold of Dimitri and tell *him* to contact Robert, wherever in Moscow he will be staying, and get the stuff off him to put in a safe place until I arrive. The point is, everything I need will be in Russia, and eventually I will also be in Russia."

"Prince Peter, I must protest—"

"It is an excellent plan," Peter declared. "Oh, if Loung is genuinely in love with my niece, he may be very angry to discover she has been used to transport plastic explosives across the border. We may even lose him. But that will no longer be rélavant. He will not betray us, because he is not a traitor. And he *cannot* betray us, because he has no idea what we are up to. That is the secret of my plan, you see, Roger. Utter simplicity allied to utter determination. No one will ever believe I simply mean to coat myself and my clothes with plastic explosives before entering Stalin's office. It is too horrible a concept for ordinary minds to grasp. Horrible! What is horrible about it? Once I squeeze that detonator, I will know nothing more about it."

"With respect, Prince Peter," Corby said, "it *is* horrible. I am talking about using an innocent young girl like Miss Hayman . . . can you imagine what the KGB will do to her if they discover what is lining her suitcase?"

"They will ask her where she got it, and she won't be able to tell them, because she won't know."

"And then . . . ?"

"They will shove an electrode up that dainty little ass. It may well do her a world of good. Anyone can see she's an impossibly spoiled brat."

"They may well kill her, Prince Peter. Or reduce her to

such a wreck she might as well be dead."

"These are risks which have to be taken," Peter said airily.

"She will certainly tell them the suitcase was given to her by you."

"That again is a risk which I will have to accept. No scheme is absolutely foolproof. But you are also assuming the very worst possibility. Why *should* the KGB search her luggage? And either way, Roger, the important thing is that the Haymans will be involved. And they will involve the United States government. And when the balloon goes up, well . . . all things are possible."

Corby stood up. "I must protest, sir, most strongly, that to involve innocent bystanders is not in the best interests of our organization. And in addition, when we put at risk the health, even the life, of a young girl who has nothing to do with our aims . . . a total innocent—"

"Who is also quite lovely to look at? Roger, perhaps young Loung is not the only one who must grow up. I thought I made that clear last night. How many innocent bystanders do you suppose are going to be involved if Russia ever drops an atom bomb on New York? As for Diana, she may well be a total innocent, but her innocence could never last, believe me. She may not know it yet, but she has been in the front line since the day she was born, just by being George Hayman's granddaughter. And my grandniece. She's lived the life of a rich little girl in America for nearly twenty years. Well, let her go out and do a bit of paying for all that luxury. I promise you, no one is going to shed a tear over what happens to Diana Hayman. In fact, the thought of her in a cell at Lubianka rather attracts me."

Corby hesitated. But he knew he could never win an ethical argument with his employer, because Peter Borodin only admitted one principle worth upholding—the downfall of Soviet Russia. He sighed. "Aren't we being optimistic in presuming Loung will succeed in bringing this sudden courtship to a successful conclusion?"

Peter Borodin smiled. "He will succeed. He's chasing the girl all the way to Paris to propose! What romantic young nincompoop could possibly resist that? And Diana is certainly romantic, wouldn't you say, Roger?"

* * *

Diana Hayman threw herself across the huge double bed and kicked off her shoes. "Honestly," she declared. "I have never been so bored in all my life."

Janice Corliss had gotten straight into the bathtub; Paris in June was hot and muggy. Now she stood in the doorway of the huge bathroom to survey her friend—some distance away, since the bedroom was on a lavish scale. They were staying at the George V Hotel, on the Rue George V, which connected the Champs Élysées with the Seine embankment. It had simply not occurred to Diana Hayman to stay anywhere else—the George V was comparable with the Savoy in appointments and service, if a trifle larger, and like the Savoy, it was where her parents usually stayed when in Europe.

By craning her neck from their window, they could see the Eiffel Tower; by walking fifty yards in the other direction, they could look at the Arc de Triomphe. Last night they had been to the Lido, this morning they had spent shopping, ending up with an expensive lunch at a boulevard restaurant. They were now apparently to relax for a couple of hours before going to Maxim's for dinner, and tomorrow night they were booked at the Moulin Rouge. They had not even begun to explore the Isle de la Cité or Notre Dame, or considered climbing the hill to the Sacre Coeur, or the Tower itself, much less visited the Louvre—and she knew Diana was planning an excursion to Versailles in the near future.

"Bored?" she asked.

"Well . . . Paris is so *romantic,*" Diana declared. "I mean, last night, looking at all those naked tits . . . it should have been sexy. It *would* have been sexy, if there'd been a man along."

"Cures like this are known as cold turkey," Janice said, wrapping herself in one of the huge white bathrobes provided by the hotel, and wandering over to the window. "All of a sudden, one morning, you'll wake up and say, now what did I ever see in men?"

Diana raised herself on her elbow, her eyes somber. "Do I *want* to feel like that?"

"To begin with, yes." Janice smiled at her. "Because only if you feel like that will you be able to look at them objectively, and decide which of them you really like, without sex getting in the way. It stands to reason that you can't possibly love a man until you know whether you like him, first."

"That is ridiculous," Diana declared. "Heaven knows what would have happened to all the great novels if women actually behaved that logically when they were falling in love."

Janice sighed, and, finding no breeze even in the open window, flapped the bathrobe open and shut in an attempt to assist the drying process. "And I really thought you were turning over a new leaf. It was you who snubbed those guys last night."

"Well . . . my French isn't all that good. And I was tired. Anyway, I don't want to make love with just anybody, Jan, no matter what you think. I really want to make love with Robert."

"Oh, not him again."

"I should've been in his arms by now," Diana said broodingly. "I just know he would have been something special. Different. Something, oh . . . fabulous."

"You *are* a nympho, you know," Janice said.

"I am not. Because there is no such thing. I was reading a book about it on the ship. I am highly sexed, and that's no crime."

"Very highly sexed."

"Could be. But that's not so uncommon either, you know. Although of course very few women will come out and admit it. The point is, I *feel*. And right now, I feel absolutely desolate." She sat up. "Jan! Make love to me."

Janice had turned back to the window. Now she faced the room again, abruptly. "Do *what?*"

Diana was undressing with great rapidity. "I need it. I'm going nuts, just thinking about Robert. Okay, you say I can't have him. Then you must take his place. It can't be just *anybody*, you see, Jan. It must be someone I really, well, love. And I don't want it to be ordinary, anymore. Push pull squeeze bite thump wallop. No more of that. It *has* to be different. Fabulous. I'm sure it would be, between you and me. Just let me take a bath first."

Janice, mouth open, watched her friend run into the bathroom. And yet she was aware of no great sense of surprise, even if she also was aware that Diana was not fooling. Diana seldom fooled.

This was something she had been watching build for the past four days. She had an idea the detonator had been Diana's meeting her great-uncle. She and that old man had taken too instant a dislike to each other, that was obvious. Hates like that usually disguised an enormous attraction, which both parties wished to reject. Janice Corliss, philosopher. But she spent a lot of her time observing life, especially Diana's life. And she could tell that Diana had been excited by the old scoundrel. Not sexually, of course. But emotionally. He was a relic of the enormously romantic past that hung above her family like a cloud. And unlike photographs in an album, or reminiscences after the third glass of brandy, he was all too real. What sort of feelings might he have aroused in someone as essentially uncertain of herself as Diana—because Janice knew just how uncertain Diana was, for all her air of utter confidence, the way she could so easily dominate a conversation or another personality. Diana was never sure whether she was a Russian princess incognito or an all-American girl acting a part. She knew she was enormously rich, but she didn't appreciate what that actually meant; she spent money like water, simply because she didn't understand its value. Yet she also wanted to live just like any other nineteen-year-old—her life was an absurd mixture of owning Ferraris and eating hamburgers at a drive-in.

And above all, she wanted to be loved, physically, to be stroked, constantly, like a cat—because she had never known the real thing. And because, Janice suspected, she was *afraid* of the real thing. Her succession of affairs had not been caused by shortcomings in the men, as she pretended, but by her own fear of surrendering, of stopping the search for the perfect lover, perhaps one model too soon. But each search had to be completed. Hence her dissatisfaction at having to flee Robert Loung.

Diana was totally amoral, Janice was sure, simply because she had never actually been taught any moral values. Her remarkable family had apparently assumed that a Hayman would be born with moral values, while all the while filling the child's head with reminiscences of their most *im*moral past, beginning with Grandmother Ilona's escapades. And however much Diana pretended to reject all that, Janice knew she had imbibed a great deal of it. Most disastrous of all had been the episode when her mother had walked in on her and Richard Malling—and simply walked out again. She had not even *said* anything, according to Diana. What price seventeen-year-old morality then?

Yet Diana's desires had always been held within certain bounds, Janice had been slowly realizing over the past forty-eight hours, merely by being on home ground. Diana was confusing love with sensation-seeking, and had always done so, while remaining emotionally cold and narcissistically in love with her own body. But in New York, where she had grown up, her more extreme desires had been kept in check, perhaps subconsciously, but very effectively. Abroad, these checks no longer obtained.

It was tempting to decide that what Diana really needed was to meet someone who would take her emotions as well as her body and put them both through the wringer. Although, even then, Janice suspected that the other person would come out the worse off. Certainly a polite young man like Robert Loung would.

And it was her problem, she supposed, at least for as long as this trip lasted.

Besides, weren't *her* inhibitions a bit loosened by being in Paris?

"I just feel . . . alive," Diana said, standing beneath the cascading water, her hair hastily tucked into a plastic cap.

Janice stood in the doorway. "I'll do anything you want me to, Di," she said, "if it's what *you* want." Diana switched off the water, so she hastily added a rider. "But I don't know anything about it. I mean, what happens."

"For God's sake," Diana said, shaking out her hair.

"I mean, do you want me to do it to you, or do you want to do it to me, or what?"

"I think," Diana said, "that we let events take their course. I just put my arms around you, like this . . ." Her body was wet, and Janice had just dried hers, but she bit her lip and kept silent. "And we press our titties against each other, and we kiss . . . oh, mmmm . . ." The telephone jangled. "Oh, Jesus Christ!" Diana released Janice, walked to the table, and picked up the phone, gazing at her friend with smoldering eyes—which suddenly seemed to catch fire. "Here?" she asked, her voice rising. "Oh, tell him to come up." She replaced the receiver. "Robert," she said. "Robert!" she shouted. "He's here in Paris. He followed us, and found us. He's coming up. Oh, he loves me, Jan. He really and truly loves me!"

"And therefore you're going to love him back," Jan remarked, in a mingle of anger and sadness, as she reached for her bathrobe again. "However briefly."

"Oh, yes," Diana said. "Oh, yes."

"Despite coming all this way to stop that kind of thing."

"I came all this way to *find* something, Jan," Diana said. "And I think I've done that. Oh, yes. I've found what I *want!*" She blew her friend a kiss. "So I'm going to grab it."

Chapter 5

"CLOSE THE DOOR," JOSEPH STALIN SAID. "AND THEN SIT DOWN, comrade."

Anna Ragosina obeyed, aware of a certain flutter of her heart. It was not merely that this man, her employer, was probably the most powerful individual in the world; it was because this was the first time she had ever been alone with him. She had actually met him only a few times in her life. The first was when he pinned the medal of a Heroine of the Soviet Union on her tunic in 1945; the second was when he ordered her to arrest Ivan Nej, following the strange death of Ivan's wife in a car accident a few weeks later. The third was when he appointed her to the North American operation. After her return from that—triumphant, at least in her own opinion—she was called to this office several times, but as she now knew, she was then already out of favor for her various indiscretions while in Washington. And the last time she saw him, he sent her into exile at Tomsk.

Now she had been back at his command for three months, yet this was the first time he had sent for her. She had known that he would, eventually. Had prepared herself for it. And still felt breathless.

She crossed her legs, and waited.

"You have now been back for some time," Stalin said. "I

have deliberately not sought you out before, because I wished you to have the opportunity of looking around, and forming certain conclusions, and because I did not wish the . . . ah, opposition to suspect that my motives in returning you to your old position were anything more than a proper decision to end your exile." He smiled. "Which was perhaps too harsh a sentence in the first place. You understand me?"

"Of course," Anna said.

"But a sentence, an exile, over which you have, as usual, triumphed," Stalin went on. "I have never seen you looking better. Or lovelier, Anna Petrovna."

"Thank you, Joseph Vissarionovich." Was he making a first sexual move? She knew better than to trust *anything* Stalin ever said, or appeared to mean.

"Tell me, how are things at Lubianka?"

"Strained," she said.

"And your opinion?"

Anna hesitated only a moment. "Undoubtedly Comrade Beria is an ambitious man who looks forward to your death for his own advantage."

"Enough to wish to hasten it?"

"I would say that."

"Have you proof of this?"

"Not yet," Anna said. "But I will procure proof, I promise you."

Stalin leaned back with a sigh. "You are a treasure, Anna Petrovna. Do you know, Ivan Nikolaievich has not yet got around to saying anything that definite. Ivan Nikolaievich . . ." Without warning his eyes drooped shut, and he scarcely seemed to breathe. He might have fallen into a deep sleep.

Anna felt herself begin to frown, and hastily cleared her forehead. Here was a possible opportunity to further herself and denigrate Ivan, and she was not going to waste it, no matter how tired Stalin might be. "Ivan Nikolaievich has other things on his mind, Joseph Vissarionovich," she said.

Stalin's eyes opened again, almost reluctantly. "What other things?"

"His first priority seems to be to bring about the exchange of his son, Gregory, the traitor who was the true cause of the collapse of my North American network."

Now Stalin's eyes were definitely open. "I remember Gregory Nej," he said. "But we already tried to effect his exchange, and the Americans were not interested."

"I have told Ivan Nikolaievich this," Anna said, "but he will not listen to me. I am afraid he gives this a higher priority than dealing with Comrade Beria."

"That is a pity," Stalin sighed. "Are you saying that Ivan Nikolaievich has not been able to cope with life in Tomsk as well as you have?"

Anna smiled. "Ivan Nikolaievich stayed sane only because I was at his side."

Stalin surveyed her sleepily. Then he said, "I should think you would keep any man sane as long as you were at his side, Anna Petrovna. Have you any idea how Ivan Nikolaievich means to effect this exchange, if the Americans are not interested?"

"I am very much afraid he means to carry out the abduction of someone he hopes the Americans will be willing to pay to regain."

"Is there such a person here in Russia?"

"No, Joseph Vissarionovich," Anna said. She did not amplify, tell him about the photograph that apparently never left Ivan's pocket. If Ivan was crazy enough to try to kidnap a Hayman out of New York, *she* didn't even want to know about it until it was done; it had been on Ivan's instructions that she had kidnapped Ilona Hayman out of Warsaw, twenty years before. And *that* had cost her five years in a labor camp.

"Hm. Keep an eye on Ivan Nikolaievich, Anna Petrovna. It may be that I made a mistake in attempting to return him to his old position. He may be past it. You will find out whether or not he is. Report to me here, personally, when you have something concrete to tell me. Now give me your hand."

Anna frowned, but leaned across the desk and extended her hand, and had to keep herself from jerking her hand away: Stalin's fingers were like blocks of ice.

"Remember it was I who brought you back, Anna. And it is I who can send you away again. But it is also I who can raise you to the heights of which you have always dreamed. Only I can do that. Find me proof of what Beria intends. And give Ivan enough rope to hang himself. Do these things for me, Anna, and the KGB will be yours. Remember! Only I can give you that. Everyone else in the Politburo hates and fears you. So if you would succeed, do not fail me."

Slowly Anna withdrew her hand. "Do you not suppose I would do these things for the good of Mother Russia, Joseph Vissarionovich?"

Stalin smiled. "No, Anna Petrovna. I do not suppose that. You will do these things for the good of Anna Petrovna Ragosina. And for fear of me. But I know that you *will* do them."

Although Anna Ragosina was single, and had every intention of remaining so, as a senior commissar she had been given the use of one of the three-room apartments in a new building to the south edge of Moscow. This was her castle, the only tangible evidence of her privileged position. It was an utterly private world, to which no one else was admitted, and which was inhabited only by her cat, Tabasco, and herself. Tabasco was a relic of the past. She was an American cat, procured when her mistress had had a luxurious—by Russian standards—apartment in Washington, D.C., as a member of the embassy staff. Those three years were the happiest of Anna's life, and that they had ended in disaster did not make them any less happy in retrospect. And anyway, she had been able to take Tabasco with her to Tomsk, and then bring her back here. The two understood each other, and adored each other.

Anna's pleasures were few. In America she had succcumbed to the lures of television and instant dinners wrapped in aluminum foil. Of these only television was also available in Russia—again, as a senior commissar, she was one of the very few people in the whole building to possess a set—but the programs were unutterably boring. Anna liked situation comedy and baseball, and above all else, American football. News programs bored her, because the news never said what was actually happening, but only what the government *said* was happening, at least in Russia; and ballet and music she found effete. But at least, now that she was again living in Moscow, she was able once more to indulge in one of her very greatest pleasures, another elic of her three years in Washington. Then she had never worn a uniform at all, for it had been part of her role as an Embassy secretary to appear as fragilely feminine as she could. Having been brought up in the KGB, having learned how to kill a man with three well-directed prods of her iron-clad fingers long before she had taught herself how to boil an egg, she had been somewhat surprised and even a little disturbed by the pleasure she had found in that new role, by the delight she had discovered in lace underwear and pretty frocks, in handbags and high-heeled shoes. These had been luxuries she had determined never to discard, and she had taken her wardrobe with her even to Tomsk. But in Tomsk the clothes had provided very little pleasure. Tomsk was too small, and she was too well known. Even in a summer frock and high heels, Anna Ragosina was still Anna Ragosina. Here in Moscow things were different. She had never been officially reported as having returned at all—just as she had never been officially reported as exiled at all. Anyway, not many people in Moscow had met her and knew what she looked like. Most were members of the KGB like herself, who would never give her away; the others were people she had had in her cells at Lubianka—and none of them were still *around* to give her away. On the streets of Moscow, and especially out of uniform, she was totally anonymous.

And it was high summer. Thus every afternoon when she left Lubianka, Anna went home to her apartment, stripped off the heavy dark-green serge tunic and skirt, and the equally distasteful green drill drawers—it was not considered necessary for female members of the KGB to wear brassieres, for the weight of the tunic effectively flattened everything beneath—kicked away the boots and hung up the revolver belt, bathed . . . and then with great care dressed herself in her lace underwear, her nylon stockings and skimpy high-heeled shoes, added a cream or pink or pale-blue nylon frock—sheer when seen against the sun—with frilly hems and a peek-a-boo bodice, and went for a walk. She knew she aroused a great deal of interest, and no doubt provoked a great deal of comment. But she wore her clothes, and walked and moved, with such total arrogance that even the young men were afraid to approach her, while their more knowing elders, making the usual mistake of assuming that she was a good ten years younger than her age, obviously carried their mistake one step further and assumed she was the mistress of some very important commissar. This she enjoyed, because actually she would have liked to be the mistress of a very important commissar. This Stalin even. Or Molotov. Or Michael Nej. She had been impressed by Michael Nej.

She had even supposed, once, that she was going to be just such a mistress. Until she had discovered that Ivan Nej was just a *little* man, and always would be.

But the illusion, created in so many minds, was not so very inferior to the reality. Her walks were the best part of her days. And while walking she could think, without fear of interruption.

Mostly she thought about pleasant, transient things. Such as men. If she could not be the mistress of Stalin, then it was certainly time she acquired a lover. This was not because she felt any need to be loved, although she enjoyed the physical act. It was because she liked to *own,* to watch a man falling head over heels in love with her beauty and her sensuality. In her time, possessing complete power of life and death over those unfortunates who had fallen into her clutches, she had been able to possess women as well as men, and had enjoyed both sexes. But women the less, because women surrendered so easily. They had lower physical thresholds for things like loneliness, and cold, and hunger, much less actual pain. Men tried to hold out. They could not, of course, but they tried.

The plain fact was, she had not had an interesting lover of either sex for three years. There had been no interesting lovers to be found in Tomsk, and there was certainly no pleasure to be got out of that worn-out ragbag Ivan Nej, whether in bed or out of it. She felt a need. Of course, probably it would have to be someone from inside the KGB itself, some young and vigorous lieutenant who would be ecstatic at being noticed by Anna Ragosina, and who would be virile enough to satisfy her enormous lust, and at the same time callow enough to weep, or even commit suicide, when she told him enough was enough. But he would have to be picked carefully . . . she frowned as she walked along.

Because other thoughts kept obtruding. Important thoughts. And rather frightening ones. They stemmed from the icy cold feel of Stalin's hand, and his obvious exhaustion. She didn't know whether Beria *had* attempted to poison the old man or not, last winter; she certainly knew that Stalin was soon going to die, of something.

And then? "The other members of the Politburo hate you and fear you," he had said. And she knew this was true. Ivan and, through him, she herself were regarded as relics of the thirties and the purges, and even before then, of the mass elimination of the kulaks, those farmers who had dared to make personal profits. They had acted, in both those causes, on Stalin's orders, and thus had become irrevocably identified with the dictator and his policies. There were men in Russia, such as Malenkov and Khrushchev, high up the Party ladder and certainly potential successors, who felt those policies had been mistaken, and had done no more than create for the world an image of Soviet brutality. They were men who wanted to liberalize the regime, even if only slightly, and to come to terms with the West, rather than regard it as a perpetual enemy. This was a dangerous deviation in Leninist thinking which Anna did not wish personally to consider. But there could be no doubt that it *would* eventually affect her personally. If Malenkov or Khrushchev were to succeed Stalin, she did not doubt for a moment that their very first act would be to get rid of Anna Ragosina and Ivan Nej. And there was only one sure way to do that: a wall and a firing squad.

She felt suddenly cold, on a warm summer evening. The thought, which had been trying to gain entry to her mind ever since her interview with Stalin, was suddenly in full control. He had promised her the moon, should she bring him proof of Beria's treachery. She was committed to supplying such proof, even if she had to manufacture it. But to what end, if Stalin died within a year, and someone else took over?

Even if Michael Nej or Molotov took over, she was finished, first because they were hardly younger than Stalin himself, and second because they hated her as much as anyone.

She found herself standing still, staring at the people walking past, without seeing any of them. She had imagined the world was about to fall into her lap. And all the time it had been falling apart beneath her feet. Yet what was she to do? Not to give Stalin what he wanted, and accept his reward, would mean, at the least, another exile to Siberia. Give him what he wanted and accept his rewards, and . . . prepare to die, within a couple of years at most?

It was an impossible choice to have to make.

"Anna! Anna Ragosina?"

She turned. At such a moment, someone had broken the rules, and recognized her in the street.

Anna stared at the intruder in total anger that slowly faded to incredulity.

"Anna?" he asked again, gazing at her frock, her high heels. "Can it really be you?"

"Nikolai?" she asked in turn. "Nikolai Ivanovich?"

Nikolai Nej took a step towards her and then stopped, glancing left and right at the interested passersby. He was actually very like his father, in his shortness and his pointed features—and his hesitancy. But Anna was not disposed to be angry with Nikolai Nej.

"Not here," she said. "Do you have an apartment?"

Another hesitation. "I share it with two others."

Her turn to hesitate. But this was too good a chance to be missed. Nikolai Ivanovich Nej! Ivan's son by his first wife, Zoe Geller. Actually, Ivan had had two sons by his first wife, as she remembered. But he had allowed them to disappear with their mother in the turmoil of the revolution; he had had no further use for Zoe Geller, the daughter of the village schoolmaster at Starogan, because he had then already determined to possess Tatiana Borodina, and it had suited him to tell the world that Zoe was dead—as she had eventually been, although not until after Ivan had bigamously married his master's daughter. What had happened to the elder boy no one had ever discovered. No doubt, like his mother, he had been one of the ten million who had starved to death or died of disease during the civil war. Just as no one had ever been interested in what had happened to the younger boy, doomed to grow up in a state orphanage, as Anna herself had done. But *his* orphanage, unlike hers, had been for the cast-off children of Party members, and that had made all the difference in his fate.

They had met in the beginning of the thirties, when she had first been working for Ivan and Nikolai had been a struggling chess player; he was a year or two older than she. By then she had already learned to hate her vicious Svengali. To seduce his son had seemed a natural, almost an inescapable, way of hitting back, especially since Nikolai also hated Ivan. But soon afterward had come her first disgrace, and her five years in a labor camp. She had seen Nikolai briefly when she had returned, just before the beginning of the Great Patriotic War; then they had both been overtaken by events. Since then, she had supposed him dead. But here he was, looking shabby, to be sure, but perfectly healthy. And he was still Ivan Nej's son, a man who still hated his father as much as she did, and was clearly still fit and virile . . . and, because he already knew most things about her, a man with whom she could relax.

He might have been made to order.

"Then we will go to my apartment," she decided. "Do not worry, *it* is not shared with anyone except my cat." It did not occur to Anna to indulge in any small talk or flirtation. She knew what she wanted, and here was a man who could relieve that want.

But he was biting his lip. "I am on my way to the Central Chess Club. There is a tournament."

"Do you still play chess?"

He shook his head. "Not in the big tournaments. I never made the master class. I am a journalist."

"Then you must take the evening off, for once." She held his hand, like any young girl with her beau; she really enjoyed gestures like this. "I thought you were dead," she remarked as they strolled along the pavement, hearts beating with anticipation of the coming moments. "Weren't you reported missing, at Kursk?"

"I was taken prisoner."

She turned her head. "You were a prisoner of the Nazis?"

"For two years." He correctly interpreted her gaze. "It was not easy."

"You *were* dead," she declared. "And have been resurrected. I am so pleased to see you!"

"But you . . . I read about what you did in the Pripet, how you became a Heroine of the Soviet Union. But then . . . I tried to find you, and you had gone. They said you had been sent to the Crimea. But when I managed to get down there last year, you weren't there, either."

"Affairs of state," Anna said. "I have been on various foreign assignments."

"And have prospered, as usual," he said admiringly. And sighed. "I suppose you still see a lot of my father?"

"We still work together," Anna said carefully.

"And is he . . . ?"

Anna showed him into the elevator. "He is well, Nikolai Ivanovich. Old, but fit."

"Does he ever speak of me?"

"No," she said. She had no desire to see a reconciliation between the two. Besides, Ivan never did speak of him. The elevator stopped, and she led him into the lobby and unlocked her door. "I did not bring you home to talk about your father. Do you know, you will be the first man ever to enter this apartment since I have lived here?"

"Anna . . ." He followed her inside and looked around in envious amazement. "That you would remember me, and still wish . . ."

"How could I ever forget you?" she asked, and stood against him to take him in her arms, and kiss him, slowly and lingeringly. "I have waited for you, Nikolai Ivanovich, for years."

"I can't believe it," he said. "I can't . . . what is that noise?"

"Tabasco. She is shut in the bedroom, and expects to be fed. We will kick her out, and shut ourselves in the bedroom instead." Anna removed the cat, gave her a saucer of milk, then shut the bedroom door and took off her frock, carefully hanging it in her closet.

"Anna," Nilolai said. "You are something out of a film. Those clothes . . ."

Anna paraded to and fro in her lace underwear. "I even have scotch whiskey," she said, and returned to the living room to fetch the bottle and two glasses. "I have everything. Except you. But now I have you as well."

"Anna . . ." He kissed her again. "Anna—my God!" He pushed her away. "I have been bitten." He sat on the bed, pulled off his shoes, and rolled down his sock to gaze at the blood welling from his ankle. "Holy Mother!"

Like so many Russians, she thought, he reached back into a long-forbidden religious past in a moment of stress.

"She must have come in when I opened the door." Anna picked up Tabasco. "Naughty pussy!" She put her out and closed the door. "She is insanely jealous." She knelt beside him, moved his hands, held his foot, and sucked the blood.

"You swallowed it," he said in consternation.

"Why not? Her teeth are quite clean." She kissed his toes. "And is it not worth a little blood, to hold me in your arms?" She sat beside him. "Soon I may bite you myself."

"My God, Anna," he muttered. "How I have missed you. How . . ." His fingers were tearing at the lace, and she hastily released her own brassiere strap, then slid down the panties herself as well. They were irreplaceable, in Moscow. Her nylons she was prepared to sacrifice, as they rolled together on the bed. He was hard, so hard. That was the principal thing she remembered about him, his penetrating hardness, which seemed to fill her from vagina to womb, and then expand sideways as well until there seemed no room for her own organs. She was a woman who normally liked a good deal of variety in her lovemaking, and a good deal of foreplay as well, but never with Nikolai. He entered, always the same way, lying on her stomach and driving the breath from her lungs, while he filled her and filled her and filled her. She always had an orgasm with Nikolai Nej. But then, she seldom failed to have an orgasm with any man. She had the power of complete concentration on whatever she happened to be doing, and when making love could combine the feelings and the desires of her genitals and her brain with a single act of will. But with Nikolai Nej that was never even necessary.

And afterward there was complete relaxation. She was even content to think about *him* for a few seconds. He was a strange character, one of the gentlest and least aggressive men she had ever known. It was difficult to imagine him in the army at all, much less being able to survive two years as a prisoner of the S.S. His adoration of her was no less strange. Did he not know she had killed, and would continue to do so? If he did not, he had to be a complete innocent. If he did, it didn't seem to worry him.

And already he was hardening again. He would keep her happy until she could find someone better, and she would be getting back at Ivan at the same time . . . She thought she might even tell Ivan, the next time *he* wanted to screw her, that she had just come from Nikolai's arms, and was therefore sated. Because Ivan could not harm her now. Not so long as she was so close and important to Stalin.

She sat up in a cold sweat, and Nikolai rolled off her with a grunt. For a moment she had forgotten the situation.

"Anna?" Nikolai asked. "What is the matter, Anna?"

She stared at him, but did not see his face, because suddenly the answer was transparently obvious. It must have been obvious all the time, only she had not recognized it. She could thank the sexual release for clearing her brain. She could hope to survive only if Stalin were to be succeeded by a man ruthless enough to continue things exactly as they were, and who would also be grateful to her, so grateful he would give her command of the KGB. That was her only hope.

And of course there was only one man in Russia who could, and would, do that.

"Ah, Anna." Ivan Nej leaned back in his chair, boots on his desk. "Come in. Come in."

Anna entered the office even more suspiciously than she had entered Stalin's a few days before. She guessed Ivan must have found out she was again seeing Nikolai, which was annoying; she had meant to tell him about that only when she was ready. Besides, it was equally annoying to be summoned to his office like some junior clerk. But patient enmity was one of her great stocks in trade; Ivan's days were already numbered. She closed the door and sat down.

"What do you think of that?" Ivan tossed her a folded newspaper. It was a Swedish daily, and Anna did not speak Swedish. But she was enough of an international linguist to gather the gist of the caption beneath the photograph Ivan obviously meant her to study. It was something like *Jewish Representatives at the Zionist Conference*. She gazed at the photograph, which was of four men and three women, standing together in the lobby of a Stockholm hotel, she estimated. The quality of the reproduction was poor, but she did not have much difficulty in identifying the middle woman of the three, who was the tallest, the oldest, as well as the most striking—she was, Anna knew, in her midsixties, and her hair was gray, but her features were as proudly handsome as ever, and she stood very erect, while she wore her very good clothes with an awareness both that they were very good clothes and that she knew how to wear them.

"Judith Petrova," she said.

"Exactly." Ivan seemed pleased, which Anna found difficult to believe. For him, Judith Petrova, who had been famous as Judith Stein before her marriage to Boris Petrov, had always meant failure. First as a friend of the Borodin girls before World War One, when he had had to black her boots, later as the mistress of his own brother during the civil war, when again, despite his hatred of her, he had had to yield to her superior social status, and lastly as the determined Zionist who had so bedeviled Stalin, and had slipped through his fingers time and again. The final disaster had come when Stalin had sent him to Israel to bring her back, and Ivan had failed. After that had come exile to Tomsk. Ivan had even tried to hit back at this woman who had always outwitted him by locking her husband, Boris Petrov, into a mental hospital. But he had failed there too. For when his son Gregory Nej had been sentenced to death for spying in the United States, George Hayman had managed to persuade President Truman to commute the death sentence—in exchange for the release of Boris Petrov, among other Jews, and the permission for him to join his wife in Israel.

Anna would have thought that Ivan's mind would curdle at the very thought of Judith Stein. But he continued to smile.

"You will observe," he remarked, "that she is in the forefront of affairs, as usual. She seems to be the head of this delegation."

Anna returned the newspaper to his desk. "This interests you?"

"Very greatly. Judith Petrova appears to have become some kind of roving goodwill ambassador for the Israelis. I suppose the Tel Aviv government is aware of her international prestige, and is using it for all it is worth. Could they fail to use her great experience in international espionage as well?"

Anna frowned. "She was never a spy."

"Oh, call it what you will. An agent provocateur. A stirrer-up of things, against the Soviet Union."

"Well," Anna said, "I suppose she hates us. Did not the Cheka execute her mother and father? On your orders?"

"Of course. The Steins helped Peter Borodin to escape capture in 1918. They deserved to die. That does not alter the facts. Judith Petrova is a woman whose every action is directed against the Soviet Union."

"She can't do us much harm now."

"You think not?" Ivan was staring at her.

Anna returned his stare. And understood his meaning. "May I remind you, Ivan Nikolaievich," she said, "that we are here to do a job?—not to engage in personal vendettas or personal dreams."

"Bah," Ivan said. "You know as well as I that there is no proof against Beria. We will just have to wait for him to make a mistake. He will; I have no doubt of that—and then we shall have him. I have told Stalin this. In the meantime, life must go on. To return Judith Petrov to Russia will be a triumph. For me, certainly. She escaped me in Jerusalem, in forty-seven—

she caused my disgrace. I have not forgiven her for that. And now . . . Do not forget that in addition to having once been Michael's mistress, she was also George Hayman's mistress for a while, and before either of *them,* she was Peter Borodin's mistress. She is important to everybody, but to the Haymans most of all. When she is arrested on a charge of commanding Israeli espionage operations against the Soviet Union . . ."

"We will never obtain proof of that."

Ivan smiled. "I propose to revert to first principles, Anna, the principles I was brought up on, and which I taught to you, remember? We arrest her first, and we let her tell us what activities she was engaged in. Because she will tell us whatever we wish, after we have had her downstairs for a while. Anyway, it does not matter what she tells us. When the Israelis and the Haymans and the whole world start to call for her release, we will be willing to bow to world opinion."

"In exchange for Gregory."

"That is correct."

Anna opened her mouth, and then closed it again. He was even more stupid, and more demented about his ridiculous son than she had supposed. But was he not playing entirely into her hands? Quite apart from the pleasure his new disgrace would give her personally, his preoccupation with this mad scheme would leave her free to pursue her own objective with total singlemindedness. "This is a stroke of genius, Ivan Nikolaievich," she said. "Absolute genius. But I would ask to have no part in it. I think that woman is bad luck, at least for me. I doubt I would be able to handle it successfully."

"Luck." Ivan's lip curled contemptuously. "I am not going to require you to handle it at all, Anna Petrovna," he said. "I want Judith Petrova all to myself. I do not want you interfering in any way."

Anna got up. "I will not do that, Ivan Nikolaievich," she said. "I give you my absolute word on that. I shall not interfere."

Lavrenti Beria marched along the corridor beneath Lubianka Street beside Anna Ragosina. "I really do not see, Comrade Ragosina, why *I* have to be involved in such things as recruitment and training problems," he protested. "You are supposed to be in complete control of such activities."

"As I am. But you are my commander, Comrade Beria," she reminded him. And as her commander, she thought contemptuously, he could merely have sent her away with a few choice words. Instead, he was doing as she wished. That was because he was terrified of her, especially now that she represented Stalin's will. It was remarkable, really. Physically, there could have been no greater contrast than between Beria and Ivan Nej. Where Ivan was short, Beria was extremely tall. Where Ivan had a thick head of hair, Beria was totally bald. Where Ivan sported a thick moustache, Beria's face was totally exposed. Where Ivan's face was all mountains and valleys, Beria's was large and featureless and bland.

But they shared one thing. Jointly heads of the most feared secret police in the world, they were both afraid of *her*. Yet Beria, at least, apparently had had the wit to plan a future for himself. It was up to her to make sure that he also had the courage to act. And if he did not, to give him that courage.

"I wish you to see for yourself," she explained, "the very poor quality of the material with which I am having to work nowadays. When I think of the boys and girls I trained before the war . . . and then of the way they were squandered, leading partisan groups behind the German lines, the way they were tortured and murdered by the Nazis—It makes me want to weep."

Beria looked skeptical.

"We could certainly have used those today, comade commissar," she said.

"Young people nowadays have it too soft," he agreed. "They do not understand that one has to be hard, to succeed in this life."

"Exactly," Anna said. "It is the system, comrade. The system. Life has been too good inside Russia these past few years. See for yourself." She opened the door to the gymnasium and led him inside, where the scent of leather and resin, and above all of human sweat, pervaded the huge, airless, underground room.

All activity within the room ceased at the entry of the two commissars, but the trainees' flushed bodies and panting chests were evidence of how hard they had been working up to that moment. There were twelve trainees, eight boys and four girls; the eldest was not more than twenty. They varied in shape and size from the tall to the short, the heavily muscled to the thin, but not one of them, after only a few weeks in Anna's gymnasium, retained even an ounce of surplus fat. This was easy to determine, for they were naked, which was how Anna liked them to be.

"How many laps?" Anna asked.

"Thirty, comrade commissar," replied the head instructor.

"Let them do five more," Anna commanded, and the instructor waved the little group into movement once more. "Watch this carefully," Anna told Beria, who was indeed watching the trainees carefully, especially the four girls. Anna smiled. But she was not prepared to anticipate her victory. She never did that.

The twelve students ran around the room another five times, starting to flag now, and were brought to a halt by a command from their instructor. The other two instructors had taken up positions by a table, on which there were twelve revolvers. These they now began throwing at the students. Three of the boys and one of the girls actually caught their weapons. The other eight, obviously distracted by the presence of the two people who controlled their entire futures, allowed the flying steel to slip through their sweaty hands and clatter on the floor; immediately they dropped to their hands and knees and started scrabbling after them. Those with the guns already in their hands opened fire on the targets, each representing a running man, at the far end of the gymnasium, perhaps thirty yards away. The room echoed with the sound of the explosions, became filled with the scent of cordite. After the very ragged volley was completed, and the last girl managed to get in her shot nine seconds after the first boy, Anna walked forward to inspect the targets. "You see?" She showed Beria. Of the twelve targets, three had bullet holes on the body itself, but only one in the chest, and that high up on the right side. Two more had been struck about the legs, and seven were unmarked. "Had this been real, and those bits of cardboard armed and returning fire, this entire squad would have been eliminated." She snapped her fingers. "Just like that."

"Well," Beria said, deprecatingly, "it must be very difficult to shoot accurately when one's hands are wet and one's heart is pounding, when one is gasping for breath and one's muscles are exhausted—"

"Are those not the usual conditions under which one *has* to shoot, comrade commissar?" Anna demanded. "We are talking here of self-defense, not assassination. The problem is pure lack of concentration, which is simply lack of mental power. Would you like *me* to show you how it should be done?"

"You?" Beria was astonished.

"Stand back," Anna commanded. "All of you." She undressed with her usual speed, and stood before them. She was obviously confident that the years in Tomsk had not made that perfect body droop.

She began to run, faster than any of the students had done. "Count the laps," she told the instructor, who obeyed with a grin, while at the same time he pressed a button to lower all the targets but one. He had seen his mistress displaying her talents before. Around and around the gymnasium Anna ran, each lap nearly a hundred yards, disappearing amid pillars and vaulting horses, ducking under low swinging ropes and trapezes, skipping over weight bars left on the floor, while the sweat started from her forehead and temples, her shoulders and armpits, her groin and her thighs, rolling downward, causing her bare feet to leave dark imprints on the stone floor. She never looked at Beria, but she had no doubt he was looking at her.

"Thirty," said the instructor.

Anna stopped, panting, turned her head to face the table, from where her revolver was already arcing through the air. She caught it in both hands, back to front, reversed it, aimed, and fired.

"One point five seconds," the instructor said.

Beria walked forward to look at the target. The bullet had entered the exact center of the chest. "That is very good," he said. "Very good indeed." His admiration seemed genuine.

"Leave," Anna commanded the students. "You too," she told the instructors. "All of you. Take the rest of the day off."

They exchanged amazed glances, but obeyed, gathering their clothes and hurrying out of the gymnasium for the showers. Carefully getting her breathing back under control, Anna walked to the table and emptied the used shells from her gun, before reloading.

"Very good," Beria said again. "You are still the best, eh, Anna Petrovna? Now I must get back to my office."

Anna closed the reloaded revolver, and turned to face him. "Do not leave yet, Lavrenti Pavlovich. I brought you down here to speak with you in private. Did you not realize that?"

Beria gazed at her naked body.

"Are you aware that I am under orders from Comrade Stalin to destroy you?" Anna asked.

Beria's jaw dropped; although she had no doubt he *was* aware of that fact, he could never have anticipated anything so brutally open. His hand twitched, because there was a holstered automatic pistol on his own belt. But he knew he had no hope of outshooting Anna, especially when her revolver was already pointing at him. "You . . ." He looked left and right, as if seeking shelter.

Anna smiled. "If I *did* intend to execute you, Lavrenti, would I tell you first?" She considered. "Yes, I probably would. I like people to know what is going to happen to them. It makes them so afraid. But I did not bring you here for that." Carefully she laid the revolver on the table. Beria's eyes followed it, as if magnetized. She could read his mind easily: he knew he still could not draw his gun and shoot her as quickly as she could reach her pistol and kill him. "Can you really pretend you did not appreciate Stalin's intention in recalling Ivan Nikolaievich and myself from Tomsk?"

Beria licked his lips. Anna guessed he was deciding it would be far too risky to acknowledge that. "I . . . he said you had suffered enough."

"Suffered!" Anna's lip curled. Then she left the table and began to move toward him, slowly. This was dangerous, as he could probably draw and fire before she could reach him, no matter how fast she was. But she did not think he was all that accurate a shot, and he must know that if she did reach him, for all that he was twice her size and weight, she would destroy him. Besides, this whole business was an enormous risk. Anna enjoyed risks; they made her adrenaline flow as nothing else could. "Of course, he wishes it done the usual way. I am to supply proof of your attempt to kill him last February."

Beria's mouth opened and then closed again. But the danger was past; she was within four feet of him. She stopped, smiling at him, putting up one hand to move strands of sweat-soaked hair from the front of her shoulders. "Of course you are innocent," she said. "But equally as a matter of course I will supply such proof—should I choose to do so."

Beria's shoulders slumped.

"But I have been thinking," she said, "how incredibly stupid it would be of you to do such a thing, when Joseph Vissarionovich is obviously declining fast. All you have to do is wait."

"Wait?" His voice was hoarse. "They hate me. All of them. They hate me."

"I know," she said. "It is because you are commander of the KGB. They hate me too."

He stared at her, and she moved closer, until they were nearly touching. Now he would be able to smell her sweat, mingling with her perfume. "But I still suggest that you wait. I think we both should wait, all the while preparing to act, the moment Stalin draws his last breath."

"Act? You? If I could . . ."

"If you could believe that? Believe it, Lavrenti Pavlovich. Believe, too, that if you wish it, I shall devote myself entirely to you. You did not enjoy the last time we were together. Perhaps I was not ready. I am ready now. I can give you the loyalty of all those boys and girls you watched just now. I can give you their *devotion*. And I can supply many more like them."

"But why?" he said.

"Because while I know that you cannot hope to survive without me, I also know that I may find it difficult to achieve all *my* aims without *you*."

"Aims?"

"When you are head of state, I want the KGB. Oh, it will always remain an instrument of your policy, Lavrenti Pavlovich. But I want the command of it."

"A woman?"

Anna put her arms around his neck, allowed her nipples to leave damp circles on his uniform jacket. "Can you think of a *man* who would be more efficient? Or who could be more eager to please you?"

Her kiss was long and slow. And victorious.

Until he took her wrists and then forced her away from him. "And Ivan Nej?" he demanded. "Where does he fit into your 'aims'?"

Anna smiled. "When the time comes, Lavrenti Pavlovich, you may give Ivan Nikolaievich to me."

* * *

It really had been absurdly easy, Anna thought. A matter of will, and thus of achievement. Obviously the road ahead was filled with pitfalls, into which the unwary might tumble. She had to keep up a pretense of antagonism to Beria, and she had to satisfy Stalin that she *was* actually working to obtain proof of treachery, without ever quite succeeding. She did not think she had to consider Ivan Nej, who was totally occupied with his absurd plans for Judith Petrova—plans that would bring him fresh disgrace, place him in her power, probably even before Stalin's demise. But she certainly had to keep Beria himself convinced of her trustworthiness, while never forgetting that *he* was as treacherous as anyone on earth. She did not pretend it was going to be easy; on the other hand, remembering what they had done to each other yesterday morning on the vaulting mattress in the gymnasium, she doubted it would be so very difficult, either.

In any event, she was fond of recalling the words of the American President Harry Truman, that those who couldn't stand the heat should stay out of the kitchen. During her years in Washington she had imbibed a great many Americanisms, and that one she rated highest of all. She was quite prepared to stand the heat, because she intended one day to be the head chef. "A woman?" Beria had said. But her little finger was worth more than the whole of any man she had ever known.

She raised her head as her door opened, after a brief knock, and gazed at her secretary, a pretty blond girl. Anna liked surrounding herself with pretty blond girls; her own dark beauty stood out so in contrast. "Well, Maria Feodorovna?" she asked.

"An item, comrade commissar," the girl said. "You once gave me a list of names, and asked that if any of these ever appeared in connection with the Soviet Union, I must bring them to your immediate attention."

"That is correct," Anna acknowledged.

"There is a woman named Hayman, who has made application for a visa to visit the Soviet Union," Maria said.

Anna frowned. "Hayman?"

"When she comes, she will be married. I think she will be on her honeymoon. Her name will then be Mrs. Robert Loung. But at present her name is Diana Hayman."

Anna stared at her, the frown slowly clearing.

"I do not know if it is important, comrade commissar, but . . ."

Her voice trailed away; she realized that her commander was not listening.

Diana Hayman? The girl from the photograph? It could not be. It simply could *not* be. But if it was . . . Diana Hayman, coming to Russia. Walking into her clutches with the innocent arrogance of her birth and position. Walking into Ivan's arms. *There* would be a tool with which to destroy him, utterly. But perhaps an unnecessary tool, if he was truly going to involve himself with Judith Petrov. Yet the girl might be valuable in so many other ways. She was John Hayman's niece. George Hayman's granddaughter. And, as Ivan had said, because she was the principal heiress, she could be considered the most important member of that entire damnable family.

If it could be true . . .

"There are particulars of this woman?" she asked.

Maria consulted her notebook. "Height five feet two inches. Weight one hundred and two pounds. Hair black. Eyes blue. Visible scars, none . . ."

"When was she born?"

"The sixth of March, 1933, New York City."

"Her parents?"

"George and Elizabeth Hayman."

It was true, Anna thought. It actually was true. Diana Hayman was coming to her. It suddenly occurred to her that, once she had at last gone out and seized her future by the scruff of the neck, fate was about to reward her far more than she had ever dared dream. Certainly, even if she had no clear idea what she intended to do with such a prize, to pass up such an opportunity as this would be criminal—it might never be repeated.

If she dared. What she was considering was what Ivan might have proposed. Would propose, if he knew about the visa application. And almost every scheme Ivan had ever thought up had turned out to be a disaster. But where was the risk in it, to her? The girl would be inside Russia, where anything could be planted in her luggage—in her very handbag.

John Hayman, she thought. This was her way to punish John Hayman.

Only Ivan must *never* know, until she was ready.

She leaned forward. "Listen to me very carefully, Maria Feodorovna," she said. "First, this application is to be seen by no one except you and me, and the officers who passed it to you. You understand me?"

"Of course, comrade commissar."

"Very good. It is known how this woman will be entering Russia?"

"The application is for a train journey, comrade commissar, beginning at Paris."

"That will come via Berlin, Warsaw, Brest-Litovsk, and Smolensk. Maria Feodorovna, I want you to find out the date of this train she will be on, take two men, and meet it at Brest-Litovsk. There you will remove this woman and her husband and their luggage. Use the customary procedure. Then bring them both to Moscow, secretly. You understand?"

"Of course, comrade commissar," Maria said, obviously not understanding at all. "This woman—is she very dangerous?"

"Oh, very dangerous," Anna said. "Very dangerous indeed."

"But then . . . why do you not just refuse her a visa?"

Anna smiled. "Because she is more dangerous outside of Russia than in it. We want her here, Maria Feodorovna. Where we can keep an eye on her. We will grant her a visa immediately."

Chapter 6

Allen Dulles gazed at John Hayman for several seconds after John had finished speaking. Then he said, "And you believe it? That he really will attempt to murder Stalin?"

"I do."

"Even if you can't figure out how he's even going to get inside the Soviet Union, much less be allowed to enter Stalin's presence with a weapon?"

"I'm pretty sure he has it all worked out."

"But you agree he's mad?"

"Mad people often have a surprising amount of cunning, Mr. Dulles."

"I'm not denying that." He gazed at the hastily written report on his desk. "I guess this has to go to the state department, but I can't imagine what they're going to make of it. I don't care to imagine what the president is going to make of it, either. We have an election coming up. Now, Harry isn't running, but he sure as hell hopes Adlai Stevenson is going to win. And he has to know that if this report of yours leaks out, a lot of people will say it's pure election-year propaganda, to prove how honest the Democrats are, when everyone in this country would actually shout for joy to hear that old Joe stopped a bullet. In addition, it'll give the Republicans an absolute field day, if Truman offers your information to the Soviets. A large part of their strategy, anyway, seems to be to claim that there are too many top officials in the administration playing footsie with the Communists."

"You don't think what I've found out is just a shade bigger than party politics?"

"You think *anything* smaller than a war comes under that heading?"

"And you?"

Dulles smiled briefly. "One of the rules of this job is that it's above politics. And maybe this report should be, too. I'm sorry, John. You've done a great job. But this is a hot potato you've turned up."

"With respect, sir," John said, "if we don't do anything about it, and Prince Peter gets where he wants, we could be on our way to World War Three. The Russians will be quite sure he was sent."

"Without decisions," Dulles said, "life would be so damned simple. We'll have a word with the British. Our best chance is for them to keep him under wraps, at least until after the election."

"I do think," Elizabeth Hayman grumbled, fiddling with her coffee spoon, "that you could have tried to find out where they were going in Paris. What they were intending to do."

John sighed. He had enough in his life of cloak-and-dagger stuff, without having to indulge in more of it to please his sister-in-law. He had proposed he come around to see Elizabeth, but she had insisted on this Lower East Side coffee shop, where they both stood out like sore thumbs. "I told you, Beth," he explained, "I had to get back in a hurry. Business."

"I don't understand that either," Elizabeth remarked. "I had the impression you were going to be in England a week or two."

"Well . . . I thought I was going for at least *a* week. But then something came up."

"So what do I do now?" she demanded. "I can't let my only daughter waltz off into the distance, without a clue where she is or what she's doing. Or perhaps with too much of a clue as to what she's doing."

"Don't you think you're making too much of the whole thing?" John asked. "In the first place, in my opinion, there is nothing, well, unnatural in the relationship between her and Janice Corliss."

"Ha," Elizabeth commented.

"And in the second, weren't they going to Paris, anyway?"

"Oh, sure. Next year. After spending a term at this London art college they're enrolled in."

"But that doesn't start until September. So they've reversed their plans, that's all. Probably because I was breathing down their necks. They'll probably be back in time to take classes. Meanwhile, you can find her easily enough, if you really want to."

"Oh, sure. I could hire a private detective. Then Diana would really flip her lid."

"I meant, you could send a telegram to each of the hotels where she might be staying. Just a keeping-in-touch greeting or something like that. One of them will bring a reply."

"Oh, really, John. There are thousands of hotels in Paris. You don't suppose she's going to be staying at the George V, or somewhere like that, if she's out to have some kind of illicit affair, do you?"

"I do *not* think she is out to have any kind of illicit affair. And I do think she may have gone to the George V or somewhere like that. Di only knows one way to live. It can't do any harm to send a cable there. And everywhere else you can think of, as I said." He leaned across the table and kissed her on the forehead. "You *are* taking this thing a bit too seriously, in my opinion. She'll get in touch when she's ready. Now I simply have to rush."

He hurried for the street, and a cab. He supposed George junior was a very happy man, but he personally couldn't live with that woman for twenty-four hours without going nuts. She wanted to control everything Diana did, while at the same time she was afraid of letting anyone find that out. Most of all, she was afraid of Diana finding out, because she knew that if that happened, she could lose the girl altogether. No one could have any doubt about Diana's strength of will, or her ability to become very angry.

How ridiculous could you get?—to be losing sleep over a poor little rich girl when the world could be on the very brink of catastrophe. Because, if Peter Borodin ever reached Moscow and carried out his threat, the Russians would most certainly suspect a British or American plot, and then . . . but surely the British would appreciate that point.

A few days later John sat at his desk, staring out the window at the building opposite, and was aroused by the *ting* of his telephone. "Your broker asked you to call, Mr. Hayman."

Broker! He dialed the private number.

"I thought you might like to hear the latest," Allen Dulles said. "According to the British, Peter Borodin left England yesterday morning for Gothenburg, Sweden."

"Oh, my God!" John said. "He must be on his way."

"We just have to keep our fingers crossed and try working on the Swedes," Dulles said. "Trouble is, they're so determined to be neutral, they'll be reluctant even to look like they're cooperating with us. I guess it's going to be an exciting fall, after all."

Robert Loung sat up in bed and stared at Peter Borodin in amazement. "Prince Peter? But—"

"Your concierge let me in." Peter looked around the small bedroom, his nose wrinkling as he took in the faded wallpaper, the threadbare carpet, the cracked washbasin. "Didn't Corby give you enough money?"

"Well . . . I didn't want to waste it." Robert got out of bed and put a kettle on the hot plate.

"My grandniece hasn't been *here,* has she?"

"Of course not!"

"Thank God for that. You simply have to remember she is used only to the very best."

Robert made coffee, frowning as he did so. "You know . . . I didn't send for you, sir."

"I know that, my dear boy." Peter dusted the one straight chair and sat down. "That's why I'm here. Tell me exactly what the problem is."

Robert gave him a cup, and sat on the bed. "There isn't any problem."

"You have been here nearly a week," Peter pointed out. "How many times have you seen Diana?"

"Every day. Twice a day. We go out in the mornings, sightseeing, and then we usually go to a show in the evenings.

Like this morning—we're going to the Louvre. We've been there twice already, but Diana wants to see it all. This evening we're going to the Crazy Horse."

"And she keeps saying no to your proposal, is that it?"

"Of course not, sir. I . . . well, I haven't asked her yet."

Peter stared at him. "You haven't *asked* her?"

"One has to go about these things in the right way," Robert explained. "Especially with a girl like Diana."

Peter continued to regard him as if he were a freak. "Have you slept with her yet?"

"Good God, no!"

"My dear Robert," Peter said, "you are behaving like a very average young man in love. That will not do at all. If I thought for a moment you were an average young man, I would not have you on my staff. In any event, there are no funds for any more of this hesitancy. I suggest you ask Diana to marry you, tonight. I further suggest that you preface that proposal by making love to her. Never forget that she is a total romantic, who has undoubtedly lived a very sheltered life. Now she is in Paris. Gay Paree! The place that young girls dream about. Do not spoil that dream by behaving like a typical tongue-tied Englishman. You have to get out and *take* her, Robert."

"Well . . ." Robert looked at once confused and embarrassed. "You make it sound like a military exercise."

"It is." Peter smiled. "It should be. Wooing a beautiful woman, Robert, *is* a military exercise. And in all military exercises there comes a time when you must send in the cavalry. My dear boy, I have great plans for you. But I wish to see you happily married first. Believe me, I know how difficult it is to concentrate on the business of one's life's work when one is unhappily in love. I have been through that mill myself. Make your play, certain that I am one hundred percent behind you. Why, I'll give the bride away myself. But you must pop the question. Now, or at least tonight. Remind her that your father was a brigadier. And no matter what she replies, invite her to lunch with me—and yourself, of course—tomorrow. But under no circumstances tell her of this little chat. Now get to it, boy."

Janice Corliss replaced the telephone. "Front desk," she said. "Your persistent pest is in the lobby. Early, as usual. So where are we going tonight? Don't tell me. The Crazy Horse Saloon. Another strip show."

"Oh, really, Jan. You can hardly describe the Lido or the Moulin Rouge as strip shows," Diana protested, sitting before the dressing mirror in her slip, and frowning at herself as she put on lipstick.

"Of course not," Janice agreed. "It will be another magnificent, artistic extravaganza in which no female will be seen clad from the waist up and all will be only just decent from the waist down."

"Well . . ." Diana applied a tissue and regarded the result. "You don't have to come if you don't want to."

"Of course not," Janice said again. "I can walk up and down the Champs Élysées like all the other prostitutes, waiting to be whisked away to the latest bout of syphilis."

"You *are* in a bad mood," Diana commented.

"Even fifth wheels get tired occasionally."

"Jan . . ." Diana took her hands. "I'm so sorry. I guess I thought you'd meet somebody, too . . ."

"I didn't come here to meet a man," Janice said. "I came here to keep *you* from meeting a man. And I've been a total failure. Okay, so this Robert seems to be a cut above the rest, but don't tell me he's *really* any different from the others. He's just slow. That's because he's English."

"Yes." Diana gazed out of the window. "As a matter of fact . . ." She turned. "Jan, *is* there somewhere you could go after the show?"

"What did you say?"

"Well . . . while we were at the Louvre, this morning, Robert did say . . . he asked, well, if he could possibly see me alone, sometime. I think he has something to say to me."

"So you can have a drink with him in the bar before we leave for the show. I'll come down a few minutes late."

"I don't think that's what he has in mind," Diana said.

"You mean it's not what *you* have in mind," Janice pointed out. "He's finally ready to make a move, you figure, and you want to have the decks cleared."

"If you want to put it that way, yes. It's been weeks—"

"Since you've had a screw, and you're horny."

Diana gazed at her, her eyes cold. "If you want to put it *that* way, yes."

"Di, I'm sorry. It's just that—"

"Look, Janice, I happen to be very fond of Robert. I think I could well be in love with him. And for the past week he has proved himself to be a complete gentleman. As you say, probably because he's English. Being with him is a treat. Now, he's made up his mind that perhaps I'm the right girl for him, and he would like to carry our relationship a stage further. I'm all for that."

"You are a *creep,*" Janice shouted in a sudden fury. "You live for sex, and nothing else at all. Okay, I'll make myself scarce. I'll go and sit on the Champs Élysées and drink coffee until it comes out of my ears. I won't be back before dawn. And when I do come back, do you know what I am going to do? I am going to go straight back to London, and I am catching the first boat back to New York. And you can stay here and screw every man in Paris, every man in France, every man in *Europe,* for Christ's sake, if you choose. I don't give a goddamn about you anymore. Not a goddamn!" She threw herself on the bed and burst into tears.

Diana gazed at her for several seconds, made a move to touch her on the shoulder, then changed her mind, and instead stepped into her dress and pulled up the zipper. She went to the door, opened it, once again hesitated, looking over her shoulder, then stepped outside and closed it behind her, very softly.

"It's terribly, well, sporting of your friend to stay out like this," Robert Loung said.

He stood on one side of the elevator as it hummed upward. Diana stood on the other, gazing at him. How little, she thought, she knew of him, even after a week of constant escorting. It had never seemed important before. She tended to get to know a man *after* sleeping with him. Or while sleeping with him. It was not possible to *know* him before then; the Bible had a point there. But that was because all the men she had ever known had had a background similar to her own. They weren't all rich, of course, but their upbringings were not so different from her own: they had learned the same things at school, had gone ice-skating in Central Park and to the movies at Radio City, had ridden on the Staten Island Ferry and probably at some time or other been to the top of the Empire State Building.

This was what nationality was all about.

But Robert Loung had never done any of those things, just as she had never been to watch the changing of the guard at Buckingham Palace, or to see the Crown Jewels in the Tower of London. She had never been to watch tennis at Wimbledon, and she had never gone ice-skating at the Richmond Rink. Robert *had* done all of those things.

Now, in Paris, they were on neutral ground. Whatever she was doing for the first time, he was also doing for the first time. And yet suddenly, for the first time in her life, she was nervous with a man. Because they both knew what they were about to do, and *she* didn't know *how* he would do it? Or because she didn't even know if he *would* do it at all? He had asked to see her alone, but he had done nothing more than hold her hand on the short walk home—the Crazy Horse Saloon was just down the street from the hotel.

Now he was expecting some kind of small talk, apparently. "Jan's a good sport," she said, without convincing even herself. Certainly it had been fairly obvious all evening that she and Janice were not actually speaking.

The elevator was stopping, thank God. She led him silently along the carpeted corridor and gave him the door key. It took him three attempts to release the lock. Well, the first time it had taken her as long, but she still had a distinct feeling of imminent disaster. "There's a bar," she said. "Fix us a drink." She stepped out of her shoes, and was pleased to hear the popping of the champagne cork. It was the floor waiter's responsibility to keep the bar stocked at all times, with everything from fruit juice to a half-bottle of champagne, but it was Robert's selection that delighted her. Not everyone would start with the best.

So here was promise. She lifted her glass against his.

"Well," he said. "Here's to . . . well, everything."

Once again, disappointment. She felt exactly like a swimmer who, having covered some distance in deep water, sees the shore at a reasonable proximity and puts her foot down in every expectation of finding sand, only to find nothing but water. And she was beginning to feel vaguely annoyed. If he had caused all this fuss between Jan and herself for nothing . . .

"There are certain things I would like you to know," he said, formally.

Totally surprised yet again, Diana sat on the bed.

"I told you my father was a brigadier, remember? Well, he wasn't. He was a major in the Royal Army Service Corps, and he was cashiered—thrown out—in 1945 for operating a racket in black-market German binoculars. They were Zeiss, you know. The very best, and very valuable."

He paused, and gazed at her. Diana realized that her mouth was open, and hastily closed it again.

"I felt you should know that," he said. "I also wish you to know that I am aware you are going to be very rich one day. I didn't know that when I fell in love with you, but your Uncle Peter told me before I came to Paris. I'm afraid *I* have absolutely nothing but what he pays me, and that's not a lot. I'm entertaining you now on borrowed money. And that great hotel I'm staying at is an absolute doss house."

Diana discovered her glass was empty. And there was only the one half-bottle. She got up, went to the telephone, and dialed room service. "Send up a bottle of Bollinger," she said. "No, make it two, please . . . No, I don't care what year it is, so long as it *has* a year." She replaced the receiver.

"Two bottles?" he asked.

"Did you say, 'fell in love with you'?" she asked.

"The third thing I would like you to know," Robert went on, "is that your great-uncle is quite unnaturally anxious that we *should* get married. And the only explanation I can think of is that he wants somehow to hit back at your family. I know he feels that they have always let him down, certainly that your grandmother and grandfather have let him down, by not giving him the one hundred percent support he feels he's entitled to. I don't really want to take sides, because I don't know the whole story. But that's how he feels."

There was a knock on the door. Diana opened it, and the waiter brought in a tray with two bottles, each in its own ice bucket. He looked around him with a faint air of surprise at seeing only two people in the suite. "Shall I open a bottle, mademoiselle?"

Diana shook her head. She wasn't sure how her voice would sound. He nodded, presented his bill for her to sign, bowed, and withdrew.

Diana leaned against the door. "Did you say that we should get *married?*" She had been right; her voice was unnaturally high and squeaky.

"Unfortunately," Robert went on, as if there had been no

interruption at all, "I work for him. I don't want you to get any wrong impressions about that. I work for him and I mean to go on working for him, because I believe in what he is doing. As my wife, well . . . you would naturally have to be involved. I think you should know all these things, because I don't want you to marry me under any false impressions. Nor do I wish you to marry me merely because your uncle likes the idea."

He paused for breath. His glass was empty, too. But she didn't suppose he was really used to opening bottles of champagne. So she did it herself, let go of the cork, and watched it remove a piece of the ceiling.

"I should have done that," he protested, and hurried forward, to receive a shirtful of froth as she turned the bottle toward him.

"Oh, I'm terribly sorry," she said, and poured some into his glass.

"My fault."

"Did you say . . ." She couldn't find her own glass, so she drank from the bottle instead, and belched. "Get *married?*"

"That's why I followed you to Paris," he explained. "To ask you to marry me."

"Oh," Diana said. "Oh!" She drank some more champagne.

"Does that mean you will, or you won't?"

She sat on the bed. "How do you know you love me?" she asked. "When you've never . . . well, been to bed with me. You've never even really kissed me."

"Do I have to do that to know that I love you?"

She considered. "I guess you don't. But most men like to find out something about the physical side first."

"And have they? With you?"

She raised her head. "I guess that's the confession *I* have to make to *you*."

He knelt beside her. "Did you really think it would bother me?"

"No." She smiled, because she had never thought about the question at all. "Besides, I always knew right off that I didn't want to marry any of them."

"And what do you think right off about me?"

"Well . . ." She hadn't considered that, either. Marriage, or even the suggestion of it, just had not crossed her mind. She held his face between her hands and kissed him on the mouth, then knelt against him, knocking over the champagne bottle in the process. "I don't know about marriage," she said. "But I do want to make love to you. Oh, how I want that."

He looked astonished. No doubt, she realized, he had never been told that by a woman before. But she was not going to stop now—she wouldn't be able to. She loosened his tie and unbuttoned his shirt.

"Di," he muttered, uneasily.

"I have to know," she said, and kissed him again. "If it could even be *possible*."

Janice Corliss stood above the bed and looked down on her friend.

Diana was naked, which was not unusual; Diana always slept naked. But she had obviously not slept alone. Her legs were spread wide in a sort of scattered fashion, as were her arms, and a pillow lay half across her face; its ruffle moved as she breathed, snoring faintly. She looked utterly abandoned, because, when she made love, Janice was sure she *was* utterly abandoned.

But she also looked, even in her sleep, enormously happy—and quite unfairly beautiful.

Janice sighed, went into the bathroom, soaked a sponge, returned to the bedroom, and squeezed it onto the upturned face. For a moment nothing happened, then Diana gave a strangled exclamation of annoyance, and rolled onto her stomach.

Janice squeezed the sponge down her back. "This place smells like a brewery," she said. She kicked something under the bed, and stooped to extricate an empty champagne bottle. "They are going to have to shampoo the carpet."

Diana got her knees up, but for the moment could make no progress with her upper half.

"Was it as good as you anticipated?"

Diana sighed, allowed her knees to give way, and rolled onto her back again, but her eyes were finally open. "Oh, yes," she said. "Oh, yes . . . Well . . . sort of. It was odd, really. I had to do everything, at first. And then he suddenly took over. Do you know, he even . . . well . . . maybe I won't tell you about that."

Janice turned away, pulled her suitcase from the bottom of the wardrobe, and opened it on a chair. Then she began taking her underclothes from the bureau drawers.

"Jan!"

"I guess I'm so superfluous I shouldn't even be breathing," Janice said.

"But Jan . . . we're going to be married."

Janice turned to face her, slowly.

"Well," Diana said. "He's asked me."

"And you've said yes."

"Well . . . sort of. I didn't really have time to think, last night. I mean, there are going to be problems. Like Mother, for one."

"You are goddamn right," Janice said. "Mother, to name but a few hundred. And Daddy. And Grandpa and Grandma. The explosion is going to make the atom bomb seem like a firecracker. You come over here, and promptly fall in love with some itinerant fortune hunter—"

"He is *not* a fortune hunter," Diana said.

"He's rich, is he?"

"Well . . . no."

"What does he have?"

"Well . . . nothing, really. He confessed he's over here on borrowed money. He's very honest. Do you know, he even confessed that his father wasn't a general at all, but only a major, who was thrown out of the army for smuggling after the war?"

"Oh, Jesus Christ," Janice commented. "Don't go on. I really don't want to know how his mother was arrested for shoplifting and his grandfather was hanged or whatever."

"I suppose you think that's very funny," Diana remarked, but she sounded more hurt than angry. "I am just trying to explain that he . . . well, he couldn't possibly be a fortune hunter."

"Oh, sure. And of course he's confessed that he didn't have a clue who you were until you told him."

"Well . . . until Uncle Peter told him."

"And you believed that, of course. Because he's so *honest*."

Rather to her own surprise, Diana still did not lose her temper. Instead she pushed herself off the bed, staggered to the bathroom, and held her face under the cold-water tap for several seconds. "Is that other bottle of champagne still around?"

Janice saw it on the table. "Yes. But the ice has melted."

"It'll still be cool. Pour me a hair of the dog, will you?"

Janice hesitated, then obliged.

"Mmmmm." Diana drank. "Have one yourself."

"Thank you, no."

"Because you are definitely leaving?"

"Yes."

"I'd kind of hoped you'd be my bridesmaid. *If* I decide to do it."

"You mean you'd kind of hoped I'd say what a great idea, I'll be right at your side," Janice told her. "Well, it's not a great idea. It stinks. Anyway, you can't do it. Your parents would have a fit."

"I'm not intending to get married *today,* or even tomorrow," Diana pointed out. "I'm just thinking of getting engaged. We'd be married in New York, of course."

Janice shrugged. "So get engaged. Move in with him. It can't make any difference after last night. You don't need me around for that. But I don't want any part of it. Especially, I don't want any part of the breach-of-promise suit you're going to have slapped on you when your Ma says to break it off."

"Oh, really, Jan—"

"Can't you see this man is in it for the dough? If he can get his hooks into you, he has a meal ticket for life. But even if he can't—he must know there is only a remote chance of that working—he has to have figured out a way to get *something* out of it."

"That's not true," Diana said.

Janice sat beside her on the bed. "Di, listen to me. He gave you a great big bang. Super. Like you said, you needed it and you wanted it and you went out and got it. I don't approve, but I *can* sympathize. So maybe he'll give you another good bang tonight, and another tomorrow night. But at the end of it all, you're going to be back where you started, wanting to ditch him. And meanwhile, because he seems to be a bit smarter than all the other jerks you've accumulated over the years, he is going to take you for everything he can. Christ almighty, even if he doesn't actually *get* anything, he'll have a field day dragging you through the courts. Di! I'll make a deal with you. I'll stay here with you for two more days. And two more nights. And I'll spend them away from here, so that you can screw him from dusk until dawn. But meanwhile, don't accept his proposal. And after three days, let's you and me fold up our tents and steal away, somewhere this Robert character can't follow us. Please, Di. Please."

Diana gazed at her for several seconds. Then she said, "You just haven't got it. I'm not going to get tired of Robert. I know that. He's . . . well, he's different. He's sincere, and he's, well . . . he's honest, Jan. Sure, he's asked me to marry him. But he doesn't want me to rush into anything, either. He knows there are going to be problems ahead. And he feels they should be tackled first, before we make any decisions. So you know what? He's found out that Uncle Peter happens to be in Paris on business. He got in touch with him and explained the situation, and Uncle Peter says he wants to see us both. We're having lunch with him today. Uncle Peter is his boss, remember. Now, he knows that Robert is in love with me, and seems to think it's great. Robert doesn't like that at all. He's afraid there may be an ulterior motive, some kind of family feud running back a couple of generations. So we're going to tackle that hurdle first, and see if we can sort it out. Does *that* sound like a fortune hunter to you? If you'd think about it, you'd see that you really are being absurd."

Janice got up and resumed packing.

"Diana! My dear girl! How beautiful you look today." Peter Borodin got up from the table and came forward to take both Diana's hands and kiss them one after the other. "But I understood that we were going to be four. Where is your friend, Miss Corliss?"

"She's gone home," Diana said.

"Because of Robert? Good heavens! The young scoundrel has been telling me how he has been badgering you."

This was not exactly the approach Diana had expected. She could feel his personality sweeping over her in an almost solid wave. Strange, she thought, it had not been so apparent when they had first met. But he had been more interested in Uncle John then. Now he was interested in her.

"He's been looking after me, you mean, Uncle Peter," she said, kissing him on the cheek in turn. "I don't know what I would have done without him."

"Ha!" He sat her down, and poured champagne from the already opened bottle.

"Not more champagne," she murmured. "It'll be coming out of my ears."

"You have already been celebrating, eh?"

"Well . . ." Diana smiled at Robert, who was looking distinctly anxious. "In a manner of speaking," she agreed.

"You mean you have accepted his proposal?"

"Well . . ."

"You do *not* wish to marry him. Ha! Very wise."

"No, no," she protested without thinking. "It's just that . . . I thought you were enthusiastic about the idea?"

"I am. For his sake. But not if you have more sense."

"Oh, I . . ." She felt herself beginning to get somewhat confused, as the fresh wine sent its alcohol racing up to her head, where there was already quite a residue. "There are so many things to be considered, Uncle Peter. Well . . . you must know of some of them."

"Of course. You are a princess of Russia."

"A—Good lord, no. Am I? I can't be."

"Snails," Peter Borodin told the maître d'. "We will have *l'escargot,* eh, my children? And then steak. *Bleu!* A bottle of Pouilly-Fumé to start, and then two of Château Batailley. 1945! Not a year after. My dear, there has not been a good claret since 1945. But of course you know that."

"No," she said. "I didn't. Uncle Peter, that is going to be an *orgy.*"

"Of course. For a Russian princess."

"Uncle Peter—"

"I am joking, of course," Peter said. "There are no longer such things as Russian princesses. They have been forbidden by Comrade Stalin. And even if they were, you are not my daughter. And I do have a daughter."

"Of course," Diana said. "Ruth Brent."

"Ruth Brent," Peter said contemptuously. "Yes. First she married an ex-Nazi—would you believe it, and her mother a Jew? And then, when he was executed, as he should have been long ago, she married an English bobby, who chooses to live in an Israeli kibbutz. Can you believe that? A Russian princess! So I will tell you this, my dear Diana: were I in possession of all my estates, I would still have disinherited that silly girl. And then, whom could I leave my fortune to? I would hope for a male nephew, of course. But there is none suitable. My younger sister is dead. *Her* male child is locked up in an American prison. My other sister has had two sons, my nephews. One is the son of a commissar—that is your uncle John, my dear girl. The other is your own father. But I suspect that your father counts being president of Hayman Newspapers as higher even than being the Prince of Starogan. So that leaves only you." The waiter had by now poured the Pouilly-Fumé, and the Prince raised his glass. "To whom I drink a toast: the most beautiful princess Russia has ever known."

"Why, Uncle Peter . . ." Diana realized she was blushing, and it was not a normal habit of hers. So carried away was he, she decided against reminding him that she, too, would one day be president of Hayman Newspapers, and that she also would probably decide that was more important than being the Princess of Starogan.

"—Who wishes to marry my very own protégé," Peter went on. "The young man I *would* recognize as my son, if I still had estates to leave him."

"Would you really, Uncle Peter?" Diana smiled at Robert, who was also flushing, and now looking more confused than ever. She gave his hand another reassuring squeeze. "Oh, I do want to marry Robert. I do love him. But what is Mother going to say?"

"Mother?"

"My mother."

"I have never met your mother," Peter said grandly, implying that omission was entirely Elizabeth's fault, and her loss, as well. "But I am still the head of the Borodin family. It is my decisions which count."

"Do you really think so?"

"Of course," Peter said. "You wish to marry Robert. You have my blessing. I cannot think of a happier match."

"But . . ." Only a few minutes ago he had said she was wise not to marry him. She wished she could have another few minutes alone, to think.

"Voilà!" Peter declared. "It is done."

"I wish it were quite that simple," Diana said. "But you see, I'm not even twenty yet, and—"

"Is that so important? Twenty is a dreadful age to get married. All Russian princesses are married before they are twenty, unless they chose to enter a convent."

"Are they really? It's legal in New York at eighteen, but I don't know what French law says—"

"French law!" Peter observed, with utter contempt. "The

law is for plebeians, not for princesses. Alas, your mother is such a plebeian, am I right?"

"Well, I wouldn't say that," Diana said loyally. "But the fact is that she didn't send me over here to get engaged. Or even with the idea that it could *happen*. I thought maybe I should write her, and tell her about Robert, and then, if you really would like to help, Uncle Peter, maybe you could write as well, and say . . . well—" She glanced at Robert and again flushed. "—that you know him, and that he works for you, and that really there's nothing phony about the setup . . . you know what I mean."

"You are thinking of Robert's father. That was just sheer misfortune. We have a great-uncle who died on the scaffold, for treason. He had married a Polish wife, and elected to fight with them against the forces of the tsar in 1863. A totally rotten egg, I can assure you."

"Sounds rather a gallant thing to do," Robert commented.

"One fights for one's tsar, or the tsar's representative," Peter said severely, "or one is a traitor." He smiled. "I am delving into history. But what I am saying is that there are skeletons in every family closet. But that did not stop your mother from marrying your father, eh?"

"I don't think she knew anything about it. And anyway . . ." Diana bit her lip. Now was not the time to point out that opposing a tyrannical tsar on behalf of a downtrodden people was hardly the same sort of crime as stealing a few dozen binoculars.

"I will, of course, write your mother if you wish. But would it change her mind?" Peter Borodin refilled her glass, and squeezed her hand. "I know these mothers. Believe me. I had one of my own, once. She was an absolute dragon. Only the family mattered. Do you know what she would do in these circumstances? She would say, 'But of course, my dear, if you love him, then you must marry him.' And immediately start working away to bring about some sort of estrangement between you."

"Oh, but . . ." Diana bit her lip. She couldn't deny that was the sort of thing her own mother would do. She was always trying to work things, to manipulate them, without ever coming out into the open. On the other hand, she suddenly remembered, Mother's principal worry over the past two years was the *ab-*

sence of an engagement, and the thought that her only daughter might not be quite orthodox in her desires. If she only knew!

But on the *other* hand, when Mother thought of an engagement, it was clearly of a suitable replacement for Richard Malling. She would see Robert as a nobody, not even an American.

What a confusing world it was!

"There comes a time," Peter went on, "when, as the poet says, you must seize life by the forelock." He paused, frowning, aware that he might not have the quotation quite right. Then he smiled brightly. "You are young, and you are in love. What could be more beautiful than that? But you are also an heiress, and the man you love is not wealthy. All the censorious forces of law and order and propriety and family will rally to prevent it happening. They will find it impossible to believe that it can be true, that you can actually *love* another human being from a different social and financial class. *Do* you love Robert?"

"Well, I . . . of course I do."

"Do you wish to be his wife?"

"Yes," she said, almost defiantly.

"Then I suggest you get married. As soon as possible. This afternoon. As soon as we have had lunch."

"But . . . that's not possible!"

"Why is it not possible? Robert already has a license."

Diana turned her head sharply.

Robert flushed. "Well, Prince Peter suggested that I get one . . . just in case."

"But—my age—"

"On my recommendation, he made it twenty-one. They are not too particular about things like that over here," Peter explained. "He also said that you had both been resident in Paris, studying art, for several months. Again, they are unlikely to try to verify that."

"But . . . Mother—"

"Mothers need to be faced with a *fait accompli,*" Peter told her. "Appear in New York, announcing that you are engaged to a man three thousand miles away on the other side of the Atlantic, and they will say, at least to themselves, Never! Appear in New York, well and truly married, with a husband at your side, and perhaps even pregnant, and they will accept the situation."

Diana shook her head, slowly. "You don't know Mother, Uncle Peter. She'll have it annulled. She'll summon up all those forces of law and order and propriety you were talking about."

"Then we must defeat her purpose. I repeat: do you *want* to marry Robert?"

"Yes," she declared, now having convinced even herself that there was nothing else in all the world she wanted so much to do.

"Then consider it done. Robert has a license. I am your most senior living relative. You will be married this afternoon, in my presence and with my blessing. Then I will tell you what you will do. You will depart on a honeymoon where no one will ever find you. A long honeymoon. Say five weeks. At the end of which, if I know my Robert, you will be pregnant." He winked at the embarrassed young man. "Now, during that time, I will get in touch with both your mother and Ilona. If necessary, I will go to America myself to see them. I will accept full responsibility for what has happened, and I will convince them that it is the best thing that *could* have happened."

"Oh, but . . . *would* you, Uncle Peter? Oh, if you would! But where could we go?"

"I have here," Prince Peter announced grandly, "two first-class rail tickets to Moscow."

"Moscow?" Diana cried.

"Moscow?" Robert demanded.

"Moscow," Peter said firmly. "That is the one place they will never think of looking for you. I also have a reservation for the honeymoon suite in the Hotel Berlin, and a full wallet of vouchers for Intourist to provide guides to take you everywhere that a visitor to Moscow should go. Everywhere that you *wish* to go, of course. Do not let the Bolsheviks interfere with your privacy."

"But . . . that's *impossible,*" Diana cried. "Moscow—we'd need visas, and—"

"Visas are all arranged," Peter told her. "You have only to give me your passports, and they will be returned tomorrow morning, with the visas attached. The Russians just stick them on, you know, and then tear them off again when you leave. A very suspicious people. You can spend tonight at the George V—you say your friend has gone. And then tomorrow . . ."

"Moscow," Diana breathed. "I've always longed to visit

Moscow. But Mother and Daddy would never hear of it."

"Surprise them."

Robert was still frowning. "I think you and I should discuss this plan, sir."

"Discuss? You and I? Anything you wish to discuss from now on, my dear boy, should be discussed in front of your wife."

"I'll agree to that," Diana said.

"Well, sir..." Robert flushed. "Don't you think it might be a little dangerous?"

"Dangerous? For whom? You are not intending to hand out subversive literature, are you? Or blow somebody up?" He smiled.

"I meant, well, Diana is of Russian descent—"

"My dear fellow, a very large proportion of the world's population is of Russian descent. I am aware that Diana's surname is a well-known one to the Russians, which is why I applied for the visa *in* her maiden name. If they didn't want a Hayman in Russia, they'd merely have turned the application down. But they have informed the British embassy here in Paris that it will be granted."

"Because I'll be Mrs. Loung," Diana said, giving Robert's hand a squeeze.

"Perhaps. There won't be time to have the passport changed, of course. But don't worry about that. You'll have a wedding certificate, and the Russians are very broadminded about things like that."

"I still feel..." Robert said.

Prince Peter finished his last snail, poured the last of the white wine, and signaled for the red to be brought forward. "I know what is on his mind. You understand that Robert works for me, Diana?"

"Why, yes."

"And I am dedicated to the destruction of the Communist state. Thus, so is he. But of course, no one knows that about him. Yet he feels it is somehow wrong for him to visit, as a tourist, a country whose government he is dedicated to bringing down. Now, can you see any sense in that? Should he not be eager to go there, to look for himself at his enemies?"

"Oh, yes," Diana said. "He may even discover they're actually not enemies at all, and then he won't have to destroy them."

Peter gazed at her from beneath arched eyebrows.

"Well," she said, "destroying people is a little passé nowadays, isn't it? You know what, Uncle Peter? I think *you* should go to Russia too, and look for yourself. And then maybe you'd change *your* mind."

"I have been to Russia," Peter said. "I lived there for the first forty years of my life. I can assure you there is absolutely no chance of me changing *my* mind. In any event, they would never let me in." He smiled, sniffed the claret cork, and nodded. When it had been poured, he raised his glass. "But you can try persuading me when you get back, if you like. So . . . a toast, to Mr. and Mrs. Robert Loung."

"*We* can't drink to that," Diana said. "So I'll propose one. To Russia!" She squeezed Robert's hand. "Don't look so fierce, darling. I think it's a great idea."

"I knew you would," Peter said. "So, this afternoon, the Hôtel de Ville. But as we are doing everything backward, such as having the wedding lunch before the wedding, I have something to show you now. A gift, that you can use on your honeymoon."

"Oh, what is it?" Diana cried, the red wine mingling with the white wine which was already mingling with the champagne to give the entire day a magnificently rosy hue.

Peter snapped his fingers and nodded to the maître d'hotel. "My wedding present," he announced. "I bought them this morning, because I knew you *were* going to get married. I always believe in giving *useful* presents, my dear."

"Oh, they're magnificent!" Diana cried, getting up in delight as the waiter approached, carrying, one in each hand, a pair of large leather suitcases, initialed in gold leaf.

Chapter 7

"OH," DIANA CRIED, AS A SHOWER OF ROSE PETALS DESCENDED on her. The size of the crowd took her by surprise. The hotel lobby was crowded with people, not one of whom she remembered seeing before in her life. They were mainly maids and bellboys, all armed with little baskets, the contents of which were now being scattered across her neat little pale-blue suit, which she had selected because she had been able to find a matching pillbox that even had a veil. "Oh, Uncle Peter!"

Peter Borodin smiled, and held her left hand; her right was firmly tucked into Robert's. He looked so proud, she thought, and happy. Well, was she not happy?

She was suddenly realizing that *this* was what she had wanted all her life. Last night they had loved and loved and *loved*. And it had somehow been different. Because she had been his wife. And now . . .

"These things just take a little organizing," Peter explained. "But the hotel is experienced at weddings. And honeymoons."

"You must be, too," she whispered, as the three of them got into the taxi. "None of this would have happened, none of this *could* have happened, without you, Uncle Peter. I don't know how I will ever be able to thank you."

"It has been my pleasure," he told her, and kissed her on the cheek. "And you will repay me by being happy. The Gare du Nord," he told the driver.

"Oh, I so wish Janice had stayed," Diana said. "She really would have loved every second of it. But I guess she's on her way across the Atlantic, by now." She stared at her uncle in sudden alarm. "Home to Mother!"

Peter merely continued to smile, holding her hand. "She can't get home for at least another three days, my dear," he said, "by which time I will have called Ilona on the transatlantic telephone, and explained the situation, and no doubt spoken with your mother as well."

"I can't help feeling *I* should have done that," Diana said.

"And as I keep telling you, that would have been a tremendous mistake. You are on your honeymoon. You must think of nothing but enjoying each other. Leave everything else to me."

They were soon at the station, and he was hurrying ahead of them to organize porters, and barking orders to be careful with the luggage.

"He just sort of takes lives over," Robert explained apologetically. "That's the way he is."

"I'm so glad that's the way he is," Diana said. "So glad. Or we wouldn't be here."

"Over this way!" Peter was beckoning them to their carriage. "This car stays with the train until Moscow Central. You're in number three. It's not the Orient Express, but it's the best the Russians have, nowadays. Now remember . . . *enjoy* yourselves."

The door banged, and a few minutes later the train started to move. Peter stood on the platform, waving them out of sight. Then he strode vigorously through the crowd and out of the station, to where the taxi was still waiting. "Very good," he said. "Very good indeed. And now . . . take me to the Soviet embassy, if you please." He sat back against the cushions, humming.

"I must see your tickets, please," the conductor said, in quite good French.

"Ah, yes. Here we are." Robert produced his travel wallet.

"And your passports."

"Yes." He found his own, looked at Diana, who gave him hers. The conductor slowly turned the pages. "We *are* married," Robert explained. "Yesterday. I have a certificate. But there was no time to have the passports changed, you see."

"I will keep these," the conductor remarked.

"Eh?"

"We cross the borders this evening, and again tomorrow. You will be sleeping. I will keep these and attend to the formalities for you."

"Oh. Well, if you would . . . that would be awfully kind of you."

"Now," the conductor said. "I show you the beds. These straps, eh . . ."

"We won't need the upper berth," Diana said.

He raised his eyebrows, looked from one to the other, clearly comparing their combined sizes with the width of the bunk.

"We're honeymooning," Diana explained.

"Hon-ey-moon-ing," the conductor said, not apparently knowing what that meant. He shrugged, and went to the door. "If you wish tea, you ring, eh? I have tea."

The door closed. The train was already gathering speed as it left Paris behind. Diana peered at the presently closed washbasin, the four sets of instructions. "But . . . they don't have any in English."

"It's a Russian train," Robert reminded her. "So there's Russian, and I suppose that's Polish underneath. Not to worry, the other two are German and French."

"I don't even speak French very well." She squeezed his hand. "You'll have to come with me to the toilet, to show me how it works."

"I speak German and Russian," he said. "Your uncle made us all learn them. But . . . don't *you* speak Russian?"

"Why should I?"

"No reason at all, I suppose." He sat down, and smiled at her. "There are so many things I don't know about you."

She sat beside him. "And quite a few I don't know about you, my darling. But that's what we're going to do for the next five weeks, isn't it? Find out all those things?"

"All the skeletons in the closets?"

"Everything," she told him. "And I am going to love them all."

So many things, Diana thought. And all of them good—because they had to be good; she refused to admit the possibility of anything being bad. Even his parents, about whom he was reluctant to speak. But she was determined to go and see them when they returned from their honeymoon, before she and Robert departed for New York. She was certain even they would be good; they were parts of Robert.

She lay in his arms, and the train rumbled through the darkness, across . . . the north German plain, she supposed. It was past midnight, and they had stopped at least twice, with a great deal of clanking and hissing and barked commands, and the tramp of heavy feet in the corridor. Border guards. But true to his word, the conductor had apparently handled everything, and they had not been disturbed. Not that it would have mattered to her, because she had hardly slept.

She supposed she was too excited, mainly at what she had done, the first open act of defiance of the monolithic social and financial world into which she had been born and in which she had been expected to take her proper place from birth. She *had* defied it before. For the past two years she had defied it almost continuously, but always secretly, and guiltily. If she hadn't defied it, she thought she would have gone mad; but she had never before had the courage to do so openly. Now she had, and she could imagine the blaze of notoriety when word got out.

And all because of a man she hardly knew. How that thought haunted her. But how much did it take to know a man? Everything she had learned about him she liked. Her body still tingled from his lovemaking, so different from any she had previously known. He was utterly tender, perhaps not any more imaginative than her other lovers, but so tender.

Besides, it was not possible to build a marriage simply on sex. She smiled to herself—she was attempting to think like Mother! But even Mother would have to agree it was not possible to build a marriage *without* sex. That was an essential foundation stone. And when it was better than any she had ever known, it had to be the best-quality concrete. Admittedly, there were things about Robert she would hope to change, with time. And fully intended to change, as soon as possible. Such as this absurd counterrevolutionary activity he had got himself into. She was not even sure what Uncle Peter's followers did. Apparently they sat around gathering information and putting out propaganda, and preparing for a sort of D-day. Which of course would never come.

He would have to be weaned from that, and from Uncle

Peter, and taken to New York. Daddy would be able to give him a position on the newspaper. Robert would understand, that as she had to prepare to take over the company, she had to live in New York.

She certainly had no intention of living anywhere else.

But Robert's involvement with Uncle Peter was in some ways splendid. Little human beings, pitting themselves, however hopelessly, against the immensity of the Soviet state. *There* was the greatest reassurance of all. There could be nothing essentially wrong with someone so idealistic, so . . . well, noble. And he was Uncle Peter's friend. Uncle Peter trusted him. There would be a crisis there, in the course of time, one she would have to play her part in overcoming. But the mere fact that Uncle Peter liked him and trusted him had to be the most reassuring thing of all. Because Uncle Peter was certainly a noble man. Irritating, at times. And certainly nutty as a fruitcake when it came to Soviet Russia. But so massively confident and reassuring . . . Uncle Peter would never have allowed her to marry anyone in whom he did not have the utmost confidence.

There was a knock on the door immediately before it slid open, and Diana realized she had been asleep after all. It was daylight outside.

The conductor smiled at her, and placed the two glasses of tea, each in a silverplate holder, on the little table that covered the washbasin. "We are coming into Berlin," he said in French. "You will wish to be awake to see Berlin."

They sat facing each other across the table in the restaurant car, eating steak tartare while drinking Bull's Blood. The restaurant car wasn't Maxim's, for either service or food, and Hungarian Bull's Blood was not exactly Château Batailley, but it really didn't matter. They were on an adventure. This morning they had breakfasted just after leaving Berlin, and half an hour ago they had left Warsaw. Now they traversed another flat, empty plain, stretching as far as the eye could see, with only occasional farms or villages, and scattered people, dreadfully poorly dressed and with pinched, anxious faces . . . but they all waved to the train as it passed.

"I suppose they're still picking up the pieces from the war," Robert said somberly.

"It seems incredible that we should have been on this train thirty-six hours," she said, "and still not reached Russia."

"Midnight," he said. "That's when the guard said we'd reach the border."

"It's still thirty-six hours without a bath," she said. "And another two days to go on the other side. You'll be hanging me out the window long before then."

"You seem to manage with your little washcloth," he said. "What really is incredible is that we should have been *married* for two whole days. Changed your mind yet?"

She blew him a kiss. "How could I? I haven't seen anyone else in all that time. I mean, not really."

They held hands to make their way back to the compartment. It had become a little world of its own, in which only they belonged. A tiny capsule in which they performed their rites of love, their eager exchange of everything—every thought, every gesture, every desire, that either of them possessed. Now she knew it was going to be all right. It was not possible to spend forty-eight consecutive hours entirely in one man's company, and not *know* that it was going to be all right.

Diana was asleep by nine; she had not slept deeply the previous night. She was only dimly aware of the train stopping, realized that at last they were at the Russian border, a place called Brest-Litovsk, she remembered. But the conductor had their tickets and passports. She nestled further into Robert's arms, then rolled over with a start as the door opened and the light was switched on.

"What the hell—" Robert sat up, hastily pulling the sheet over Diana's breasts, while they both stared at the green-uniformed border guards, two of them, armed with submachine guns, and at a pretty blond young woman, wearing civilian clothes.

"Mr. and Mrs. Loung?" the woman asked in French.

"Yes," Robert said. "What's the matter?"

"I do not think anything is the matter," Marie said. "May I ask your destination?"

"Why, Moscow, of course."

"But your tickets are for Brest-Litovsk."

"For— That's impossible!"

"It is so," she said. "Somebody has made a mistake. It is no matter. My name is Maria. I am from Intourist, eh? If you will come with me, I will have your tickets corrected." She regarded his naked chest. "It will be necessary to put something on."

"But—" He looked down at Diana.

"Your wife should come too," Maria agreed.

"You're darned right," Diana said, in English. "I'm not letting you wander off into the night with *her*."

"But . . . what about the train?" Robert asked. "Will it wait for us?"

Maria smiled. "Of course. At Brest-Litovsk, the train waits for three hours. It is the track, you see. In Europe, they use a different gauge than in Russia." Her tone indicated that the Europeans were hopelessly backward. "Thus it is necessary to move the train from this track to the proper track."

"Move the train?"

"Well . . ." She shrugged. "It is a system of shuntings. Very jerky. You will be better off in the station. But we should make haste. I will wait for you in the corridor."

The door closed, and Robert gazed at Diana. "That seems a bit odd. How on earth could the old boy have made such a mistake? I'm sure I checked those tickets, anyway, and they seemed all right to me."

"Ah, well." Diana got out of bed, pulled on a pair of briefs and then slacks, added a cashmere sweater, dragged a comb through her hair, and stuck her toes into sandals. "It's just a glimpse of Russian bureaucracy at work. We'd better play ball, or they'll send us back." She waited for him to finish dressing, then opened the door. "Ready when you are, Comrade Mademoiselle."

Maria smiled, and escorted them off the train. The platform was a blaze of light, and was actually extremely large; it was also crowded with people, forming a line that stretched all the way to the single ticket window, Diana observed with a sinking heart, some distance away.

Robert had come to the same conclusion. "Did you say three hours? We'll never get to the front in time."

"Bah," Maria said. "These are peasants. They are always traveling to and fro. Stefan will help you. Stefan!" she called, and spoke rapidly in Russian.

"What's she saying?" Diana asked.

"It's incredible," Robert said. "She's telling him to push all the people aside and take me to the head of the line. In Russia? I thought there were no classes here."

"Lesson number one," Diana said. "But then, people think there are no classes in America, either."

"You accompany Stefan, Mr. Loung," Maria said. "It will not take too long. You come with me, Mrs. Loung."

"Where?"

Maria produced her smile again. "To the ladies' waiting room. You do not want to stand around a drafty platform in the middle of the night. There is a samovar in the waiting room, and we will have a cup of tea. Haste, Stefan, haste!" she commanded.

Diana followed her, casting an anxious glance at the train, which was at last commencing to move off, puffing and hissing. "Are you sure it isn't going anywhere?"

"Nowhere at all," Maria assured her, "until you are ready to rejoin it. Here we are. Do sit down."

Diana looked around her with interest. She told herself that it was time to stop feeling irritated and confused and therefore worried, and start to take in what she was seeing. It was very unlikely that she would ever be in Russia again. To her surprise the women's waiting room, which looked like any waiting room anywhere, was empty, except for a picture of Lenin, and a large, stout woman who was behind a small counter at the far end of the room; the only furniture was a table and six straight chairs. On one of these Diana sat, while Maria spoke to the woman in Russian, and she started getting out cups and saucers and pouring tea.

"Russian tea," Maria explained. "It is very good, but very strong. You will not need sugar."

"I had some on the train," Diana told her. "It was delicious." She sipped, and frowned. This certainly wasn't delicious. It had a vaguely bitter taste, as if it had been left steeping for too long. But Maria was drinking hers quite happily, and Diana felt it would be discourteous not to do the same. She held her breath and drained the mug. "How long will Robert—my husband—be?"

"Not long, I think," Maria said, gazing at her in a fixed manner. "The only trouble will be if there is someone else booked into your compartment, from here to Moscow."

"Oh, my God! What would we do then?"

Maria smiled. "It is unlikely. And even if it has happened—

well, we shall simply tell the other person he must wait for the next train, eh? You are in my care now, Mrs. Loung."

How reassuring she was, Diana thought, even if her face had suddenly grown quite fuzzy. I must not be really awake yet, she thought, and then frowned, as her fingers relaxed of their own accord and the glass mug fell and smashed on the floor. "Oh," she said. "I'm so terribly sorry." At least, that was what she meant to say, but the words seemed to be coming from an old phonograph in desperate need of winding. She tried to stand up, because the dregs had spilled on her pants, and then she fell forward, on top of the glass.

Anna Ragosina raised her head from the papers she had been studying, and half-frowned at Maria. "You should be in Brest-Litovsk."

"I should be here, comrade commissar. With the . . . goods you required. They are downstairs."

"So soon?" Anna got up and came around the desk. "That is splendid work. You are a treasure. And no one knows of it?"

"No one," Maria said. "Even Stefan does not really understand what is happening. I have put the man in cell thirty-four in the male block . . ."

Anna nodded. That was an isolation cell.

"And the woman in cell forty-seven in the female block."

Cell forty-seven was where women were put when they were intended never to appear again.

"That is very good," Anna said. "You have told the guards no one is to go near them?"

"Yes, comrade commissar."

"And they are still under sedation?"

"Yes, comrade commissar." Maria looked at her watch. "I gave the last injection three hours ago. They will not wake up for another four hours."

"You are a treasure," Anna said again, and returned behind her desk. "Take the rest of the afternoon off. But I shall require you, four hours from now, when I go down to see them."

"Of course, comrade commissar." But Maria did not move.

"Yes?" Anna asked.

"There is something else, comrade commissar." Maria was clearly repressing enormous excitement.

"What?" Anna's voice was immediately watchful.

"I searched their luggage, comrade commissar," Maria said. "I took it apart on the plane, while we were flying here."

"I did not tell you to do that."

Maria licked her lips, but she did not lose any confidence. "I felt I should. And comrade commissar, I discovered that each of their suitcases has a false bottom."

"Oh, yes," Anna commented, without great interest.

"And the space within each false bottom, comrade commissar, is packed with plastic explosive."

It occurred to Anna Ragosina that when fortune started running your way, it really bubbled. In kidnapping Diana Hayman she had been reacting to a purely private urge, knowing that she was taking an enormous risk, but certain that if she could not achieve everything she intended through the girl, she could at least have her disappear forever, and sit out any international fracas that might result.

Now she was absolutely in the clear, by the merest chance. But no one would ever know that, except for Maria, and Maria would never betray her. To everyone else, when she chose to make known what had happened—should she ever choose to do that—she would seem to possess an almost demoniac prescience.

But what on earth were these two children doing, traveling with enough plastic explosive to destroy this building? Finding *that* out was going to be a pleasure.

"Do you want assistance, comrade commissar?" the head jailer asked hopefully.

Anna shook her head. "We will be able to manage, thank you. Should we need assistance, we will call for it." She walked down the corridor, the keys swinging from her hand, Maria just behind her.

Down here was a world that usually repelled and terrified visitors, even if their reason for being here was innocent. It was a world of abrasive odors, a mixture of disinfectant, sweat, and fear. It was a world of disturbing sounds—grunts and groans from behind closed doors, sometimes even demented screams. It was a world of utter loneliness, utter helplessness against the forces that surrounded and dominated it and its inmates.

It was her world, because she was that dominating force.

And when one reached the lower level, there was not even any sound or smell, because down here each cell was soundproofed, utterly isolated from the world of human beings. Now only her heels and those of Maria, immediately behind her, broke the silence. And the rasp of the spy window as she slid it aside, to look into cell number thirty-four.

A two-hundred-and-fifty-watt naked bulb glared in the ceiling, which was too high to be reached by any inmate driven insane by the constant brilliance. There was no furniture in the room—nothing but a capped valve set into the stone wall and the body of a man. He had been stripped of his clothing, and lay on his side, facing the door, his hands secured behind his back. He was a young man, and handsome. He might be one of her more promising projects, Anna thought, if she could ever spare him the time. But he was merely a stepping-stone to mastery over the girl.

Maria was already undressing, hanging her clothes on the hooks that waited on the corridor wall. Anna followed her example. Her techniques never varied. She knew from years of experience that the only way even to attempt to resist her interrogation was to concentrate intensely. Breaking down or eliminating that concentration was more than fifty percent of the task ahead. But she knew how it could be done. Maria, again without instruction, had proceeded down the corridor to remove the hose from its bracket on the wall. It was a very short length of hose, only four feet long, but it ended in an adjustable nozzle, which could be altered as required to provide a wide blast or a needle-thin jet.

Anna unlocked the door and stepped inside. Maria followed her and closed the door again behind her. Now no sound would escape the cell. Maria went to the valve in the corner and unscrewed the cap. Instantly a considerable flow of water gushed out, rapidly covering the floor of the cell; patiently Maria screwed the end of the hose into the valve, and the gush ceased. The cell floor was already half an inch deep in water, lapping at their bare feet.

The water slurped around the man's face, and he moved feebly. Anna stooped, thrust her fingers into his hair, and raised his head. Maria switched on the hose, and a broad gush of water splashed on Robert Loung's face. His eyes opened, closed again, and then opened again. Maria turned off the water, and

Anna released his head. It fell into the water with a splash.

This time Robert rolled, realized for the first time that his wrists were tied behind his back, and struggled to come to rest against the wall. Anna and Maria took a shoulder each and dragged him into a sitting position.

His head turned, to look at Maria. And then back the other way, rapidly, to look at Anna. He could not believe his eyes.

"Tell me," Anna said, using her most seductive voice, "about the explosives."

He stared at her, unable to keep his gaze from drifting down her body, turned to look at Maria again, and then, with an almost visible effort, shut his mind to them, and stared at the door instead. "Where am I?"

"In cell number thirty-four," Anna told him.

That got him looking at her again. "You . . . my God! Where is my wife?"

"She is in cell number forty-seven," Anna explained. "Both cells are in Lubianka Prison, here in Moscow."

"In Moscow? But . . . we were in Brest-Litovsk!"

"We transferred you here by aircraft," Anna told him. "As you may know, smuggling explosives into the Soviet Union is a grave matter. Thus we felt that we could better get to the bottom of it here at Lubianka. We have so many more facilities here for obtaining satisfactory answers. I am sure your wife will tell us all we wish to know when we visit her. We shall be doing that when we leave here."

"What explosives are you talking about?"

Anna frowned; there had been a truly sincere quality of incomprehension in his voice. "You do not know?" she asked. "You do not know that your suitcase and that of your wife are packed with explosives in the false bottoms?"

Robert stared at her, the color draining from his face. "Oh, my *God!*" he said again. "Oh, Jesus Christ!"

Anna smiled. "You have been hoodwinked, perhaps? Then all you have to do is tell me who provided you with the suitcases."

He opened his mouth, and then bit his lip. She could almost see his brain whirling around and around. He knew the answer, but he was afraid to give it. She raised her head to look at Maria and gave a slight nod. Maria picked up the hose and stood above him. Robert stared at her in bewildered apprehension as she slowly and deliberately twisted the nozzle, until it was all but closed. Then she switched it on. The jet, as thin and as hard and as sharp as an icepick, struck him between the eyes. This was Maria's opening specialty, because it required great skill; that jet, mistakenly—or deliberately—directed into an eye, could destroy the sight. Robert's body jerked and he rolled away from the wall. Maria's jet scoured down his shoulders and back, and he instinctively rolled again. This time the jet played on his genitals. He screamed and tried to draw up his knees, but Anna caught his ankles and held him on his back.

"Enough," she said.

Maria switched off the jet.

Anna released him, and knelt beside the gasping man. "With that jet," she told him, "Maria can castrate you. It will take time, but we have all the time in the world. And we find it enjoyable, as well, to watch, and listen, and know what is happening to you. And when we have finished with you, we will visit your pretty little wife, and introduce *her* to the pleasures of the hose. We can render her sterile with the hose. We can even rupture her and watch her die, with the hose. And even if we do neither of those things, once we have used the hose, she will never be the same again. Do you know what Maria calls her hose, when used on a woman? The big prick."

Robert stared at her, straining against the handcuffs. "Who *are* you?" he whispered. "You are a devil from hell."

"I am Anna Ragosina," Anna told him, with some pride. "And I *am* a devil from hell, to those who oppose me. But you know . . ." She ran her fingers into his hair. "I can be very nice to those who please me. And so can Maria."

Robert gazed at her.

Anna shrugged. "Make him feel," she told Maria.

"No," he gasped. "Listen . . . Miss Ragosina . . . If I tell you who gave us the suitcases, who must have planted the explosive, will you release Diana? My wife? She knows nothing of this, I swear to you."

"You have my word," Anna told him. "I wish only to discover the truth."

"He is a self-confessed terrorist," Anna told the jailer. "But I do not wish him beaten or harmed in any way, for the moment.

Put some furniture in his cell, feed him, and give him clothes to wear and some books to read. Treat him well, you understand me?"

"Of course, comrade commissar," the jailer said. "He did not take long."

"No," Anna said. "He did not take long. He is in love."

She and Maria, both dried and fully dressed now, left the men's section of the prison and went to the women's. Here the head jailer was a woman of nearly sixty; she had been there ever since the first day Anna had descended these steps, twenty-five years before, and hardly seemed to have changed. She was tall and thin and raw-boned and vicious; as her hair had turned gray, her viciousness had increased. She regarded Anna with a mixture of contempt and apprehension. "You have come for forty-seven," she remarked.

"Why, yes," Anna said, and frowned. "You have not touched her?"

"I was told to leave her alone," the woman said.

Anna nodded. "Maria will look after her, until further orders."

"She has no name," the woman commented.

Anna gazed at her. "That is right, comrade. Until further orders, she has no name."

When they reached cell forty-seven, Anna opened the peephole. Her heart was pounding pleasantly. She could have spent an hour amusing herself with the young man, but she had been in a hurry to get to the woman. After all, Robert Loung was just a name and a body; this girl was a Hayman. If Anna could not have John Hayman in one of her cells, then a close relative would be an adequate substitute, for the present. And this girl was one of the wealthiest heiresses in America. Her life would have been one of pampering, of luxury, of being surrounded by the obsequious. Her reactions to what was about to happen to her would be composed of outrage, anger, incredulity, and then, probably very quickly, total fear and subjection, because she would be in a world of which she could know nothing, about which she could not even have a suspicion.

And judging by the photograph in Ivan's pocket, she might even be pretty.

She stared through the peephole, and felt her flesh begin to tingle. The scene was exactly the same as in cell thirty-four, except for the sex of the inmate. Anna's heart slowed while her nostrils dilated. Until now she had not formed any clear idea of what she expected to see, had been content to await the reality. A girl, after all, was only a girl. Now she realized that Ivan's photograph not only must have been taken several years ago, but had also been a bad print of a poor picture.

She remembered having Ruth Borodina, the daughter of the prince of Starogan, in this cell, fourteen years ago. Ruth Borodina's mother had been Rachel Stein, the younger sister of the famous Judith Petrov. The exquisite loveliness of the Jewish girl and the flamboyant handsomeness of the Borodin prince had produced a small, dark delight. Ruth Borodina had been one of the most enjoyable episodes of Anna's life. But if Ruth Borodina had also been lying on that floor, right this minute, she would not have warranted a second glance.

Anna found it was almost difficult to control her breathing. Besides the flawless beauty of the face, the delicious upturn of the nose, the arrogant tilt of the sleeping lips, and the wealth of silky black hair that clouded past her shoulders, the body looked faultless, too. Ruth Borodina had been thin. This girl, certainly no taller, suggested nothing but firm flesh, with only a trace of rib as she breathed. Anna gazed at small but full breasts, smooth thighs, slender but well-muscled legs . . . and felt almost sick with anticipation, and at the same time suddenly angry, that she should not have been the first to look upon such perfection, much less to touch it.

She closed the peephole and turned her head. Maria as usual was undressing. "What are you doing?" Anna demanded. Her voice could be uncommonly harsh.

Maria looked up in surprise.

"Put your clothes on," Anna snapped.

"But—"

"This girl does not need interrogation," Anna said. "Her husband has told us all we need to know. Why was she stripped? I gave no orders to do that."

Maria opened her mouth, and closed it again. "It is normal procedure," she muttered.

"Normal procedure," Anna sneered. "We do not have normal procedures, Maria Feodorovna. I suppose you searched her as well?"

"I . . . of course, comrade commissar." Maria's cheeks were

pink, and she gave a cry and staggered against the wall as Anna's hand slashed across her face. Anna could knock a man unconscious with that hand, and even though she had deliberately held back some of her strength, Maria's lip burst into streaming blood and her face turned white.

"How much longer will she remain unconscious?" Anna asked.

"If—if she is not disturbed," Maria gasped, "another hour, at least."

"An hour," Anna said. "Very well. Have the cell furnished, immediately. Have food prepared. And wine, and vodka. She will be thirsty when she wakes. Have her dressed. But not touched more than necessary. Have this done within half an hour, Maria, and then leave her. I will return shortly."

Diana Hayman was aware of a peculiar sensation, that of spinning through space at great speed; her stomach felt light and her brain seemed unhinged. She gasped for breath and had a tingling sensation in her toes and fingers. But gradually the movement slowed and stopped, and she could risk opening her eyes.

She gazed at a ceiling, which contained a bulb shaded with blue, so that the light was diffused, and almost pleasant.

She seemed to be lying on a bed, and was fully dressed, yet surprisingly she was *aware* of sensation, as if her most private parts had been investigated by curious fingers. Something to do with the kaleidoscopic dreams that had been swirling through her unconscious mind.

She took a long breath, and tried to concentrate. She remembered dropping her teacup, and then . . . nothing else. Except the dreams.

Robert! She sat up, stared left and right, while the room seemed to be moving, only slowly settling down and allowing her to see. It was a large room, furnished, at first glance, with a table and chairs in addition to the cot she was lying on—but there were bars on the little window in the door, and no other windows at all. There were no carpets on the floor, either, and only the single light bulb above her head. She was definitely in some sort of prison.

She realized she was not alone, and looked anxiously at the far end of the bed, where a woman sat. Her mouth sagged in surprise mingled with relief. It was not merely that the woman was quite exceptionally lovely, with coloring remarkably similar to her own. She was much older, of course, but her actual age was impossible to guess. Her quite splendid features were framed in center-parted, straight black hair, almost suggesting a Madonna. But the truly remarkable thing about her was her clothes, a frilly pink party dress, high-heeled shoes, nylons . . . she might have stepped straight out of a New York cocktail party, though a party of a few years before. And most reassuring of all, she was smiling, in a most relaxed and friendly fashion.

"Mrs. Loung," she said. "Diana. I am so glad you have awakened. How do you feel?"

Diana opened her mouth, and then closed it again. Her throat was too dry to speak.

Anna understood. She got up and poured a glass of water from the pitcher on the table, and Diana realized that the table was set for a meal, and had wine waiting as well as water. But for the moment she wanted only water, her throat was so dry. She drank without thinking, and only then remembered that this whole ghastly nightmare had begun with a cup of tea.

Anna had noticed the change of expression. "Those injections do make one very thirsty," she agreed.

"Injections?"

"They were necessary. To bring you here in safety."

"Bring me where?" Diana asked. She was aware of an immense desire to shout and scream, and rant and rave. But equally, of the absolute imperative to do none of those things, to remain calm and cool. She was Diana Hayman. Whatever happened to her, she wanted to have happen. Therefore, when something like this happened, it had to be a mistake—which would soon be rectified. She just had to remember that.

"You are in Lubianka Prison, in Moscow," Anna explained. She saw Diana's eyes widen in amazement. "I am Anna Ragosina. Perhaps you have heard of me?"

Diana frowned. She had heard the name, had heard it used by her Uncle John, but in what context she couldn't for the life of her remember, at this moment.

"No?" Anna was clearly disappointed. "Well, I am a colonel in the KGB. Do you know what that is?"

Diana's chin moved slowly up and down. "The Russian secret police."

Anna smiled contemptuously. "The letters stand for Komitet

Gosudarstvennoy Bezopasnosti. In English, the Committee for State Security."

"That's what I said," Diana pointed out. "The secret police."

"I see I have many things to teach you," Anna said.

"Yes," Diana said, seeking, as she always did, even if subconsciously, to take control of the conversation. "Such as, what has happened to my husband?"

"He is well," Anna said. "I spoke to him not twenty minutes ago. Tell me, are you not hungry? You have not eaten for at least twelve hours."

Diana looked at her wrist. But her watch had been removed, together with her wedding and signet rings. Robert had not had the time to buy her an engagement ring.

"Your jewelry will be returned to you, soon," Anna promised. "Will you not eat?"

Diana realized that she *was* hungry. In fact, she was ravenous. At the very mention of the word *food,* her mouth had filled with saliva.

"It is all for you," Anna said. "I will sit with you, but I have already eaten."

Diana gazed at the table and the food. It was all cold, some sort of Russian version of smörgåsbord, as far as she could make out. But it still looked delicious.

"Do not be afraid," Anna said. "It is not drugged."

Perhaps this was a chance to regain the initiative, which would certainly be lost the moment she started to eat. "But the tea in Brest-Litovsk was?"

Anna shrugged. "I have told you it was necessary. You and your husband are very naughty children."

"Children?" Diana was already lowering herself into one of the chairs; now her head came up. But she could no longer stop herself; she took a mouthful of salted herring, and the saliva threatened to choke her as she swallowed.

"Is it not childish, to attempt to smuggle explosives into the Soviet Union?"

"To—" Diana was swallowing her next mouthful of food, and again nearly choked. "To do *what?*"

"I am forgetting," Anna said. "According to your husband . . . Robert, is it, such a nice boy . . . you had no knowledge of that. It was your Uncle Peter's doing. Oh, we know *he* is a criminal. Can you imagine, sending you into Russia with your suitcases filled with plastic explosive? On your honeymoon?"

The nearly paralyzing hunger was beginning to fade, and she could think again. And nothing of what she was hearing was making any sense at all. This woman was clearly under a total misapprehension as to the true situation, and therefore the sooner she was corrected, the better. "I don't believe a word you are saying," she declared. "I have never heard such a load of rubbish in my entire life. I think you want to be very careful what you are doing, Comrade Ragosina, or whoever you are. I think very possibly you don't quite understand who I am."

"Oh, I know who you are," Anna said, and poured them each a glass of vodka. "Why else do you think I would be trying to help you? I know your family well. We are good friends. Your uncle and I once fought shoulder to shoulder against the Nazis. I would hate to see you harmed. But the facts are there. Your Uncle Peter filled the false bottoms in your two suitcases with plastic explosives. Now tell me, did he not give you the suitcases in the first place?"

Diana gazed at her with her mouth open.

"Exactly," Anna smiled. "Now, do you know what my job demands I do? Interrogate you until you scream. Until you admit things you had never thought of, until I suggested them to you. And then put you on trial before a people's court. You are guilty of a very grave offense, an offense which carries the death penalty. And your husband works for Prince Peter Borodin. You cannot deny that."

Suddenly Diana felt very tired. She wanted time to herself, to think, to figure, to plan. She drank some vodka, under the impression it was water, and choked.

"It is very strong," Anna said, "for those who are not used to it."

Diana got her breathing under control. "How do you *know* all this?"

"Your husband told me."

"Robert admitted all of *that?*"

"Why not? He is in love with you, and he wished to save you from any misfortune."

"Oh, my God!" Diana said.

"So, is it not all true?"

"We knew *nothing* about it," Diana cried. "Uncle Peter . . . my God, I cannot believe it! He seemed so kind, so generous, so . . ." She bit her lip. She had not intended to give way to any outbursts like that. But the panic rising in her stomach was giving her acute indigestion.

"So two-faced," Anna said sadly. "I'm afraid he is like that. But there we are. The damage is done. It is not as if I alone had any jurisdiction over this affair. I am merely an employee of the state, who must perform her duty. It is the merest chance that I, who also happen to know your family, was assigned at all. But even so, I am told that I must prosecute it to the very maximum. Of course, I do not think you *are* in any grave danger. Perhaps a year or two in a labor camp . . . that is not very nice." She stretched out her hand, gently smoothed Diana's hair, left the hand lying on her shoulder. "They will cut off your hair. All of your hair. They will shave your scalp and then they will shave your body. To prevent lice, they will say. That is not very nice at all. When they are finished with you it is difficult to believe you are human. And then they will beat you whenever you make a mistake. But as they will not tell you what *is* a mistake, you will not know, and so they will beat you at least once every day, until they tire of you."

Slowly Diana closed her mouth. She felt that if she left it open it would scream of its own volition. So she took a long breath and said, as quietly as she could, "Why are you telling me all this?"

"Because it is what is going to happen to you. But as I have said, you are Diana Hayman, and I believe you *are* innocent of willful involvement in this business, so I do not think you will have to endure it for more than two years. And of course, your family will seek to have you exchanged, as soon as possible. Two years in a labor camp is very bad. Two days, two *hours* in a labor camp is hell. But you at least will survive. Your husband . . ." Anna sighed. "I am afraid he will be sentenced to death."

"To—but he's as innocent as I am," Diana declared, her voice rising, despite her constant inner voice reminding that she *must* keep control over herself.

"Do you know?—I believe he may be," Anna agreed. "But the facts are against him. He works for this Peter Borodin. He has told us this—"

"You've tortured him," Diana shouted.

"Of course not. It was not necessary. We merely told him we were going to torture *you.*"

Diana's hands clasped themselves around her throat.

Anna smiled, and she removed her hand from Diana's shoulder, reluctantly. "Of course we were not going to do that either. This is part of the sequence. But there it is. He has confessed to his relationship with Peter Borodin, and there is no way he can possibly deny the presence of the explosive."

"Unless *you* planted it," Diana said.

Anna looked shocked. "We do not do that sort of thing, Miss Hayman—I beg your pardon, Mrs. Loung."

"But he is *innocent.*" Diana got her voice back under control. "You know that. You have just said so. And anyway, do you really suppose he would involve me in such a scheme? You yourself told me that he loves me, that he confessed only to save me from . . . from ill treatment."

"That is what he claimed," Anna said. "But who knows? He might just be a total coward."

"Robert? That's not possible."

Anna shrugged. "You did not think that your uncle would involve you in such a thing, either, did you? And how well do you know this man? You are on your honeymoon, are you not? You have had a few screws. *That* is the extent of your knowledge."

Diana bit her lip. That much *was* true.

"Exactly." Anna got up. "Ah, well, I don't suppose you will miss him very much when he is gone." She walked to the door.

"No!" Diana shouted, also getting up. She hated herself, but she knew she was going to beg. She had never begged for anything in her life—she had never had to. But Robert was her husband, no matter what this woman had suggested of him. "Please, Miss Ragosina. Colonel. Please! He is innocent. I know he is innocent. And I love him. You must help him. Help us!"

Anna, her hand on the door hasp, made a moue. "You do not know what you are asking," she said. "You could be putting my career in jeopardy. In Russia that is not a good thing to do."

"Please!" Diana said again. "If you know my family, you will know that they are very rich. They will reward you, believe me. Anything you wish. Just help Robert."

Anna hesitated, then left the door and came back to stand almost against her, and put her arm around her waist. "You *do* love him, don't you? My dear, dear girl. But what good do you suppose your family's dollars can do me, here in Russia?"

"There must be something—"

"Oh, there are a great number of things," Anna said. "But not dollars. Dollars can do nothing for me. My life is a lonely one, and a misunderstood one. I am a servant of the state, and as such, I must do some terrible things from time to time. I do not enjoy doing these things, but I know they are necessary. And then I return to my lonely apartment, and I weep myself to sleep, for lack of any true companionship. If you knew how my heart yearns to share itself with another, with another perhaps as beautiful as yourself . . . such wondrous beauty . . ." Her left arm was still around Diana's waist; now her right hand came to rest on Diana's stomach, and moved upward, carrying the cashmere sweater with it, exposing and stroking the flesh beneath, reaching up for the breasts. Thoughts kaleidoscoped through Diana's mind. This woman wanted *her*. Nothing else. And Anna Ragosina could presumably save Robert's life, if she was in charge of the investigation. So must she lie back and enjoy it, as she had been prepared to enjoy it with Janice? But that had been a game, and she had been the leader. This woman was not a girl with whom she might reach some mutual *experience*. For all her beauty and apparent sympathy, this was a colonel in the KGB, who would do nothing which did not have a purpose, a goal, a triumph at the end of it. She had told Robert she would torture *her,* to get what she wanted from him. And now she was saying that Robert would be executed, unless Diana made love to her. But she had not actually provided any proof that she even held Robert, much less that there *was* explosive in their suitcases.

"Such beauty," Anna said, gently moving Diana toward the cot, making her sit down, still holding her breasts, and at the same time bringing her face forward for a kiss.

My God, Diana thought, I am about to be raped. She stared into Anna's eyes, and found the hardest, coldest blue she had ever seen, glittering sapphires that were now glowing with a mixture of triumph and passion. An unholy glow that took her beauty and turned it inside out, making it quite hideously evil.

Diana felt she was standing on the edge of a very deep pit, into which all her senses were beckoning her to fall, and remain—and never reemerge.

But that was impossible. She was Diana Hayman, and had things to do with her life. She could not simply become this woman's victim. She could only live, and die, as what she was.

She stared at Anna's smile. Her instincts warned her that this woman could not be combated by conventional physical means. She could only be resisted by some totally unexpected and even unthinkable assault.

"My dear girl," Anna said, playing with Diana's nipples. "My dear, dear girl."

Diana took a long breath, and with all the strength in her jaws, bit Anna on the nose.

Chapter 8

ANNA SCREAMED, A MINGLE OF PAIN AND OUTRAGE, AND JERKED away, while Diana stared at her in consternation. She had not realized just how hard she could bite, or how sharp her teeth were; she watched the blood bubbling from the deep cut on the bridge of Anna's nose and come coursing down her nostrils and across her lips to drip from her chin.

The scream, clearly not from the prisoner, caused the door to burst open, and several female warders to rush in.

"I'm sorry," Diana said, genuinely contrite at what she had done. "I guess it was a reflex."

"You . . ." Anna pointed, her whole face twisted. "Strip her and stretch her on the table. Bring pepper. By God, they are going to hear you scream in New York."

She spoke in Russian, and Diana did not understand what was about to happen to her until she was seized by several pairs of hands, her sweater pulled over her head, her slacks wrenched down her legs. "You . . . stop it!" she shouted, becoming angry herself. "Stop it, you harpies. Let me go!"

She gasped for breath as she was lifted bodily from the floor and thumped onto the table, scattering plates and bottles, held by her wrists and ankles as she attempted to sit up.

"Pepper," Anna stormed, having found her handkerchief and pressing it against her nose in an attempt to stem the flow of blood. "Where is the pepper? What the devil do *you* want?"

she demanded of Maria, who had appeared in the doorway, her own face still puffy from Anna's blow, staring at her commander and the scene beyond in amazement.

"You have been wounded, comrade commissar," she cried.

"Of course I have not been wounded, you cretin," Anna bawled. "And nobody sent for you. Get out. Get out! Where is that pepper? Hold her down. Spread her legs. By God—"

"But comrade commissar," Maria said. "Commissar Beria wishes to see you, immediately."

"Well, he can wait," Anna snapped, "until I am finished with her."

"He said it was a most urgent matter," Maria protested.

Anna hesitated, looked at Diana, who was still attempting to fight her assailants, not speaking, now, but gasping for breath, face flushed and breasts heaving, hair scattered and legs kicking. One of the women came hurrying in with a bag of peppers. Anna chewed her lip. But the girl would only improve by waiting. "Tie her to the table," she commanded. "Tie her so tightly she cannot move a muscle. And then leave her. I will come back to her soon enough." She stood above Diana.

"I said I was sorry," Diana gasped. "I'm just . . . not that sort of girl, I guess."

"I am going to make you *feel,*" Anna told her. "From the tip of your toes to the top of your head, you are going to *feel*. Lie there, and think about what is going to happen to you, Miss Diana *Hayman*." Still holding the handkerchief to her nose, she hurried from the cell.

"Anna Petrovna!" Lavrenti Beria peered at the woman who had so suddenly become the most important thing in his life. "What is the matter?"

"Oh . . ." Anna removed the handkerchief, briefly, gazed at the blood, and restored the cloth against the wound. "I . . . I fell. Against my desk. So I have cut my nose."

"Cut your nose? But your entire face is covered in blood."

Anna glared at him for a moment, then pulled open the door of his private washroom, stared at the mirror in total consternation; her face was indeed a red mask. Hastily she turned on the faucet, scooped cold water in her hands, reached for a towel, aware that Beria had followed her, was standing against her, his hands on her thighs; he was so constantly aroused in her company that she sometimes wondered if he had ever had another woman at all.

And the emotion, amazingly, appeared to be genuine. As she straightened he put his arm around her shoulders, and despite the silent protest of her petulant shrug, held her hand away from her face. "My God! But you should have that seen to. It is a deep wound. Your desk, you say? Your desk has a serrated edge? It is possible the bone could be broken."

"Do not be absurd," Anna told him. "Of course the bone is not broken. It is a cut, that is all."

Beria kissed her on the forehead, and returned behind his desk. "You should still have it seen to," he repeated. "You could be scarred for life."

"Bah!" Anna said, and threw herself into a chair. "I was extremely busy, Lavrenti Pavlovich. I hope this is as important as you claim."

"It is." Beria leaned forward, looked left and right with a most conspiratorial air. "I have received a cypher message from our people in Paris."

"Paris?" Anna frowned. The Loungs had begun their journey in Paris.

"Indeed. They have received a visit at the embassy there—you will never guess from whom."

"Ah . . ." Anna's hesitation lasted only a moment. "Prince Peter Borodin."

Beria frowned and leaned back in his chair. "How did you know that?"

"I use my head. Besides, it was a guess."

"Indeed?" Beria leaned forward again. "And what do you suppose this archtraitor, this archenemy of the Soviet Union and everything we stand for, had to say?"

"I would say he is threatening you, us, with some catastrophe, if we do not agree to some preposterous proposal of his."

"Ha!" Beria leaned back again, and now he was smiling. "You are wrong."

Anna removed the handkerchief, gazed at the still-fresh blood, and replaced it again.

"I will tell you what the prince had to say," Beria said. "It was quite a tale. Briefly, he said that he is tired of opposing the Soviet Union and the great Communist movement. He is an old man and knows he is shortly to die. Russia is his home.

He was born here, the last of many, many Borodins, and he wishes to die here. He asks to be allowed to return."

Anna studied him. Thoughts, possibilities, were beginning to leap about her brain, despite the pain and the anger, and the almost sickening desire that kept dragging her concentration down to cell number forty-seven.

Beria continued to smile. "You do not believe me? It is true. And as he knows that he is not welcome here, he has offered to buy his way in."

"With what?" Anna asked.

"Information. He claims to have information of vital importance to the security of the Soviet Union."

"And you believe this?"

"Do you?"

Anna considered. It was all very obvious. Peter Borodin wished to get into Russia to link up with Robert Loung and the two suitcases filled with plastic explosive. Anna could not believe her good luck. The whole world was falling into her hands. If she still intended to make that little bitch suffer as no woman had ever suffered before in history, it was still all in her own hands. And it was going to remain in her hands, until she was ready. Until she knew for sure what Peter Borodin intended to accomplish. Until he had utterly betrayed himself, and Robert Loung—and thus Diana Hayman as well.

"It is certainly possible that he could possess information of use to us," she said. "He has a network of agents throughout Europe. We know this. We know that some of them are even in the Soviet Union. He also has good connections in America. His sister is married to George Hayman, the publisher, one of the most powerful men in the United States. I think he might well be worth listening to."

"He insists that his information can only be divulged to the very highest authority."

Anna smiled. "In this context, that is you and I, Lavrenti Pavlovich."

"Will not Ivan Nej wish to muscle in?"

"Undoubtedly. But Ivan Nej is not here."

"Not here? Where is he?"

Anna shrugged. "Vacationing in the Crimea or some such place. He was born down there, you know. Well, in the Basin of the Don. So this could not have happened at a better time.

I think we should offer Prince Borodin a safe conduct into the Soviet Union. It can always be revoked. I think it will be very amusing, and informative, to hear what he has to say, and arrest him afterward. I think things are working out very well for us."

"Well . . ." Beria scratched his bald head. "If you are confident that it will not be dangerous."

"It can be dangerous to cross the street, Lavrenti Pavlovich," Anna reminded him. "But it is necessary if one wishes to get to the other side. I am quite sure that I—we—can handle Prince Borodin. Now, I have things to do."

"Such as having your nose seen to."

Anna's smile was cold. "Such as attending to my desk, Lavrenti. I intend to smooth down the rough corners, so to speak."

"Let me get this straight," Elizabeth Hayman said to Janice Corliss. "Having gone to London with Diana, and then to Paris, you simply abandoned her, and came home? In *Paris?*"

Janice glanced from Elizabeth to George Hayman, Jr., who was trying to look sympathetic, in strong contrast to his wife, who looked ready to strangle her. "Well . . . I didn't exactly go as a chaperon, you know, Mrs. Hayman. Oh, what the hell. Sure, I went as a chaperon. There are certain things about your daughter you just have to know, sometime."

"Really?" Elizabeth's voice was like a steel rasp.

"Yes. Well . . . Di likes men. Not just the way most girls like them. I mean, she can't keep her hands off them, Mrs. Hayman. Or her mind. She falls in love with them quicker than you can spit. Why, she's had eight affairs in the past two years, to my certain knowledge."

"Eight . . . *affairs?* Do you mean . . . ?"

"Sure, I mean sleeping together. She doesn't brag about it. I think she's even ashamed of it. But that didn't stop her doing it."

"I don't believe you," Elizabeth declared.

Janice looked at George junior.

"Maybe you'd better amplify," he said quietly.

"Well, what's there to add?" Janice asked.

"Perhaps one or two names would help."

Janice considered, and then shook her head. "No, I couldn't

do that, Mr. Hayman. It would be letting Diana down, and let's face it, the guys were all headed for nowhere. They never even knew what hit them until it was too late. Di would meet a guy, and they'd date, and neck a bit, and next thing they were in love. Or she was. The point is, she's not promiscuous. Not really. She just genuinely falls in love with them, one after the other. And then falls out of love with them, a few weeks, sometimes even a few days, later." She looked from face to face. "It's a fact."

"And the trip to Europe was intended to break the sequence," George junior observed.

"That is ridiculous," Elizabeth declared. "She went to Europe to have a secret . . ." She gazed at Janice, her mouth open.

Janice shook her head again. "Di knows what you've been thinking about us, Mrs. Hayman. But it just isn't true. She has to have a confidante. I guess we all do. But she goes for *men.* I tried to tell her she was going to fall flat on her face one of these days, and she promised me that for all the time we were in Europe, there weren't going to *be* any men. And I believed her. So what happens? She falls for this English guy she meets at her Uncle Peter's place. I think he works for the prince. And next thing, he asks her to marry him."

"Marry him?" Elizabeth cried.

"Right. And I'm pretty sure she said yes. I tried to reason with her, explain that he was just another guy, and she'd have fallen out of love with him in another week, but she wouldn't listen."

"Marry him?" Elizabeth repeated. "How can she marry anyone without my—our—permission?"

"I told her you wouldn't approve, Mrs. Hayman. I told her this Robert Loung was probably after a payoff from you, and she just got angry. I could see I wasn't doing her any good, and I figured the best thing I could do was come home and tell you what's going on. I'm sorry, Mrs. Hayman, but that's the way it is."

Elizabeth continued to gaze at her for several seconds, then she got up and strode over to the telephone.

"Who are you calling?" George asked.

"I am booking seats on the next flight for Paris," Elizabeth said. "And then I am going to have a word with your mother about this ridiculous brother of hers. Because when I get to

Paris, I am going to have him locked up. *And* this man Robert Loung. And, if necessary, Diana as well. It might do her some good."

"Look, first let's phone the George V Hotel, and have a word with Diana." He smiled at Janice. "And thanks a million for coming home, Janice. I guess we'll handle it from here on."

"I thought you'd like to know," Allen Dulles said, "that this uncle of yours has disappeared. The Swedish government has no record of his entering their country. Of course, he could have done so illegally, and they are trying to find something out, but for the time being—"

"I don't think he went to Sweden," John said, his voice as grim as his face. "I think he may have gone to France."

"France? How do you figure that?"

"Just a hunch. There's a family brouhaha going on at the moment. And I'm the number-one black sheep. You remember telling me to introduce my niece to Uncle Peter, to give a reason for calling on him?"

"That's right." Dulles was frowning.

"Well, her friend has come hurrying back across the Atlantic to tell us that Diana appears to have fallen in love with one of Uncle Peter's cohorts, who followed her to Paris, and it's possible they're going to elope. According to this girl Janice, Uncle Peter may have gone, too. Diana had a lunch date with him the day Janice left to come home."

"Paris," Dulles said. "Well, we'll get in touch with them right away. How long ago was this lunch date?"

"Four days ago," John muttered.

"Four *days?"*

John sighed. "Well . . . this girl had to come home, Mr. Dulles."

"For heaven's sake. He could have gone anywhere in four days."

"I know that, and I've been checking. The moment he found out what was going on, yesterday, my brother—Diana's father—telephoned her Paris hotel and was told that Miss Hayman had indeed got married, to this Robert Loung."

"Married?"

"You are starting to sound like Diana's mother, sir. Sure,

it wasn't legal, since she's not of age. But that's a detail. The bad news is that, according to the people at the hotel, Diana and her husband left Paris three days ago, on their honeymoon. They were going to Russia, Mr. Dulles."

Dulles stared at him for several seconds. Then he said, very quietly, "Holy Moses!"

"And I think you will find that Prince Peter has also gone to Russia," John added.

"You mean Diana is working for him?"

"Oh, God, I don't know. Her husband certainly is. But does that matter, Mr. Dulles? Whoever goes to Russia with Peter Borodin is going to wind up against a wall, after having been torn apart by the KGB. By Anna Ragosina. God, it makes my blood run cold."

"Because she's your niece."

"Sure, because she's my niece. But also because she's an innocent young girl."

"Even if she's become involved in an assassination plot?"

"I don't think she has," John insisted. "I think she's been hoodwinked or coerced. But that won't matter to the Russians."

"And it shouldn't matter to us," Dulles reminded him. "You're working for the United States, John, not the Haymans, even if they are your own family. You understood that when you came to us." He shot John a suspicious glance. "Have you told anyone else about this?"

"No, sir."

"Not even the old man?"

"I'm trying to avoid the old man, believe me. Mr. Dulles, I've got to do something about it. I've got to try to get Diana back before she's either executed or reduced to a walking wreck. I *must*."

Dulles shook his head. "Can't be done. There's no way we can become involved. You'll just have to keep your fingers crossed."

John leaned forward. "Mr. Dulles, we want to stop this assassination if we can, don't we? Simply because we can't tell what the consequences will be. Okay. I think maybe I can do that. Listen to me, sir. I know this Ragosina woman very well."

"Sure," Dulles said. "And from what I've read in your reports, the next time she sees you she's going to shoot first and make a positive identification later."

"Sir, the important thing is that I know she'll talk with me. I can use my own father, as well, if I have to. You have to let me try, Mr. Dulles."

Dulles continued to study him for some time, then he sighed in turn. "Whatever you do, you're on your own. I'll give you leave of absence, but no support. I'm not even going to remember this conversation, when you close that door behind you." He smiled, and held out his hand. "But by God, I wish you luck, John."

"His excellency, Prince Peter Borodin," Lavrenti Beria announced, with the air of a magician producing an outsize rabbit from his hat.

Anna nodded, while Peter Borodin stared at her. No doubt he had heard of her, as she had heard of him—but if he made a remark about the bandage on her nose . . . As for the prince, he was a distinct disappointment, because of his obvious age. "I trust you had a good journey, Comrade Borodin?"

"Indeed," Peter said, and sat down, crossing one immaculate knee over the other. He would be a pleasure to destroy, Anna thought, just because of his arrogance.

"Colonel Ragosina is my aide," Beria explained. "We are the people you have come to see."

"I came to see Premier Stalin," Peter said. "And Molotov, and Nej . . . Michael Nej, that is. I will deal only with the very highest."

Anna snorted, but Beria continued to smile. "*We* are the very highest, Prince Peter," he said gently. "We control the state. You will see no one until you have convinced us that you have something to offer."

"And then?" Peter asked.

"That will depend upon what you have to say."

"I think Comrade Borodin should tell us exactly what he wants from us, comrade commissar," Anna said. "It may be of use in future discussions."

Beria glanced at her, then nodded. "As you wish. Prince Peter?"

"I have told you what I want," Peter said. "I am a Russian, born and bred. Circumstances have forced me to oppose the present government in this country, to attempt to bring it down. I owed this to my ancestors, and those of my family murdered by the Bolsheviks. Well, I have failed. And now I do not have much of my life left. So, I surrender. I would like to live out the last few years of my life in the surroundings I have always loved so well."

"How touching," Anna murmured.

"Thus I offer you information which I believe is of vital importance to the Soviet government, and in return I ask nothing more than the right to live here. But of course I also wish to make my peace with the men against whom I have fought for so long," Peter said. "Premier Stalin, and Vyacheslav Molotov, and Michael Nej."

"Very laudable," Anna commented. "We shall certainly see to that, in due course. Now, Comrade Borodin, we have arranged accommodation for you at the Hotel Berlin—"

"We have?" Beria asked in surprise.

"Of course," Anna said. "Comrade Borodin is an honored visitor to our country. I trust the Berlin will be satisfactory, Comrade Borodin?"

"Oh, very satisfactory," Peter said. "It could not be better. Why, I believe my grandniece is staying there at this time, with her husband. It will be pleasant to meet them again."

"Grandniece?" Beria demanded. "Your grandniece is in Russia?" He looked at Anna again.

"I think I recall approving an application for a visa for a Miss Diana Hayman," Anna said.

"And she is staying at the Berlin?"

"That I cannot say."

"Oh, she will be there," Peter said.

"Then you will have a happy reunion, as you say, Comrade Borodin. Now, we wish to know what you have to tell us."

Peter Borodin looked from one to the other. "It is information of a most serious nature."

"Yes?"

"Well . . . you will recall that some months ago, Premier Stalin was most seriously ill."

Beria and Anna looked at each other. "That is so," Anna said. Beria was obviously incapable of speaking. "He suffered a heart attack."

"Nonsense," Peter said scornfully. "He was poisoned."

"Poisoned?" Beria cried.

"Yes," Peter said.

"How do you know this?" Anna asked.

"My agents know everything," Peter pointed out.

"Indeed? And who is supposed to have attempted this poisoning?"

"His doctors."

"His *doctors?*"

Beria settled back in his chair with a thump.

"Several of them were Jewish, were they not?"

"Why, yes," Anna said. "That is true enough. Are you suggesting—"

"There is an international conspiracy, controlled from Tel Aviv, aimed at eliminating all the top Russian leaders," Peter said triumphantly. "They will work through the medical, because here in Russia a great number of your doctors are Jewish, and those that are not have Jewish sympathies."

"Is that a fact?" Anna asked.

"Of course."

"Well, that is very interesting," Anna said. "We shall have to investigate what you say, and see if we can get to the bottom of this. We are indeed grateful, Comrade Borodin. Indeed, as you claim, you *have* probably done the Soviet Union an enormous service. Now, may I suggest you go to your hotel, and perhaps see your grandniece? My chauffeur will drive you. And we will be in touch with you as soon as we have evaluated your information. Until then, of course, you are the guest of the Soviet government."

"Ah . . . yes." Peter Borodin got up, looking faintly taken aback at his summary dismissal. "It has been a pleasure." He made to hold out his hand, changed his mind, and left the office.

Anna gazed at Beria, and then burst out laughing.

"He is mad," Beria said. "Stark, raving mad. But you know . . ."

"I know that he nearly gave *you* a heart attack," Anna said.

"He should have died long ago," Beria commented. "Now I would like you to arrange that happy event, immediately. Today. This very afternoon."

Anna shook her head. "I think that would be a mistake. And a waste. I don't think he is really mad at all."

"You mean he may possess actual information? My God . . ." Beria wiped his brow.

Anna continued to smile. "I doubt he possesses *anything* of any value. He has merely created a reasonable scenario, and is one of those foolish men who underestimate everyone else. He assumes we will fall for his ludicrous story. Were he even to suspect there is some truth in it, he would probably be amazed. Well, I think we should humor him. I will arrest one or two doctors and have them sign confessions. Oh, they will be Jews, of course, so there is nothing for you to worry about." She gave him a quick, penetrating glance. "None of the people you employed *were* Jews?"

"Of course not. But I do not understand what is happening, Anna Petrovna. I am in a total fog. What is all this about his grandniece?"

Anna shrugged, partly to disguise her contempt; she wondered if this man would ever realize that he had been in a total fog since the day of his birth. "I have no idea. I saw an application for a visa, for this girl and her husband, and I approved it. There was no reason not to. Presumably they are staying at the Berlin, as Borodin claims. They may even be part of whatever he is plotting. The important thing is for us to discover what that is. And the easiest way to do that is to give him enough rope to hang himself. He will not keep us waiting very long."

"Well . . . it is your baby, Anna. I would have him run over by a bus, this very afternoon. He is a dangerous man."

"He is not dangerous, Lavrenti Pavlovich," Anna assured him. Because, she thought to herself, he will not be able to find his grandniece and her husband, nor their two suitcases filled with explosive. She wondered what he would do then. She was certain Prince Peter Borodin was about to embark upon a trying few days, which might produce some interesting results.

"Well," Beria was saying, "just remember that there are one or two people who must *not* be arrested, under any circumstances. Do you understand me?"

Anna smiled. Obviously he was referring to the doctors who had actually administered poisons, and who could therefore implicate him. What a fool this man was! If anyone should have been run over by a bus, those two were at the top of the list.

In every way he continued to put himself more and more in her power.

"Of course, Lavrenti Pavlovich," she murmured.

* * *

"Anna Petrovna!" Ivan Nej leaned forward over his desk to peer at her. "What has happened to your nose?"

"I tripped and fell," Anna said, very calmly; she had been preparing herself for this moment. "How was your trip? The Crimea must have been pleasant at this time of year, although I don't see much evidence of a suntan."

"The Crimea." Ivan snorted. "You think I have been to the Crimea?"

"That is where you said you were going," Anna said patiently.

"I have been to Hungary," Ivan declared pompously.

Anna waited.

"Your nose," he said. "Is it broken?"

"No, it is not broken," Anna snapped. "It is a trifle bruised, that is all. So you have been to Hungary. How very exciting for you. And now you have summoned me here to tell me this tremendous item of news. Commissar Nej has been to Hungary. Do you want front-page headlines in *Pravda?*"

Ivan raised his eyebrows. "You are not in a good mood, my Anna."

"I am very busy right now."

"With this mysterious prisoner in cell number forty-seven? Who is she?"

Anna shrugged. "A subversive. She and I are . . . getting to know one another. I think she may well have something to tell us, one day." She frowned at him. "You have not been poking your nose into my affairs, I hope, Ivan Nikolaievich? This investigation is at a very delicate stage."

"I would not dream of it," Ivan assured her. "In any event, I have been warned off. I, Ivan Nikolaievich Nej, have been told by that harpy you employ down there, that I cannot even look at this woman. Keeping a prisoner masked, indeed! That is medieval. And it is ridiculous as well as annoying. I think you should remember that at the end of the day, Anna Petrovna, your affairs are also *my* affairs."

"I promise that all will be revealed to you in good time, Ivan Nikolaievich." Anna got up. "But I must return to her. She consumes a lot of my time."

"And are you not interested in what I was doing in Hungary?" Ivan asked.

Anna's frown returned. "Weren't you taking a vacation?"

"A vacation? Ha! Let me tell you, Anna Petrovna, Ivan Nej never takes a vacation. I went to Hungary to be as close as I could safely be to Italy, because I wished personally to take charge of some goods from Rome. You will recall the goods of which I speak."

Anna's head came up. "You have done it?"

Ivan smiled, and rose to open the door for her. "Come."

"You are mad," Anna declared. "I do not believe you."

Ivan was opening another door. "Here we are," he said.

Anna stepped inside. She was in a small room, hardly more than a closet, one wall of which was entirely glass. But it was one-way glass, and to the person on the other side, the window would appear as a mirror. Anna stood against the glass and stared at Judith Petrova.

"Judith Petrova?" Lavrenti Beria rose from his seat like a disturbed pheasant. "He has kidnapped Judith Petrova? From *Rome?* My God!" He stared at Anna. "And you can smile? Has she been harmed?"

"She does not appear to be harmed," Anna said. "From what I saw of her. She was fully dressed. Unconscious, of course; she had been drugged. But she was lying on a settee and I did not see any bruises, or even any signs of assault. It must have been a very smooth operation. Very unusual, for Ivan Nej."

Beria continued to stare at her. "You knew this was going to happen?"

Anna shrugged. "I had heard him speak of it, but it seemed such a crazy idea I told him I did not wish to know about it. I never thought he would actually do it, anyway."

"But he has done it. The absurd fool! Does he not realize that one cannot just go around kidnapping people for the hell of it? Especially well-known people like Judith Petrova?"

"Well, it *can* be done," Anna said. "After all, Ivan has done it."

"And what is going to happen now? I will tell you. All hell is going to break loose, at any moment."

"I should think you are probably right."

"And you find this prospect amusing?"

"I think the situation is filled with possibilities, all of which we may be able to turn to our advantage. Consider these points."

She held up her hand and ticked off her fingers. "One. We have Peter Borodin here in Russia—we do not know why, but we shall find out in due course just by waiting and watching. However, he claims his reason for being here is to give us information on a Jewish plot to murder Premier Stalin."

"Which we know is absolute nonsense."

"Of course. But only *we* know that. Now, number two. Ivan has kidnapped a very prominent international Zionist, who is also an Israeli citizen. I can tell you why he has done it."

"Yes?"

"He wishes to offer her in exchange for his son Gregory."

Beria's mouth opened, and then closed again. "But . . . the man is an absolute thug. A Siberian bandit. Does he really suppose he can get away with something like that?"

Once again Anna shrugged. "*He* thinks he can. His idea, as he outlined it to me, was to concoct some kind of a Jewish plot to which Judith would be made to confess, by suitable interrogation. I personally doubt that a woman like Judith Petrova would confess to anything, even if he used red-hot pincers. He seems to have forgotten that she survived three years in Ravensbrück Concentration Camp. However, this is Ivan's idea. With this plot he hopes to withstand the storm of international protest which, as you have said, is going to break approximately tomorrow morning. And then, having provided a legitimate reason for holding Judith Petrova, and indeed for putting her on trial, he will magnanimously offer to exchange her for the leading KGB officer in prison in the United States. You must admit that the little man thinks big."

"He is mad," Beria declared. "My God! We have to stop him."

"I don't think we should do that at all. I think we should help him as much as possible. We can, you know." Anna leaned forward. "Lavrenti Pavlovich, don't you see? We *have* a Jewish plot which we do not want—Peter Borodin's 'poisoners.' Ivan has a Jewish prisoner for whom he desperately needs a plot. Don't you see the possibilities?"

Beria's brows drew together. "You mean that we should offer him *our* plot? And get him off the hook? You are betraying me, Anna Petrovna."

Anna sighed. "My intention is to get the hook so firmly wedged in Ivan's maw that he will never be able to spit it out.

There is going to be a fuss, which will be bad for Russia's image, unless there actually *is* a plot. But there *is* a plot; Peter Borodin says so. So we hand him over to Ivan. They love each other, anyway, the way a mongoose loves a cobra. Now then, Lavrenti Pavlovich, listen very carefully. This woman Petrova was once Borodin's mistress. He will be faced with a difficult but irrevocable decision: either sustain his pretended plot to the limit, and sacrifice Judith Petrova, or admit it was all a fabrication, and sacrifice himself. I think he will sacrifice the woman. Then Ivan will believe the whole world has fallen into his lap, for it will appear to have been a stroke of genius for him to arrest Judith Petrova before the plot even broke. He will be the man of the moment. But even more important, the existence of such a plot will set all Russia, all the world—and, comrade, all the Politburo—by the ears. They will be able to talk of nothing else, to think of nothing else, for some time to come. You and I will be ignored, to live our little lives, and forward *our* little ambitions, in peace. Is that not an attractive prospect?"

Beria's face had gone completely blank. Clearly he had lost her drift some time before. "How can we benefit from all this? Will it not make Ivan still more powerful?"

"Briefly. But men who swell up too fast burst with the loudest pop. You see, when we are ready, Lavrenti Pavlovich, we can prove that there never *was* a plot."

Beria frowned. "How can we do that?"

"I already possess the necessary proof," Anna said. "Everything Peter Borodin has pretended has been a lie. I have under arrest one of his people, a courier who was attempting to smuggle a large quantity of plastic explosives into Russia, and who was intending to rendezvous with Borodin at an appropriate moment."

Beria's frown deepened. "You never told me of this."

"It is a routine matter. But this young man will tell the whole truth whenever I am ready. He and I have reached quite a rapport."

"My God," Beria commented. "You frighten me, Anna. You always have."

"You should be grateful that I frighten other people more. Thus, at the most appropriate moment for us, I will prove that the whole scheme was devised by Ivan, and of course, by Stalin himself, and his henchmen, Michael Nej and Molotov, to forward some aim of their own, in defiance of morals and international opinion. There is a large body within the Politburo which already feels that this has been happening too often. I think, when the time comes, that *we* will emerge as the true heroes of the hour, dedicated servants of the state who have pursued our own investigations in the interest of truth and justice, regardless of the fact that it meant opposing even our own beloved leader."

Beria scratched his bald head. "But . . . what of Peter Borodin's *actual* plot? The one we are waiting to discover?"

"You mean what he intends to blow up? I think this may well force him into the open even quicker than we had hoped. I think he is probably a very worried man. Do you know that his grandniece and her husband have not yet arrived at the Berlin? Nobody knows what has happened to them, except that they did board a train for Moscow in Paris. It is plain to me that they also are couriers of his, and they too have gone astray. But all of that is surely irrelevant compared to the opportunity to snare Ivan. I promise you, Comrade Borodin will not even blow his nose without my office knowing of it thirty seconds later. He is absolutely no danger to anyone, except himself. But he is a very useful weapon indeed, for us, if properly used."

"You are a remarkable woman, Anna. I wish you did not like to live quite so dangerously."

Anna blew him a kiss. "It is only necessary to *live*." She got up. "I must go."

"But you will come to see me tonight, Anna Petrovna," Beria said. "I will need you tonight."

Yes, he would need her, because he was terrified, and only in her arms could he regain even a modicum of courage, she thought contemptuously. "Why, yes," she said. "I will come to you tonight." She would even come willingly, because she was on her way down to cell number forty-seven, and that always made her want sex.

The excitement over the imaginary Jewish plot would prevent anyone—and especially Ivan—from interesting himself in the fate of Diana Hayman, Anna told herself complacently. By the time she was ready to unveil her prisoner, it would be a simple matter to implicate Diana Hayman, as well, in this Jewish plot. If it became necessary.

* * *

Judith Stein Petrova was aware of being in the middle of a nightmare. A nightmare she had endured on too many occasions in the past. Only in the last two years had she imagined it over, forever.

Presumably it had to do with having been born a Jew. For some reason known only to God, hers was a nation destined to suffer. Not for any expiation of their refusal to accept that Jesus Christ was the last redeemer, certainly. She had no doubts about this. But for being the most successful people ever to walk the earth. Thus persecutions, by less successful but more powerful peoples, had afflicted them time and time again throughout the years, and in almost every nation in Europe. Only the non-Christian countries, those ruled by the Muslims and the heathens, had been prepared to accept such an industrious and self-conscious—in the truest sense of the word—enclave in their midst without protest. Those, and the bursting, emergent, impious and yet deeply religious United States. Wherever state religion had marched hand in hand with state government, the Jews had been on the receiving end of every decision dictated by tyranny and chauvinism.

And nowhere more so than in Russia. In Russia, for centuries, it had been a slow and hateful persecution, under the tsars and then under the Soviets. This was where she had made her biggest mistake. As a young Jew, fervent and angry at the way her people had been treated and were being treated, she had easily slipped into the postures of a revolutionary—and many of her fellow revolutionaries had been Jews. Equally many had not. She would remember to her dying day her amazement at discovering that the utterly lovely young matron building a barricade next to her in Moscow in the autumn of 1905 had been the Princess Ilona Roditcheva, née Borodina. Out of that chance meeting had sprung a remarkable friendship, and a great number of other things besides. But Ilona had only been playing at revolution because of an unhappy marriage; when the going had got really rough, she had simply fled across the Atlantic to her lover. Judith Stein had been genuinely involved, and had found herself condemned to death for a crime in which she had actually had no part, a sentence carelessly commuted to a living death in Siberia by the tsar, and then, even more carelessly, remitted altogether in a spur-of-the-moment amnesty. Flight had not come into it. Nor would she have wished to flee, then, because during those terrible, unforgettable years, she had discovered that there were many Jews as fervent and determined as herself, and even more talented. Men like Trotsky had been serious, and had risen to the top of the Soviet hierarchy as Jews. In him she had seen the hope of the future. But even he had stumbled and fallen. The lesser lights such as herself—mistress in turn of Prince Peter Borodin and Michael Nej and George Hayman—had had to fight and struggle and commit crimes and prostitute themselves just to keep alive. And she and so many others had survived only to fall into the hands of Hitler's thugs. Yet she had endured even that, had made a good marriage to Boris Petrov, and with the help of her many friends, had been able to devote her declining years to furthering the cause of her own people, in their own land. She had come to regard herself as the archetypal survivor. And now, with a role to play as a goodwill ambassador for her friends Ben-Gurion and Weizmann, she thought of herself as a successful and even happy woman, a woman who had already suffered her full quota of life's traumas.

Instead of which . . . She had no memory of what had happened in Rome. She had attended a meeting and had then taken a taxi to her hotel. She had opened the door of her bedroom, and had awakened on a plane to Moscow. It was a typical Soviet pattern, one she had experienced before, and had overcome before—with the help of her friends. Now her friends would not even be aware of what had happened to her, because there was no *reason* for it to have happened. Nothing she had done in the past few years could remotely have harmed Soviet Russia in any way. There was the possibility of a deep-seated determination to destroy her emanating from those dark men who dominated the Kremlin, but surely they would have had her killed, not kidnapped. What was the point of holding captive someone who could tell them nothing of importance? And everyone else would follow the same reasoning. Sometimes she thought she had gone mad—or worse, that she was the only sane person left in a maniacal world.

And, having been arrested by the tsar's secret police in her girlhood, and then by the Cheka as a young woman, she found it equally frightening to realize that this time no one had yet attempted to hurt her, either by word or deed. No one, indeed, had even attempted to communicate with her, and for her to attempt to carry on a conversation with her warden was a total waste of time. She had experienced both Nazi and Bolshevik methods, and she knew that in one respect they were exactly alike—the initial phase of captivity was a carefully designed destruction of personality, of dignity and self-awareness and even of humanity, and thus, finally, of will, by means of humiliations, of body searches that were virtual rapes, of sleeplessness, of disorientation, of physical mistreatment calculated to make one grovel rather than suffer pain. The pain came later. She had not even been searched, this time. Or if she had, while she was unconscious, it must have been done in the gentlest fashion, without even seriously disarranging her clothing. Now she sat in a not-uncomfortable cell, and though she had been here for at least three days—they had taken away her watch, so it was impossible to avoid *some* disorientation—and in that time had not been allowed a bath, was aware that her makeup had dissolved and her hair was a tangled mess, she had at least been fed regularly, had been allowed to sleep as she chose, and had received not a single kick or even a threat. It was as if she had been kidnapped for no other purpose than to remove her from circulation.

Perhaps it was all part of a new form of torture. Because it was torture for her, and it would be torture for Boris, for her niece, Ruth, for everyone who would be wondering where and with whom she had gone. She was hardly sure herself, now. But for her knowledge of Russian she would not even know she was in Russian hands, and though she assumed she was in Moscow, that was only a guess.

Yet she would know, eventually, the answers to everything. Of that single fact she was certain.

And so a new nightmare was about to reveal itself. For the cell door was opening. Judith Petrova stood up, knowing that, since it was not mealtime, this could not be the wooden-faced young woman who normally attended her. She caught her breath, as she stared at Ivan Nej.

This was the one possibility that had not occurred to her, that she would come face to face with this man, who had polished her boots on the occasion of her visit to Starogan as a guest of Prince Peter Borodin in 1914, had eventually murdered her parents, had hounded her for thirty years, and only five years before had attempted to kidnap her from the center of Jerusalem. There he had overreached himself, and thanks to Nigel Brent he had failed. She had been told that failure had caused his disgrace and exile, perhaps even his death. But here he was, wearing the uniform of a general in the KGB, as unchangingly hateful as ever.

"Judith Stein," he said. "Or should I say Petrova? And how is your charming niece? And that muscular blockhead of an English policeman she married? And of course my old friend Boris?"

Judith licked her lips.

Ivan smiled. "You are confused, and afraid. That is natural. But you bring these things upon yourself, Judith Petrova. Josef Vissarionovich himself once said to me, 'Judith is a born conspirator, Ivan Nikolaievich. She will come to a bad end.' And he was right. Well, we have treated most of your conspiracies with contempt, but when you seek to conspire against the lives of our very leaders, why, it is necessary to do something about it."

"Against—" Judith sat down on the bed. Ivan had this effect upon so many people, that of taking away their strength, their ability to stand, much less think with any clarity. "I have conspired against no one."

Ivan wagged his finger at her. "You must not treat me like a fool, Judith. Those days are past. Not even Michael will intervene on your behalf, when he sees the evidence against you."

"Evidence?" she shouted, her self-control threatening to snap. "What evidence? You have kidnapped me for some purpose of your own. What, are you still brooding on what happened in Jerusalem? You failed then, Ivan Nej, and you will fail again now. You have committed an international crime. Do you suppose you can possibly get away with it? When it is learned what you have done—"

"All your rich and powerful friends are going to come rushing to your aid?" Ivan shook his head. "No, no, Judith. This time you have gone too far. Come. There is someone I wish you to meet."

He held the door of the cell open for her in an almost gentlemanly gesture. There was no way she could refuse his invitation, even had she wanted to—she was at once too agitated and too curious, because it was dawning on her that Ivan was *not* playing a game: he genuinely believed he had evidence against her.

She allowed him to escort her down the corridor, and up the flight of stairs she remembered so well, was shown into his office, and gazed in astonishment at Peter Borodin.

"Anna Petrovna, you should have been there. I do not know when I have enjoyed myself more," Ivan declared, beaming. "They were lovers once, you know. Years and years ago. When he was Prince of Starogan. He even took her to Starogan to meet his mother! He was a fool even then. You can imagine how his mother received her. I mean to say—a Russian prince and the daughter of a Jewish lawyer! I remember, because I was there. And she remembered too. You should have seen the way she flushed, put her hands to her hair, tried to straighten her dress. You would have relished that."

"No doubt she also remembers that, after having taken her virginity, he then married her sister," Anna said—with deliberate cruelty, because Ivan had coveted Rachel Stein, as well.

The amusement left Ivan's face. "Yes," he said. "Do you know, I *hate* that man. I hate him more than any human being in the world, except perhaps George Hayman. And to have him here... You are a treasure, Anna Petrovna. I only wish you had told me sooner."

"I knew you were very busy, Ivan Nikolaievich," Anna murmured. "And I was only trying to help. How could I know that you were already aware of this Jewish plot? I think perhaps you could have told *me,* sooner."

For a moment Ivan's face went as blank as Beria's. He was obviously confused by her involved machinations. But he had his triumph in his hand, and soon started beaming again. "Anyway, I can tell you, it has been a treat. To have Peter Borodin having to be polite to me, to know I can destroy him with a snap of my fingers, and then to confront him with Judith Stein and tell him she is seriously involved—because of course he knows that she isn't. Do you know?—for a moment I thought he was going to attempt to withdraw his deposition, pretend it was all a fabrication, in order to save her. But he does not have that kind of courage. So he was forced to agree. You should have seen the expression on her face. And when she learned that there really is a plot, and that it was Peter himself who brought it to our attention . . . I thought she was going to hit him. Certainly, I would not have liked to have been in his shoes, after some of the things she said to him. He must have shriveled up inside. I tell you, it was the most enjoyable morning I have spent in a long time."

"I am so pleased for you," Anna said. "You realize, however, that there is an international storm brewing?"

"Of course. But we can thumb our noses at world opinion, because we possess the facts, do we not, Anna Petrovna?"

Anna smiled. *"You* possess the facts, Ivan Nikolaievich," she reminded him. "I had no part in it, except to agree that Prince Peter should come to Russia. It will be your triumph, and yours alone."

"Well, that is very generous of you, Anna."

"It is a pleasure. I am pleased for you. I wish you every success. And I look forward to seeing Gregory Ivanovich back at Lubianka in the near future. Now I must go."

"Down to cell number forty-seven? This creature is becoming a habit, Anna. You should never let your enjoyment of the job obscure the purpose for which the job was undertaken."

Anna's smile was cold. "In this case, Ivan Nikolaievich, the two are synonymous."

Chapter 9

YET THERE REMAINED IN ANNA THE NAGGING SUSPICION THAT Ivan could possibly be right. Diana Hayman *was* becoming an obsession; she found herself thinking about Diana constantly. It was upsetting, disturbing—and utterly delightful. It was a dream, like being able to see and touch a reincarnation of herself as a girl.

She could love Diana Hayman. Perhaps she already did. Certainly she *would,* once the silly girl learned to surrender.

But she hated her as well, because of her name and her background. As long as she remembered that, she was safe.

Maria stood at attention at the door to the observation chamber. It was her duty to make sure no one entered the chamber while her mistress was with the prisoner. Maria's face remained cold and angry, although the bruise had long faded. The silly bitch was still remembering the slap—and, Anna knew, she was also jealous of this new plaything. But Anna was not disposed to waste her time worrying about Maria's feelings; the girl was utterly her creature, and would always remain so for the simple reason that, once known as Anna Ragosina's assistant, she could never belong to anyone else. And Maria was well aware of that fact.

So Anna merely nodded in response to the salute, and stood at the window, which from within the cell looked like any other of the concrete blocks. She did this every day, partly to satisfy herself that her little bird had not in some way managed to fly away, partly to make sure that Diana was being properly cared for. Anna was well aware that her fastidiousness, her attention to pleasant details, was considered by some of her subordinates as almost a weakness. Such ignorance amused her. She had survived a labor camp, and she had survived the war in the Pripet Marshes; if the occasion were forced on her, she would willingly forget such luxuries as she presently enjoyed. But while she could indulge them, she delighted in them. And in providing them for her victims. She did not like the smell of sweat and fear and human excretions. Thus at her command Diana Hayman was bathed and perfumed every morning, just as she was fed three times a day and given a glass of wine with lunch and dinner; Anna did not wish Miss Hayman—she preferred to consider her as a Hayman rather than as Mrs. Loung—to misunderstand a single moment of her imprisonment through any dulling of the senses.

She nodded again. "Very good," she said, and went down the stairs to the lower level. She herself carried the keys to cell number forty-seven, and she opened the door for herself and closed it behind her.

The girl sat against the wall, naked, her wrists in handcuffs, which in turn were secured to boltrings set in the concrete four feet apart. She could move, but she could not bring either hand closer than her shoulder, and therefore it was impossible for her to reach behind her head and remove the black velvet mask that covered her face from her chin to her forehead, with slits for her eyes and nose and lips. She sat on a cushion to save her from the discomfort of the floor.

When the door opened the girl looked up, her shoulders momentarily squaring themselves, as the muscles in her thighs and belly tensed, an entrancing gesture of awareness, which lifted her breasts away from her chest, and gave the whole superb image life.

Anna reached behind the girl's head and released the mask, lifting it away and laying it on the bed at the other side of the room. Then she squatted before Diana. "And how are we today?" she asked.

The girl gazed at her, and Anna felt the strange mixture of desire and anger and utter frustration that always overtook her at this moment, rising in her belly and her brain. She had early recognized that here in this spoiled, pampered American was a will almost as strong as her own; the prospect of bending it as required had been at least as attractive as the thought of exploring all that beauty. But things had not turned out as she had expected, or wanted. That first day, in her anger, she had used her pepper with brutal effect; Diana had screamed and wept and her body had twisted and arched. It had been horribly beautiful, as unforgettable an experience as Anna had ever enjoyed—and she had never considered for a moment the possibility that it would not lead to total, abject surrender. As it had—apparently. When Diana had been washed, trembling and still weeping, her nipples swollen to twice their normal size, she had submitted to violation without a word, without a gesture of protest. As she had submitted ever since, to whatever Anna had chosen to inflict upon her. Physically. But at the same time she had closed her mind, shut it away behind steel doors that had so far proved impenetrable. And the penetration of which had become the most important thing in Anna's life. If Ivan were to know that, or Beria...

But they would never know. And so long as she did conquer this girl in the end... if only she could be totally confident that she *would*, eventually.

She released the handcuffs, allowed Diana slowly to massage her wrists, and then said, "It is time for your exercise."

Without a word, Diana Hayman got to her feet and began to jog on the spot, muscles trembling, breasts jumping, black hair fluttering in the self-created breeze. Anna sat on the bed to watch her, desire now uppermost. When the girl was finished, when that beautiful white sweet-smelling flesh was tinged pink with exertion and coated with a fine mist of sweat, she would summon her to this bed, and amuse herself... and the girl would accept it, and gaze at her, and say not a word, move not a muscle.

She might as well go back to her apartment and masturbate.

It was a pattern with which she was perfectly familiar. To close the mind while allowing the body total surrender to forces too strong for it was part of KGB and presumably American secret-service training. She herself had survived the labor camp only by practicing such a device. What was not familiar and was most disturbing was the certainty that this girl had never received any such training, that she was drawing entirely upon some inner strength—or even more frightening, some inner certainty that, because she was Diana Hayman, she must triumph in the end. Anna had an uneasy suspicion that this was indeed the case, and that in this one girl she possessed a textbook example of why the Americans, no matter how many things they did wrong, usually *did* triumph in the end. That was the most terrifying thought of all.

Of course, she could reflect, the situation was of her own manufacture, and could be ended whenever she chose. No one, not even the daughter of a millionaire, could fight her by closing her mind over any period of time, were she to use *all* the methods at her disposal. She could whip this girl with her steel-tipped knout until her flesh was in ribbons, or she could use the water jet as a lance, or she could put pepper between her legs until she went mad, or she could merely seize her and *beat* her, as she so often felt like doing . . . but any of those would mean physical as well as mental destruction. Anna knew she was greedy. She wanted to conquer this mind, absolutely. But she wanted the body to remain as entrancing as it now was.

Diana lay on her back with her legs in the air and bicycled. She followed exactly the program Anna had outlined for her.

Anna leaned against the wall, watching. "Today," she said, "your husband is to be whipped."

Diana's legs faltered for a single second, and then the movements resumed.

"Do you not love your husband?" Anna asked. "He loves you. He screams your name, whenever he is in pain."

Diana had finished the exercise. Her legs came down and her body came up, in a single graceful movement, so that she was standing. She was breathing only a little bit harder than normal.

"Perhaps you do not believe me," Anna said. In fact she knew perfectly well that Diana did *not* believe her. She had made a mistake in the beginning, because she had been so confident of success, in telling the girl that her husband was safe and unharmed, and had even been released. When she had reversed this and said he was still a prisoner, and was being subjected to daily beatings, Diana had obviously preferred to believe the earlier version. Of course, Loung could be brought before her, could even be beaten in her presence. But Anna's instincts told her this would be an even greater mistake. She suspected that Diana's reaction to seeing her husband tortured would be a withdrawal into an even more remote and inaccessible fortress. Besides, Robert Loung's willingness to cooperate—because of his anger at Peter Borodin for having placed his bride in such a position, and his relief and gratitude to *her* for having, he thought, released Diana—made him far too valuable a trump card in the power play she knew was coming, to be carelessly squandered for personal gratification.

Such self-control, she thought proudly, was the true answer to stupid little men like Ivan, who could even imagine that she, Anna Ragosina, would ever allow herself to become *obsessed*.

And yet, to bring some spark of reaction from that impassive face . . .

"He screams your name," she said again, "whenever I coat his penis with pepper."

Diana gazed at her.

And Anna's self-control suddenly snapped. "You little bitch!" She propelled herself forward and seized Diana's hair, dragging the girl to her knees while she slapped her face twice, sending the head jerking to and fro, and then releasing her so that she fell over. "Say something!" she shouted.

Diana slowly pushed herself to her knees. Tears dribbled down her cheeks from the force of the blow, but her emotions were in check. "Something like . . . 'fuck off'?" she suggested.

Anna stared at her, while her fingers curled into fists and her shoulder muscles tensed and she knew that in one moment she was going to grab this girl by the throat and throttle the life out of her. And then she laughed as she realized what a fool she was being, because there *was* a way to mutilate this girl, physically, and therefore perhaps mentally as well—and yet know that the destruction was only temporary. It was something that should have been done a long time ago; she had indeed been neglecting her duty.

She got to her feet, strode across the cell, and opened the door. "Maria! I want this prisoner shaved. Every single hair. Shave her until she looks like an egg." She turned to look at Diana again, and Diana gazed at her. "Call me when you are ready," Anna said. "Give her an hour to think about what is going to happen to her. Then we will hear what she has to say."

She stamped up the stairs to her office, threw herself into her chair, glared at the male secretary who waited hesitantly in the doorway. "Well?"

"The courier from the Washington embassy has been to see you, comrade colonel," the man said. "I told him you could not be disturbed, and he left this envelope for you."

"For me? From Washington?" Anna sat up, curiosity getting the better of her anger. She took the envelope, slit it open, and scanned the single sheet of paper inside.

"Checkmate; your game," she read. "Just tell us what you want. John."

"No one seems to want to *know,*" George Hayman, Jr., shouted. He stood in the center of his parents' living room, and gazed from face to face. "I've tried everything reasonable. *Everything!*"

Here, his father thought, was one of the richest and most powerful men in the world, reduced to something approaching hysteria because he had for the first time encountered a situation neither his money nor his power could control. Well, would he himself not have acted the same? Somehow he did not think so. His youth had been composed of situations he could not control. Perhaps his son had lived too sheltered a life.

Which did not make his distress any less disturbing.

"My dear boy," Ilona said. "Oh, my dear boy. Don't you think it's possible she may just be afraid to contact you, until she knows you won't try to have the marriage annulled?"

"Sure she may be afraid," George junior conceded, soothed as ever by his mother's calm voice. He sat down beside her on the sofa. "But tell me, how is she going to learn our reaction to the marriage unless she gets in touch? And tell me, too, how she's managed to disappear so completely, if there isn't something fishy going on. Nobody I've employed can find a hair of her."

"Have you contacted the state department?" George senior asked. "If you feel she's behind the Iron Curtain—"

"The people at the state department are the most useless of all. They seem to think we should've kept her closer to home. And they made it perfectly clear that they have more important things to do than worry about the spoiled daughters of millionaires."

"The police—" Ilona suggested.

"Don't you think I've been to them too? So she's under twenty-one. So they can put out a description and ask for her to come home. They've done that through Interpol. But Interpol doesn't work behind the Iron Curtain."

"And you feel positive that's where she is?" George asked gently. "Europe is a big continent."

George junior sighed. "I don't know anything, Dad, and that's what's so terrifying. She married some man I have never even heard of, much less seen or met. They get on a train in Paris, bound for Moscow. At least they said they were going to. Nobody actually saw the tickets. The train gets to Moscow, and they aren't on it. As far as I'm concerned, that's a kidnapping. But nobody wants to know about that either."

"*Can* a man kidnap his own wife?" Ilona asked.

"Are you talking about legal definitions? As a matter of fact, yes. But he may have been kidnapped too, for all I know. For all anyone knows. Except, as I say, that nobody *wants* to know. 'How can it be a kidnapping?' the police ask me. 'There's been no ransom demand. The moment you get a ransom demand, Mr. Hayman, you come to us, and we'll take it from there.' Like hell they will. 'Suppose she's been murdered,' I asked them, 'and there never is a ransom demand?' 'How can there be a murder?' they ask me. 'There's no body. The very moment we find a body, Mr. Hayman, we'll take it from there.' Jesus Christ! This is my daughter they're talking about. I feel as if I'm going stark, raving mad. Elizabeth is already halfway there. In Paris she just about had a breakdown. Well, so did I. Now she's under sedation, most of the day. Four weeks, and nothing. And Uncle Peter is involved too. I'm sure of that."

"Oh, really, George!" Ilona said. "I know Peter is a bit soft in the head, but you can't really think he'd kidnap his own grandniece."

"Why not? He once kidnapped his own sister. Besides, I can't afford to be sure of anything, anymore, Mother. Oh, yes, I can be sure of one thing. That there are a whole lot of people who know more about this than they are prepared to let on. The state department, for one. And you want to know who else? John. My own brother. He won't see me."

"Won't see you?" George frowned.

"He's too busy. Or he's out of town. Always busy, or out

of town. He's never been this busy before. Even Natasha doesn't seem to know what he's doing. But he's too busy to see me. Me! George Hayman, Jr. I own the *American People* newspaper. I snap my fingers and I get things done. And I'm being given the runaround like any clerk. By God—!"

It occurred to George that his son was closer to a nervous breakdown than he had suspected. He turned his head in some relief as the front door banged, and they all gazed at Felicity, framed in the living-room doorway, face composed but remote as she looked from one to the other.

"Hello, George," she said. "Any news of Diana?"

"No," George junior said. "No news at all."

"Poor thing," Felicity remarked. "She's probably in a cell somewhere, just like Gregory." She left the doorway and climbed the stairs.

George stared at his father. "If I thought for one moment—"

"Well, don't," George said. "That's too farfetched even for Ivan Nej. And he isn't in power anymore. The Soviets are becoming civilized, son. You just have to accept that."

"You were saying that just before the purges began in 1935," George junior pointed out. "If they're so civilized, how come they won't give me a visa to go see for myself?"

"Well, maybe they don't want a big-time American publisher nosing around."

"Yeah? How come the private detective I tried to send over there was denied a visa too? I think Felicity just may be right. What's the quote? Out of the mouths of babes . . . ? Well, if those goddamned reds have hurt Diana . . . You say they don't want a big-time publisher nosing around? By God, they are going to get the biggest anti-Soviet campaign in history thrown at them. Starting right now." He got up. "I'll see you."

"Hold it just one moment," George said. "Do you seriously think something like that is going to help Diana? Do you think such a campaign can do anything but harm, with an election coming up fast? George, I hate to pull rank on you . . ."

George junior sighed. "Oh, sure, I know. I have to have a sense of responsibility, and the *People* has to have a sense of responsibility too. But for God's sake, Dad, my daughter— She could be dead in a ditch someplace, and we don't even *know.*"

"Yes." George got up also and freshened their drinks. "You

say you think John knows something? That's not just because he was in London with her when this thing started?"

"No, it's not," George junior said. "I'm not imagining the fact that he *is* avoiding me. And the state department is certainly giving me the cold shoulder, and—"

"Where's the connection? John doesn't work for the government." George bit his lip, aware that he had spoken a trifle too brusquely. The subterfuge John, and therefore he, too, had been forced to practice for the past seven years had always bothered him, mainly because he had known it couldn't work forever.

But George junior apparently suspected nothing. "Okay," he agreed. "But he *was* acting for them when he went to London, right? He was going to feel out what Uncle Peter was up to, or something like that. For the state department. Don't look at me like that. It was as plain as the nose on your face. I think something happened, or was happening, or is happening, which is linked to the state department, to Uncle Peter's disappearance, and to Diana's disappearance. And I think John knows what it is."

"If anything had happened to Diana, anything serious, and John knew of it," Ilona declared, "he would have told us, no matter whom he was working for."

"I know that," George junior conceded. "That is the only thought that's kept me sane. But I still want to know what's happened to my daughter."

"Exactly," his father agreed. "Leave it to me. I'll talk with John. He won't avoid *me*."

They sat together in a quiet corner of the country club bar, and watched the golfers at work. "You have to understand," George Hayman explained, stirring his martini, "that George is feeling pretty desperate. And Elizabeth is becoming ill over this. After all, Diana is their only child. She's also the heiress to the whole shebang, you know. If anything has happened to her . . . Now, Ilona and I both feel that it *is* just an elopement, or I wouldn't be sitting here talking to you. We feel it's most likely that Diana and this husband of hers are shacked up somewhere in Germany, or maybe Scandinavia. Buying a ticket for Moscow is the simplest thing in the world; getting there is next to impossible. I mean, how could they have obtained their visas so quickly? Then it would have been even simpler for them to leave the train at any one of several stations, and take another one going in another direction. But George can't accept this solution, mainly because of the fact that we can't locate Peter either, and that Janice Corliss apparently told George and Elizabeth that Robert Loung is connected with Peter's organization. Frankly, if I thought that Diana had somehow got herself mixed up in Peter's harebrained schemes, I'd be having hysterics myself."

John Hayman gazed at his stepfather. "So?"

"Well . . . hell, John, I don't want to interfere with your job in any way. But it just so happens that I *know* what you really do. And you know that. So I'm pretty sure that your trip to Europe *was* for the FBI, and that if you went to see Peter you were, in fact, working. Now that George junior has got that idea as well, without realizing how close he is to the truth . . . I just have to *know,* if Diana is in any way connected with Peter, and if there *is* something sinister about her disappearance."

John's shoulders sagged. "Dad, I don't work for the FBI anymore."

George's brows drew together. "You expect me to believe that?"

"It happens to be the truth."

George's frown deepened. He had known John since he was an infant, and he could tell he was speaking the truth. But not all of it. "So who *do* you work for? You're still with that 'advertising agency'?"

"Sure."

"So you're still working for the government."

"Sure."

"But not the FBI," George said thoughtfully. "Something so secret you can't even tell me. Okay. I can't push that one any further. But John, you have to tell me if you know anything, anything at all, about what has happened to Diana."

John continued to meet his gaze. "I don't know anything at all about what has happened to Diana," he said. "As you say, she's probably honeymooning, and will come back when she's good and ready."

But this time, George knew his stepson was lying.

Sunday lunch at Cold Spring Harbor. A lonely Sunday lunch. Two elderly people, each sitting at an end of a vast dining table, gazing at each other. No sound, but the occasional rattle of cutlery from the kitchen.

There had been occasions like this before, for each of them; in the recognition of that fact lay the great solace of age and experience. The great weakness of age and experience was the dwindling certainty of the future. Both George and Ilona could remember lunching with Ilona's parents in the huge, airy house in Port Arthur, listening to the Japanese shells exploding closer and closer to the doomed Russian city. But they had been young enough to be sure of their personal immortality. George could remember the dreadful loneliness that had followed their enforced separation, the necessity to eat and sleep and shave and go through the motions of living, when he had not known if he would ever see her again—but he was only twenty-eight then. And although she had undoubtedly felt the same, she was only nineteen. Words such as "ever," or even more, "never," had encompassed an enormous amount of time, time they had had to spare.

They had been separated and alone during the First World War, and again during the Second. They had known the tragedy of Rachel Borodin's death and then of Tattie's murder, and more recently they had watched, helplessly, the growing tragedy of Felicity's involvement with Gregory Nej. But always, around them, had been the swelling happiness of their children, and then their children's children. And that happiness had been typified by the Sunday lunches at this very table. Suddenly, a thing of the past.

"I know how she feels," Ilona said. "If I had managed to get away that night from Starogan, and ride to Sevastopol, and join you . . . Children do these things, George."

He smiled at her. "You mean you now know that you would have been making a mistake?"

She blew him a kiss. "I mean I would have done it—I *tried* to do it!—without considering what it might mean to my mother. But the fact is, I would have done it even if I *had* known the grief it would cause. Because I was in love. No doubt Diana is in love with her Mr. Loung."

"And would you not have written your mother, just as soon as it was safe to do so?" George asked.

Ilona sighed. "Yes. Yes . . . but perhaps it is not yet safe for Diana to write Elizabeth."

"Five weeks?"

She sighed again. "You think something *has* happened to her?"

It was George's turn to sigh. "I don't know. I honestly and truly don't know, my love. Common sense tells me nothing *can* have happened, that she's just a lovely young girl with an urge to live. But at the same time . . . If only we could locate Peter. If only we could find some trace of where she's gone. Of *anything*."

"But there is something else bothering you."

George finished his wine. He had never been able to keep any secrets from this woman. "Yes. But . . ."

"Something to do with John?"

"I was going to say, I'd be grateful if you didn't ask."

Ilona gazed at him. "I've known for a long time there was something between you and John," she said. "Some secret deal. You know, I loved to think of it. The private looks you exchange, the total intimacy . . . when I think that he isn't even your son, that—" She sat very straight. "George! What about Michael?"

"What do you mean?"

"Well, what about asking Michael to help? George junior thinks that Diana may in fact have gone to Russia, and gotten into some trouble there. Michael would be able to find out for us."

"Um."

"George, this is no time for pride."

"I have none, where Diana is concerned. Believe me. But . . . I don't think we can ever forget that Michael is a Soviet commissar first, and our friend second. Suppose—just suppose—that Diana *has* in some way become associated with Peter and his crazy schemes. It's not impossible, you know. If we ask Michael to find her, it could put her in real danger."

Ilona bit her lip. "I never thought of that."

"We just have to be patient, I guess. And trust in . . . well, in Providence, maybe . . ." He frowned as a car's wheels scraped on the gravel outside. "Callers?"

Ilona got up, listened to Redmond, the butler, talking with someone, and faced the door as the big Irishman opened it. Through the window she could see the black Buick with the diplomatic corps license plates waiting by the steps.

"Excuse me, Mr. Hayman, Mrs. Hayman," Redmond said.

"But there is a Russian gentleman to see you, a Mr. Michael Nej. He claims to be an ambassador, or something. I showed him into the living room."

Michael Nej was accompanied by his wife and his daughter, both of whom the Haymans knew well. Catherine Nej was in her early fifties, her heavy dark hair and equally heavy features betraying her Tartar blood as explicitly as when George and Ilona had first encountered her amid the battered ruins of Sevastopol, some thirty years before. Nona took after her mother; both women, with their high cheekbones, dark coloring, and somewhat docile eyes presented a strong contrast to Michael's fairness, and their stolid manner contrasted, too, with his impression of quickness. But George, who had lived with this family during the terrible winter of 1941–42 when the Germans had been at the gates of Leningrad, knew that they both possessed in full measure the patient, determined courage of the average Russian, just as they also possessed the typical Russian reverence for authority, evidenced by the way they stood back to allow their husband and father, who also happened to be a senior commissar, to be greeted first.

"Michael!" Ilona cried. "How good of you to stop by. Is this a farewell visit?"

"Well . . ." Michael flushed. "For Catherine and myself, certainly. Nona is remaining in your country to study."

"How marvelous!" Ilona said. "You must be sure to visit with us whenever you're in New York. Catherine, how lovely to see you. And you're looking so well."

George could only marvel at the way his wife could turn on the charm, even after everything that had happened, even knowing that Felicity was at this moment visiting the Russian spy, this man's nephew, who had completed the ruin of her life. And even with the various dreadful fates which could have overtaken Diana, plucking at her heartstrings.

Thus he must do the same. He shook hands. "Good to see you, Michael. We knew you were going back, but not so soon." He had heard about Michael's departure for Moscow in the spring, and since his return to New York there had been considerable speculation about whether he would stay; only recently had come the announcement of a permanent move back to Moscow.

"I'm leaving on tonight's flight."

George raised his eyebrows. "I assume this is a promotion?"

"And not a sentence of exile to Siberia? It is a promotion, George. Joseph needs me in Moscow."

"Congratulations. Redmond, I think we'll have champagne cocktails."

"At three in the afternoon?" Michael remarked. "I think tea would be better."

"Champagne can be drunk at any hour of the night or day," George pointed out. "And we're not big on tea. Cocktails, Redmond."

Redmond gravely inclined his head, and withdrew.

"Besides, we were just talking about you," Ilona told Michael.

"About me?"

"Well . . ." She looked at George.

"I think Michael should tell us why he called," George said.

"Well . . . I wanted to say good-bye, of course," Michael said. "But I also had to see you before I left, George. Something has come up."

Ilona turned her head sharply.

"To do with us?" George asked softly.

"Indirectly."

"Would you like to see me alone?"

Michael hesitated. "No," he said at last. "I think what I have to say may be of interest to Ilona as well."

"Oh," Ilona said. "Well . . ." She gazed at George. "I suggest we all sit down and listen. Ah, Redmond, thank you." She took a glass of champagne, seated herself, and patted the cushions beside her for Nona to join her.

"It really is, well . . . the most terrible thing," Michael said, remaining standing. "But fortunately, circumstances, well . . . may permit a happy ending."

"I sincerely hope so," George agreed. "Tell us."

"You will perhaps have heard," Michael said, "that Premier Stalin was gravely ill last winter?"

"He had a heart attack," George said.

"He was poisoned."

"What?" George sat up.

"Unsuccessfully, of course. He has a very strong constitution. But he *was* poisoned, George. I have to tell you that

Joseph suspected this from the beginning. That was why I was summoned back in March, as you may remember. He was very concerned."

"That would be putting it mildly, I suspect," George said, his thoughts tumbling. What on earth did an attempted assassination of Stalin have to do with him? Him, of all people. Michael had not asked him to treat anything that was said in confidence, so he must know this would be headline news in the *People* tomorrow morning.

"Well," Michael said, "we naturally had to get to the bottom of it. But it was a difficult task. Several . . . avenues were explored. But only recently has the truth become known. I must say, this is a case where Ivan must be given the highest credit."

"Ivan?" George cried.

"Joseph had him recalled from Tomsk to head the investigation," Michael explained. "There is no one better."

"But . . . the man is a murderer," George protested.

"I know. I do not condone anything he has done, believe me, George. But this was an affair of national security, and as I have said, there is none better."

"And Ivan has solved this assassination attempt?" Ilona asked.

"Yes. It is quite terrible. You will hardly credit it, but there is a Jewish conspiracy."

"A Jewish conspiracy?" George cried. "Oh, come now, Michael!"

Michael shook his head. "I know you are a Zionist supporter, George. But these are dangerous people. They always have been."

"They are also very pragmatic. Tell me what they could possibly hope to gain by bumping off Stalin, except a whole bucketful of trouble."

"I do not know what they hoped to gain, George. I only know the facts. But George, that is not the worst of it. The plot was masterminded by Judith."

"By—" George's jaw dropped, and he looked at his wife.

She met his glance for a moment, then looked at Catherine Nej, who appeared embarrassed; she was well aware of the curious, intimate, almost incestuous relationship shared by these people, including her own husband, years before she had ever come into their lives.

"Do you suggest *that* is impossible?" Michael demanded.

"God knows I have always loved that woman, but you know that she's a born conspirator, George. There was the Stolypin assassination—"

"She always denied any implication in that," George pointed out. "*You* implicated her by running to her for shelter."

"Do you not suppose I had reason? Then what about the Rasputin assassination? She has never denied being implicated in *that*. And since then, all her machinations on behalf of the Zionists—"

"I'm sorry, Michael," George said, "but I have to dismiss all that as a load of crap."

"That may be," Michael said. "But the fact is that she is in Moscow under arrest—"

"Judith?" Ilona cried.

"You have arrested Judith Stein?" George shouted. "Judith is in Ivan's hands?"

"She is in Lubianka, yes. I am assured that she has not been harmed, and that she will not be subjected to any serious interrogation. However, she is guilty of a very grave crime, George."

"That is nonsense, Michael, and you know it," George insisted. "And let me tell you something. If Ivan has been given some alleged conspiracy to nail and thinks the short answer is to kidnap Judith—well, all hell is going to break loose. I'm surprised it hasn't already."

"Perhaps you will stop to think *why* it hasn't," Michael said quietly.

George frowned at him.

"Judith has now been held in Lubianka for several days, after being taken from her Rome hotel—"

"You *admit* this?"

"To you. I will deny it to anyone else. But the fact is that although Tel Aviv must be aware that she has disappeared, the story has not been released. Think about that, George. But even more important, we possess proof positive that the plot not only exists, but that Judith is very deeply involved."

"Proof," George sneered, angrily. "Some pseudo-confession—"

"George," Michael interrupted, and looked at Ilona. "Ilona. What I have to say will come as a great shock to you. It came as a great shock to me. I said that Ivan was called to take charge of the investigation. This is true. But he did not get to the root of the matter. Given time, he might well have done so. However, he was saved the time, by the receipt of information from a source which, having regard to past history, must be considered impeccable."

"Oh, yes?"

"The information, George, was supplied to the KGB by Peter Borodin himself," Michael said.

George and Ilona stared at him blankly, and then at each other.

"Peter?" Ilona asked at last. "You expect us to believe that Peter would tell Ivan of an impending Jewish assassination plot directed at Stalin?"

"That is correct."

"That is the most absurd thing I have ever heard," George declared.

"I agree it is astonishing, on the surface. But it has happened. And can even be explained. Peter himself has explained it. He admits he has spent his entire life fighting the Soviet concept of peace and social justice. He admits that he has failed. Now that he knows his life is drawing to a close, he wishes to make his peace with the Motherland, to return there to die. Well, he knew he would not exactly be welcome. But his network of agents—and even you will have to admit that he *does* employ a vast network of agents, George—had turned up this plot, and so he offered it to us in return for political asylum in Russia."

"Peter?" Ilona echoed. "My brother Peter wishes to return to Russia?"

"He is there now."

"Oh, my God!"

"And Peter has accused *Judith* of being implicated in this plot?" George asked.

"To her face."

"Jesus Christ! Really . . . the man is mad. You must know that, Michael. Stark, raving mad."

Michael shrugged. "He does not appear mad to our people."

"And what was Judith's reaction to this accusation?" George went on.

"She denied it, of course. She became quite angry, I understand. But then, she would deny it, would she not? Her denials will accomplish very little. Arrests are now being made, and out of those will certainly come enough confessions to implicate her as completely as Peter claims."

"You mean that by the time Ivan gets through with them, the poor wretches will confess to anything he tells them to. My God! I suppose, if he's back in the saddle, Anna Ragosina is too."

"Comrade Ragosina has also been rehabilitated, yes," Michael admitted. "And is undoubtedly assisting in the investigation. I do not care to know too much about their methods, because I do not approve of them, as you know. But they are certainly effective. Judith's guilt *will* be substantiated, George."

George gazed at him. "So why are you telling me all this?"

"Don't you care about Judith?"

"Of course I care about Judith," George snapped. "And I am going to move heaven and earth to get her out of there, Michael. You can take my word for it. My newspapers are going to launch an anti-Soviet campaign the likes of which you won't even have dreamed of in your worst nightmare. By God, they are! And you can tell both Ivan and Joe Stalin just that."

"I have come here to save you that bother," Michael said. "I am here to save a great deal of international fuss, and to save Judith as well."

George's brows slowly drew together.

"I wish to save her too, you see," Michael said gently. "So, believe it or not, does Ivan, if only for the sake of peace. And so does Joseph Vissarionovich. Yet she is guilty, and she must stand trial. At that trial she will almost certainly be convicted of a crime which carries the death sentence. Do you wish that to happen?"

"You are doing the talking," George said.

"Well . . . she *will* have to stand trial, of course. But this can be expedited. I imagine the whole thing can be completed by Christmas. Once she has been convicted, it is our wish that she be saved from the firing squad. This can be done, George, if your people are amenable to reason. More amenable than they have been in the past."

George gazed at him, comprehending. "You want Gregory back," he said.

"Yes," Michael agreed. "That is what we want, George."

George snorted. "I really dislike being taken for such a fool, Michael."

Michael raised his eyebrows.

"What you have been saying is the most bare-faced attempt at blackmail I have ever heard. Jewish plot indeed!"

Michael felt inside his breast pocket, took out a photograph, and gave it to George without a word. George studied it, while his brain continued to teem. But the photograph, taken inside an office, was certainly of Peter Borodin, Judith Petrova, and Ivan Nej, all talking together, and very obviously neither Peter nor Judith was aware it was being taken. Indeed, from the expression on Judith's face, she was shouting something at the moment the shutter had closed. Nor, no matter how closely he studied the print, could George detect any sign of superimposing or faking in any way.

"I still don't believe there's a plot," he said, somewhat lamely.

Michael shrugged. "You have a happy ability to believe whatever you wish, and to disbelieve whatever you wish, George. I can assure you that there *is* a plot, that Judith is going to stand trial, and that she is going to be condemned to death. And that only you can save her life."

"Me? I don't run the United States government."

"Nevertheless, you are an important man. You own a powerful newspaper. You can talk to the right people. I beg you, George, to use your influence. You will know that your government has not been amenable to reason over Gregory in the past. I would beg you to make them see reason now."

"The United States government has *never* been amenable to blackmail, Michael."

"I would ask you not to consider the situation in those terms, George. We of the Soviet Union prefer to consider ourselves as realists, and we are just as pragmatic as the Israelis. It is the result which matters, not the sometimes circuitous path of arriving at that result. Judith's life is in danger. Gregory's life is being squandered in prison. Both of those are needless tragedies. And now they can both be avoided, if you will but forget for an instant your peculiar concept of ethics."

George continued to glare at him, and Ilona hastily rang the bell for Redmond. "I think we should all have another cocktail," she said. "And then, perhaps we can talk about something *you* may be able to do for *us,* Michael."

"Anything at all, Ilona," he promised.

"Forget it," George said.

"But George—" Ilona protested.

"Forget it," George repeated. "Let's just have another cocktail, and talk about something else."

Ilona raised her eyebrows, but accepted his decision, until the Nejs had left, after an uncomfortable further half-hour. "I don't understand," she said, when the front door had closed. "If *he* wants *your* help—"

"He doesn't want my help," George told her. "He has just presented me with a fait accompli and an ultimatum. I take it or I leave it. And I *did* think he was our friend. But I suppose that at bottom he's just as big a thug as any of them. When I think . . . for God's sake, he and Judith lived together as man and wife for two *years*."

Ilona did not look impressed. No doubt, George thought, she was remembering that Michael had been *her* lover, and had fathered John, long before that, that Michael had only turned to Judith because *she* was no longer available.

Equally, perhaps, she was remembering that Judith had interfered in *their* lives, very nearly disastrously, even if quite without meaning to. Judith Stein *had* attracted trouble throughout her life, because of her peculiar combination of beauty and intensity.

"I still think he would have helped us trace Diana," Ilona said.

"Michael doesn't know anything about Diana, my darling. If the Soviets had her, don't you think she'd be part of the deal? Hell, she'd *be* the deal. They wouldn't need Judith at all."

"But Peter has gone to Russia, and George junior thinks that Diana may also have gone to Russia—"

"That's exactly it," George said. "She *may* have gone to Russia. But the Soviets apparently don't know that. We may have to play that card, in time, but I'm sure as hell going to keep it up my sleeve for a day or two yet."

"But George, what *are* you going to do?"

George smiled at her. "Go to Washington. What else can I do?"

Chapter 10

IT WAS THREE YEARS SINCE GEORGE HAD BEEN INSIDE THE Oval Office. Once, in the days of Hoover and Roosevelt, he had visited here more frequently. Although George was a dedicated Republican, even Roosevelt had found his international stature, and more important, his personal relationships with the main Soviet leaders, too valuable to be neglected—thus his brief unofficial ambassadorship to Russia in 1941, and those unforgettable days in Leningrad, when he had stood shoulder to shoulder with Michael Nej against the gray torrent of Nazi ambition.

But even then they had understood their alliance was a matter of temporary expediency—although they had hoped their friendship would endure. The murder of Tattie, and Gregory Nej's treachery, had changed that. George had been happy to accept another roving ambassadorship from Harry Truman, to find out what was really happening behind the Iron Curtain in the days immediately following the end of the war. But since Gregory's arrest he had stepped down from the international scene, partly because he had been hoodwinked by the boy's personality and charm, which had left him feeling utterly guilty over what had happened. Yet Truman was happy to see him, and with his secretary of state, Dean Acheson, to listen to him with courteous patience.

When George had finished, however, the president sat up

and placed his elbows on his desk with his fingertips resting against each other in front of his face, a familiar gesture that George knew and feared. "You realize that is pure blackmail, George."

"I do, Mr. President. I told Nej so."

"It's so barefaced," Truman went on, "I'm surprised they have the nerve to try it at all. This woman Stein, or Petrov, or whatever she now calls herself, isn't even a United States citizen. Why didn't the Soviets at least go to Tel Aviv first?"

George waited.

Truman cleared his throat. "I know she's an old friend of yours, George, but I have to tell you that this government is not going to be blackmailed by anybody, at any time. Least of all by the Soviets, and least of all at this time. In another couple of months I am leaving this office for good."

"And you figure that to exchange Gregory Nej right now would be to hang a millstone around Adlai Stevenson's neck, is that it?"

Truman gave one of his rare, quick smiles. "I guess Adlai has a millstone around his neck already, George. It's called Dwight Eisenhower. And I thought you knew me better than to think I'd play politics with international affairs. I couldn't hand a concession like that to either of them. What would happen the next time we nail a Russian spy? They'd just look around the world until they found someone who might be interesting to us, and they'd snatch him, or her, and they'd say, Now let's talk. We don't do business that way, and by God, we're going to show the rest of the world that they can't either. Not with us, anyway."

"I should remind you, sir, that the Soviets are perfectly capable of carrying out their threat and putting Mrs. Petrov against a wall," George said.

"That wouldn't do their international reputation any good, Mr. Hayman," Acheson said. "I would guess they're bluffing. After all, it isn't as if this Gregory Nej was of any real importance to them."

"That's where you're wrong," George said. "That's where I think our handling of the Soviets has always been wrong. We expect to deal with the *office* in foreign affairs—the office of the president, or of the prime minister—because we expect foreigners to deal with *this* office when they come to us. As you just said, Mr. President, in a couple of months time you are leaving this office once and for all, without any looking back over your shoulder. So I'm not talking to Harry S Truman. I'm talking to the president of the United States, and again, as you have just said, the reason you can't exchange Gregory—one reason—is that the president of the United States, whether it's you or Stevenson or Eisenhower, can't be seen to be blackmailed. Equally, when we're talking to Prime Minister Churchill we're talking to the Prime Minister, not the man. And the same goes for almost everywhere else in Western Europe. That just isn't so in Russia, though, or anywhere in Asia, for that matter. The man *isn't* the office over there. The office is the man. It's no use addressing yourself to 'the premier of the USSR.' You're dealing with Joe Stalin, because Joe Stalin is going to remain in office until he dies or is overthrown. Therefore he isn't working for the state, for the continuity of his office in the hands of a successor. He is working for Joe Stalin. And for Joe Stalin's friends and accomplices—and they are accomplices, you know. In mass murder. Ivan Nej happens to be one of the closest of those friends, which is why *he* has gotten away with murder, mass and individual, time and again. These men didn't get where they are by kissing babies and shaking hands with their parents. They reached the top by shooting people, both parents and babies. So now that they're in charge they don't see life in terms of opinion polls; they see it as them or us. And Gregory Nej happens to be one of them, because he's Ivan's son. Ivan wants him back, and thus Joe wants him back. And in getting him back, they're not going to give a damn about world opinion."

Truman gazed at him for several seconds. Then he said, "Quite a speech, George. And quite some thinking, too. Maybe you're right. I tell you what. You let us think about it." He pointed his finger in a warning: "No promises. It's not our baby. But we'll consider the situation from every possible angle. I can't offer you more than that."

"Mr. President," Allen Dulles said, "you've met John Hayman."

"I have." Harry Truman shook hands. "You have to forgive me, Hayman, if I sometimes feel there are just too many people with your name in this world of ours. Sit down. I've read your report. Mr. Dulles thinks this uncle of yours means what he says."

John carefully lowered himself into a chair, sitting almost at attention. "Yes, sir."

"Well, we didn't take it too seriously when you first put it forward, because we didn't see how a man like Peter Borodin was ever going to get inside Russia. Now he seems to have gone and done it. And therefore you think this Jewish plot is all a fabrication, to enable him to get close to Stalin?"

"To gain him admittance in the first place, sir. But Stalin is certainly his goal."

Truman stroked his chin, gazing at John. "And what happens if he reaches that goal?"

"I don't know, sir. Nobody knows. But I do know that while Stalin may be one of the most brutal leaders on earth, he doesn't want war with anyone right now. Oh, he'll push and he'll prod. He'll even take overt action, as in Berlin, if he thinks it's worth the risk. But he won't go as far as shooting. He showed that in Berlin, too. I couldn't make that estimate of his successor, because I don't know who that may be."

"Isn't there at least a chance such a successor could be your own father?"

"No, sir, I don't think so. Michael Nej is too old, and he is personally unambitious. Besides, he has lived in Stalin's shadow for too long."

"Too bad. It would be an interesting situation, him over there and you over here." Truman leaned back in his chair and glanced at Dulles. "So you both think that such an assassination would not be in the best interests of this country."

"We do, Mr. President," Dulles said.

"So what do you recommend? That we blow the whole thing? Borodin would be shot, of course. Assuming they even believe us."

"They won't believe us," Dulles said. "This business is littered with imponderables. But it is our opinion that we should get Borodin out of there, as peacefully and as rapidly as possible. I don't know the truth about this so-called Jewish plot. My information is that there *was* an attempt on Stalin's life last winter. The Russian Jews could have been involved, and Borodin's outfit may have learned of it—his people may even have been involved, because we know that several of his agents are Jews. But either way, I'd say that is an internal Russian matter. On the other hand, we know Judith Petrov is innocent of involvement, and we want Peter Borodin out of there before he starts something. I would say that is most definitely in the interests of the United States."

"So we yield to blackmail."

Dulles smiled. "Let's say we bend a little, sir. And we do a little blackmailing of our own. Let them have Gregory Nej. In exchange for Judith Petrov *and* Peter Borodin."

"You think they'll go for that? Isn't he the chief witness?"

"If we are right in all our assessments, Mr. President, they are more interested in Gregory Nej than in any plots. They can always secure confessions. They're pretty good at that. If they've nabbed Judith Petrov simply to make an exchange, and if George Hayman is right about how badly they want young Nej—I think he *is* right—they may be happy to see the last of Peter Borodin as well."

"Did you talk to the Israelis about this?"

"No, sir. And I don't mean to until it's done. They're going wild over there ever since the story broke. They wanted it kept hushed up at least until they had exhausted every possibility of getting Mrs. Petrov out of Russia quietly, which does make you think that there *could* be some involvement. The important thing is, they don't know *we've* been approached. Nobody knows we've been approached. It could be quite a coup for you, Mr. President, if it were to come out that you had stepped in and offered Gregory Nej in exchange."

Truman grinned. "I thought you voted Republican."

"When I'm off duty," Dulles explained.

Truman nodded. "So stay *on* duty, Allen. Hayman, we'll arrange the exchange. You can tell your stepfather. But it's confidential until it happens. Not a word in a newspaper. Got me?"

They lunched at Dulles's club. "I have to tell you that I'm proud of you," Dulles said, "for not bringing up the subject of your niece."

"I didn't think it would help."

"I think it would have damn well hindered. But it must have been a temptation. So what's new?"

"Not a damned thing."

Dulles studied his protégé. "You don't think you could be barking up the wrong tree?"

"If I thought that, Mr. Dulles, I'd be out there singing in the rain."

"You're really fond of this girl?"

"Sure I am. But it's not just that. It's not just that she's beautiful and charming and just plain nice. It's that she's the lynchpin holding my family together. I don't want to start thinking about what happens if she's gone for good. I can see some of the evidence of it. Her mother's having a nervous breakdown. George junior is totally uninterested in anything, even the election, which could bring the first Republican president in twenty years. Mother and George visibly aging every day—and they don't have that much room left to maneuver."

"Still, now you have something good to tell them."

"Sure. And I'm grateful. But Judith is a friend. Even Uncle Peter isn't close anymore—the whole family regards him as a dangerous lunatic."

"Yeah." Dulles sighed. "Well, I stand by my offer. If this female Dracula does reply, you have carte blanche, so long as you don't openly involve the firm."

"And if she doesn't?"

"It sure as hell won't mean your niece is in a Lubianka cell, John. Quite the reverse in my opinion. Think about this. With all this talk of exchanging going on, and with the reds knowing it's your family they have to deal with, because of Gregory . . . if Anna Ragosina and Ivan Nej had your Diana, wouldn't they be shouting it from the hilltops?"

"Mr. Dulles," John said, "I don't know a hell of a lot about Ivan Nej, other than that I'd like one day to sight him down the barrel of a Magnum. Gregory is his son, so maybe he has feelings. But I can tell you this: Anna doesn't give a damn *what* happens to Gregory Nej, and she doesn't ever do the obvious, or even the normal thing. My instincts tell me she's got Diana. I also know she's got my note. If both those are true, and she's not replying, and Diana hasn't been thrown into this deal, then Anna is following some plan of her own." He shrugged. "Either way, we'll just have to be patient, and when the time comes, be as tough as she is, until we get Diana back."

"Ruth?" George Hayman shouted into the telephone. "Ruth? . . . God almighty, what a line! Are you there, Ruth?"

He glared over the receiver at John, who was frowning. He hadn't been able to stop his stepfather from making this call, and he trusted him implicitly, but he knew that George could become overexcited. "What time is it in Israel?" George asked him.

"Ah . . . eleven in the morning here . . . maybe six in the evening? Seven?"

"They must be awake. Ruth? Hi! Is that you?" His face broke into a smile. "Sure, it's me, George. Home. I don't travel much anymore. Ruth, how're things?"

His face grew somber as he listened. "Yeah," he said. "Yeah. I'm with you there. Yeah. How's Boris bearing up? Yeah. He's tough. Ruth, listen to me. Can you hear me? Well, listen. We're doing all we can over here. The state department is helping. Even the president is helping. The president. Yes, that's what I said, the president. And Ruth, it's going to work out. I can't tell you how, or when. Judith may have to stand trial in Russia. She *will* have to stand trial. No . . . Ruth, listen to me, she's not going to come to any harm. I give you my word. She will have to stand trial, and she may even be convicted, but we're going to get her out before she comes to any harm. Listen to me, Ruth. It's going to be all right. I've given you my word . . . No. Under no circumstances. You tell Nigel to stay right where he belongs, next to you and the kids. There is no point in his trying to be a hero. This simply isn't his league, and we're going to look after things from this end. Just sit tight, and trust us over here, Ruth. It's going to be all right. Yeah. She sends you hers, too. It's going to be all right, Ruth. It's going to be all right."

He replaced the receiver and wiped his brow with his handkerchief. "I don't think I did so well," he said. "When I said she'd have to stand trial, Ruth nearly jumped straight through the telephone. They're close, you know. Judith may only be her aunt, but they're as close as mother and daughter, especially after surviving Ravensbrück together."

"You need a drink," Ilona said. "I guess we all do." She waved Redmond forward with his jug of punch.

"I think I got them just in time," George said, taking a deep gulp of the liquid. "Nigel was planning to set off on some kind of singlehanded invasion of the Soviet Union. She says the government in Tel Aviv doesn't seem able to help, simply because the Soviets won't talk to them. Won't even admit or deny that the rumors in the papers are true."

"Still, as you told her, it *is* going to be all right." Ilona held his hand, waiting for his agitation to subside. If she could regard Michael's affair with Judith with some skepticism, knowing it for what it was—a simple bargain for survival on the woman's part—she never could forget that Judith had made *her* husband happy at a crucial period of his life, and contrary to George's suspicions, she had long forgiven the woman with whom she had shared so much. Now she gazed above his head at John. "It *is* going to be all right?"

"We hope so."

"It would be so wonderful," Natasha said. John's wife was thinking of the family she had come to regard as her own; she had only met Judith Stein once, and she had never met Peter Borodin.

"What I can't understand," Ilona said thoughtfully, "is why the state department keeps coming to you, John. If Truman intended to allow the exchange, why didn't he just tell George there and then?"

"Because he didn't know whether or not he could allow the exchange then," George said hastily. "And they came back through John because John was involved with Peter in the beginning, and did that little job for them last summer. They wanted to know if Peter would be willing to be brought out. Isn't that so, John?"

"Yes," John said. "That's about it, Mother."

But he knew Ilona wasn't convinced, and soon after pleaded a headache as an excuse for going home early.

"You don't know what a difference it will make to her, if everything goes as we hope," George said, walking down the stairs with him while Natasha and the children received their farewell hugs from Ilona. "It's not just helping Judith . . . We both can't help feeling that with Gregory back in Russia, Felicity may just come to her senses. If only we could hear something positive about Diana, now . . ." He glanced at his stepson.

"I wish that too," John said.

"But she's not a part of this game? Hell, John, you can tell me that."

John sighed. "As far as we *know* she's not a part of this game, Dad."

"But *you* feel she's involved? You know that George junior is planning to go over there as soon as the election is over?"

"To Russia?"

"No. They won't give him a visa, although he keeps applying. No, what he means to do is take the train from Paris, the same Moscow train that Diana took, and stop at every station, armed with photographs of Diana. Then catch the next Moscow train through, and so on."

"Hasn't he had detectives doing that for the past couple of months?" John said.

George shrugged. "He feels they may have missed something. Anyway, none of them have been allowed past West Berlin."

"And George thinks he will be? Without a visa?"

"He's going to try. And he'll make one hell of a stink if they turn him back."

"It's not really what the president of Hayman Newspapers Incorporated is best suited for. What will the stockholders think about it all?"

"God knows. I'm coming out of retirement to hold the fort until he gets back. I can't stop him, John. He won't be the same until he's been and seen for himself, and tried for himself. He says it may take six months. Okay, so it takes six months. Just so long as he turns something up. It sure would be good if you could turn something up first."

"If we do, Dad, you'll be the first to know," John promised. Which was a lie, he knew. His hands were tight on the wheel as he drove back, Natasha silent beside him. She was used to his moods, and if they had been more intense than usual recently, she was prepared to accept that too. She was a Hayman now, and Diana's disappearance had affected her no less than anyone else.

And him, most of all? Because of what he suspected, and feared? He had never properly put what he suspected into words, even for himself. But everything pointed to the same thing. Diana had been hooked into joining Peter's organization—and only as a safeguard for Peter himself rather than for any skill she might possess. So if Peter had left for Russia to further his assassination plans, immediately after she had left for Russia on her honeymoon, then she was almost certainly there as well, with her so-called husband—John could not believe there was any genuine love between them, at least on Loung's part. And they were awaiting the opportunity to put a bullet into Stalin. It was difficult to believe that a girl like Diana could ever contemplate murdering anybody, but he had been trained to accept facts, just as Anna Ragosina and Ivan Nej and the KGB did. There was no way Peter Borodin could have fooled Anna. There was no way she would not be aware of everything he was doing, and every agent he had within Russia. Therefore she either already held Diana and was not talking about it for some reason of her own—and that was a pretty horrible thought—or she knew where Diana was, and was capable of picking her up whenever she chose. So he had blundered in, acting on that instinctive certainty, and offered . . . what? He had had some vague idea that it might be Gregory Nej they wanted . . . and he had been as innocent as everyone else in supposing the Russians did not already have *that* one all worked out.

So what could he offer now, that Anna might possibly wish? He knew of only one thing—himself. Anna had never forgiven him for destroying her American network, or even for threatening to burn her, that night in Washington. So, was he prepared to commit suicide for the sake of his niece? Or at least accept exile in his mother country? He had been born there, and his father was returning there to complete his life's work. To a society John personally abhorred. Perhaps he *was* prepared to risk all that, for the family that had given him so much even though he did not actually belong to it. And with the confidence that his father would never let Anna actually kill him.

But what would Natasha say to that? She had fled Russia to be with him, and because she hated the Soviet ruthlessness, which had included the murder of her parents by the KGB, even more than he did. What would she feel about the two very American children now wrestling in the back seat? How could he possibly justify taking *them* to Russia?

But how could he condemn Diana to a living death, either?

As if it mattered. Anna had not even bothered to reply. She was not interested in *anything* he had to offer.

Or else the girl was already dead.

The cell door opened. "You have a visitor," the guard said. "Let's go."

Gregory Nej sat up in surprise and looked at the calendar on his wall. Apart from a framed photograph of Felicity Hayman, it was the only decoration to be seen.

"Today is not visiting day," he protested, and stroked his chin. He hadn't even shaved.

The guard grinned. "I don't think this guy will mind."

He was not an unfriendly man. None of the guards had ever been unfriendly, much to Gregory's surprise. He had accepted, when sentenced, that he must look forward to nothing but beatings and ill treatment; once one was known as an enemy of the state, one lost the right even to be a human being. Thus he had been continually surprised, and pleased, to find that this was not necessarily the case in America. The guards understood that even as a spy, Gregory had been doing a job. He had succeeded in his assignment, too, which had earned their respect—and he had been taken before he could escape, which had provided them with an adequate sense of justice. Besides, he was a model prisoner, except when pushed.

He had been pushed, more than once, in the beginning; the other prisoners had not been as understanding as the guards. Here was a man who had sought and been granted political asylum, been accepted with open arms by the highest in the land, and then betrayed all that trust. That the highest in the land had welcomed him only because he was related to them, and because he had something to offer, as a captain in the KGB, cut no ice with the murderers and rapists and arsonists and robbers who populated Sing Sing. A traitor was the obvious butt of their cruel, often savage, humor. But Gregory Nej *had* been an officer in the KGB. Not only had he been trained to kill with his bare hands, and was determined enough to use that skill, but he was also a big man; he took after his mother Tatiana Borodina in size, even if his somewhat sharp features were those of his father, Ivan Nej. He was not an easy man to bully. And if he had been prepared to accept mistreatment by the guards as part of his sentence, he also possessed the savage instincts of a man for whom life has come to an end. This had early been recognized by both guards and inmates. When two of the latter had been removed to the prison hospital with broken ribs—Gregory had carefully restrained his blows—the remainder of the prisoners had decided to ignore his existence. The prison superintendent had felt obliged to punish him with a week in solitary confinement. Gregory had not minded. He was not afraid of his fellows, but he had no wish to hurt any of them, and he did not enjoy the waves of hatred he could *feel* surging at him when in their company.

Thus he had come to this cell, away from the main blocks. In fact, it was possible to say that he had been in solitary confinement ever since his second week in Sing Sing. But this suited him admirably. The cell was comfortable; he had been allowed to furnish it as he wished, and also been allowed all the books and writing material he wished, and had found that for the first time in his life he had been able to relax, and think, for himself and about himself, rather than of his place in the Soviet hierarchy.

His books were the most valuable things he had ever owned, because they were books about America and Americans, and he wanted to learn everything he could about this unique country to which so many people were fleeing. But the books were as nothing, compared with visiting day. He had not been able entirely to close his mind to the outside world.

He had expected nothing of Sundays, made himself expect nothing, from the beginning. He had known Felicity was the only member of the family, the only person in America, who would even consider visiting him for the pleasure of seeing his face; if he had received a few visits from his Uncle Michael, these had been duty calls—the Soviet ambassador to the United Nations could not really be seen hobnobbing with a convicted spy. But he had accepted that even Felicity would soon abandon him. They had loved, desperately and earnestly, but also illegally, and it had been a love of the body more than the mind, at least on his part. Felicity was the first American woman he had really known. He had been fascinated by her clothes and her jewelry, by the way she took owning a car, and driving it herself, for granted, by her perfume and her magnificent hair, by her superb body, which she also seemed to take for granted, and above all by the product of all of these things, her quite unconscious arrogance. She was Felicity Hayman. That alone guaranteed her a place among the stars.

That she was also lonely, and still grieving the fiancé she had lost in the war, and at odds with her family, had not in any way lessened her beauty or her appeal, but it had made her vulnerable—a vulnerability of which he had taken shameless advantage, because it had guaranteed his acceptance in America. A defector who immediately embarks upon a love affair with his first cousin, to the scandal of polite society, can hardly also be conceived of as a spy. Even Anna, he thought, after her initial surprise and anger, had realized it was a stroke of genius.

But by the time Anna had thought that, the carefully calculated maneuver was becoming a reality. Having had so much time to himself during the past three years, his feelings for Felicity were easy to rationalize, in retrospect. She was physically very like his mother, as she was like his Aunt Ilona, Felicity's own mother. He had grown up in Tatiana's shadow, and he had adored her, though she was less like a mother than a flamboyant, amoral older sister. She had been murdered by his own father, as he now knew. But in her place had come Felicity. And then there was the ease with which he could dominate Felicity. The only other woman Gregory had ever made love to was Anna Ragosina, and there could be no possibility of any man ever dominating Anna.

But Felicity . . . she had been a virgin, something he had not suspected. And she had fallen madly, wildly, in love with the man who had taken her virginity. That was not so strange. And she had stayed in love, perhaps because she was in many ways a socialist herself, at heart—a theoretical socialist, the most absurd kind, who believed in equality but would renounce none of her own wealth and privilege. But where he had been educated to regard such people with contempt, he had found her fascinating. And now she owed him her life, because when it had come to a choice between Felicity and prison on the one hand, and Anna Ragosina and Russia and fame on the other, he had, with total irrationality, chosen Felicity.

But that she should love him so much that she had continued to come to see him, every Sunday, for three years, despite the pressure that he guessed was being put on her by her family, despite the way she was criticized by the press, despite the fact that in all that time they had not even been able to hold hands . . . in a few months she was going to be forty years old. Could *that* be the reason? That she was clinging to the only bit of real youth she had ever enjoyed?

But today was not visiting day, and therefore not Felicity. He squared his shoulders as he entered the interview room, then stopped in surprise. "Mr. Hayman?" he said.

"Good morning, Gregory," John Hayman said. "Why don't you sit down? I have something to say to you."

Gregory waited, heart pounding. But then, his heart always pounded immediately before he saw her. Seeing her involved so many memories, so much desire. And now, so much confusion.

Felicity was, as always, beautifully dressed. She wore a pale blue woolen dress; her head was bare, her golden hair free. She wore no jewelry except for the gold band he had given her, and that was on the third finger of her right hand. She looked cheerfully composed; as she was not normally a cheerful person, he guessed that she carefully created the mood for his benefit.

She sat opposite him, and smiled at him. "Hi. I've brought you some shortcake. I gave it to the guard. Or rather, he took it. Do you think he's going to break it up, looking for a gun or something?"

"He doesn't usually," Gregory said. His hands lay on the table in front of him, hers in front of her; they were only twelve inches apart. But it was against the rules to bridge those twelve inches, and there were two guards in the room with them, watching their every movement.

"Mother and Father send you their regards," Felicity said. This was a continuing lie, as he well knew. "They saw your Uncle Michael, just before he left last week. Did you see him?"

"Yes," Gregory said. "He came to say good-bye."

"They said he's looking very well," Felicity said. "As are Catherine and Nona. Nona is staying in the U.S. to study. Did you know that? She's coming to visit with us whenever she can."

"Yes," he said. "Uncle Michael told me. Felicity . . ." He drew a long breath. "I'm to be exchanged."

The faintest of lines gathered between her eyes, and her mouth opened, not sagging, but merely surprised.

"Your brother John came to see me," Gregory explained. "I'm not sure how he's involved, or even how it's all happening. But apparently I'm to be exchanged for your Uncle Peter—my Uncle Peter as well, I suppose—and a friend of your mother and father, Judith Petrov."

Felicity caught her breath. "When?"

"Not for a few months yet. But it is going to happen."

"Oh," she said. Her eyes filled with tears. "I'm so happy for you, Gregory. So happy."

"Are you?"

"Of course. You'll be free. You'll be going back to Russia. You'll—"

"And you?"

She shrugged. "I'll find something else to do with my Sundays, I guess."

He gazed at her, and she gazed back, the tears now dribbling down her cheeks.

"I'm not going to go," he said.

Her head came up sharply.

"They can't make me," he said. "I do not wish to return to Russia. How can I go back to the man who murdered my mother? They must understand that. How can I leave you? They cannot make me go. I received American citizenship. That's why I'm here now. And I've served three years of my sentence. They tell me I'll be eligible for parole after seven more years. Even with a life sentence, I'll be eligible for parole."

"Seven years," she murmured.

"Only seven years," he said. "I'll only be forty."

"I'll be . . ." she bit her lip.

"Forty-six. But I'll still love you, Felicity. When I'm released, we'll be married."

"First cousins?"

"Nobody will stop us then. Not if you'll wait for me."

"Oh, I'll wait for you, Gregory. For ever and ever. But you . . . seven more years?"

"I've worked it out," he said. "That's only three hundred and sixty-four Sundays. We can manage three hundred and sixty-four Sundays, Felicity. I know we can."

"Let me get this straight," Harry Truman said. "This character doesn't *want* to be exchanged? He doesn't *want* to go home to Russia, Home, and Beauty? To his father? To his Uncle Joe? To all his comrades in Lubianka Prison?"

"That's about the size of it, sir," John Hayman said, and glanced at Allen Dulles.

"For God's sake, why not?" Truman demanded.

"Well, sir, as he explained it to me," John said, having received the nod from his superior, "he no longer supports the Soviet system. Apparently he's felt this way for a long time, even when he was still spying, but he didn't know how to stop."

"That's a damned unlikely story, for a start," Truman snorted.

"I believe it's true, sir," John said. "Then, while he was over here, he discovered that his father murdered his mother. I know it seemed like a car accident, but it was actually a political execution, because Madame Nej was planning to leave Russia with her English lover and settle in the West, and while Stalin did not feel he could publicly refuse so famous a dancer permission to emigrate, he also felt it would be detrimental to the Soviet state. So naturally Gregory has turned against his father as well. Then, in addition, he fell out with the KGB officer that he reported to, and in fact attacked her when she wanted to kill my sister Felicity. If he hadn't done so, Felicity would be dead, and we—the FBI, that is—wouldn't have been able to arrest Colonel Ragosina."

"I know all of that," Truman said. "That's why this Nej is in prison instead of pushing up daisies."

"Yes, sir. And finally, he has done a lot of reading and thinking during the three years he's been in prison, and he has come to the decision that he would rather be an American than a Russian."

"But he *is* a Russian."

"Because we took his American citizenship away from him, for treason. But he did receive it, you may remember, sir, when we thought he was on the up and up. Now he plans to serve out his sentence, get paroled at the earliest possible moment, and then reapply for citizenship."

Truman looked at Dulles. "Can he do that?"

"I think it's technically possible, sir," Dulles said. "Whether or not he'll get it is another matter."

"And what about *our* requirements, for getting Judith Petrov and Borodin out of Russia, just as quickly as possible?"

Dulles shrugged. "It looks as if we may have to rethink that one."

"Like hell it does," Truman said. "Now you listen to me, both of you. This man Nej is a traitor. Sure, we gave him political asylum, and citizenship. Because he hoodwinked your family, Hayman, into believing in him, we gave him everything he asked for. And in return he helped to lift the most important secrets this country has ever had to lose. Now you tell me he wants to be a model citizen. I would have to have my head examined to believe that. To *risk* believing that. In addition, he's very important to our plans right this moment—back in Russia. I'm afraid he is going to have to bite the bullet. We didn't ask him to come here. Now we're asking him to go, pretty damn quick. And he is going. That's an order." He looked at each of their faces in turn. "Got me?"

"Let me get this straight," George Hayman said, sitting up in his deck chair—early fall Sundays at Cold Spring Harbor were almost as warm as those in June, although the leaves were falling. "He says he isn't *going?*"

"Right," John said, and glanced uneasily at Felicity.

"Can he do that?" Ilona asked.

"No," John said.

"What did you say?" Felicity cried.

"Simply that, Felicity. Gregory is a convicted traitor, and damned lucky to be alive when he could have been sent to the electric chair. Now we have a chance to make a deal with the Russians and he won't play. Well, it's not his choice to make. He's going, whether he likes it or not."

"You can't," Felicity shouted. "You can't make him! This is a free country, isn't it? Isn't that what you're always prating about? What's free about a country which just deports people?"

"We're trying to keep it free, for our own people," John said patiently. "That means getting rid of enemy spies."

"Gregory isn't a spy anymore. He wants to *be* one of our people."

"He happens to have been a traitor first," John said.

"It's a conspiracy," Felicity stormed. She glared from face to face. "You all just want to get rid of him, because he and I happen to be in love."

"Felicity—" Her mother put an arm around her shoulders. "—of course we don't want to get rid of him. But he has to go. We have to get Judith and Peter out of Russia."

"Why?" Felicity shouted, shrugging Ilona off. "Why do they matter, and Gregory not?"

Ilona looked at George helplessly.

George sighed. "Because he is a Russian, Felicity. He is an officer in the KGB, and no matter what he may have told you, he remains an officer in the KGB. His people, his own father, want him back. And we don't want him here. So as John says, he simply has to go."

Once again Felicity looked from face to face, her own flushed and angry. "You just want to separate us," she said again, in a lower tone. "Well, it won't work. If you send Gregory back to Russia, then I'm going with him. Back to Russia."

"She's just distraught," Natasha observed, staring through the windshield of the car at the road unfolding in the beams of the headlights.

"Felicity has been distraught since December 7, 1941. That's going on eleven years," John pointed out. "I'd say it's just about a permanent condition."

"You mean she might actually try to do it?"

"I'd say so."

"But . . . surely George can lock her up, or something."

"Would that really be a solution, Natasha? Locking up your own daughter for the rest of her life? It would probably be better to let her go."

"To Russia?" Natasha shivered, and hugged herself. "I'm even sorry for Gregory, having to go back. I don't really understand why he has to. I mean, this Petrov woman—"

"Is just a friend. And not even an American. But there are important issues at stake. And Gregory *is* a spy."

"*Was* a spy, John. Felicity was quite right there. If he's genuinely realized how terrible the Soviet system is, why *shouldn't* he be allowed to stay? It takes some decision, you know, to abandon your country. Think of me. You asked me to marry you, back in 1932, and we didn't get around to it. I couldn't make up my mind to leave Russia, until 1940. And *then* we didn't actually make it until 1945."

"Not the same thing at all." John slowed for the bridge, and then the canyons of Manhattan. "You had your career. And then there was the war."

"I had the umbrella of Tattie and the Soviet state protecting me, because I could dance. I was reluctant to leave that umbrella and take my chances in the outside world, even with you, and even with the Haymans willing to give me an even greater umbrella. I was afraid to leave Russia. It sounds incredible now, even to me, but it was true. Better the devil you know, remember? I'm sure the same thing applies to Gregory, and he didn't have half as much going for him."

"What *does* an officer in the KGB have going for him, outside Russia? The KGB murdered your parents, Natasha."

"Gregory didn't. He was a child at the time."

"Oh, for God's sake, I don't know what we're arguing about," John said. "There is simply no way that Gregory is not going back to Russia. As for Felicity . . . well, we have to hope that George and Mother can talk some sense into her." He parked in the underground garage, and they rode the elevator in silence. He found himself wondering if there was some way Gregory might be able to do something about locating Diana. He was sure the guy was decent enough at heart—in fact, he even felt sorry for him. But he didn't know if he could be trusted that far.

They had not taken the children to Cold Spring Harbor this time, because they had suspected it was going to be a trying day. "You're home early," the baby-sitter said. "There are some letters. No calls, though. And Alexander . . ." She wandered off with Natasha to show her Alex's latest escapade, while John flicked through the mail, finding nothing of importance until he saw an envelope with the crest of the Soviet embassy. Heart pounding, he slit it open. It contained but a single sheet of paper.

"I shall be at the Park Star Hotel, Stockholm, from the first through the sixth of November. Anna."

Chapter 11

NATASHA WALKED THROUGH THE GARDEN AT COLD SPRING Harbor with her mother-in-law. "I suppose it means that he is moving up in the world," she said, "being sent abroad this often to interview clients. This is the second time this year, you know. But I should so love to be able to go with him. I do miss him so."

"Still, it's only for a few days at a time," Ilona said. "Natasha, what *is* John doing now?"

"He's in advertising, Ilona. You know that."

"I meant, what sort of job is he actually doing? You spoke about interviewing clients . . ."

"Well, that's what he does."

"He must have to interview clients here in America, too."

"Of course."

"Then doesn't he take them out to dinner, with their wives and you along?"

Natasha frowned. "No. He never does that."

"He never even brings them home?"

"No. He—"

"Doesn't he talk about his work with you? What about his colleagues? You know, office parties, dinners and the like."

Natasha's frown deepened. "He doesn't seem to have them."

"But you've been to his office, haven't you?"

"Oh, yes. I went once. About three years ago."

"Once? Three *years* ago?"

"Well . . . John doesn't think it's a good thing for wives to badger their husbands in the office."

"Does he ever bring work home?"

"Oh, yes, quite often. And sometimes he tries out slogans on me."

"Mmm," Ilona commented thoughtfully, and looked across the lawn to where her son and George sat in deck chairs, talking. She wished she could hear what they were saying. Certainly they remained very close—closer than George was with his own children, she sometimes thought. But then, in the last few weeks John had been the only rock to which they had been able to cling. Sometimes, indeed, she felt near to despair. George junior getting set to embark upon some wild expedition to Europe, which she was sure would bring nothing but trouble, and which would certainly be discovered and publicize Diana's disappearance, something they had hitherto managed to avoid. Then there was Felicity, still exuding determination to accompany Gregory Nej to Russia; she was indeed suddenly tremendously excited about the whole idea, for she would be able to live with Gregory again next year, instead of having to wait for seven. She was even claiming that she had always wanted to visit Russia—and she was apparently quite prepared to become a Communist herself.

Compared with them, John was so sane and sensible. But so mysterious as well. She could not help but remember that he had once worked for Peter. A long time ago, and they had apparently quarreled, but . . . why had he gone to see Peter in London? And why was he so involved in the coming exchange, which was entirely a government matter? Unless, again, it was something to do with Peter?

But he and George were such close friends, seemed to trust each other so absolutely—and she knew that George disapproved of Peter's activities. She *wished* she could hear what they were saying.

"First week in November," George remarked. "You could miss the election."

"I'm not sure my vote will be very relevant," John said.

"But you're looking forward to the trip. Because you have a lead, is that it?"

John gazed at his stepfather. "Yes," he said. "I think we may have a lead, at last."

Stockholm in November. The days were already shortened to a scant eight hours, and the temperature seldom rose above freezing. The harbor was iced over and there was snow on the ground. Yet Stockholm in winter was perhaps even more beautiful and certainly more alive than Stockholm in the summer. John had a feeling that the Swedes looked on summer with a certain suspicion; it was at once brief and alien, and if as a nation they seemed to rip off their clothing and head for the nearest lake or beach the moment it was warm enough to do so, it was with the exuberance of children let out of school for a half-day off, well aware that the real business of living must recommence after a few hours.

Lining up for a taxi outside the Central Station at six o'clock in the evening, he slapped gloved but frozen hands together, and stamped equally feelingless feet up and down on the snow. But when John's turn eventually arrived, the taxi was warm, and only moments later they were gliding down Mälarstrand and turning into the hotel forecourt.

"Mr. Hayman," the desk clerk said, "indeed we have a room for you. It is number 417, next door to number 419, you understand; there is a connecting door." He neither smiled nor smirked, looked neither knowing nor censorious; Sweden *was* the land of the free, at least when it came to human relationships.

But *he* was not Swedish, and he was aware that his heart was pounding most painfully. It would have done so, probably, no matter who the woman waiting for him upstairs was—he had not slept with another woman since Natasha had accepted his proposal of marriage, twelve years before. The knowledge that the woman waiting was Anna Ragosina made him almost sick with a mixture of excitement and apprehension. Throughout his journey he had refused to let himself think about it, about what he was actually doing, and to this moment had almost succeeded. He was doing his job, even if on this occasion he had a personal involvement in the outcome. Mundane thoughts such as the possible betrayal of Natasha, the physical and mental health of Diana, should not be allowed to come into it at all. Even the fact that he was dealing with Anna

Ragosina—and he knew the real Anna, a conscienceless killer, a spitting, furious, vicious creature—should not be allowed to come into it at all; she was merely the Russian commissar who, he was sure, held Diana.

But that unemotional review of the situation was made nonsense by reality, and now reality was about to emerge most decisively.

Room 417 was comfortably and, as he had expected, warmly furnished: twin beds, an entire wall of desks and bureaus and vanity mirrors, and harborside windows concealed behind draperies. The bellhop placed his suitcase on the rack, received a tip without comment, and left. And John stood in the center of the room and gazed at the door that connected with 419. He moved closer, stared at it. He certainly did not intend to make the first move . . . but the door was unlocked on his side. And therefore on hers as well?

He had been traveling all day, and despite the cold was in need of a bath. He stripped off his clothes, unpacked clean ones, stepped beneath a steaming shower . . . and felt the hairs on the back of his neck slowly rise as a gentle scent filled the room. He peered through the steam and saw her, standing just beyond the bathroom door, holding a glass in each hand.

Anna Ragosina. Wearing a crimson dressing gown and high-heeled mules, her hair loose on her shoulders, her face totally relaxed and quite beautiful in its perfect symmetry. Except . . . he frowned.

"I know," Anna said. "There is a scar on my nose. But you will not ask how I got it, and I will not tell you." She smiled at him. "This is Bollinger," she said. "They tell me it is very good. I do not know about these things. Is it the best?"

John shut off the water and reached for a towel. "It is just about the best."

"Welcome to Stockholm."

He stepped from the shower stall, instinctively wrapped the towel around his waist, and then remembered that not only was it not necessary, but that it *was* necessary to match this woman, from sophisticated carelessness to downright amorality, if he was ever going to defeat her. So he hung the towel on the rail and took his glass from her fingers. Their flesh touched, and he really did not know what was going to happen next; her gaze remained on his face, but he knew she was aware of his body. Then she released him and walked into the bedroom, to sit down with one leg draped across the other, the dressing gown falling away to uncover her knees and calves.

"It's my pleasure to be here," he said, realizing his response was somewhat banal.

"I do not think we will go down to dinner," Anna said. "I have ordered smörgåsbord in my room, at eight. We have so much to discuss, have we not, John?"

He drank some more champagne. "And you are on an expense-account trip." Why *did* she make him feel, and talk, like a schoolboy?

"Of course. Are you not also on an expense-account trip, for the FBI?"

He hesitated. While she could never even guess at the existence of the CIA, a lot might still depend on his answer. "Let's say I'm here in an unofficial capacity."

"Ah. You are acting for your family. For Diana's parents."

"They do not even know where I am, Anna. I am acting for myself. But you are admitting that you hold Diana."

"She fell into my hands, John. Such a sweet child, although a very foolish one."

"And is she still a sweet child?"

"She is to me."

He went into her room, wondering if she would follow him. But he should have known Anna better than that. She was not afraid of anything he might find in her room, and undoubtedly she would not be carrying a weapon; Anna had always trusted her bare hands as much as any gun. He picked up the bottle and returned to refill their glasses.

"Tell me what you want in exchange for Diana."

Anna gazed at him over the rim of her champagne glass. "I want so many things, John. And do you know, I nearly always get what I want? But you are not just going to negotiate and leave, are you? I am booked in here for the next five days. So are you. Courtesy of the Soviet government. Is that not a triumph you would wish to relish?"

"I'm sure I shall. But I'd rather negotiate first, and . . . well, talk after."

Anna shook her head. "That is not how we do things. You and I have quite a history between us, John Hayman."

He waited, drinking champagne. It was beginning to get to him. But had he not known what she would want first, before he ever arrived here? Had he not been suppressing his excitement throughout the journey? So he *would* be betraying Natasha; he had come here prepared to do that, because he had known it would be necessary. And was it because he had wanted to, for so very long, ever since he and Anna were comrades in the Pripet Marsh? That question he was not prepared to answer.

"I once threatened to beat you with a steel-tipped whip," Anna said thoughtfully. "I was very young. And you once threatened to set me on my own hot stove. You were not very young. But you were very angry. And in between, the Pripet. . . . Do you ever think back to those days?"

"Very often."

Anna sighed. "Life was so uncomplicated, then. We killed Germans, or the Germans killed us. But you managed to complicate even something as simple as that. You hit me once, do you remember?"

"I thought it was necessary at the time."

"Oh, it was, or I would have cut the breasts from that girl. But do you suppose you saved her from anything? She was an SS secretary. Do you suppose, after she was taken away by our soldiers, she would not rather have died there and then?"

"I can at least *hope* she survived," John said, "whatever they did to her."

"You are like a knight of old, who would take the entire weight of the world—the female world, anyway—on his shoulders." Anna shrugged. "That is a waste of time. But I have often thought, you must have been very angry with me, to hit me so hard. Just as you were very angry with me when you wished to burn my bottom. I have thought that there were times, like those, when you must have hated me."

"I won't deny that."

"And times when you loved me?"

"There were times when I wanted to *make* love to you."

"While hating me. I find that quite fascinating."

"You wouldn't have, at the time."

"Do you not think so? Have you never thought that pain and pleasure—I am talking about agony and ecstasy—are very close together? Tell me what you would do to me, John, if you had me entirely in your power, with no risk of recrimination, with nothing to consider except your physical gratification."

He gazed at her. "I didn't come several thousand miles to play dirty games, Anna."

She finished her drink, held the glass out for a refill. "I didn't bring you several thousand miles to play games either, John. I brought you here to negotiate the release of your niece. The negotiations have already started. I would like you to make love to me, or beat me, or torture me, or whatever you really wish to do to me. I would like you to do that tonight. After we have had supper." She smiled at him. "And then I wish to do the same to you. But you see, I am prepared to be generous. You can have first . . . bite."

"You can't be serious," he said.

She raised her eyebrows. "Have you ever known me not to be serious? I have been told that I have absolutely no sense of humor." She cocked her head as a gentle knock sounded on the door of the other room. "Our dinner. I will get it. There is no necessity to put anything on. Just give me five minutes and then come in."

She closed the connecting door behind her, while he gazed after her in the total bemusement to which she so easily reduced him—and everyone else, he surmised. The wildest of thoughts kept kaleidoscoping through his brain, but uppermost was the knowledge that she *was* Anna Ragosina, and he had let her out of his sight . . . he had only her word that it was their dinner, and not some of her people coming to kidnap him, or that she would not tamper with the food. But it was absurd to worry about such things. He was here; if she wished either to lay him out or have him kidnapped, or even have him murdered, she would do it no matter what steps he now took. He had come here in full knowledge of that possibility. But also in the knowledge that there was no reason for her to do any of those things. He had come here to bargain. No, to surrender. As she well knew.

But what she was suggesting . . . the five minutes were up. He opened the door and stepped into the other room.

She stood by the window, and had taken off her robe. Although he had seen her naked before, there is a world of difference between seeing a woman naked when she swims in a river, as Anna had done in the Pripet, or when one is trying to frighten her, as in Washington, but when one has no thoughts of sex in mind or is trying desperately to reject such thoughts—and seeing her naked when one knows that in a very few minutes all that flesh and blood and bone and muscle, as well as that brain, is going to be in one's possession. Thus, now he looked at square shoulders, large breasts, beginning to sag, but in a still-sensuous way, hard belly with ridges of muscle disguising the tight rib cage, hips that were wider than he had supposed, because of the trimness suggested by the uniform in which they were usually encased, an enormous bush of pubic hair that seemed physically to spread the muscular thighs, perfectly formed legs, feet which had not a mark on them. She did not look forty. From the neck down she scarcely looked thirty, and her face was remarkably unlined. But her blue eyes were both utterly ageless, and utterly old. Those eyes had looked on death so many times that her own life must have come to seem an eternity.

"Let us eat," she said, "and drink some more champagne." Another bottle waited in its bucket on the table beside the open sandwiches. "And talk. And plan." She smiled at him. "Do you know, I am quite excited?"

Was it possible to believe that? She *looked* excited; her eyes sparkled and her mouth was soft. And certainly she could tell *he* was excited; eating a meal with a beautiful, naked woman with whom he had never yet made love was not something he could take in his stride.

"You are afraid," Anna remarked, "of totally releasing your desires. You think that in some way this will corrupt you, soil you, weaken you. So many men have this absurd point of view. Have you never stopped to think that it could instead cleanse you, and make you stronger?"

"I could agree with that," he said, "except for the knowledge that, having, as you put it, cleansed myself once, I would wish to do so again and again—which would in time weaken me, because it would become an obsession."

"You *have* thought about it. I am so glad. An obsession . . . I cannot see anything wrong in being obsessed by sex, from time to time. Perhaps you suppose the woman would object. Not if you have the right woman, John." She leaned forward, and with her tongue stroked his mouth. A moment later she was in his arms, half kneeling on his lap, their bodies locked together in the tightest embrace he had ever known, while her tongue, which tasted like nectar, seemed to fill his mouth. Had he not waited twenty years for this moment?

But she was away again, laughing, her hand drooping between his legs to give him a quick caress before she sat on the opposite side of the table. "You will make love to me, or do anything you wish to me," she said, "until you are satisfied. Until you are sated. I undertake to obey you utterly until then. But you must undertake to be governed by me, afterward. Until *I* am sated."

He stared at her, realizing that she meant what she said. *This* was what she wanted.

"We shall, of course, mutually undertake not to harm each other," Anna went on. "That is, we may mark the skin, but the skin must not be broken. And of course we shall not kill each other. Do you agree?"

"How do you know I will be able to resist killing you, Anna, when I have you at my mercy?"

Anna smiled at him. "Because I alone can give you back Diana."

"I do not yet have any proof that you possess her."

Anna got up, walked to her dressing table, and picked up a photograph. "She is a beautiful girl."

John looked at the print, his mind consumed by the increasing awareness of his body. It was certainly Diana, chained naked to the wall of a cell. And there was no reason to doubt the cell was in Lubianka; he had been inside such a cell himself. He raised his head. "Is it necessary to keep her naked and chained, like an animal?"

Anna shrugged. "That photo was taken some weeks ago, when she was constantly being recalcitrant. Her behavior has improved since then. And you can see that her condition is excellent." She returned to the dressing table, opened a drawer, and took out a handful of leather thongs. "But you can bind me just like that, if you choose, John." She went to the bed, and lay down across it. "Only I do not think you will find that necessary."

She was, of course, in total control of the situation. In every way. He was not only mentally unprepared for such a sudden plunge into a world of pure hedonism—he had already been stimulated almost to bursting point.

He stood above her, looking down on her, terribly aware of her gaze. With an act of will he made himself kneel beside her, and possess her, as best he was able, with his mouth, kissing her lips, finding her tongue again, kissing each nipple and taking them between his own lips to suck, kissing her groin and her toes, rolling her on her stomach, trying to will himself to hurt her, and finding himself quite unable to do so, because at this moment he could not even hate her; he made himself go through the motions of exploring her with his fingertips, and he was curious that so much perfect femininity should conceal so much total depravity. And so he moved her hair to kiss the nape of her neck, gently pulled the gown beneath her arms, and then being overwhelmed by his own desires, collapsed on top of her. She had to rise to her knees herself, carrying his weight, and direct him, before sinking to the mattress again, with him imprisoned inside her for a single tumultuous, orgasmic spasm.

He rolled away from her and lay on his back. Anna rose on her elbow to smile at him. "Perhaps the next time you will do better," she said.

He gazed at her, eyes lazy.

"You did not attempt to hurt me. You did not even make me cry out," she pointed out. "I would have thought you would accomplish that, John."

He reached for her, to bring her down to him, and she evaded his hands with a twist of her body and a flurry of her hair. "No, no," she said. "You have had your chance. Now it is *my* turn."

"You'll have a difficult job," he told her, "right this minute."

Anna continued to smile. "But I am not in a hurry, as you were, John. We have all night. And you must remember our bargain."

She washed him, with cold water. He gasped, and remained still with an effort. She dried him instantly, but left him tingling and alive, and already half restored. But as she had said, she was not in a hurry. Where he had spent seconds, she spent minutes; minutes with his face, kissing, sucking, licking, touching. Minutes with his feet. Minutes with his chest and nipples. Minutes which brought him to full erection and full readiness half an hour before he would have thought it possible, only again to be washed in freezing water. Desire was not removed, only capability, while the lump in his groin seemed to grow and grow.

Minutes on his back, her nails scouring his flesh, but gently, so as not to break the flesh. Minutes when she hit and slapped him, panting with the effort and with her own emotion, but using only the flat of her hands, again so as to leave no permanent mark. Minutes when she masturbated herself, while holding him, before a third cold-water treatment. And then at last, she lay on his chest, and moved her body on his. He did not know what to believe, whether he was to receive another douche. When he discovered that he was not, he seemed to be sinking into her and into her and into her, or, as she lay on him, perhaps it was the other way around. But that she was as aroused as he could not be doubted. She gasped and moaned, screamed and used her nails, this time as weapons, and exploded into a tumultuous ecstasy.

And he matched her surge for surge.

Then they slept, their heads together, their legs intertwined. He would have wished to sleep forever, because he dreaded the thought of awakening. But Anna had no such fears. He hardly seemed to have closed his eyes when she was shaking him awake and switching on the light. "Now," she said. "Let us negotiate."

John sighed, and looked at his watch; but it was actually seven in the morning. "I thought we had already done that."

"We have merely cleared the air."

"Then let's clear some more air." He was shacked up with a she-devil, and might as well enjoy it—he knew that the awakening, when it came, was going to be painful. He reached for her, but she slipped away with her usual ease and got out of bed.

"No, no," she said. "We have merely established that there is a basis *for* negotiation. Now let us commence." She went into the shower. "Tell me about this proposed exchange of Gregory Nej. Will your people really do it?"

"Of course. They have agreed to it."

"I think you are fools." There was a moment's hiatus while the water poured, then she emerged, leaving damp imprints on the carpet, toweling her hair. "Is this woman Petrova so important to you?"

"She's a human being." He sat up to watch her. "But it is Prince Peter we really want."

"Is that so? Why? He has come to us voluntarily. He wishes to live in Russia, and die in Russia. Until that happens, he wishes to cooperate with us."

"We want him out."

"Before he does something foolish? Is it something to do with the explosives?"

"The . . . did you say *explosives?*" Suddenly even the beauty before him was irrelevant.

"Did you not know about that? No, I suppose you did not."

"Anna—"

"Peter Borodin sent two of his aides into Russia, each carrying a suitcase packed with plastic explosives. Their names were . . . let me see . . . so difficult to remember these things—" She smiled at him. "One was called Robert Loung. And the other was a woman. What *was* her name?"

John leaped out of bed and seized her wet shoulders. "You are trying to tell me that Diana was carrying a suitcase packed with plastic explosives?"

"Of course. Why else do you suppose she was arrested? She denies it, of course. She is so innocent. She even denies working for this uncle of yours; but that is equally absurd, would you not say? Because he came along behind them, unaware that they were both under arrest, with a rendezvous all arranged—at the Hotel Berlin, would you believe it? Oh, of course he had to have a reason for coming, so he offered us this ridiculous story about a Jewish plot to assassinate Stalin—"

"You mean, you know that isn't true?"

Anna shrugged her shoulders free and dried them. "Of course. Do you not imagine *I* know who tried to assassinate Stalin?"

"Oh, my God," he said. "My God, my God, my God!" He felt he was caught in a web spun by the biggest spider in all history. "But you're letting it happen—?"

Anna sat before her mirror to make up her face. "Why should I not let it happen? There are far too many Jews in the world as it is. Besides, things like this distract people. That is always good."

"But Diana—"

"In view of the evidence I possess, she would be executed within a week of my placing her on trial. I may still have that done. I have not made up my mind. Tell me about the explosives. Where were they to be planted?"

"The explosives." He tried to think. Two suitcases of plastic explosives, to assassinate Stalin? Where *had* Peter been planning to plant it? Where could he possibly *hope* to plant it? Stalin did not often appear in public. And even when he did, Moscow wasn't the sort of place one could go around planting plastic explosives without being noticed.

"Well?" She began to brush her hair.

"I'm trying to think," he said. "But I just can't. Anyway, does it matter, since you have the explosives?"

"I'm sure he has other sources of supply." She put on her dressing gown, sat down at the desk, and dialed room service. "I would like a liter of orange juice, very cold, please; a liter of coffee, very hot; no milk or sugar; a bottle of champagne, very cold; and four eggs, boiled, very soft. I will need two glasses, two cups, and two spoons. Thank you."

"Is that your breakfast every morning?" he asked.

"Only when I am with a delightful man. You are a delightful man, John." She sat beside him and kissed him on the nose. "Is that why you wish Prince Peter back? Because something has gone astray with your plans?"

"We have nothing to do with Prince Peter, Anna, believe me. We did know he was planning something, but we didn't know what it was."

"Now you do?"

"Now I'm no further ahead, except that you tell me it's something to do with explosives. But since he's coming out anyway—"

"He isn't," Anna said. "He doesn't want to. I told you. He wants to die in Russia."

"Did you say—he's not coming out?" John asked.

"That's right."

"But it was agreed—"

"Certainly. But he does not wish to return to the West. Believe me, we have put no sort of pressure on him to stay. I will admit I would cheerfully have had him shot, but Ivan is concerned only with getting that stupid son of his back, and he feels we have obtained everything that is worthwhile from Prince Peter. But, as I said, the prince does not wish to go." She went to the door at the knock, allowed the waiter to wheel in the breakfast cart, signed the check, closed and locked the door again. "Now, you know, John, that we would never dream of forcing someone to act against his, or her, will. Would your people?"

John opened his mouth and then closed it again. To tell her the truth about Gregory would help no one, and could only harm him.

"Breakfast," Anna said, adding champagne to a glass of orange juice, and handing it to him. "This knowledge will not of course become apparent to your people until they are at the prescribed place, with Gregory. Do you think they will then call the whole thing off? Ivan is very nervous about it. He wishes to force Prince Peter to go, but it has been pointed out to him that this would be very bad publicity. It would be better for the prince to have a heart attack, perhaps, that would *prevent* his going. This can be arranged, of course. But I personally feel that it is really Judith Petrova your people want, and that they will accept the situation. After all, it will be sprung upon them and they will have to make an instant decision."

It occurred to John that if he ever made the mistake of confusing this succubus with a human being, she would very rapidly bring him back to earth again, by her careless decisions to kill, or not to kill, other human beings. He could not resist a probe. "What makes you think I shall not tell our people what is going to happen?"

"Because you will not be there. You are *here*, John, to negotiate the release of Diana."

"Ah. And you'll substitute her for Uncle Peter, if necessary."

"Oh, no," Anna said. "Oh, no, no, no, no, no. She is an entirely different matter. Peter and Judith Petrova are Ivan's, to exchange for whomever he wishes. Diana is mine."

John sighed. Why, knowing her so well, understanding her so well, did he keep making the equally serious mistake of supposing this woman would *ever* act in a rational, or even a reasonable, manner? But he dared not push the subject of Diana; Anna would get around to that whenever she was ready. "But you are actually pleased Peter is staying. May I ask why?"

"Of course. I should hate to let him slip away, or die for that matter, without discovering what he is really up to, with his explosives and his agents. I am still hoping you will tell me."

"I have told you that I don't know."

"What I meant was, I am still hoping you will find out, in the course of time, and then tell me."

He gazed at her. It was a temptation to tell her now, if only to watch the expression on her face as she realized the time bomb with which she was so carelessly playing. But he wanted time to think about this new situation. He wanted time to make up his mind whether or not he could condemn his own uncle to death—because that was what he would be doing. But more important than either of those, he might need his knowledge as a bargaining counter when it came to Diana.

"So maybe I will," he agreed.

Anna smiled. "I am sure you will, John." She got out of bed, sat at the breakfast cart, and broke an egg. "I have enormous hopes of you. Do you know, when I agreed to meet you here, I had no idea *what* I wanted? I had vague thoughts . . . but I did not know if they would be practical. Are you not going to eat?"

He sat opposite her. "And now you have decided?"

"I think I have. I think you would be a fair exchange for Diana."

At least she had not succeeded in surprising him; he even felt a little disappointed, and raised his glass. "Well, I'd say, as *you* always say, that you've had what you wanted."

Anna poured coffee. "One night?" She shook her head. "We have barely scratched the surface of our relationship."

"Okay. So I'll stay the full five days. You can have Diana brought here while we scratch a few more surfaces."

Anna sipped her coffee, gazing at him over the cup. "I do not think even five days will be sufficient, John Hayman," she said. "I want you always, from this minute on."

John swallowed half his egg before he really meant to. "Maybe" he said, when he had gotten his breath back, "you should amplify that statement."

"Of course. We shall leave the hotel today. You will come with me. We shall take the ship that is waiting in the harbor, and sail to Leningrad. You will defect, John."

"Defect?"

"I do not intend to keep you hidden away for the rest of your life," she told him. "I intend to wear you on my sleeve, so to speak. That means the maximum publicity. Photographs, television and radio interviews, everything we can think of, with you smiling at the camera and saying how happy you are to be serving Mother Russia at last. We don't want anyone being able to say you were kidnapped or coerced. Besides, the publicity will be good for my image. My ultimate triumph, so to speak. While Ivan schemes and scrapes to regain his puerile son, I am engaged in subverting one of America's leading FBI agents."

John drank his champagne mixture slowly. He had to give himself time to evaluate the situation, to understand what was really being proposed, to control his temper and his emotions at the same time. He could only take refuge in words. "No one in America except my immediate contacts knows that I work for the FBI, or have ever done so."

"Then we will tell them. Banner headlines."

"And I was never anything but an insignificant cog in the machine."

"We shall make you important, John. When our journalists are finished with you, you will appear more important that J. Edgar Hoover himself."

"And you really think I am going to agree to that?"

"It is entirely up to you. You are free to walk through that door, at any time. Of course, should you do so, I will be left with no alternative but to put Diana on trial, after she has been suitably interrogated. Until this moment she has been very well treated. She is in the pink of health. But this is because she has been a privileged prisoner. Were I to withdraw those privileges, well . . . it would be unfortunate. She is such a lovely girl."

"I should kill you."

Anna smiled. "I do not think that would help Diana."

"And do you really suppose, if I agreed to your obscene proposal, that I would be any good to you in bed?"

Anna shrugged. "I think so." She gave a delightful little laugh. "You might be able to become more enthusiastic than you were last night. But I think, when *you* really think about it, you will understand that you are being absurd. You are wasting your life, at the moment. You have just told me, and I believe you, that you are a very unimportant member of the FBI. And you are nearly forty-five years old. What lies ahead of you, John? Oh, no doubt you will inherit some money from your mother. But will you inherit enough to have, for example, the power of your half-brother? Will you ever be anything more than a very unimportant member of American society? Why do you not stop to consider what I am offering you? To begin with, you belong in Russia. You are a Russian by birth and by parentage. More, your real father is one of the most senior members of the Politburo. I can tell you that he will be absolutely delighted should you make the right decision. Do you suppose you will be assigned merely to amuse me? I would hope that you *will* do that, of course. I think if you will consider the matter you will realize that you and I are made for each other, in every way. But that is for our leisure hours. I see a tremendous future opening in front of you. You will be my principal aide. And I can tell you in confidence that in the not too distant future I am going to command the KGB. It has all been decided."

He could only stare at her. "You really think you can take the world, and everyone in it, and reshape it and them to your own requirements, your own desires? You really think that, Anna?"

"Now you are being a silly emotional male again, John. One of my first tasks will be to rid you of that weakness. I am not reshaping the world and everyone in it. I am reshaping *you,* for the better."

Her calm certainty was breathtaking. The only way to combat Anna was by brute force, as he had in Washington. He should throw the champagne in her face, and then take her earlier advice and return to his room, lock the door, dress, and catch the first plane out of here.

But that would mean leaving Diana behind. Forever.

Besides . . . he got up, walked to the window, drew the blinds, and blinked at the brilliance of the morning as the rising sun played on the snowy streets. He was being asked to defect. As an FBI agent. No one, least of all Anna, had any idea he worked for the CIA.

So he, a CIA agent, was being *asked* to defect. To join the KGB. To take his place in the very nerve center of every secret Soviet activity. Only someone with Anna's colossal arrogance and total confidence could contemplate such a step. But was it not obvious that Anna's only weakness *was* her colossal arrogance and total confidence? He was actually being given the opportunity to take advantage of Anna Ragosina's weakness. Dare he refuse such a chance?

And thus desert Natasha, and the children? Be reviled the

length and breadth of the States? Not entirely. Surely Allen Dulles would know what he had really done and why. But Dulles would not be able to tell anybody what he knew.

He would also be able to reach Peter Borodin. Certainly he would be able to stop his uncle from carrying out his mad scheme, possibly even to save his life. And he would be saving Diana.

Nor need it be forever. Surely, once Diana was safe . . . but this was Anna Ragosina he was dealing with. The only mistake *he* could make would be to imagine for a moment he could fool her. If he defected, he would have to make it seem convincing in every way, until . . . Dulles got him out? But Dulles might well feel that an agent could never be removed from such a valuable situation.

How *could* he just walk away from Natasha and the children, perhaps forever? Of course, Anna, once she became tired of him, might well agree to their being brought over. But would Natasha wish to come? Would she not hate him as much as anyone else was going to hate him, when the news broke? Would it not be better for her to stay in America—and trust that when he got back, Dulles would vouch for him, and his devotion to duty? Even for his heroism in accepting such a dangerous assignment?

When he got back. *If* he got back.

"I see the idea at least interests you," Anna said. "Believe me, John, I will make it worth your while. Quite apart from myself, I will see that you have anything and everything you wish, from women to whiskey."

He turned. "I have everything I wish. A wife, and children."

Anna's nostrils dilated. "We shall have to consider them, in due course."

"If we do not consider them now, they will hate me for defecting."

"All America will hate you, John. But we in Russia will love you. As will your wife, eventually. *If* she loves you."

"And Diana?"

"Will be returned to her family. With her husband."

"When?"

"Ah . . ." A shadow flickered across her eyes. "In due course."

"You must take me for a fool."

"Believe me, John, I wish to take you for what you are—

a very bold and even dangerous man. But you must not take me for a fool, either. Diana will be set free when you have established yourself in your new position. It should not take long. When you have convinced the world that you have truly defected, and when you have carried out one or two small tasks for me, then she will be set free."

"Do you expect me to accept that?"

"I expect you to accept that you have no choice. I would also ask you to be sensible—what reason could I possibly have for holding the girl, once I am sure that I have you?"

John hesitated. But as she had said, he had no choice but to trust her. "Then I wish to see her, as soon as I get to Russia."

"Why?"

"Because, my dear Anna, how else can I be sure she is in the excellent condition you insist she is in?"

Anna smiled. "I have told you she is perfectly well. But she is not immediately available. She is in Siberia. It is best if she stays there until she can leave Russia."

"You have sent Diana to *Siberia?*"

"Oh, stop worrying. Not to a labor camp. To a private prison of mine. Where she would be absolutely safe from Ivan, you understand. Don't you see? He does not even know I have her. He has been so wrapped up in his own affairs he has lost touch with the department. But were he to find out— You know Ivan, John. Would you like to think of him getting his filthy hands on that lovely girl? And he would certainly wish to use her for political ends."

"Which of course would never occur to you," John remarked, with heavy sarcasm.

"Now you are getting angry with me again," she said. "I know . . . now you wish to hurt me. Perhaps to beat me."

"Yes," he said. "Now I wish to hurt you, very much."

She gave a delighted laugh. "Then you accept my proposition? Because if you do, you can hurt me. As often as you like." She leaned forward to kiss him. "Starting right now."

George Hayman, Jr., opened the door of his half-brother's New York apartment and gazed at his father and mother, his face as somber as theirs.

"Well?" George asked. "How is she?"

George junior shrugged. "She's under sedation. Elizabeth

is with her, and the nurse. At least this shock has shaken Elizabeth out of *her* condition."

"And the children?"

"They're at our place. They're being looked after." He stared at his mother. Ilona had not spoken, was as beautifully dressed and groomed as ever, but she seemed twenty years older. "I'm sorry, Mother. Believe me, I am sorry. I still find it hard to believe."

Ilona walked across the room and sat down on the sofa, her back very straight. George thought that she had never looked quite so much a princess as she did at that moment. "Why can you not believe it?" she asked, her voice low. "Aren't you both thinking that it's strange this has not happened before? *I* think it is strange. I have thought for some time that John has been acting strangely. Ever since he returned from Russia in 1945. Now I know why. I think I knew why some time ago. But I foolishly refused to believe my senses. Because no matter how well we are educated, how carefully we are brought up, we are what we are. John is the son of a Russian Bolshevik commissar. It had to come out, some time. Is that not what *you* are thinking?"

George junior bit his lip.

George sighed, and sat beside his wife. "We simply don't know what pressures were brought to bear."

"Did he look like a man on whom pressure was being brought to bear?" Ilona asked.

"Well . . ." George junior said, "television directors can play funny tricks with their cameras. Interviews can be edited to make exactly the reverse of what was said come out."

"That is nonsense, and you know it," Ilona said. "My family! Do you know what I went through to bring you all into the world? The disgrace and the humiliation, the trauma and the terror? I did it all because I loved your father. As I love him still." For a moment her eyes softened, as she looked at George. "And now I feel like begging his forgiveness. He knew what John was before he accepted him as his son. But you—rushing off on some absurd chase—"

"I *have* to go now, Mother," George junior protested. "You must see that. My God, if I don't find Diana . . ."

"It's been six months," Ilona said bitterly. "Can't you understand that she is dead?" She glanced at her son, but her gaze softened only momentarily. "Sometimes one has to face facts, as I should have faced facts about John years ago. Diana is a Borodin. Borodins are a cursed race. They have been cursed for generations. Do you know something, my son? Since the moment my grandfather died, in 1904, no member of my family has died in bed? Every one of them has been murdered or committed suicide or been shot down. Every one! Now you go off and get yourself shot as well. You are half Borodin. And Felicity . . . fleeing with her Communist lover. Well . . ." She gave a harsh laugh. "At least John will be there to greet her."

"Ilona," her husband said, and took her hand.

She freed herself, and stood up. "With them gone, you are the only child I have left, George." She stared for a moment, and then turned away. "I must go to Natasha. There is some hope for *her*. She only *married* a Borodin."

She swept down the corridor.

"I've never seen her in a mood like this," George junior said.

"John is her firstborn," George said. "But you're right. She's never been like this before."

"What do you think is going to happen about Gregory's exchange, now?" George junior asked.

"I should think it will go ahead as planned," George said. "The defection of an advertising agent isn't likely to involve state security. It's more a family affair."

"An advertising agent?" George junior looked into his father's eyes. "The Russians claim John was a bigwig in the FBI."

"And we deny it."

"Wouldn't we? But wouldn't it fit John's mode of life these last few years? Even Mother's suspicions? Come on, Dad, you knew, didn't you?"

"If I did, I wouldn't confess it to anyone," George told him. "Not even to you, son."

George junior hesitated, and then sighed. "Of course you couldn't. But the thought of an FBI agent, who also happens to be my own brother, defecting . . . Maybe he's a plant. That would be just great."

"Yeah." George wished he could sound convincing. Because not even *he* knew what John had been doing this last couple of years—except that it was something utterly secret. But to believe that John would become a traitor for the love of Anna Ragosina, as the Soviets claimed . . . But the Soviets also claimed it had been out of a sense of responsibility toward his father. That was the truly imponderable factor, and the circumstance that made everything plausible. And raised so many other ugly possibilities as well.

"Do you think I'm doing the wrong thing in going to look for Diana myself?" George junior asked.

"I know you'll never sleep again until you do."

"But you also think she's dead, don't you?"

George hesitated, and then shook his head. "Nobody's dead until you see the body. You go find her and bring her back." He clapped his son on the shoulder. "I wish to God I were coming with you. I have half a mind to, anyway. But I may have something for you before you go."

"What?" George junior's head jerked.

"I have no idea, right this minute. But I'm lunching tomorrow with Allen Dulles. He made the date, and he's come up from Washington especially to keep it. He's with the state department, you know, or at least an offshoot of it. He might just have something to tell us."

Chapter 12

THE FEMALE GUARD TOUCH JUDITH PETROV ON THE ARM, AND without a word Judith got up, climbed the short flight of stairs, and stood in the square box facing the judge's podium. This was a familiar box, a familiar position; the three judges, already in their seats, were familiar, as were the prosecutor and her own defense lawyer, an amiable young man whose principal requirement seemed to be that he agree with all rulings of the court. Familiar, and yet unfamiliar. Real, and yet nightmarish. It was quite impossible for her to decide where the nightmare ended, and reality began. To attempt to decide would be too horrible.

It was impossible to convince herself that she had now been in Russia for eight months, and in a cell in Lubianka throughout that time. Eight months without seeing Boris or Ruth or Nigel, without even being allowed a letter from them. Or to them. Eight months in which the earth might have opened and swallowed her up, for all anyone knew. That could not be real.

It might have seemed more real had she suffered the sort of imprisonment she had known in the past. But for those six months she had neither been beaten nor threatened nor even *humiliated*. She had occupied a comfortable cell. She had been fed, well fed, three times a day. She exercised twice a day. She had been given books to read, although no newspapers, and she had been bathed every other day and given clean clothes to wear. Certainly the silent young women who had attended her were elements of a nightmare, but a strangely distant, passive nightmare.

Yet it was there. It had begun with her meeting with Prince Peter. How strange that she had once loved that man. But she had not loved him for long; she had come to understand too much about him. Yet, in her anger at the murder of her mother and father, she had willingly worked with him in his vain attempts to organize counterrevolution and international intervention in Russia. And he had come to her rescue during Hitler's war. For that she had been grateful, even if after 1945 their paths had separated again, as he had resumed his impossibly fanatical opposition to Bolshevism, and she had found a better goal in the erection of the Israeli state. But now . . . He had not changed; that was the dreadful point. He was still flawlessly dressed, flawlessly handsome—allowing for his age—flawlessly mannered. And still flawlessly mad, mad with hatred, not only against the peasants who had deprived him of home and family and prerogatives, but now, it seemed, against the whole world. So mad, and thus so convincing, that he had almost convinced her—as he had certainly convinced the Russians—of her involvement in this doctors' conspiracy he claimed to have uncovered.

For three weeks she had been denying these accusations. The other accused, reduced to shambling figures by a few weeks in Beria's cells, had confessed, been sentenced to terms varying from death to long imprisonment, and been removed. She, tall and strong and healthy and vigorous, and obviously unharmed, had denied everything, time and again, to the growing amusement of the court. Denied while the evidence against her, even implicating her by name, had, however false, been allowed to grow, feeding upon her past exploits, the fact that she *would* once have been capable of planning and carrying out a vast international conspiracy to commit murder . . . until her denials had seemed absurd even to herself.

But now it was done. She became aware that the courtroom was crowded. There had always been a horde of journalists; the regime had given the Doctors' Trial, as they called it, the maximum publicity. Now they seemed even more anxious than ever to witness and report the final act. There were men in uniform, as well, and women. No doubt Ivan Nej was here.

Probably even Peter Borodin was here. But she did not wish to look at any of them. She could only gaze at the judges, denying and defiant to the last.

"Judith Stein Petrova," said the chairman, "you have been found guilty, by reason of the overwhelming evidence against you, of subversion and treason and acts of war against the Soviet state. Have you anything to say before sentence is passed upon you?"

Judith opened her mouth, and then closed it again. Even she was tired of denying and denouncing. She seemed about to be overwhelmed by utter exhaustion.

The judge waited for several seconds, then raised his head to look at the court. "The sentence is death by firing squad," he said, "to be carried out immediately."

The guard touched Judith on the arm, and she turned for the stairs, discovering as she did so that she had mysteriously and silently acquired three more wardresses, standing close, watching her as she moved. They feared a hysterical outburst, perhaps, or a collapse. They did not know that she had stood in a very similar court, and been condemned to death in very similar terms, once before; the only difference between 1953 and 1911 was that then there had been a portrait of Tsar Nicholas II hanging on the wall behind the judges instead of one of Lenin, and that then the death was to be by hanging, instead of firing squad. And that time she had been a bruised and battered wreck of a woman, Prince Roditchev's victim, whereas now she had never been healthier. The fools, she thought, smiling at the women; they did not realize how much things had actually improved, in the past forty years.

Yet she knew despair lurked very close at the edges of her consciousness. She had been telling herself that to be condemned again would be rather like being struck by lightning twice; it seemed to go against the laws of nature. She had anticipated massive diplomatic interference by the Israeli government. But of course, as had been pointed out to her repeatedly during the trial, she had fled Russia without giving up her citizenship. In the eyes of the law, she was still a Russian, and therefore the Soviet state refused to recognize any claims that she might be something else.

Worst of all was the awareness of her innocence, on both

occasions. She was the victim of a madman's prank. She should hate him. She should shriek to the world, "God curse you, Peter Borodin, and may you rot forever in hell." Well, she did hate him, but more for what he had caused to be done to others, than for what he had done to her. She had accumulated a vast store of dignity over the years, as well as a sufficient store of fatalism. Now she even regretted having denied the charges, as her denials had made so little difference. Better to have stood in silence, throughout the whole three weeks. But at least she could die in silence.

Immediately. How immediately *was* immediately? There were more guards waiting for her at the foot of the stairs, to walk her along the corridor to the private entrance, where the van would be waiting to take her back to the prison. That at least was certain; she would not be executed at the courthouse. But would she be taken back to her cell, for a last private communion with herself? Would she be offered a meal? Would she be allowed to use the bathroom? Suddenly she was desperate to use the bathroom, though she had felt no particular urge earlier. But one could not be shot with a full bladder.

The door opened, and there was daylight. Briefly. Because the car door was also opened, and the interior was gloomy, since the blinds were drawn. Waiting for her were guards . . . guards? Judith halted in the doorway, staring in consternation. There were two people wearing uniforms, certainly. One, an incredibly beautiful woman, whom she did not remember ever having seen before. The other was John Hayman.

Judith fainted.

Judith realized she was on a train, lying on a berth in a sleeping compartment. She felt no pain, but exhaustion numbed her body and mind. She wondered if she was dead.

"We are coming into Berlin," a woman said. "It is only a short distance further. She will have to be wakened."

A damp cloth was placed on her forehead. Judith opened her eyes, and gazed at John Hayman once again. And it was definitely John Hayman. She closed her eyes once more.

"Mrs. Petrov . . . Aunt Judith . . ." John said, using the name he had given her in his teens, when they had been such good friends. "You must wake up now." He shook her very gently. "There is nothing to be afraid of now, Aunt Judith. Your sentence was only a formality. You are on your way to be exchanged."

Judith slowly pushed herself up in the seat, stared at him and past him, at the lovely woman she also remembered from the car, who also wore a Russian uniform.

"We have not met formally," Anna said. "I am Colonel Ragosina. Captain Hayman is right. You are to be exchanged, very soon after we have passed through Berlin. Perhaps you would like to wash your face and clean your teeth. The basin is there. Or would you like a glass of vodka?"

Judith looked at John. "Captain Hayman?" she asked. "You . . . are a captain in the KGB?"

John would not lower his eyes. "Yes," he said.

"But . . . no," she decided. "It cannot be true." She looked at the woman again, her eyes flickering as she realized that she had heard the name Ragosina before. Often. It was a name to be afraid of, and hate. Anna Ragosina was the woman who had kidnapped Ruth Borodina, Judith's niece, and held her captive for two years, years which even now Ruth would never speak of . . . and had then returned her to Nazi Germany, and the certainty of persecution. This was the most vicious possible product of the Soviet system. And John was working with her? "It cannot be true," she said again. "I will not believe it."

"Aunt Judith," John said. "It is true. I am an officer in the KGB. But it is also true that you are to be exchanged, tonight. There is nothing more for you to be afraid of."

They remained in the closed and shuttered compartment while the train halted in Berlin. Again Anna Ragosina offered her a glass of vodka, and again she refused. With every moment she was aware of an increasing sense of outrage, not merely against John, for this obscene prank he was playing, but against the whole Soviet state. She was to be exchanged, when several other equally innocent people had already been shot. How could she accept that? But how could she not accept it, either? As she had suspected, the nightmare was growing more deeply terrible as it fastened itself about her. But John . . . she stared at him, willing him to give her some signal that it was not true, that he was in fact rescuing her from the KGB like the greatest of Scarlet Pimpernels.

If that were so, of course, he would not dare give her a

signal, until they were both safe. On that slender thread she hung her sanity, as she watched the pair of them smile at each other and talk, realizing that these two were far more than just colleagues.

The train was moving again. Berlin was two hours behind them when they stopped at a lonely, deserted station, which was suddenly filled with armed men who escorted her and her captors off the train and into a truck. They drove for a while, and then came to a bridge, across a river. It was a big river, running to the northwest, Judith estimated. Therefore it was the Elbe, and over there was West Germany, and freedom. Freedom for her, if she could believe in freedom again. For anyone.

The driver of the truck flashed his headlights three times, and there came an answering flash from the far side. "It is time," Anna Ragosina said. The temperature on this February night was freezing, and she wrapped herself in her green army greatcoat before stepping down from the tailgate. John followed and turned to hold up his arms to assist Judith, but she ignored him and climbed down by herself. She had begun to suspect this nightmare was never going to end, would only become more nightmarish by the minute. Otherwise John would have already thrown off this absurd disguise, and killed these Russians, and run with her across the bridge . . .

"Cover us," Anna told the leader of the men who had accompanied them in the truck. He nodded, drew an automatic pistol, and moved to the left of the bridge. Two of his men went with him; the other three went to the right. "Remember," Anna said, "that should anything go wrong, we all die. But you will die first." She indicated the bridge. Judith stepped onto the steel surface, with John at one side, Anna at the other.

"I should have thought," Judith remarked, "that Ivan would be capable of doing his own dirty work."

"Walk," Anna commanded.

There were several people at the far side of the bridge, and now three of these left the land and also stepped onto the steel. Two others waited on the very end of the bridge, and John could just make out the flutter of a skirt. Now it was necessary to close his mind to the next ten minutes.

Such a procedure, closing his mind to reality, had not been

necessary before, because in Russia, as Anna had prophesied and promised, he was surrounded by friends, or people who were determined to appear as friends. His father's joyful reaction, he had no doubt, had been genuine. Catherine, his stepmother, had been no less delighted. Neither seemed to consider for a moment that his defection might be anything less than a genuine awakening of his mind and spirit, a general disillusionment with the faults of capitalism. Only the fact that he had come as a protégé of Anna had seemed to bother his father in the slightest. Michael Nej had said, "We must talk, John," while looking past him at Anna. "We must talk."

So even his father was afraid of the woman, which was not reassuring. And so far there had been no opportunity to talk; Anna had seen to that.

Others had been more skeptical. Stalin, whom he had last met when the great man had pinned the Medal of Lenin on his tunic in 1945, was certainly one of those, as was his Uncle Ivan. But they were all under the spell of Anna Ragosina.

The others who might have mattered, men like Beria and Molotov, merely seemed bemused by the whole thing. If they were skeptical of anything, it was of the amount of publicity being devoted to his flight. They doubted his value. But Anna remained totally confident in what she had done.

As usual, she had managed to surprise him with their relationship, which was quite unlike what he had expected, and indeed, feared. Far from being the constant companions she had promised, they actually saw very little of each other. She had made him embark upon a most severe course of physical training, in the company of men and women half his age; but the fact that he was her chosen lieutenant, and that she often dropped in to oversee his training, and occasionally take part in it herself, protected him from any contempt. She had also procured for him an apartment of his own, consisting of three rooms, and this she had filled with Communist literature, which he was required to read; there was also a television set which he was required to watch, for two or three hours a night. She was going about her duties of subverting him and making him into a KGB officer with the same intensity with which she approached everything else; again, the fact that he was *her* lieutenant protected him from demonstrations of the jealousy he was sure his arrival—and installation in an office next to hers—had aroused in the minds of her other subordinates, and especially the cold-eyed blond girl named Maria.

It had all happened so fast, and his days had been kept so filled, that he had had very little time to reflect on what he had done, and what was happening to him, and what the eventual outcome might be. And on the evenings when he did begin to reflect, there would be a knock on his door, and there she was, almost as if she could read his mind from a distance and was eager to empty his brain of any thought but sex, to exhaust them both with her apparently insatiable desires. That this did not happen more often surprised him. Amazingly, and disturbingly, it also concerned him, because he did not doubt that Anna had sex with *someone* every night. And for that he had given up everything. No, that was a lie. It had to be a lie, and it *was* a lie. When the time and the summons came, he would destroy her without a moment's hesitation. He had to believe that, or loathe himself. He *had* to believe that.

Just as he had to believe that such a summons, such a time, *would* come.

But meanwhile, her suggestion that on the nights she was unavailable he should invite one of the female secretaries from Lubianka to his apartment did not appeal to him. Or if it did appeal—because some of them were extraordinarily pretty young women, and they were all apparently as amoral as Anna herself—he was not prepared to give way to temptation. He had betrayed Natasha with Anna as a deliberate act, he hoped, of eventual sabotage against the Soviet Union; to sleep with any other woman, though, would be a true betrayal.

More disturbing than his speculation about the other men in Anna's life, however, was the realization that the longer he existed beneath the blanket of her power and protection, which seemed to extend throughout the Soviet system, the more rapidly the outside world became meaningless. The outside world only existed so far as the Soviet news agencies allowed it to exist. Thus not only had the reactions of Natasha and the children, of his mother and stepfather, his brother and his sister, and possibly most important of all, his employers, become unimportant, because he had no idea what they might be. But even the reason for his being here had suddenly receded in importance. Anna assured him that Diana was in good health, in a safe place, and was being well cared for—and that she would be released when the time was right. This he had to believe, because he had no choice—but also because he wanted to believe it. And she made the reasons for her delaying Diana's release very plausible: in no way could it be linked to his defection. That had to be accepted by the world as an entirely voluntary act—although she had suggested that she would be willing, for the sake of his family, to make it appear that, *after* his defection, he had discovered that his niece was under arrest for smuggling explosives into the Soviet Union, and had persuaded the authorities to forgive her and send her home.

It would happen when Anna was ready.

He was not even disturbed by the fact that he had not yet been able to be alone with his Uncle Peter. They had met, and Peter, after staring at him for several seconds, had turned and left the room.

John had been relieved; there had always been at least a chance that Uncle Peter, coming face to face with him inside Russia, with the man who knew what he was here for, might have panicked and given himself away. This he had not done. There remained, of course, the chance that he might seek to complete his self-imposed mission as soon as possible, but so far as John could gather, there did not seem to be any chance of his uncle being allowed near Premier Stalin. For the past six weeks, he had been too occupied in giving evidence about the doctors he had incriminated—and in any event, John had been told that Stalin had no desire to meet him. In addition, he had been reassured to learn that Peter Borodin's every movement was so closely watched that there was absolutely no chance of his obtaining any more explosives.

But all of that was irrelevant at this moment. Because now he was about to step out from beneath the cloying red umbrella that had sheltered him for three months, into the very cold light of day. The process, carefully designed by Anna—who had insisted upon handling this exchange herself, to provide the final proof to the outside world that John was totally hers—had begun with Judith Petrov's reaction to seeing him in a KGB uniform. But Judith's shock and disgust had only been the predawn half-light, because even in the darkness he saw who he was about to meet. Gregory, of course. But he had also recognized the man standing beside Gregory as an old comrade in arms, Arthur Garrison, who had been his immediate superior in the FBI. It figured that the exchange would have been given to the FBI to conduct; not only had they been the ones to arrest Gregory in the first place, but Allen Dulles would not wish the Russians even to suspect the existence of the CIA. That was a hopeful sign, for it meant that Dulles might be hoping John had not revealed the formation of this new counterespionage organization.

But Garrison was unlikely to know anything more than that his old buddy was a traitor.

And even Arthur Garrison was not the biggest hurdle, for John had also recognized the fluttering skirt, and the bulk of the man standing beside it, at the far end of the bridge. His brother and sister were over there.

Slowly, Judith, Anna, and John walked along the bridge, while the American party did the same. They both halted when they were about twelve feet apart. John moved slightly forward; Anna had instructed him to act as commander of the operation.

Garrison stared at him. "You've come a long way, *comrade,*" he remarked. He was a big man who suggested an occasionally friendly grizzly bear; this evening the occasion was lacking.

John ignored him. "Welcome home, Gregory," he said.

Gregory gazed at him. "I wish to protest," he said. "I do not wish to return to Russia."

"Well, I'd keep that to myself, if I were you," John said. "Mrs. Petrov certainly wishes to leave."

"There was to be another," said the second FBI man. "A Prince Peter Borodin."

"He does not wish to be exchanged, either," John said.

"Yeah?" Garrison inquired. "So it's a setup."

"Not at all," John said. "It is a simple exchange, Mrs. Petrov for Captain Nej. When Peter Borodin is ready to leave Russia, he will leave Russia. We have no desire to keep him, but we certainly will not force him to go. He is Russian-born, and has just performed a valuable service for the state."

He could feel Judith's contemptuous gaze burning the side of his neck, but kept his eyes fixed on Garrison.

"Yeah?" Garrison demanded again. "Well, fuck you, too." And he moved with tremendous speed, swinging a fist at John, which missed, went over his shoulder, brought Garrison's body thudding into his, and carried them both to the bridge rail. It was a chest-high rail, yet the force of Garrison's swing, combined with the weight of his body, somehow arched John over the side, and sent him plummeting down toward the icy waters of the river.

Vaguely John heard Anna shouting orders, and the other FBI man also shouting, telling the Russians, as well as his own people hidden on the far bank, not to shoot. But there were more important thoughts running through his mind, of how Garrison was not the man to miss with a punch, of how a hand had seized his trousers to lift him and almost throw him over the bridge rail, and of how Garrison was splashing into the river beside him.

John broke the surface, gasping for breath, the cold striking through his clothes. Desperately he thrust a foot down and found bottom, while Garrison, already on his feet, loomed above him. "For God's sake," he gasped.

"Grapple," Garrison commanded, and threw both arms around him again; they were in only five feet of water, but standing was difficult with the icy current tugging at them and seeming to wrap iron bands around their thighs—indeed they could only breast it by holding on to each other. "Allen says you'll either kill me or listen. Christ, what a job!"

"Hurry up," John snapped, attempting to give a good impression of fighting desperately. He could see Anna looking down on them from the bank, still shouting orders, and knew that within seconds KGB men would be in here to rescue him.

"Just to say hi," Garrison said. "We'll be in touch, but it may take time. This exchange on the level?"

"It has to be."

"And your sister?"

"Her too, if that's what she wants. No foul-ups."

"Okay, kid. Did I ever tell you you're one hell of a guy? Now lay me out."

The Russians were splashing into the river. Garrison pulled away, and half stepped back; John took a deep breath and swung with all his strength, connecting with the point of Garrison's jaw in a blow that seemed to push his fist into his wrist and his elbow into his forearm. Garrison went down without a sound, dipping into the water. John seized his shoulders, and the KGB men helped drag him to the bank.

"Let the bastard drown," Anna shouted from above them.

Between them they pulled Garrison on to dry land. "He was a friend, once," John said. "I guess you can't blame him."

"You will catch pneumonia," Anna said. "Fetch some blankets." She gazed at the other FBI man, who had so completely forgotten protocol as to cross the bridge into East German territory, and was also halfway down the bank—John wondered if he had not been party to Garrison's ruse. "As for you—"

"What can I say, ma'am?" the man said. "Seems Garrison lost his head."

It occurred to Judith that in all the confusion she should have tried to run, tried to do *something*. But Gregory Nej, standing next to her, hardly moved either, only turned his head to watch what was happening. No doubt he also knew that there was nowhere for either of them to run to, once the two greatest powers in the world had decided to take over their immediate destinies. In any event, though both Anna Ragosina and the other FBI man had run off, within seconds Judith and Gregory were again surrounded by men, from both sides of the bridge.

She gazed at Gregory Nej, who shrugged. "I do not understand either, Mrs. Petrov," he said.

"But you do not wish to go back," Judith said. "You are at least sane. Believe me, young man, I am sorry to be the cause of this."

Gregory shrugged. "At least I can feel that my surrender has accomplished *some* good, Mrs. Petrov."

Anna Ragosina had returned, accompanied by the FBI man, and by two Russians carrying the unconscious body of Arthur Garrison. "You," she snapped at Gregory. "Your very presence causes disaster." She pointed at Garrison. "I hope he will be severely disciplined," she told the other FBI man. "He might well have killed Captain Hayman."

"Yeah," the American agreed. "Aren't too many people in our outfit who'd mind too much, Colonel. Now, there's this girl says she won't leave Captain Nej . . ."

"You wish her to come?" Anna asked Gregory.

"No," he said. "I do not wish it. But it is what *she* wishes. And we love each other. And—"

"And in typical bourgeois fashion, you are sentimentally incapable of making a decision about it," Anna said contemptuously. "So I will make it for you. The woman is welcome, if she comes entirely of her own free will. It is all arranged." She walked forward, to stand before Felicity. "So: You recovered. Do you know how fortunate you are? When I shoot someone, that person usually dies."

Felicity gazed at the woman who had tried to murder her. "Yes, comrade," she said, her voice, as ever, slightly breathless.

"I should say that I am sorry for what happened in Washington," Anna said. "But I am not. If you wish to live in Russia, you must accept Russian discipline. I hope you understand that."

"I understand that," Felicity said.

"You will also have to work," Anna said. "If you understand the meaning of the word. But you will at least be with your lover, without censure. You must decide now, if you wish to come. You will not be able to change your mind afterward."

"I am here because I wish to come," Felicity said.

"Felicity—" George junior said, his tone a plea.

Felicity hesitated, half turned her head. "Forget it, George."

"You *can* still change your mind. Mother would be so happy if you were to go back."

"Mother doesn't understand," Felicity said. "She never has. Any more than any of the rest of you."

"Are you *quite* ready?" Anna inquired.

"Quite ready," Felicity said.

"Then join your lover. Make haste. We must all make haste, if your brother is not to die of exposure."

Felicity stepped forward and gazed at Judith.

"You are *shit,*" Judith remarked quietly. "I would scrape you from my shoe."

Felicity turned away and hurried over the bridge; Gregory had waited for her, and now he put his arm around her shoulder.

Anna glanced at George junior without interest, and turned to follow.

"Madame Ragosina," George junior said.

Anna checked, and looked at him.

"John is my brother too," he said.

"Ah," Anna commented.

"You seem to have gained a great triumph here," George junior said. "You have secured two of my mother's three children—I should think you can afford to be generous with the remainder."

Anna frowned at him. "What do you want of me?"

"I want a visa to enter the Soviet Union. I have applied many times, and been refused. I do not wish to come as a newspaperman. I wish to come as a private citizen. I have lost my daughter. My only daughter. A girl named Diana. She entered your country last summer, and disappeared. I would like to search for her, or at least discover what happened to her."

"Of course," Anna said. "John's brother. You are Diana's father! How stupid of me. I should have known at once."

"You have heard of her? Please, Madame Ragosina, my wife and I are desperate. She is my only child."

Anna gazed at him for several seconds; Judith wondered if it was occurring to her that, no matter where Diana Hayman might be, she had at this moment the opportunity to remove almost the entire Hayman clan into Russia, with their complete agreement. However, she appeared to resist the temptation. "John has told me the story," she said at last. "It is very sad. My heart bleeds for you. I will see what can be done about getting you a visa, comrade. I will even mount a search for your daughter, myself, and see if she can be found. If she is in Russia, I will find her. I promise you that. And then she will be returned to you." She smiled. "She can make up the missing half of the exchange."

"If you would do that, madame," George said, "I would be in your debt forever."

"Consider it done, comrade," Anna said. "And perhaps you will then alter your image of us, and have your newspaper alter *its* image, too. I give you my word, I will find your daughter. If she can be found, anywhere within the Soviet Union." She saluted, and turned to walk back across the bridge.

"God," Garrison muttered, slowly coming to. "Oh, God. To think I taught that bugger how to punch."

"Wrap him in blankets," said the other FBI man. "And give him a slug of brandy. We have to get out of here. Mrs. Petrov, come with me, please. I won't feel happy until you're out of Germany."

Judith had been standing almost as if turned to stone. Now she walked toward the car. George held the door for her.

"I think she meant what she said," George remarked. "Hell, Aunt Judith, both John and Felicity are doing what they seem to want to do. And if this Madame Ragosina *will* help . . . maybe the Reds aren't so bad, after all."

Judith gazed at him, and then got into the car.

Garrison drank brandy deeply, sighed, shivered, and rubbed his jaw. "Well," he said, "at least we got you out, lady. You should be happy about that."

"Yes," Judith said.

The car engine started, and they turned onto the road; the two other cars followed them. The Russians had already disappeared into the night.

"So what do you aim to do now?"

"Go home," Judith told him. "Go home to Israel, to my husband and my niece and her family, and never leave them again. And try to forget that Russia ever existed." She hugged herself, and stared out the window, at the darkness. "And the Haymans too," she muttered.

Michael Nej's apartment, an unusually large one, glowed with light, and throbbed with laughter, much of it supplied by the host and his brother. The vodka had been flowing for some time, and the two commissars had allowed themselves to become discreetly drunk. John thought that Felicity was also more than a little tight, and he himself had put away a lot of alcohol.

He supposed it was because they suffered from a common affliction—a feeling of total disbelief in their circumstances, a disbelief shared, but not enjoyed as much, by the other two members of the party, Catherine and Gregory.

"To have you back," Ivan said, embracing his son for what must have been the fiftieth time, "safe and sound, after an American prison—"

"I have told you that I was not ill-treated, Father," Gregory said. "And you must understand that I did not wish to come back."

"You have been brainwashed, of course," Ivan complained, sniffing. "Now we have you home we will soon have you rehabilitated. And to have brought this beautiful, charming young lady—" He seized Felicity's hand and kissed it, again for the fiftieth time. "Do you know, my dear, you are like a reincarnation of my dear Tatiana and my dear Svetlana?"

And you are like a rerun of a very old movie, John thought.

But Felicity was smiling at her uncle. "That is so kind of you," she said. Her eyes were filled with tears. But they were caused, John guessed, not merely by this family get-together. The entire day, the days on the train from Berlin, the entire past few weeks must have been traumatic. Now she was moving in a wonderworld of adventure and strangeness, for which her sheltered life could have given little preparation. Nor could she, knowing only Gregory, believe any of the things he and his brother and father had told her about Russia, and about the KGB, and about Ivan Nej in particular. Throughout today, her first in Moscow, Ivan had been charm itself, and in addition she had been greeted by bands and photographers, by Stalin and Molotov and Beria themselves, been embraced by them—no movie star had ever had such a reception. And she would sleep tonight in Gregory's arms, free from fear and recrimination and guilt, so John did not suppose she would awaken from her euphoric dream in a hurry.

Certainly he could not speed the process. He was still on trial, even if Anna had decided not to intrude upon the family reunion; on the trip back to Moscow she had not troubled to hide her dislike and contempt for both Gregory and Felicity—but also, he thought with some relief, her satisfaction at the way he had apparently handled Garrison.

He did, however, look forward to having several long chats with Gregory, in the course of time. Gregory despite his protests, was apparently to be returned to his duties in the KGB; he had been a captain of instructors. And John himself was still being instructed. He thought he would give a great deal to know exactly what was going on inside his cousin's handsome head. He believed Gregory when he claimed he would have preferred to remain in the U.S.—but it was essential to know why. Because of Felicity? Because he had been able to observe the far higher standard of living there? Or because of a real disillusionment with the Soviet system, arising from his realization that much of the anti-American propaganda he had been fed in Russia *was* just propaganda, and intensified by his anger on learning that his father had killed his mother. That anger still showed; it was even possible to suppose that Gregory nursed notions of revenge against the little man who was sitting beside him and displaying such bourgeois emotions. That would be an interesting, and useful, consideration. On the other hand, how long would Gregory's anger last, surrounded as he was by the apparent adulation of the Russian press and people? And leaders? He had also been embraced by the premier at the train depot, in front of newsreel and television cameras. Now he was to resume his career, whether he liked it or not; and under the auspices of his father, he would no doubt go very far, however much Anna Ragosina disliked and distrusted him.

A dislike and a distrust which made John's job that much more difficult. He could not be seen to be too friendly to his younger cousin. But at the same time, he *had* to find out, at some stage, whether or not Gregory was truly an American at heart, or still a Russian. It would be risky, but it was a necessary part of the job he had taken on, and he could pursue it with the more courage and optimism now he knew that Dulles was solidly behind him. What a relief *that* was!

And it was a job which had to be undertaken before the reverse brainwashing gathered strength, and Gregory once again became a Soviet automaton.

"Are you suffering no ill effects from your ducking? From that criminal assault?" Michael Nej asked, standing beside his son at the window, to watch the snow clouding down over Moscow.

"Not so far," John said. "I don't think I've stood still long enough for any ill effects to catch up to me."

Michael smiled. "You are too happy. We are all too happy. I have never seen Ivan so happy. I did not suppose he had it in him. But to have his son back, when he had thought him lost forever . . ." He glanced at John. "I too know that happiness, John."

Deceiving this man was the most distasteful part of the entire business. But, John thought bitterly, he had been deceiving *someone,* somewhere, ever since he could remember. Deceit had almost become a part of his nature. And Michael Nej, despite being his father—and, John believed, a truly decent man—was still a Bolshevik, who held life to be important only if it could be useful to the state. It was difficult to believe that such a man would not even sacrifice his own son, if he considered it necessary.

He said, "It is a happy occasion for me, as well, Father."

Michael said, "But it is still clouded, perhaps. I can understand that. You must be thinking of your mother, and Natasha . . ." Another quick glance. "And the children. It must have been a great wrench to leave them."

"Mother, certainly," John agreed. "I doubt she will ever understand. But I am hoping that Natasha and the children will be able to join me here, soon."

"You have been in touch with them?"

"No," John said. "But Anna Ragosina has promised to try to arrange it."

"Anna Ragosina," Michael said thoughtfully. "You are very much her protégé."

"Well, we have known each other for a very long time," John explained. "Do not forget that we fought shoulder to shoulder in the Pripet for four years."

"And planned this defection then?"

John hesitated. He constantly had to be aware of traps. Even from his own father? "Perhaps," he said. "But at that time I had no intention of actually returning to Russia to live."

"And what changed your mind?"

"A great many things, Father. I do not really wish to discuss them."

"I quite understand," Michael said. "Believe me, just to have you here is sufficient. However, I feel that I must warn you . . . Comrade Ragosina, while undoubtedly a woman of great force of character and great talent, and an invaluable member of the KGB, is also utterly ruthless and self centered."

John nodded. "I know that, Father."

"Then you will know not to trust her as fully as she may require you to," Michael went on. "But there is something more, of which I feel I must warn you. In her ambition, which is at times quite remarkable, Comrade Ragosina has more than once overreached herself, and has had to be disciplined. When these things happen, the star is usually accompanied into decline by those satellites which have been seen to be flying too close to it, if you follow me."

"I think I do," John said.

"I hope so, because should such an event again occur, even though you have my word that I will do all in my power to help you—providing, of course, you have done nothing subversive against the Soviet Union—your career could suffer a setback that would take years to overcome. Anna is undoubtedly a woman from whom to learn, but it would be in your interests to look out for yourself at all times." Michael gazed at his son. "In particular, it might well be to your advantage to report to me anything out of the ordinary that you may encounter, or that may be suggested to you in the course of your work."

"I'm not sure I'm cut out to be a spy," John said.

Michael smiled, and clapped him on the shoulder. "How can you be a spy in Russia, where you keep the interests of the Soviet state always in mind, and are determined to serve them at all times? I am giving you advice, as a father should. I but wish you to consider what I have said, very carefully. Now, I have a surprise for you." He turned to face the room. "For you all."

The others listened with polite interest.

"We are all Nejs and Borodins gathered here tonight," Michael announced. "For very many years the two halves of the family have been enemies. I would hope that this occasion, in which representatives of both families are gathered together here in Moscow, is but the first step in the direction of a general rapprochement between the Haymans and ourselves. To further this aim, in which I am sure you will all wish to agree with me, and assist me, I have invited Prince Peter Borodin to join us here for drinks after dinner." He looked at his watch. "I invited him for nine o'clock, and it is now nine o'clock."

They listened to a knocking on the door, and Michael smiled. "And Prince Borodin is always punctual."

Peter Borodin entered the apartment with a slightly defiant air, but he shook hands with Michael confidently enough. "Do you know a man follows me, wherever I go?" he said. "Will your government never learn to trust me, Comrade Nej?"

"Like most governments, it takes a long time to learn anything," Michael said jocularly. "Do *you* know, Prince Peter, I sometimes suspect that there is a man following *me*, as well. Now let me see—Ivan you know, of course."

Peter nodded to the little man, his former servant, who was clearly highly amused.

"My wife, I think, you have also met."

Peter bent over Catherine's hand. "Of course. In London, in 1946."

Catherine was clearly bewildered by the occasion and merely nodded.

"My nephew, Gregory Nej."

"I met you in London also, in 1946," Peter said, shaking hands with some warmth. "You fooled me as much as everyone else. I thought you were about to defect, long before George and Ilona did. But all the while you were out to steal the atomic secrets. You really must be congratulated."

"I assure you," Gregory said, "I really had very little to do with it. I was simply there."

"My boy," Peter said, "most success depends on being in the right place at the right time. And the Americans certainly had it coming. Oh, indeed. I have never seen such a willful squandering of total supremacy. Truly, as the Good Book says, those whom God would destroy—"

"That is not a quote from the Bible, Uncle Peter," Felicity said quietly. "It was first written by an English professor of history in the seventeenth century named James Duport."

Peter stared at her. "Felicity?" he asked. "You are a most amazing child. I saw you on the television news, and I could not believe it then."

"Gregory and I are to be married," Felicity explained.

"Bless my soul," Peter remarked. "Bless my soul."

"And John, of course, you know very well," Michael said.

"I do not think Uncle Peter approves of me, either," John said.

"My dear fellow, I just find myself unable to keep up with your multicolored coat," Peter said. He had optimistically decided to accept the fact that John, for whatever reason of his own, did not mean to betray him, and was determined to be affable.

"As I occasionally also find yours a little changeable," John reminded him, looking into his eyes.

Peter flushed, and Michael came to the rescue. "The important thing is," he said, "that we are all Russians, and that all of us have at last come to our senses. I would hope and pray that those others of our family will also, in the course of time, come to their senses and return here to live. That would be a famous occasion." He handed Peter a full glass of vodka and raised his own. "I would like to propose a toast. To all the Borodins, Haymans, and Nejs in the world, and to Mother Russia."

"Hear, hear," Ivan said, and drank, as did the others.

"And now, another toast," Michael said, smiling at Gregory and Felicity. "To the happy couple, whom neither family, politics, nor even prison bars have been able to separate."

Once again the glasses were raised, to hover as there came a knock on the door. Instantly the room was filled with tension, and John gained an insight into the precariousness of existence even for senior commissars or members of the Politburo itself, whose careers, or lives, could be terminated by just such an unexpected knock.

"I had better see who it is," Michael said, giving Catherine a quick and reassuring smile. His voice sounded more mystified than concerned, in some contrast to his brother, who had turned quite white. He went to the door, and opened it. Those inside the room could see that there were two men waiting there, but men who saluted Michael most courteously, before standing aside to admit a short, stocky man wearing a gray uniform jacket and black trousers, his face half-concealed beneath a walrus moustache.

"Michael Nikolaievich," Stalin said, "forgive this intrusion into your family party, but I could not let such an auspicious occasion pass without coming personally to wish you all every happiness in your newfound unity. Perhaps you will introduce me." He smiled genially at the room. "But I do not need introducing. I know you all. Except you, comrade. Will you not introduce yourself?" He stood before Peter Borodin.

For a moment the entire room seemed petrified, although only John had any idea what might be about to happen. Then Peter Borodin moved, raising his right hand—not to take Stalin's but to reach into his inside breast pocket and draw a small automatic pistol. The two women gasped; Ivan dropped his vodka glass to shatter on the floor; Gregory instinctively stepped in front of Felicity, pushing her into a chair. Michael ran forward. But he could not reach Peter in time.

These thoughts flashed through John's mind, even as he realized that, apart from Peter himself, he was the only armed man in the room; Anna had insisted that he always carry his pistol. And now it had to be used, or his mission would have failed before it could even be begun.

Before those thoughts could even crystallize, he had drawn, and fired, with his usual accuracy, his bullet striking Peter Borodin in the left eye and nearly blowing away his skull, before Peter could also squeeze his own trigger. John stared at his uncle in horror as the immaculately clad figure sprawled over a chair and then hit the floor, blood and brains spurting from the gaping wound.

But Joseph Stalin was lying beside his would-be assassin.

Chapter 13

"MMM, COMRADE," ANNA RAGOSINA MURMURED. "DO IT again. Oh, do it again."

She nestled ever deeper into her bed, enjoying the caress. To think that she had actually supposed John Hayman could replace this. But of course that was an absurdity. He was too inhibited, because of his upbringing, and he was also too conscious of having been blackmailed into his present position.

But somehow, no matter what his background or his reason for being in Russia, she doubted he would ever have been as good a lover as Nikolai Ivanovich Nej. It occurred to Anna that she was learning, perhaps a trifle late, what all women eventually learn—that it is not good looks or fine manners or smooth talk or beautiful gifts that denote the one man who will be *everything;* it is the man's desire to give pleasure to his lover, and most men only wished to take. Nikolai was short and a trifle plump and certainly not handsome; like his father he was nearsighted. He was a failed chess player and a second-rate journalist. He had neither money nor power, he did not bathe often enough, and his clothes were appalling. But he adored her with a desperation that almost made her love him back, and he had an exquisite pair of hands, which he used only for her delight, and he backed them up with an exquisitely knowledgeable penis. He could send her into orgasm after orgasm, whether she was in the mood or not—and very often she was most definitely *not* in the mood. Making love to Lavrenti Beria, which had to be done at least twice a week if only to reassure him that she was utterly faithful to him alone, left her feeling ready to scream. Making love to John, much as she enjoyed the physical feel of him and understood the need to bind him emotionally to her just as thoroughly as she did Beria, was very little better, because she was aware of the tension between them at all times. In comparison, Nikolai was like a dream. She knew he was useless at everything but lovemaking, and he wanted nothing of her except her body. He did not even have to be deceived—he *knew* he was only one among several, and being Nikolai, he presumed he was at the bottom of the list, and wanted only the crumbs she let fall from her table.

And when she *was* in the mood—like tonight—he could raise her to a pitch of ecstasy she sometimes thought she would not survive, an enormous, satisfying desire that was what she really wanted more than anything else in life.

She could afford to be honest about this, at least with herself. Once, perhaps, she had been driven onward by hatred. But that had been expiated long ago. Now she sought the rewards, the good things in life, and her ambition was directed toward achieving the power that would secure these things for her for the rest of her life. Even when she tortured some poor subversive into madness, nowadays she did it because she genuinely enjoyed doing it, rather than for any desire to obtain information or to prove herself the deadliest woman in the world.

Yet she could also be proud that she kept herself, and her desires, under such careful control; she allowed Nikolai to visit her only twice a week, and she kept one night every week entirely for herself, taking two sleeping pills, putting pads over her eyes, and sleeping for twelve hours; she even fed Tabasco sleeping pills in her milk that night, so that the cat should not disturb her. That one long night a week rejuvenated her, gave her the bubbling energy to cope with whatever might lie ahead.

Such was her control, she had not even been down to cell number forty-seven since her return from Stockholm. She did not wish again to be aroused by the girl, since she had decided to let her go. But before that could happen, a program of disorientation must be completed, so that Diana Hayman's mind would become a jungle of places and people and events, not one of which would be clearly remembered, and therefore when she tried to tell her terrible tale, as she undoubtedly would, she would stumble and be uncertain, and convince her listeners merely that she was suffering a breakdown. This was a lengthy process—it was the main reason why the girl's release had been delayed. But it would soon be completed.

But to visit her would certainly arouse *her*, and were Diana to say or do anything to irritate her, Anna might well do her an injury; she was well aware that her desire for Diana was separated from a vicious loathing by the narrowest of margins—and now the desire was absent.

She wondered if John would be more relaxed after Diana's release. Perhaps. But never as relaxed as this. Shudders tore through her frame, leaving her feeling almost sick with sated desire. She gasped, and lay on her back, arms flung wide and legs spread as wide as she could manage, while Nikolai kissed her armpits. And then Anna watched the bedroom door opening in total amazement, because no one would dare enter her bedroom uninvited . . . and she stared at Lavrenti Beria.

Beria blinked into the gloom. Not only was he very nearsighted, but he obviously could not believe what he was seeing. "Anna?" he asked. "Is that you, Anna?"

Anna sat up. She was very angry. Not merely at being interrupted on one of her nights off, so to speak, but because she knew there was going to be a scene. Therefore it was necessary for her to attack first. "You cretin," she snapped. "What do you mean by coming here?" she demanded. He was, after all, afraid of her.

"Anna?" he asked again, scratching his bald head. "There is a man with you!"

"An old friend," Anna explained, getting out of bed and praying that Nikolai, who was lying on his stomach with his face in the pillow, would have the sense to remain like that. "We met yesterday for the first time in years, and wished to have a talk."

"To *talk?*"

Anna held his arm and took him through into the living room, kicking the bedroom door shut behind her; she did not bother with a dressing gown—she knew how distracting Beria found the sight of her naked body. "That is what I said. Then we decided to sleep together. That is all. It has nothing to do with *our* relationship, Lavrenti."

"To sleep together," he repeated in bewilderment, and sat down on the sofa.

Anna knelt beside him. "Well, my dear one, I knew that you were not available, and . . . I felt randy. It is as simple as that. Now, I shall make us some coffee, and—"

"Anna," Beria said, "do you ever sleep with Captain Hayman?"

Anna raised her eyebrows. "Of course not."

"How do I know that?"

"Because I am telling you," she pointed out. "I recruited Hayman because he is the sort of man we are going to need—well, when we need him." She could never be sure, despite her precautions, that Ivan might not have had her apartment bugged. Besides, Nikolai might be listening. Of course Nikolai was absolutely trustworthy, but that did not mean she intended to trust him.

"When we need him! My God, Anna!" Beria rose from the settee. "I almost forgot why I came, seeing you in bed with that lout. Anna . . . Stalin . . ."

Anna, already on her way into the kitchen, halted, and turned, frowning. "What about Stalin?"

"It is incredible," Beria babbled. "You will not believe it—"

"How can I believe it, unless you tell me what it is?" Anna came back across the room, held his shoulders. *"Tell* me, Lavrenti."

"Joseph Vissarionovich . . ." Beria gasped for breath. "He went to a party at Michael Nej's last night. A celebration for Gregory Nej's homecoming. And Peter Borodin was there."

Anna's frown deepened. "Go on."

"Borodin drew a pistol. How he smuggled a weapon in—how he even got hold of it in the first place—is a mystery. He had been searched, you know, in the lobby. At least, checked out with a metal detector. Oh, I can tell you, heads are going to roll."

Anna was conscious of a curious and contradictory feeling; it was as if her heart had slowed, while her brain was suddenly racing ahead. "Borodin shot Stalin?" she asked.

"He was going to," Beria said. "But your friend Hayman beat him to it."

"What?" Anna shouted. "John Hayman shot Stalin?"

"Oh, no, no, of course not. He shot Borodin. His own uncle. Would you believe it?"

Anna's knees gave way, and she sat on a straight chair. John had shot his uncle? She almost wanted to weep with joy. Because, despite everything, she had not been able to bring herself completely to believe in John. Of course he was being blackmailed. She knew he resented this, and thus had known she would have to be at her most persuasively charming best to overcome that resentment and turn him into the trusted aide she sought. She had even supposed she had been succeeding, until that strange incident with the American, Garrison, three days ago. It had been almost as if John had *wanted* to fall into the river; certainly he could hardly have tumbled over that guardrail by accident. She had been brooding on it ever since. But now, if he had shot his own uncle, to protect Stalin . . . She smiled at Beria. "I told you he would be invaluable."

"Yes," Beria said. "But you don't understand . . . Stalin . . ."

Anna's frown was back, and she was on her feet again. "What about him?"

"He suffered a stroke, and perhaps another heart attack. He is gravely ill, Anna. He may even die, this time."

"Come in, comrade captain," Anna said. "The hero of Soviet Russia."

John snapped to attention before her desk; Anna was a stickler for protocol in public. "Do you really think so, comrade colonel?" he asked. "Do you know what the so-called 'gun' was?"

"A wooden facsimile, carved by the Prince himself," Anna said. "Yes. I have seen it. Very ingenious. It was the only weapon which could possibly have got through the metal detector. Yet it did contain a hammer and a pin and a real bullet. That guard must have heard something on the detector. He is being disciplined."

"It is probable that the whole thing would have collapsed, if fired, and possibly destroyed the hand of the man who fired it," John told her.

"But also the man at whom it was aimed. So it remained a deadly, if perhaps suicidal, weapon. Do you suppose your uncle came to Russia with that in mind? Sacrificed all those Jews and those doctors, all but sacrificed his own ex-mistress, for the sake of a shot at Stalin? That is real hatred, eh? It is a pity we shall never know the truth of it. In any event, that is by the by. You did not know what it was your uncle held in his hand. It looked like a gun, and there was your leader, standing before it. You acted with splendid speed and resolution."

"And shot my own uncle," John said.

"Oh, comrade, that is what makes your deed so heroic. Now close the door and sit down. I wish to talk with you about a very important matter."

John frowned, but he obeyed.

"And relax, just a little," Anna said. "You are aware that Premier Stalin is very gravely ill?"

"I thought he was dead, for a few moments," John confessed.

"Yes. Well, that may well be the outcome. His is not a young man, and he has a weak heart. No doubt you realize the importance of such an event, should it happen. Or perhaps I should say, when it happens."

"No doubt you are going to tell me," John observed.

Anna frowned at him for a moment, and then smiled. "To be sure. Why else do you suppose I brought you to Russia? The point is that Premier Stalin has never designated a successor. Therefore we may anticipate the same sort of power struggle as followed Lenin's death in 1924. That, you may remember, took five years to resolve. Five years in which the Soviet state nearly fell apart. And we were not a world power, then, with the Americans just waiting for us to collapse."

"You would all live a great deal longer, and probably be a great deal happier, if you could get it through your heads that America is not just waiting to wipe you out," John said. "We—I mean, they—could have done it more than once in the past, you know."

Anna smiled briefly. "We are not here to argue political motives, John. We are here to make sure, for the good of everyone, that such a situation is never allowed to occur again. Agreed?"

"Agreed," John said. He could only listen, and try to absorb, while his thoughts continued to spin and he hardly knew whether he was standing on his head or his heels. He *had* shot his own uncle. It *had* been a reflex movement, born of the knowledge that he had to keep Stalin alive, or at least prevent his murder. Those were facts; they could be considered as aspects of the bizarre job he had taken upon himself.

What was distressing was that he felt no remorse. It was as if he had been carrying out a preordained task. Was it because he had always known that Peter Borodin was a dangerous lunatic who would one day have to be stopped? Or because of sheer outrage that the man should have involved Diana, and thus himself, in his mad schemes, cost them both so much misery, and the girl, perhaps, her very sanity? Either way, those were not points of view likely to be understood by his mother, or by anyone in the outside world, when the news of his "heroism" was released. Now it seemed that he had taken an irrevocable step, even greater than that of accompanying Anna back to Russia. *That* could be explained by necessity, and by Allen Dulles. Killing Uncle Peter had been a personal decision, with which not everyone could possibly agree. Especially the man's sister.

And now . . .

"We—that is, the KGB," Anna was saying, "must therefore endeavor to control events, so that the succession takes place in the most orderly manner, and so that Premier Stalin is succeeded by the most suitable man for the immense job that lies ahead. Do you understand me?"

"I wish to know what you have in mind."

"I am about to tell you. This responsibility *must* be ours in the KGB, because there is no other body in the state capable of exercising that prerogative, and doing so successfully. It therefore merely remains for us to decide who the most suitable successor to Premier Stalin is. You will no doubt agree with me that Molotov is too old. The same, unfortunately, has to be said about your own father. Believe me, he would have been our first choice. But he is nearly as old as Premier Stalin, and I am sure he would be the first to understand that it would be a very shortsighted policy to invite a recurrence of the present situation in the immediate future. Both he and Molotov will of course be expected to continue in their present positions and with their present responsibilities. But considering all the circumstances, I am sure you will agree that there is only one possible candidate for supreme power in the Soviet Union whom we as an organization can possibly support."

"There is?" John asked.

"Of course. Lavrenti Beria."

"Beria? But he is the commander of the KGB."

"Is that an insuperable hindrance to his taking control? Rather, I would suggest that it facilitates it. And guarantees his success."

John stared at her, as a monstrous suspicion seemed to erupt in his mind. Anna's next words gave it immediate confirmation.

"Unfortunately," she went on, "there are elements in Soviet society who will have different ideas. We may refer to these as the young guard. Men like Malenkov and Khrushchev. Men who were boys during the revolution, who never knew Lenin, and who would change the essential and vital character of the Soviet Union. Those elements will have to be dealt with."

"Dealt with? This is a conspiracy," John said. "A conspiracy for which you and Comrade Beria have been planning!"

"It is always necessary to plan one's progress through life," Anna said quietly. "As you say, Comrade Beria and I have been planning our actions following Premier Stalin's death for some time. There are a great number of areas in which we do not see eye to eye, but we understand one simple fact: that while we can mutually destroy each other, while we work together we are invincible. Thus we have been working to strengthen our joint positions. Why do you think I brought you here? To have you at my side during the coming crisis. Because there will *be* a crisis. And when it breaks, I will know that standing behind me is someone entirely dependent upon me and therefore entirely loyal to me, but at the same time capable and determined. That is a great reassurance to me, John."

"You and Beria," John muttered, still unable to believe what he had just been told. "The two of you, carving Russia up. He takes the premiership, and you take the KGB."

"Why, yes." Anna gave a quick smile. "You will no doubt agree with me that I have the better bargain. Now, as I was saying, Malenkov and Khrushchev and their clique will have to be dealt with. I would prefer to avoid any mass executions, because such things are always bad for our reputation abroad. And I would hope this can be done. They are sensible men, and they will assume they have time on their side, and will thus accept the *fait accompli*. That is my hope. However, there is, regrettably, one man who will *have* to be disposed of, simply because he is inexorably opposed to Lavrenti Beria and all he stands for. I am speaking of your Uncle Ivan."

"Isn't he the man who made you everything you are?"

Anna snorted. "Do not make me laugh. Ivan made me what I am simply because he wanted what I am. I, as a human being, never existed for him. When he no longer required me, he sent me off to a labor camp. Do you know what they *did* to me, in that camp? There were women there who knew my name, whom I had interrogated . . ." She gave a little shudder. "I have long intended to settle with Ivan Nej one day. Now it would seem that day is coming closer." Another quick smile. "And having disposed of one uncle, John, you should not find the other one much of a psychological problem. However, the point is that he does have some elements within the KGB who will probably remain loyal to him. These must be eliminated at the same time."

"Will *that* not be bad for our reputation?" John asked, realizing, even as he said it, that sarcasm was always wasted on Anna.

"I do not think so," she said seriously. "Members of the KGB are always regarded as thugs. The executions of one or two will cause no stir at all. The execution of Ivan Nej will be hailed as a blessing. Even Judith Petrova will wish to shake your hand after that, John."

"And my father will be allowed to watch his brother die, and still be maintained in office?"

"He will certainly be maintained in office. But do not worry about your father either, John. In his heart he loathes his brother, and feels contempt for him. I know these things. I have seen them together. Now, here is a list of the men and women whom we cannot afford to trust, and who must be dealt with. I wish you to study that list, and commit it to memory, and then destroy it. This is very important. So is the matter of timing. We do not intend to make any overt move until Premier Stalin actually dies, but the moment he does, everything must start happening. The very moment. Now, I am going to be completely occupied with taking over the Politburo. And to be frank, with bolstering Lavrenti Pavlovich. Therefore I am putting you in command of the Elimination Section. I have already informed all the section commanders I know I can trust that you are to be obeyed without question, on receipt of a single code word from this office. That word must be uttered by myself, over the general intercom throughout Lubianka. The word will be *challenge*. Once I utter that word you will be sure of one hundred percent support from my people. You may well be opposed by certain of Ivan's creatures, but those who may be dangerous are on that list in any event. They must be destroyed without hesitation." She smiled at him. "There is no risk of your having to execute a friend, at any rate."

John allowed his eye to flicker down the list. Maria Kalinova! He raised his head. "Maria Kalinova? Surely she cannot be loyal to Ivan? Is she not your aide?"

"She was, before you came. Now she has been displaced. I do not actually know if she is working for Ivan or not, but I have not trusted her for some time, anyway. And do not feel sorry for her, John. She most certainly hates you. Were the situation reversed, she would have no hesitation in killing *you*."

John was still reading. "Gregory Nej?"

"That is essential," Anna declared. "Not only is he Ivan's son, but I do not trust *him* at all. Do not forget he spent four years in an American prison, and that he betrayed my organization in America even before that. I believe he may well be a plant. But do not worry about your sister," she went on hastily. "I give you my word that no harm will befall her. We will send her back to America, to your mother. She will like that. Your mother, I mean."

John's thoughts seemed to be rushing around in circles. But one fact was slowly becoming dominant. Here was the true Anna Ragosina, the creature of whom he had only caught glimpses in the past. Some of those glimpses had been terrifying enough, and he had rejected what they had indicated, or explained them away. First, because she was Ivan's creature. And then because she was fighting a war. Whatever she had done had perhaps been forced upon her. But now she sat behind her desk, smiling and looking as lovely as ever, having just condemned some fifty people to death without trial or mercy. Among them were some who had been her closest associates. As he was now her closest associate, he realized with something of a shock. Was there any emotion at all in that icy brain, that slow-beating heart? Could she even *feel*, except when she deliberately allowed herself to do so, for her own pleasure?

In his memoirs, he recalled, he had described her as the

most dangerous woman in the world. And he had not even known the half of it.

And yet, as usual, she still held all the trump cards, the ultimate weapons. If he were to lean cross this desk and squeeze the life from that body, he would still not be rescuing Diana. Diana! For nine months she had been the plaything of this lizardlike monster.

"Are there any questions?" Anna asked, taking back the list.

"Yes," he said. "If there is going to be some kind of a palace revolution, accompanied by a bloodbath, I would like Diana to be safe before it starts. I have now waited four months for you to carry out your part of our bargain. I think that is long enough. I also think I have proved my loyalty sufficiently even for you. I want Diana to be sent across the border into West Germany immediately, before Stalin dies."

"*You* think? *You* want?" Anna's eyes for just a second were as cold as ice. Then she smiled. "Perhaps it's just as well. I will have to see if she is ready."

"Ready? What the hell are you doing to her?"

This time Anna's eyes were hooded, as she realized she had made a slip. "It is no concern of yours. I have told you that she is alive and well, and she *is*. The very moment I can move her, I will."

"I would like to see her."

"That is impossible," Anna said. "She is in Siberia. I have told you that."

"And I think she is here in Lubianka."

Anna frowned at him. "Are you accusing me of lying?"

"I don't think you know what the truth is, Anna," John said. "You spoke of seeing if she was ready," he pointed out. "You can hardly do that in less than a week, if she is in Siberia. And you are not going to leave Moscow right this minute, with so much at stake, are you, Anna? If she *is* all right, what is wrong with letting me see her?"

Anna continued to gaze at him for several seconds. "I do not know," she said at last, speaking very quietly, "if you are under the mistaken impression that what I have just told you in some way gives you a hold over me, John. If so, you had better think again. You may have saved Premier Stalin's life, but I am his most trusted agent; I report to him every month, and he has given me carte blanche to conduct affairs as I see fit. No matter what I am accused of, or who does the accusing, my word will be accepted against that of anyone else in Russia, anyone else in the world, as long as he lives. The moment he dies, my law will become that of the state. I am inviting you to accompany me to the very heights. If you choose not to do that, you may well find your name on that list, and that of your addlepated father as well. I do not intend to play you false about the girl. I have said that she will be returned to her family, and that will happen. When *I* am ready. Although, once again, I should point out that should you cease to be my friend and become my enemy, all bets, as they say in your country, are off. You will have betrayed our bargain, and I will therefore have no choice but to execute the girl as well." She smiled. "But you are a sensible man. You and I understand each other, John. Now go back to your duties, and hold yourself in readiness for a summons from me."

He stared at her. There could be no doubt that she was very angry indeed. Her eyes had become black pits, and her nostrils dilated as she breathed. He had dared the lightning, and had very nearly been struck.

But having destroyed his resistance, as she saw it, she was, as ever, prepared to be magnanimous. "And tonight I shall come along and see you. It is not your night, but I shall still come, John. Will you not like that?"

She might have been speaking to a child. It did not seem to occur to her that he too could be very angry.

How narrow is the border between duty and desire, between love and hate, between *I wish* and *I must?* Narrow, John Hayman wondered, or impenetrable?

He lay on his back on his bed, and listened to the clock ticking. Sometimes he thought he could still hear her heels on the stairs. Certainly he could still feel her body on his. Now it was just after midnight, and he was again alone. She had come, with clinical detachment, to cement him to her side, and then had hurried off. She had somewhere to go at one o'clock in the morning. Because this had not been his regular night?

And yet, while he resented her abrupt departure, he was glad of it. He needed to think, and that was not possible while in the presence of Anna, or even knowing that she was coming to see him.

Had he nearly throttled her as she had lain in his arms? The thought, the desire, had certainly crossed his mind. But he had controlled it. Because Anna, even a dead Anna—supposing he had been able to do it before *she* killed *him*—had to be opposed by a mental power superior to her own. Even in death, she would command too many forces for him to overcome—unless he could first think his way through the maze of plot and counterplot which she represented.

So now was the time to think. She was gone, and he did not know when time would run out.

She sought nothing less than the supreme power. The elevation of Beria to the premiership could be regarded as both temporary and irrelevant; while he was there, he would do what Anna told him to do. When she no longer needed him, he would no longer be there.

That was the salient, the only truly important point. He, John Hayman, had stumbled upon the greatest conspiracy in recent Russian history. No, that was incorrect. He had been deliberately introduced to the conspiracy, because he was meant to play a leading part in bringing about the conspirators' triumph. Of course Anna had wanted him, the man she remembered from the Pripet, the man without a country or even a heritage that he dared remember, the bastard son of a Russian commissar and a princess. A man, as she had smilingly told him, who would have no friends among those he was designated to destroy.

A man who would then have outlived his usefulness, perhaps? He could no longer even pretend that she felt anything for him at all.

But *feeling,* personality, were distorting his thoughts again. He could not allow that. He was a CIA operative . . . who was slowly realizing that he might have it in his power to decide the course of history. There could be no comparison between a Russia ruled by Lavrenti Beria, in turn ruled by Anna Ragosina, and any other conceivable organization. He did not know either Malenkov or Khrushchev, or any of the other younger men who might aspire to take Stalin's place. But he did know that they had not been educated by the KGB, that they had not been part of the bloody feuds that had distorted the revolution. Hopefully they would be willing to accept advice and guidance from Party veterans like his own father, and might also be prepared to guide their country in the direction of rapprochement with the West.

They at least represented hope.

A Russia ruled by Anna Ragosina would seem as if Ivan the Terrible again stalked this land, and where Ivan the Terrible had ruled a relatively small, turbulent, ineffective country, Anna would be taking over the second most powerful nation on earth. Logic told him she had to be stopped. Therefore she had to be condemned to death. That was the only way to stop Anna.

But what would merely executing Anna achieve? The conspiracy would remain, except that without her to guide it, no one could say what would happen. A Beria in control, without Anna, might even be worse than Anna in control—history taught that at least strong tyrants were safer than weak ones.

No, the entire conspiracy had to be brought down. By him? He would be committing suicide. He could not doubt that. As she had reminded him, he had come here as her creature, and was totally identified in that role. Even if he betrayed her, they would almost certainly put him against a wall beside her; not even his father, relegated to the status of ineffective elder statesman, would be able to prevent that. He wondered what they would say to each other, just before the bullets smashed home?

But that was beside the point. What he was really trying to convince himself of was that his role here was finished. He had been given the most perfect assignment in the history of international espionage, and after three months he was going to blow it, because there was nothing else he could do. Dulles would not be amused.

But Dulles would not understand the true situation. He had come here less as a spy than as a hostage for the release of Diana. To destroy Anna and her entire conspiracy would nevertheless leave him a failure if he did not also rescue Diana. He did not even know if the rest of her life would be worth living, after having spent nine months in Anna's custody, but now he did know that Anna had no intention of letting her go. So, as Anna herself had said, he intended to ride to her rescue like a knight in shining armor . . . without even knowing where she was, or how they could cross thousands of miles of Russian territory to safety.

But he had a few ideas on how that could be accomplished.

It was simply a matter of planning his steps slowly and carefully—but not too slowly. Of deciding whom he could trust, and whom he could not. And then of acting, with utter determination and conviction.

Of taking his life into his hands. But he had done that often enough before.

John got out of bed and began to dress.

Michael Nej looked at his son with somber eyes. "If what you say is true . . ."

"Do you doubt it?"

Michael shook his head. "No, I do not doubt it. It was I who warned you against her ambition, remember? And even Ivan is aware that she is no longer the devoted assistant she once was. Beria! There is a two-faced monster! Stalin was quite right not to trust him."

"Beria might appear as a monster to the world," John said, "but he is a harmless middle-aged lecher, compared with Anna Ragosina."

"No doubt. No doubt." Michael got up, paced his living room floor, and glanced a little anxiously at the door to the bedroom; but Catherine slept soundly. "The question is, what must be done?"

"Surely you should put the matter to Stalin himself," John said. "Or is he too ill to understand?"

"By no means," Michael said. "But . . ." He chewed his lip. "Anna Ragosina, as you may have observed, seldom bluffs. It is true that she visits Joseph at least once a month, and sees him alone. I think he *has* decided to trust her above everyone else."

"Above even you?"

"Who can say? He is an old man, and ill . . ."

"But if he already distrusts Beria, Father, and Anna is working *with* Beria . . ."

"I can only give him your word for that," Michael reminded him. "And if it is something he does not wish to hear . . . He is given to violent moods. You do not know him. To go to him with this tale might well be to sign our own death warrants. Can you imagine if he were to hand us over to that woman?"

John stared at his father. If he had never been able to feel any true affinity for this man, he had also never felt anything less than respect for him—for his courage as a revolutionary, and as the general who had led the Red Army of the South to final victory over Denikin and Peter Borodin, despite first suffering several calamitous defeats. But this man standing before him was frightened of dying, when there were so many other lives at stake. And was still capable of convincing himself that he was doing the right thing.

"Besides," Michael was saying, "there is no proof of *anything*. Only what she has told you."

He was right. Anna had even taken back the list of names.

"No, no," Michael decided. "I know what we will do. I will tell *Ivan* about this plot, and we will await events. When Joseph Vissarionovich dies, if he dies—because he still may not—then we will be ready for any overt act from either Anna Ragosina or Beria. Once they have shown their hands, we will know what to do."

And meanwhile, John thought, you will pray—no, because you do not pray, at least not openly; but you will certainly hope, very fervently—that Joseph Vissarionovich will not die, or that Beria will change his mind or lose his nerve . . . that anything will happen which will keep you from involving yourself in such a dangerous crisis.

"When they show their hands, Father," he said quietly, "it will be by murdering Ivan and all of his associates."

"But you are the one designated to do that," Michael reminded him. "And you are not going to carry out those orders, are you?"

John gazed at him, and then nodded. "As you say," he agreed. "I am not going to carry out those orders, Father."

"Rather, you are going to act with us."

John looked at him for several more seconds. So now he was going to deceive his own father. But he had done that from the moment he had entered this room, in not telling him about Diana. He had wanted to, had even intended to—which would have meant telling him what he really planned to do. Something had held him back, for which he must now thank God.

"Of course," he lied. "When the time comes."

They lay together, body to body, cheek to cheek, legs intertwined, and fingers also. Because they loved with such a desperate earnestness, they often slept this way, as they had before their world had fallen apart. Now they were together again, but in a world which showed no immediate sign of coming back together.

Felicity Hayman was well aware that she was regarded as slow by her family. When one is so regarded by one's nearest and dearest, over a long period of time, it is very easy to accept such a crushing verdict. But Felicity was both a Hayman and a Borodin. She knew she was not slow. In fact, she knew she was at least as intelligent and quick-witted as any of her famous relatives. She was also more sensitive. In 1940, on the rebound from an unhappy love affair with a boy her mother disapproved of, she had become engaged to a Navy lieutenant. She had known it to be a rebound—caused entirely by parental opposition to a prospective son-in-law who was neither a millionaire nor had any prospect of becoming one—but yet she had been prepared to love David, to throw herself entirely into the business of being his wife, and in time the mother of his children; her family was delighted, as David, the son of a prominent New York banker, was exactly what they had wanted for her. And then Pearl Harbor had happened. David's body had never been found. She had spent several years waiting for him mysteriously to reappear, and more years coming to terms with the fact that he wouldn't.

She had turned inward, voluntarily. Her family had not understood that she wanted only to be left alone. They had endlessly sought to entertain her. When their Russian cousin had arrived for a much anticipated vacation, it had seemed to them natural that Felicity, with so little to do with her time, would show him around. She was seven years older than he, and could look after him. And it would do her good.

Instead, she and Gregory had fallen in love—she with the total, passionate commitment of a woman who had never wanted anything but to love; he, she now knew, as an act of strategy. Yet the act had soon enough become reality.

Once again the family had not understood, their lack of understanding accentuated by such evocative words as "incest," and it was their vendetta, as far as she was concerned, that had been mainly responsible for Gregory being sent to prison. After that she had hated them, and America.

She had always felt a sense of insecurity that she should have been born to wealth and power simply because her name was Hayman—a sense of guilt, even, that she should have so much, while so many people had so little. Identifying with the teeming millions in Russia, who seemed to have seized control of their own destinies, had been simple. And when, in addition, it had brought her and Gregory together again . . .

But he was utterly unhappy. She had always considered it wayward of him, his desire to identify himself with America and Americans rather than with Russia and Russians. Of course she had been filled by her family with absurd tales of the horrors of the Bolshevik regime; she had dismissed them as propaganda. Gregory himself had told her that his father, for reasons of state, had executed his mother, and that he could never forgive him for that, which she thought quite understandable. But she had somehow managed to romanticize this incident—after all, Tatiana had been running away with another man—until it seemed nothing more than a skeleton in the family closet.

Not anymore. It was not merely that Ivan Nej, her own father-in-law, she kept reminding herself, actually looked like a murderer. One need not, of course, like one's father-in-law. And certainly all the other bigwigs she had met, from Stalin down, seemed very anxious to entertain her, and smile at her, and be nice to her. While to find John himself, her own half-brother, ensconced in the midst of these people, as comfortable as he had always been in America, should have been reassuring. Instead, she had found it intensely disturbing. There was apparently just as much a hierarchy in Russia as there was in the United States, a hierarchy not of wealth and property and family as much as place in the Party, achievements for the Party. Not being the dimwit her family supposed her to be, Felicity could readily understand that place in the Party lent itself far more readily to corruption than place in the family or place in the social register, which had to be earned by a few generations rather than a few devious deeds.

But the common people in both countries remained the common people. In America they were those who did not have a lot of money in the bank or did not claim descent from the passengers on the *Mayflower*. In Russia they were those who had not found favor with Joseph Stalin. Suddenly, America actually seemed more democratic.

Gregory had known these things all the time. She was just

finding them out. But he had been forced to burn his bridges, and she had followed his example voluntarily. America was closed to them, now and forever, barring a miracle. And at least they had each other. But oh, how she wished time could be stopped, and perhaps turned back.

She sighed, and rolled onto her back . . . and gazed at her brother, framed in the doorway.

Gregory Nej pulled his nose thoughtfully, and glanced at Felicity, who was staring at him.

"You do know, don't you," John said.

"The man would be in one of the cells in row thirty," Gregory said. "Diana would probably be in cell forty-seven, in the women's block, if she has been in the special custody of Anna Ragosina."

"In Lubianka."

"That is correct. Down beneath the street. Beneath even the ordinary cells. It is a special world down there." He glanced at Felicity again. "A terrible world."

"But you can take me to it," John pressed.

"I can do that. It will be very dangerous. There are guards, and doors . . . it would be to risk our lives."

"I have told you, Gregory, that your life is already written off, in Anna's eyes. *All* of our lives are. Perhaps you feel I should stay, and fight against her, with your father and mine, and let Diana go to hell."

"No," Gregory said. "I do not feel that. I do not even feel that about myself. If they wish to destroy themselves, that is probably a good thing."

"Then you will help me?"

Gregory gazed at Felicity. Her gaze was unreadable; he knew she would not attempt to influence this decision.

"And afterward?" Gregory asked.

"Afterward? If you help Diana and me, and Felicity, to get out of here, no one will refuse you entry to the United States, Gregory. Or citizenship."

"I meant, after we have taken your niece from the cell," Gregory explained. "Have you considered what happens then?"

John bit his lip. "Well, I thought if we waited until Stalin actually died, and Anna gave her password, then I would have carte blanche, at least within Lubianka—"

"Within Lubianka," Gregory said contemptuously. "Have you any idea how many hundreds of miles Lubianka is from the border? The Polish border, John. To all intents and purposes, that is Russia. Then there is East Germany. That journey takes three days by train. In winter it will take even longer by car. Have you considered that?"

"Things here will be in one hell of a mess," John said lamely.

"Not for three days. Within six hours of Stalin's death, either Anna and Beria will be in control, or my father and yours will be in control. Either way, they will send someone after us. And then. . . . I do not know about your father, but mine does not forgive. He never forgave my mother for deserting him, and he will never forgive me."

John sighed, and looked at Felicity.

"But I do not think, even with your warning, that they will win," Gregory went on. "I think they are already condemned to death. Both of them. Your father as well, if you desert Anna."

"Does that concern you?"

"My father deserves to die," Gregory said. "I was thinking of yours."

John hesitated. "My father must fight his own battle, now," he said. "He has before. I wish to know if you will help me."

Gregory turned to Felicity once again. "We opposed Anna Ragosina once before," he said, "and she all but killed you. If she takes us now, she will kill you slowly, as she has no doubt already killed Diana, at least her mind. It is for some shattered hulk of a woman that Johnnie is asking you to risk your life."

Felicity did not lower her gaze. "I will go wherever you go, Gregory," she said.

Gregory got up and walked to the little bar in the corner of the room, poured himself a glass of vodka, and drank it. "I am a fully qualified pilot," he said, gazing at the wall. "Did you know that, John?"

John's heart started to pound. "Then you will help us?"

Gregory turned, his face suddenly harder than John had ever seen it before. He opened his mouth, and stopped as the telephone suddenly jangled.

All three of them stared at the instrument, and then at the clock on the mantelpiece. It was three in the morning.

Slowly Gregory crossed the room and picked up the receiver. "Yes," he said. "No, I was awake. Yes. Yes, I see. Of course. In the morning."

He replaced the receiver, and gazed at them. "That was my father," he said. "He telephoned to tell me that Premier Stalin died half an hour ago."

Chapter 14

FLICKER, FLICKER, FLICKER WENT THE LIGHT. BANG, BANG, bang went the noise within her head. Seethe, seethe, seethe, coursed the flesh on her bottom, where she had been whipped, and on which she was now sitting, moving, seeking some relief.

Was she also making a noise, moaning or screaming? She had no idea. She often did moan or scream, even when by herself, and only realized she was doing it when, briefly, the noise stopped.

This present hell had begun with the lights. When? She had no means of knowing. Weeks and weeks ago. Perhaps years. The last definite incident she could recall had been the day they had shaved her. That had been the most terrible experience of her life, to that moment, because one of the girls had held a mirror, so that she could see what was happening to herself, and she had not been able to stop looking. Anna Ragosina herself had done the final shaving, removing every last hair from her head, every last hair from her body, smiling at her while she did it, understanding that for a girl as beautiful as Diana, this was degradation. Yet she had not screamed, then. Then she had still wanted to oppose them, oppose Anna Ragosina, with stoic dignity.

And after she had been shaved, she had been left alone for a long time. The guards had brought her meals, seen that she exercised, walked with her to empty her latrine bucket, but they had never spoken to her, nor had they attempted to ill-treat her in any way; she had come to the conclusion that she was too horrible a sight even to interest them. She had never seen Anna again, since the day of the shaving. It had even been possible to suppose that she had been removed from control, that someone else was now in command of the women's section. It had been possible to hope, and put her faith in patience. Insensibly, she had relaxed.

Then, one day, without warning, there had been the light. Several lights. The entire roof of the cell had seemed to be filled with lights, glaring down. Lights too bright to be resisted, even with tightly closed lids. Lights that precluded sleep. For days there had been no sleep.

Then there had been the music. They had stripped her and chained her to the wall, as in her first days in here, and they had clamped earphones to her head, and for days there had been no cessation of sound. The lights had been bad. The noise was sheer torture. She had realized they were trying to drive her mad.

Was she mad? She did not know what madness was. Had she ever known?

The days of light and the days of noise had been succeeded by days of utter, silent darkness. At first she had not noticed the difference. Lights continued to glow before her eyes, her brain continued to throb. When the silence had finally penetrated her consciousness, she had slept deeply, through sheer exhaustion. Yet it had not been possible to sleep long, because the darkness was not tranquil, it was a stealthy, crowded darkness. It kept being filled, with *them*. She would hear her door open, and not know who was there. They would come in, and touch her, while she could not see them; she presumed they were using some kind of infrared glasses. They would play with her, she supposed, as a cat might play with a mouse.

Or had she dreamed them, and their horrible fingers? That was the problem, separating dreams from reality.

Then suddenly the lights were back, and she was being squirted with a hose. She discovered that her wrists were free, and she could move. The water had been ice cold and as hard as a whip. It had played up and down her body and she had screamed and shrunk away from it, before becoming angry and attempting to charge the naked women who were laughing at her. But the jet had merely knocked her over again, sent her cowering and gasping and weeping against the far wall. But she had not begged them to stop. She had refused to do that. And in time they had gone away.

Sometimes she was beaten, by the same laughing women. She was never kicked or punched or slapped, which might conceivably leave permanent marks or damage. Always they used a leather strap, used it with exquisitely savage cunning and knowledge. But there had been no more assaults with red pepper; that was apparently the prerogative of Anna alone.

Yet there had been things nearly as bad—the sexual assaults, which took place at random, and left her ashamed of her own femininity. To think that once she had wanted sex at least once in every day.

And then there was Robert. She would be taken to an observation room, and allowed to see him. Sometimes he was just chained to the wall of his cell, as she often was. But once he had been being beaten. And once he had been in bed with two naked women, his wrists tied behind his back. Another time it had been two men. Shameful, horrifying, distressing . . . if real. But *was* Robert real? Had he ever been real? It seemed like a dream out of a long distant past, that they had lain together in a bed in a luxurious Paris hotel, and loved, and talked, and planned. What really distressed her was that if he was real, then perhaps from time to time he was being taken to observe *her*, a caricature of the woman he had married.

Now the hair was growing again. She had no mirror, but she could see it on her groin, and she could feel it on her head. What did that mean in terms of how much time had passed since the shaving?

When was now? Every day was a kaleidoscope of noise and light and water and sex and beatings—every day. Or was every day actually a month, a year, an eternity? In the tomb that was her cell, she could form no idea of time. Even meals did not help, because these were also part of the process of breaking her down into madness. Sometimes she would be given an enormous meal, and then another one surely no more than one hour later; when she could not eat they would force her mouth open and cram the food in until she vomited. And then there were times when she was sure she had had nothing to eat for forty-eight hours or more, and would almost be ready to gnaw her own flesh.

But she could think these things, still. She could attempt to combat, still. She had been combatting . . . from the beginning. It was impossible to be sure how long ago that had been. Then she had never had any doubts that rescue, and revenge, were only days, perhaps hours, away. She was Diana Hayman. All the forces of wealth and privilege and even righteousness in the world must be hurrying to rescue her. In that mood, she had tried to fight them. Once, she recalled, she had bitten Anna. A very long time ago. How strange, that she could not clearly remember what Anna looked like. But she could remember the bite, and the frightful assault with pepper that had followed. Then, she recalled, she had begged even as she had screamed. The assault had been renewed, twice afterward, and each time had reduced her to a screaming, begging, *thing*. Now that, the pepper, *would* have driven her mad. Yet strangely, its use had been discontinued. She did not understand that at all, although she had some idea it was because Anna had lost interest in her.

But she had not lost interest in Anna. Hating Anna had kept her sane, then. She had not actually been aware of the emotion, at first. She had not know what it was, because she had never before in her life had occasion to hate anyone. When she had found herself dreaming of sitting on Anna's chest and slowly throttling the life from that lovely, vicious face, she had wanted to reject her thoughts as obscene. But obscene things were being done to her, and she had come to realize her own hatred was the pathway to salvation. Or at least survival.

Now she doubted. Because she could no longer convince herself that even Anna was a real human being, and not a figment of her imagination. She had come, and then she had disappeared. For an eternity. Certainly years and years and years. Years in which *she* had lain here, and suffered, and hated, but not Anna. One could not hate a dream, even when the dream was a nightmare. That way *was* madness.

Besides, there were a great many other, more immediate things to hate. There was the girl, Maria, who came in here every day to torment her. There was Peter Borodin, for involving her in this mess. There was Robert . . . but Robert, by the evidence of her own eyes, was in this mess with her. Or *were* those just pictures in her brain? She couldn't be sure. She couldn't be sure of anything.

Except that if she *was* still sane, she was holding on by the most slender of margins, and hatred had nothing to do with that. Because hatred had progressed from Robert, to her mother and father, for allowing her to be born, and then even back to her grandparents, and everyone in the dreadful chain of ancestorship who had been responsible for such a total catastrophe as she had become. But the most hateful thing of all was the bag of flesh and bone and pain in which she was so totally imprisoned.

Unless perhaps she too was not real, but a creature in a nightmare.

But gradually she had worked out a system of survival, within herself, within her body prison, which was imprisoned in a cell, which was imprisoned within the vicious laughter and mistreatment of the women. In the first place, since the women could not be escaped, could not even be fought with any hope of success, they had to be accepted, and if possible, neutralized. The key to this was the mental breakfall. She had taken judo classes at college, and knew all about physical breakfalls. The system was the same, used mentally; instead of resistance, there was acceptance, a merging of the force that was her own pain and terror and hate with the immense force that was causing her that misery. Thus, forget dignity, and scream. And scream and scream and scream. Scream and weep. Never beg. That was unnecessary and would serve no purpose. But scream until your lungs would burst, allowing your mind and your body to absorb every spasm of fear or pain.

That was for coping with people. It was when she was alone that survival was most difficult, because being alone started the doubts all over again, the wondering how much of what was happening to her was real, how much of anything that *had* happened to her, ever since she had left New York on the *Queen Mary,* was real. To consider accepting even a small proportion of what had happened since that day as real *would* have been to go mad.

It was far safer to drift back in time, to areas about which she had no doubt. Once upon a time there had been a girl, Diana, for whom life had really been very simple. There was a great deal about that girl that had been too simple to be acceptable, to the hairless creature in the cell. But there were aspects of her life on which she could allow herself to concentrate. She could stand on the deck of her father's yacht, her hands on the helm, and she could sail, far away out of her cell and beyond the reach of the hateful, stealthy fingers, of the hose and the strap, the music and the lights. She could be alive, and real, then, feeling every change of wind, suggesting every change of sail, often relinquishing the helm and going forward to handle the sheets and feel the salt spray splashing on her cheeks, and sometimes she could even enjoy the thrill and the apprehensions of a storm, with sail shortened, with Father and Mother and herself in oilskins, with huge waves creaming up to the bow and seeming about to overwhelm the ketch before fading away to either side in roaring foam. Then she had been alive! Just as she could feel her hands on the wheel of her Ferrari, guiding it along the expressway on her way out to Cold Spring Harbor. There was always a considerable amount of other traffic on the expressway, some of it fast, some slow, and some doing surprising things. She had to concentrate, to twist the wheel to and fro, to avoid that massive truck, overtake that little convertible, smile and wave to the children by the curb who had been waving at her.

Those were ways of overcoming the mental collapse that constantly threatened to overtake her. They could not of course be used to counter the pain of the strap or the hose, the torment of the manhandling; that would have been to lose them altogether. They could not even be used to help her through the daily round of exercises, running on the spot, pushups, bicycling on her back, which would invariably be prolonged until she was all but unconscious with effort and exhaustion, but which she dared not stop until so commanded because any slackening would immediately be followed by the sting of the strap. Then she had to summon up more potent, more mind-consuming assistance yet, such as trying to remember the names of all Shakespeare's plays, in historical order, or reciting to herself all the Roman emperors, from Caesar Augustus to Romulus Augustulus. Often she enjoyed a certain triumph at seeing the bewilderment in the faces of her tormentors, when for all her obvious pain her mind had equally obviously escaped their presence, concentrating upon some distant objective.

Yet presumably they *were* winning, and they knew that. They were winning because every day—or every period of time between one torment and the next, she did not know what each period actually represented—more and more things became unreal, and could not be believed. She had come close to disaster recently, when she had been indulging her ship-and-sea dream, and had been awakened by the hose. That was pure coincidence, but the hateful cold water, driving the breath from her lungs even as it stung her flesh and brought shuddering tears to her eyes, had broken through her consciousness at the same moment as a dream wave had broken over the yacht, and for a moment even that reality had been lost, submerged in the terror and the disgust of the hose. She did not know if she dared risk that dream again, or if she would awaken, screaming. And it had been her favorite, the safest refuge.

So they *were* winning. They had no idea what was going on inside her head, but even so they knew what they were doing, and knew, too, the end result for which they aimed, that of driving every coherent thought from her brain, of reducing her to a mindless, shivering jelly, who would be able to respond only with shrinking movements and pitiful whispers when they came to her, and for the rest would sit and stare vacantly into space.

And, as she had clearly been mistaken in supposing the whole world was rushing to her aid, and there was no hope of her ever emerging from this cell, would that not be a blessing? Was she not merely increasing her own torment, by continuing to think and to feel, and therefore hope? Would not the oblivion of madness be far preferable to her present existence?

But that way would lie total surrender for her, and total victory for her tormentors. She *must* continue to fight them, and fight them, and fight them, and . . . her muscles tensed, as she listened to feet outside, to the key turning in the lock. She could not keep from drawing up her knees and preparing her body for whatever was about to happen to it.

The door opened, and she stared at the woman standing there. It was as if a huge light had been switched on in her brain. Because this face was utterly familiar, utterly remembered, as was everything else about the woman. Even the scar on her nose. She was real. Anna was real. Therefore everything that had happened was real. Every moment of pain, and every moment of humiliation. She had dreamed none of it, imagined none of it. It was real, and she was real, and no matter what they had done to her, she was not yet mad.

* * *

Anna closed the door behind her and stepped into the cell. Her first reaction was one of surprise, that so little had changed. But then, she herself had ordered that this girl was to reveal no physical evidence of anything that might have happened to her. Therefore her body *was* unchanged; no doubt her flesh was unnaturally white, from her months below ground, and of course the skin on her wrists had been rubbed raw so often there were certainly going to be permanent marks there. But her hair had come back, and she was again quite absurdly beautiful.

Her hair, Anna thought, and went closer, to stand immediately above Diana. The black silk was streaked with white. There was a considerable change, but something that could happen to anyone.

She adjusted the light switch to stop the flicker, switched off the taped music and removed the earphones, pulled off the velvet face mask. She had commanded that this continue to be used even though she had doubted that Ivan would be able to recognize the girl, now.

"Say something," she commanded.

"Anna," Diana said. "Do you know, I had almost forgotten what you looked like?"

Anna frowned, and stooped, to stare into her eyes; she *would* have expected them to change, to take on the irrational flare of a broken mind. But there was nothing irrational about those cool blue irises.

"Maybe you'd forgotten what I looked like, too," Diana said. "I guess I must have changed. But you haven't. Did you know you still have a scar on your nose?"

For a moment Anna's hand almost moved, to slap her insolent face. But she controlled herself. There was a mystery here. "They told me you were all but ready," she remarked, half to herself.

"You mean they told you that I had gone mad?" Diana asked. "Maybe I have. Maybe I *did*. But I'm sane now, comrade. The moment I saw you, I became sane. So what are you going to do to me today?"

She *was* afraid, of course. Anna could see that she was trembling, every muscle jumping of its own accord, and her lips as well. But she still wished to resist. And she was a long way from having lost her mind.

Haymans, Anna thought, with angry, envious contempt.

But she still held this girl's very existence in the palm of her hand. She straightened. "I think," she said, "that I am going to have to use sterner methods on you. That means I will have to break a promise."

Diana frowned at her.

"I was going to release you, you know," Anna said. "I promised your uncle I would do so, and I was going to keep my word. Just as soon as your mind had collapsed. But you have a tough little mind, haven't you, Diana? I think you will have to go to Siberia, after all, and stay there, where no one will know where to look for you, until I can spare the time to look after you myself. Yes, that will be best. I will arrange it."

"Siberia," Diana muttered. "I have always wanted to go to Siberia. My grandparents first met and fell in love in Siberia. But for Siberia, I wouldn't be here at all. Comrade . . . may I ask that my husband be allowed to accompany me?"

Anna gave a brief laugh; the girl was, after all, on the very brink of madness. One more little push might well do the trick. "You may ask. But he, I think, I shall execute. After a suitable trial, of course; I will need someone to distract the people's mind. And he did smuggle explosives into the country, and he was poor Peter Borodin's accomplice. Oh, yes, poor Peter Borodin."

"Poor?" Diana whispered.

"Of course, you did not know that your great-uncle is dead," Anna said. "Executed by your Uncle John. It is all in the family. But there are so many things you do not know, my dear Diana, which would surprise you. You do not know, for instance, that your Uncle John is now a captain in the KGB, working for me. The Americans are calling him a traitor, of course, but they are so shortsighted about these things. John is one hundred percent Russian, and knows it. And now he has come home. To me, Diana. Why, do you know, not three hours ago I was in his bed? He is *such* good company."

Diana stared at her with her mouth open. "I don't believe you," she said. "I don't believe a word you are saying."

Anna shrugged. "You don't have to believe me. It is true. Why should I waste my time in lying to you? Siberia! And then, when things have settled down here, I will come to see you, and perhaps drive you mad myself. But right now, I have a treat for you. You may sleep for a couple of hours. And when you wake up, you will know what I have been saying is true."

She reached for the door, and it opened, suddenly and violently. A female jailer entered the room, equally violently, stumbling across the floor and cannoning into Anna, who lost her balance and in turn cannoned into the wall. She gave an exclamation of fury, slapped the girl aside, and stared at Gregory Nej, who stood before her with a revolver in his hand. "You—" She looked past him at Felicity Hayman, and then... Her jaw slowly sagged open, while her brain seemed to freeze. Robert Loung? Wearing an ill-fitting and obviously hastily donned KGB uniform?

"Have you lost your senses?" she whispered, even as icy fingers started to claw at her heart. Because then she saw, coming in last and closing the door behind himself, John Hayman.

"It's a long way to Siberia, Anna," John said. "And as I said, you did *not* have the time to get there and back."

Anna stared at him, and then at Gregory and Felicity; Robert Loung was already kneeling beside Diana. Now Gregory stepped forward and plucked the pistol from her holster. Anna discovered she was panting. She wanted to attack him, and destroy him. But she knew that of all the men in the world, this was the one she could not equal. She had taught him everything he knew, and then had had to attack him once before—and been defeated.

"Robert?" Diana whispered. "Oh, God, Robert!" She attempted to draw up her legs, to shrink away from him.

"We're leaving this place," Robert said, drawing the bolts from the rings.

Diana started to weep, silently, huge tears rolling down her cheeks from tightly closed eyes. She did not want to look at any of them, because *they* could not be real—the sight of Anna had after all driven her out of her mind.

"Help him, Felicity," John said quietly. Felicity carried a bundle of clothing in her hands.

"You have lost your senses," Anna said, beginning to recover. "Do you really suppose you can come here, into Lubianka, and behave like this?"

"Anna," John said. "This was a poor time to indulge yourself. Stalin is dead."

Her mouth formed a little O, as she glanced at Gregory, as if seeking confirmation. But Gregory continued to stare at her, and to point his revolver at her; he knew how dangerous she was, even when bemused and unarmed.

"So all hell is about to break loose," John told her, "if it hasn't already. You were going to control that hell, Anna. But you preferred your little games, instead."

Anna got her breathing under control. She looked down at Diana, who had been released and was leaning against Robert, eyes still tightly shut, while Felicity attempted to help her dress in the green uniform of the KGB. Then she looked back at John. "So why are you not carrying out your orders?" she asked. "Listen to me. Obey me, cooperate, and I will send this girl home. Tomorrow. Today. I swear it."

"No dice," John said, and looked at his watch. "Get a move on, Felicity."

"Come on, Di," Felicity said. "Come on, little girl. Don't you want to go home, now?"

"You will never get away with it," Anna said, her voice beginning to snarl. "And when you are caught—"

"You, at least, are going to know nothing about it," John said.

Anna glared at him as she understood the menace in his voice. She whipped her head around to stare at Gregory, recoiled from the coldness in the boy's eyes, looked down at the guard, who cowered on the floor, and then looked back at Diana again. They had got her skirt on, and Robert was buttoning her tunic. Then they sat her down to pull on her boots.

"Are you real?" Diana whispered. "Really real?" She had stopped weeping, but after looking into Robert's eyes for a moment, she buried her face in his tunic.

"Di!" John stooped beside her. "This is Anna Ragosina. Do you know Anna Ragosina?"

Diana raised her head and stared at her tormentor. "Yes," she said. "Oh, yes. I know Anna Ragosina."

"Has she ill-treated you?"

Diana's nostrils flared. "Pepper," she said. "She used pepper."

John glanced at Anna, whose nostrils were also dilated.

"She is also a mass murderess, a conspirator, and the most vicious woman who ever lived," John said. "Well, we are going to make sure that she never commits any more crimes. Is there anything you wish to say to her, anything—" He drew a long breath. "—you wish to do to her, before she dies?"

"Dies?" Anna snapped. "Me? You mean to kill *me? You* cannot do that, John Hayman. And neither can you, Gregory. *You,* execute me? Either of you?" She gazed at Diana as the girl slowly got to her feet, and twisted her lips into a ghastly facsimile of a smile. "The uniform becomes you, Diana," she said. "Why do you not stay and become one of my aides? Like these . . . creatures?"

But suddenly *she* was afraid, as Diana stared at her. In the past she had enjoyed flirting with ill-treatment, even flirting with death; it had always been on her terms, with her in a position to call a halt whenever she had had enough. Now . . . she could feel her own muscles jumping, knew her own lips were trembling, and clamped them tightly shut with a vicious snap. She could not believe this was happening. She could not understand *how* it had happened.

But far more important, she knew there was so much she should be doing, so much that was vital to her, and to Russia.

And instead of doing anything, was she to die, in one of her own prison cells? That was impossible. Both of these men *were* her creatures. They had slept with her, worshipped at the shrine that was her beauty. Both of these men.

But she was facing the two women she had tormented, and Robert Loung.

"I would like to shoot her," Felicity said, and flushed, as though surprised at her own anger.

Anna inhaled, sharply.

Without a word, John gave his sister Anna's own gun.

Felicity looked at it in horror, for several seconds. Then, as though impelled by an outside force she could not resist, she wrapped her fingers around the butt.

"You cannot," Anna gasped. "You cannot. Listen . . ." She knew she was babbling. "You wish to escape Lubianka? Escape Russia? You cannot do so, unless I help you. I will take you out of here, comrades—John . . ." She was gazing at the knuckles on Felicity's right hand, where the skin was whitening.

"No," Diana said.

Felicity's head turned to look at her niece.

Diana was staring at Anna. Now she could remember, with absolute clarity, everything that had been done to her. Anna was less a woman than a female devil, yet she lived and breathed. She was undoubtedly a murderess, many times over, again as John had accused her, yet at the end of the day she could still tremble with fear.

She was worthy of hate, but Diana was suddenly realizing that *she* was too exhilarated to hate, or wish to punish. Too exhilarated for her own good. Sometime very soon she was going to collapse into hysterical tears. When that happened, she might again hate enough to kill. But for the moment she only knew that all her confidence, all her determination, had not been futile after all.

So how could she hate this creature whose only pleasure was tormenting others? Who had never actually stood on the deck of an ocean-going yacht and felt the spray on her face, never held the wheel of a Ferrari in her hands, felt the enormous power beneath her foot? Nor could she hate the terrified, limited, knowledgeless girl at her feet. Perhaps she had even been one of the tormentors. Diana couldn't be sure. But she knew that to kill either of them would make her no better than they were.

"Di," John said, gently.

"Can we get out of here, Uncle John?" Diana asked. *"Can we?"*

"I think we can. If we hurry. But not with her chasing behind us."

"She won't be chasing behind us. Leave her here with her friend. Leave her and lock her in and throw away the key."

Slowly Anna released her breath; with an effort she kept herself from smiling. But after all, she was Anna Ragosina. These people lacked the courage to kill her.

"She must die," Gregory said. "There is no other way to stop her. Besides, she deserves to die."

"No," Diana said again. "Just leave her here, and throw away the key."

"They'll get her out soon enough," John told her.

"So let them," Diana said. "But for an hour or two she'll have been chained to that wall, with the light flickering and the music playing. I just want her to feel something of what I felt, for a while. I want her to think about that." She gazed at the woman. "And I want you to remember me, Anna, and remember that you didn't *win*. You couldn't remember, if you were dead."

Lavrenti Beria panted up the steps and into the lower hall of Lubianka Prison, ignored the sleepy night clerks who hastily came to attention, and stared at John Hayman, hurrying toward him. "You have heard the news?" he demanded.

John snapped to attention, as did the people behind him. "I have heard the news, comrade commissar."

"And where is Colonel Ragosina?"

"I do not know, comrade commissar."

"My God!" Beria said. "At a time like this, she just takes herself off . . . I have been to her apartment, and she is not there. But the sentry outside says she came here—"

"And left again, to my knowledge, comrade commissar," John said. "I understood she was going to attend the Politburo meeting."

"One has been called for eight o'clock, yes," Beria said. "But it is now only three."

"No doubt Colonel Ragosina has returned home to prepare herself," John told him. "You must have missed her on the way, comrade commissar. I know that she intended you both to attend that meeting, because that is where the important decisions are to be made."

"But—" Beria gazed around the empty desks as if expecting to see each one supporting a dead body.

"There is nothing for you to concern yourself with here, comrade commissar," John assured him. "I have my instructions, and I know what to do. My people also know what to do. This is a picked squad I have assembled here. We will not fail you. Go and prepare yourself for the meeting, comrade commissar, and leave the details to us."

Beria gazed at him. The American was in a state of high excitement, he could tell; his cheeks were flushed and he was breathing heavily. On the other hand, the people at his back looked absolutely determined. There were two men, both grim-faced, and two women, equally determined looking. All four were armed. Beria frowned. It was occurring to him that both the women—one was strikingly blonde and the other was equally dark although with streaks of premature grayness in her hair—

bore a facial resemblance to Hayman himself. Clearly his eyes were playing him tricks, through nervousness.

And then he remembered that the blond woman was actually Hayman's sister; he had met her at the train depot.

And the men . . . one was Gregory Nej!

John had been watching his eyes, reading his changing expressions. "Captain Nej is one of us, comrade commissar," he said. "He hates his father for the murder of his mother. He has asked to carry out the execution himself. Colonel Ragosina has approved this."

"Yes," Beria muttered. "Yes." He wished Anna would keep him more informed of what was going on. But this Hayman was her most trusted aide; and certainly the fellow had killed his own uncle without hesitation. Besides, he had too much on his mind, thinking about the coming Politburo meeting, which he had to dominate. He could only pray that Anna *was* planning to attend. Certainly he had to find her before then. "Well . . . good fortune, Captain Hayman," he said. "Good fortune. The fate of Russia may well be in your hands."

Ivan Nej opened the door of Anna Ragosina's office, pistol in hand. But the office was in darkness. He switched on the light, looked left and right, and holstered the pistol. He was dressed in uniform, although it was not yet daylight outside—and incongruously, he carried a paper bag in his left hand. "Empty," he said.

Maria Kalinova stood just behind him. She too was armed and trembling with excitement. "Perhaps she is at home, comrade commissar."

"I have been to her home, Kalinova. She is not there. Nor can I find Hayman at *his* home. I wonder if he has played us false?"

"How can he have done that, comrade commissar?" Maria asked. "Once he told his father about the plot—"

"He is Ragosina's creature," Ivan said darkly. "There could be another plot, of which he has not told anyone. They may be waiting, or doing— They must be found, Kalinova. She must, anyway. You have worked with her for years. You must know her habits. Her haunts."

Maria hesitated, then snapped her fingers. "Cell number forty-seven."

Ivan raised his eyebrows.

"There . . . there is an important prisoner in forty-seven," Maria said, still hesitantly. She could not be sure what Ivan's reaction would be when he discovered just who that prisoner was. But she was committed now; if he had been speaking the truth when he had told her she was on Anna's death list, she had no choice. In any event, she had every intention of getting even with the bitch, for that slap.

"The woman in the mask," Ivan said thoughtfully. "Yes. You mean Anna visits her in the middle of the night?"

"Sometimes," Maria said.

"And she could be down there now, amusing herself, while her plans go astray? I would find that very interesting." He ran down the stairs, still carrying his paper bag, Maria at his heels. In the lobby of the women's section he encountered the senior warden, clearly just out of bed and very annoyed. Waiting with her were two very worried-looking assistants.

"Comrade commissar," the warden said. "I wish to be informed of what is going on. These girls tell me Warden Smislova has disappeared while on sole duty. And all these rumors—"

"These rumors are all facts, comrade," Ivan said. "Come with me." He led them to the observation chamber overlooking cell forty-seven.

"That girl will have to be *whipped,*" the head warden said. "Deserting her post. Do you know, comrade commissar, that we have thirty-three inmates in here? And she just walks away from them? I am going to take the skin from her bones."

Ivan waved her to be quiet as he removed the panel and peered through. He remained looking down for several seconds, then closed the panel, turned to face the women, and smiled. Maria instinctively took a step backward; not even Anna had ever looked quite so malevolently pleased.

"Where is the key to that cell?" he asked.

"I no longer have charge of it," the senior warden said, and looked at Maria. "Comrade Kalinova . . ."

"Colonel Ragosina took it from me yesterday," Maria said.

"Ah," Ivan said. "Then we will break the lock. Come."

He led them down the stairs to the lowest level, drew his pistol, and fired six times into the lock. The bullets whined and ricocheted around the corridor, driving the women back to the safety of the stairs, but the lock gave. Ivan opened the door and led the women into the cell. They stared at the warden, lying bound hand and foot in the corner, and at Anna, naked and chained to the wall, earphones clamped to her head, eyes glaring at them.

"Warden Smislova," the head warden snapped. "What are you doing lying on the floor in that disgusting condition? You are going to be whipped."

"But, comrade," Smislova whined.

"I suggest you remove her," Ivan said. "Take her upstairs and whip her, or do whatever you wish. But get out."

"Release me," Anna was bawling. "This instant. Now."

Ivan watched the two other girls unfastening Smislova's bonds and pulling her to her feet. Between them they pushed her through the door. Smislova had burst into tears. "Comrade commissar," she shouted at Anna. "Tell them what happened. Tell them—"

"If you do not release me this instant—" Anna hissed.

Ivan turned off the music, removed the earphones, and handed them to Maria, who stood attentively at his shoulder; but like him, she was smiling.

"My dear Anna," Ivan said. "You do get yourself into some remarkable situations."

"Very funny," Anna snapped. "Get these chains off me. By God—"

"Who did this?"

"Who do you think did this, you cretin?" Anna shouted. "Your filthy son. He is an American agent. I always knew he was. And Hayman. By Christ, when I get my hands on them—"

Ivan frowned at her. "My son? And Hayman? Hayman I could understand. I always knew you made a mistake there. But Gregory . . . Where have they gone?"

"They mean to flee Russia," Anna shouted. "They have the women with them. Let me go. Maria, release me this instant."

"Leave Russia?" Ivan said thoughtfully. "I wonder how they mean to do that. In *winter?*"

"Captain Nej is a qualified pilot, comrade commissar," Maria suggested. "And there is the military airport just south of Moscow, with two planes specially reserved for the use of the KGB. If your son and Hayman were to appear there . . . It is well known that Hayman is Colonel Ragosina's assistant, and that Gregory Nej is your son. No one would think of refusing them a demand for an aircraft."

"Gregory," Ivan said, his fingers curling into fists. "My own son. Betraying me . . ." He looked at Anna. "How long have you been here?"

"Oh, how should I know?" she screamed at him. "Maybe three hours. Are you going to let me go? There is much to be done."

"Three hours," Ivan mused. "And it is now six o'clock. Say an hour to reach the airport and have the plane serviced . . . they could be very nearly at the Polish border by now."

"They can never make West Germany without refueling," Maria remarked. "That is more than twelve hundred miles."

Ivan gazed at her thoughtfully. "Then they will know that. Gregory is my son. He has a brain." He snapped his fingers. "Sweden. That is five hundred miles closer. They could make Sweden. But they will hardly have reached the coast as yet. We will stop them. Oh, yes, we will stop them. Come with me, Maria Feodorovna."

"Ivan!" Anna stormed. "Take off these chains at once. There are things to do. If Stalin is indeed dead, there will have to be a Politburo meeting. I must be there."

"Stalin is indeed dead, Anna. And there is indeed to be a Politburo meeting." Ivan looked at his watch. "It is called for eight o'clock. But you do not really want to be there, Anna. Politburo meetings are such a bore."

"Ivan," Anna said, no longer shouting, but loading her voice with menace. "If you do not release me this instant, I swear, so help me God, that I—"

Ivan shook his finger at her. "You seem to be forgetting that there is no God, Anna. The state, which we both serve, has decreed this. And thus you are revealing a deviationist streak which I find most disturbing. All in all, I think you are well situated where you are." He smiled at her, and chucked her under the chin. "You look very pretty, plastered against that wall. And while you remain there you cannot get into any mischief. By all reports, you have been getting into a great deal of mischief recently. Do not worry. I will come back, as soon as the meetings ends, and tell you exactly what was said, and what was decided."

"Let me stay with her, comrade commissar," Maria requested.

Ivan looked at her, eyebrows raised.

Maria gave a pretty flush. "I could perhaps . . . find out things for you," she suggested.

"You little bitch," Anna snarled, every muscle and tendon in her body standing out as she strained against the chains. "You . . ."

Ivan was smiling again. "I think that may be a splendid idea, Maria Feodorovna. But not right now. I need you at this moment, Maria Feodorovna. But I promise that you will have the interrogation of Colonel Ragosina, when the time comes. Let her remain there a while longer, and contemplate the future. But I am not going to leave you entirely alone, Anna Petrovna. I have brought you some company. Your favorite company." He walked to the door, turned, and threw the paper bag onto Anna's lap. From inside it the body of Tabasco the cat rolled onto the floor.

The little twin-engined aircraft shuddered as a fierce squall of wind and rain struck it, while lightning carved serrated patterns across the heavy clouds. It was a six-seater trainer, and for that reason Gregory had chosen it over the immensely faster jet trainer, which could only carry four. Its range was a theoretical seven hundred and fifty miles, which he had calculated should just carry them to the Swedish coast, but he had felt obliged to fly as low as he could, to stay off the majority of radar screens, and this was the fourth storm they had been forced to plunge through. Now he was casting anxious glances at the fuel gauges, which were reading just under half full.

"Do you think we'll make it?" John, sitting in the copilot's seat, asked him.

"We will make it," Gregory said. "Providing no diversions are necessary." He looked over his shoulder to give a reassuring smile to Felicity, who was alone in a center seat; Robert and Diana were in the back, hidden in the darkness. "We should soon sight the coast."

"Are they still talking about us?" Felicity wanted to know.

"I have lost that conversation," Gregory said. "But they are certainly looking. The weather is on our side, providing it clears before Sweden."

He turned back to the controls and glanced at John. There was no need for him to spell out what the alternatives were. They *had* no alternatives.

Did she want an alternative? Diana wondered. The whole thing seemed unreal—even the fact that it was actually morning, although there was as yet no sign of daylight. But that was no more unreal than everything else which had happened. When they had mounted the steps in Lubianka—she had no recollection of ever descending them into her prison—and had come face to face with the tall, moon-faced, worried-looking man whom John had later told her was at the very top of the KGB, she had almost felt as if she were watching a movie, in which she was one of the characters. When they had stepped outside into the crisp, freezing air of the courtyard, and she had inhaled, her lungs, after nine months of air conditioning, had felt as though they might explode.

She had stared at the lights of Moscow as they drove from the city, Robert's arm around her shoulders. This was where they had been going to honeymoon, visiting theaters and museums, eating in restaurants . . . nine months ago, they had told her. She had shivered, and Robert's arm had tightened. Thank God he had not tried to do more than that, had not even kissed her on the cheek. She had not known if she would have been able to accept even that without shuddering.

But of course, he had also spent nine months inside Lubianka, suffering as she had suffered, breathing the same air, smelling the same smells. She had supposed he was trying to comfort her; but was he not also seeking comfort for himself? And *could* they comfort each other, ever again? She had not even properly remembered what he looked like. Could she still be his, or anyone's, wife? Could they live together, make love together, after what they had endured? She had read stories of wartime marriages, undertaken after a courtship of hours, followed, after perhaps a weekend's honeymoon together, by several months of separation, at the end of which the couple had discovered that they did not even like each other—and they had not necessarily suffered any physical hardship during that time. *She* had always felt that way about her boyfriends after just a few weeks of seeing them almost every day.

Could Robert possibly be any different?

The radio spluttered in Gregory's ear. "This is Riga control," the voice said. "Riga control. I am speaking to the unidentified aircraft flying northwest at a height of eight hundred feet. We have you on radar. Identify yourself, or you will be shot down."

Gregory glanced at John, who shrugged.

"If we're inside the Riga control zone, the coast can't be *that* far away," John said. He peered through the windshield. The rain had stopped, and the wind had momentarily dropped, but all was still dark as they flew through the buffeting clouds.

"What are they saying?" Felicity asked.

"They wish us to identify ourselves," Gregory told her. "But they will have to work that out for themselves."

So now was the crunch, Diana thought. It did not really seem to matter. She was still thinking about Anna Ragosina. How strange, she thought, that she had *not* wanted to hurt her. It must have been because *she* had triumphed. All her being, all her strength, had been directed toward surviving until she could be rescued. And she had achieved that. Anna Ragosina could never harm her, once she had reached that goal. But if she was ever to be taken back . . . she jerked her head as the clouds suddenly parted at the same time as the first lazy fingers of dawn peeped into the northern landscape.

"Houses," John said, pointing to the right.

"Captain Gregory Nej," the radio said. "We have reason to believe it is you piloting the unidentified aircraft in the northern sector. Come in, Captain Nej."

Diana leaned forward to stare out at the flat Latvian landscape, the distant red roofs. Robert rested his hand on hers, and she instinctively squeezed his fingers.

"Captain Nej," the voice said, "we have a message for you from the commander of the KGB in Moscow, your own father. You are instructed by Commissar Nej to land immediately and surrender yourself and your passengers."

Gregory looked at John.

John glanced at his watch. It was only just past seven o'clock; the Politburo meeting could not possibly have taken place yet. "He sounds confident," he remarked. "Maybe they've already pulled a countercoup."

"Captain Nej," the voice droned. "If you do not land your aircraft within five minutes, our interceptor fighters will bring you down. They have orders to shoot, Captain Nej. Five minutes. Why commit suicide, Captain Nej?"

Gregory looked left and right, at the cloudbanks that still hovered to either side of them.

"Well, glory be," John said. "There's the coast."

The two women and Robert craned their necks to glimpse the yellow sand, the pale ribbon of surf, and the blue beyond.

"Yippee!" Diana shouted. "We've made it."

"And there are the fighters," Gregory said, pointing to the southern cloudbank, from which three MIG jets were just emerging.

Chapter 15

"OH, GOD," FELICITY SAID.

Somehow she had never believed it would come to this, because since Gregory's release she had discovered an immense faith in the future, something she had never possessed since the day David had been pronounced missing, believed dead. They could not possibly be shot down now, with their lives still in front of them.

Diana felt Robert's fingers tightening on hers until she thought the bones of her hand would crack; but she had no desire to pull herself free.

"The man mentioned five minutes," John said, and pointed in turn. "Look at those clouds."

About two miles to their right was a thunderhead, scoop upon scoop of solid black cloud, reaching upward fifteen, perhaps twenty thousand feet. Gregory sucked air into his lungs. Throughout the flight from Moscow he had attempted to avoid such formations, and even so had felt the little plane being buffeted before the wind and the electricity generated by those giant mushrooms. But wind and even electricity were preferable to being torn apart by cannonfire.

"Tighten those belts," he said, and made a hard right turn. The plane almost stood on one wingtip, the gray Baltic Sea now only five hundred feet beneath them, the three jets three thousand feet higher up and closing fast, before straightening and climbing almost vertically as Gregory pulled back on the wheel.

Diana felt the blood draining from her brain, and black spots appeared in front of her eyes. Nothing Anna Ragosina had done to her had been quite as painful as the sudden pressure on her ears. But this pain was acceptable; she was on her way home.

"Captain Nej," the radio said. "This is Flight Commander Raskov. Do not be a fool. You cannot escape. Put down."

Sudden grayness, almost as dark as the night that had just ended. For a moment they seemed almost to be sitting on the clouds, then they struck the first air pocket and dropped about fifty feet. Once again Gregory sent them soaring into the murk.

"Go in, go in," Raskov was shouting. "Ground control, give me a radar fix."

There was a vivid flash of lightning, and the plane seemed to fall on its side, and keep on falling; the instantaneous crash of the thunderclap made it rattle like an old tin can. Diana buried her head in Robert's shoulder, felt his arm go around her.

"Well, what do you know?" Gregory remarked in surprise. "We still seem to have our electrics."

There was another stomach-rending drop, and then another soar, and with it, a sudden whistling howl that threw them the other way.

"Jesus *Christ!*" John shouted. "That was a MIG."

"I have seen the enemy, commander." A voice sounded on the radio.

"Where? Where?"

"I do not know, commander. They have gone again."

"Fool," Raskov bawled. "Ground control, give me a radar fix."

"I can no longer tell which one is the enemy," ground control complained.

Gregory was climbing again into the clouds, once more forcing them to accept the unacceptable G-force. Diana gasped, and tried to swallow, found she could not. Then they had leveled out, and she looked ahead at a patch of blue sky, beyond the cloud. She gasped, and felt tears rolling down her cheeks, and gasped again as she realized that three aircraft were entering the clear air at the same moment, each from a different direction. Two were MIGs, hurtling toward each other at a combined speed of very nearly a thousand miles per hour. Gregory thrust the wheel forward, and the trainer sank down again toward the cloud layer, while tracer shot whined immediately above their heads. Their trainer had a glass roof, and they all looked up, throats dry with horror. The first fighter tried to roll away from the second, but too late; its wingtip caught the belly of the other. There was a huge flash of light, and an enormous explosion. The trainer rolled over and they hung upside down for a moment, dangling in their belts, then Gregory had it under control again, watching his altimeter, which was racing downward at hundreds of feet per second.

"Commander, commander," said Riga control. "Two of your planes have disappeared."

"Disappeared?" Raskov shouted. "Say again. Say again. *Disappeared?*"

Gregory kept on diving, until his altimeter showed a thousand feet. But still they could not see the sea, so thick was the cloud.

"Now a third aircraft has disappeared," Riga control said. "There is only one left. Commander Raskov, are you there? Give your altitude."

"Of course I am here," Raskov snapped. "Five thousand feet."

"Your adversary has gone down, I think," Riga control said.

"Gone down?" Raskov demanded. "Gone down where?"

"Well, you are over the sea, are you not, comrade commander," ground control said, a trifle wearily. "You are instructed to return to base. We will send out a ship to search for wreckage."

"But my aircraft," Raskov complained. "My flight squadron! What has happened to my flight squadron?"

"There!" John said, looking down. "Holy Christ!"

The cloud ceiling was finally parting, and the gray sea was not more than two hundred feet below them. Gregory pulled the wheel back toward his stomach, and they leveled off. "Here we stay," he announced.

John pointed at the fuel gauges; they were below a quarter full. "How much further?"

"I have no idea," Gregory said. "My navigational instruments are useless at this height." He looked over his shoulder.

"There are lifebelts under your seats. Please put them on. But be sure to refasten your seatbelts afterward."

Robert released Diana, reached beneath their seats, and pulled out the yellow inflatable vests; Felicity was already wriggling into hers.

John looked down. "Do you have any idea what the temperature of that water is likely to be?"

"Well," Gregory said, "we can see that it is not actually freezing. So I would say that if we ditch we will survive about five seconds."

John stared at him.

"Would you prefer to surrender?" Gregory asked.

"If we go in, we're dead," Robert said into Diana's ear. "You understand that?"

"Yes," she said. "I understand that."

"But you're not afraid?"

"Yes," she said. "I am afraid." She turned her head to look into his eyes. "But I'm not going back, Robert."

He kissed her on the lips. He felt her start to withdraw, and then she seemed to change her mind. "I love you," he said. "I don't know how to say how sorry I am for everything that has happened . . ."

"Then don't," she suggested. "He was my uncle, remember? He was only your employer. I should say to *you* how sorry I am. But that's over, Robert. Say, do you know, I have no idea what day it is? What month, even?"

"It is March 5, 1953," he told her.

"Well, glory be," she said. "Tomorrow is my birthday."

He squeezed her hand. "You'll make it, Diana."

Felicity stared past Gregory's head at the sea, unending and unchanging in front of them, and at the gauges, whose needles were imperceptibly dropping toward zero. On the map in the atlas, the Baltic Sea had never been wider than her finger. It just couldn't go on this long. She wondered if their compass was faulty. But even if it was, they had to reach land somewhere, sometime.

"Look!" she cried, pointing ahead of them at the three small trawlers.

"Do we ditch?" John asked.

"No," Gregory said.

They passed the trawlers barely above mast height; they looked down on the men gazing up at them.

"They're Swedish," John said, gazing at the blue flags with the yellow crosses.

"If we went in, we would not live long enough to be picked up," Gregory reminded him.

John was staring at the gauges. One was showing empty. He looked ahead. Nothing but gray sea. The trawlers were out of sight behind.

The starboard engine coughed, spluttered, caught again, and died.

"Oh, God," Felicity whispered. "Oh, God!"

Robert's hand was back, closing on Diana's, holding it tighter and tighter.

"There," John shouted. "Oh, Christ, there!"

Yellow sand dunes, gleaming in the morning mist, perhaps four miles away. Four miles . . . the port engine coughed.

"Stand by to abandon," Gregory said, his voice absolutely calm. "The entire roof comes off, or it should. Do not release your belts until the plane comes to a complete halt."

The port engine coughed, and died.

"Going down!" Gregory snapped.

There was a tremendous surge of water, breaking right over them as they hit, before they bobbed up again, careering onward now, being thrown right and left as they bounded across the shallow waves.

"She will sink in twenty seconds," Gregory said, and released the roof.

"Free your belts," John shouted.

Robert grasped Felicity's thighs and gave her a push. She stepped onto the wing, lost her balance, and fell into the sea. The cold drove all the breath from her lungs, but she discovered she was standing up. And the plane could not sink, because it was sitting on the bottom in four feet of water.

Diana fell into her arms, and they hugged each other, then realized their legs were going numb. Holding hands they splashed across the sandbank and onto the beach, to face khaki-clad soldiers who had suddenly appeared. One of the men shouted at them in Swedish.

Felicity looked back to where Gregory was also coming ashore, blood streaming down his face from a cut on the forehead. But he was not seriously harmed, and John and Robert were beside him.

She turned back to face the soldiers, and raised her arms in the air. "We surrender," she said. "Don't any of you speak English? Or even American?"

Even the small corner of Idlewild International Airport to which the military aircraft had been directed seemed crowded. "Hayman Newspapers, you see," George explained, having used his privilege to follow George junior on board. "This is the scoop of the year for them. Think you can face them?"

Diana hesitated, looked left and right at the four people who had dared all with her. Was it only forty-eight hours ago? Forty-eight tumultuous hours. She had not been alone once in all that time, except to sleep for a few of those hours—and she had slept.

But they were waiting for *her*. She was the one whose release was the news flashed to an astonished world, up to that moment hardly aware of her captivity. The other stories, those of John and Gregory and Felicity and Robert, important in themselves, were being made irrelevant besides that of the heiress who had died and then miraculously been brought back to life. The news of her return seemed almost as important as that of Stalin's death.

She drew a deep breath, smiled at Robert, and nodded. George junior, still holding her hand, led her to the gangway. Applause broke out from the watching people, and flashbulbs gleamed even at that distance. Diana went down the steps, and was in her mother's arms, with Ilona and Natasha immediately beyond, smiling through their tears.

"Oh, Di," Elizabeth said. "Oh, Di." She held her at arm's length to gaze at the gray steaks in the black hair, then caught her close again. "Oh, Di!"

Embrace after embrace. Janice Corliss and her parents. People she had never even seen before, but who she gathered were big in the state department. She looked back at the others leaving the aircraft, pulled herself free, and ran to Robert. "Mother!" she gasped. "This is—"

"I know," Elizabeth said. "Welcome to America, Robert."

John faced Natasha, who was smiling through her tears. "Natasha?"

"I knew," she whispered, holding him close. "I knew. Allen Dulles told Father, and Father told me. I knew, John. Oh, I'm so proud of you, and so glad to have you back."

"Captain Nej?" There were two men of the lantern-jawed variety. Gregory had encountered them before, one in particular.

"Yes," he said wearily.

"Will you come with us, please?"

"Now wait just one moment," George said. He had deliberately stayed at the side of Gregory and Felicity.

"Protective custody, Mr. Hayman," Arthur Garrison explained. "This character can't be the most popular guy in Russia, right this minute."

"I'm going with him," Felicity declared, "wherever."

Garrison shrugged. "Be our guest, Miss Hayman."

"Miss Hayman." A reporter, bolder than his fellows, stood at Diana's elbow. "Miss Hayman . . . I'd like to hear your thoughts on Russia."

Diana looked at him. And then tucked her arm under Robert's. "I can't tell you anything about Russia," she said. "I was honeymooning. And my name is Loung, not Hayman."

But she knew it was not going to be quite as simple as that. It would not have been simple even without their experience. Robert was not only being overwhelmed by America, by New York, by being in the public eye, and today, by the house at Cold Spring Harbor—there was also the family itself.

It had been Mother's decision that they should accept Ilona's invitation and stay out at Cold Spring Harbor for a few days. "Until things settle down," Elizabeth had said. This made sense. Undoubtedly there would be reporters, and just plain gawkers, hanging around the New York apartment for some time to come. Cold Spring Harbor was safe.

But Mother had an ulterior motive. Here she and Ilona could get to know Robert—as they had been doing, with relentless determination, all day. After an early supper, she and Robert had been escorted up to their bedroom rather as if they had just completed a seventeenth-century marriage, with the attendant parents and well-wishers determined to oversee the consummation. Then they had been left alone.

And finally, only one thing truly mattered: not what Mother and Grandmother thought of it all, but what *she* thought of it all.

She stood at the window and gazed out at the beach on

which she had played and made sand castles on so many days of her life, and beyond, invisible in the darkness, at Long Island Sound, where she had helmed that yacht that had kept her sane for so many weeks. She still could not believe she was home. Even now she could feel the cold stone wall against which she had been chained; whenever there was a footstep in the hallway outside she turned, heart constricting, waiting breathlessly, as if for the door to open and the hose or the strap to be brought in. These fears had to be overcome, she told herself. She was no mindless ninny. She was Diana Hayman Loung. Anna Ragosina had not succeeded in breaking her spirit, when she had had her inside Lubianka. It would be too ridiculous to allow her spirit to break, now that she was free.

And safe. Nobody could be more safe than in Cold Spring Harbor, and in George Hayman's house, a haven within the haven that was Long Island, within the haven that was the United States of America. Nobody could touch her here, unless she wanted him to.

And that was the biggest fear of all. She wore a dressing gown, and nothing else. Mother had bought her a matching nightdress, but in the well-heated bedroom, she would not even have worn a dressing gown, had she been alone. Now she was wondering if she should *not* have put on the nightdress, after all.

She wondered how the others were getting along. Gregory, whisked off to detention by the state department—would he ever be able to live his own life, without grim-faced men standing at his side? But Felicity had also been at his side, and clearly intended to remain there. Gregory and Felicity had never seemed to have any doubts about each other. John had also been summoned to Washington, and Natasha had stayed with him, of course; the children were out here at Cold Spring Harbor, in the care of their grandmother. But Natasha had seemed to know what John had been doing, and to understand. And throughout their separation she had remained in safety and comfort.

She had not known that just down the corridor . . . Diana turned, as the bathroom door closed. He had been very careful not to encroach upon her privacy in any way, had even changed in the bathroom. He wore a dressing gown very like hers, as it too had been chosen by Mother. And he had ignored the pajamas laid out for him; she could see no sign of trouser legs beneath the robe.

"You've quite a family," he said.

"One becomes used to them," she said.

"Your father has offered me a job. I don't know anything about newspaper work, but he said I'd learn." He shrugged. "I tried to argue, but he also said you weren't ever being allowed out of their sight again, or at least not for a long, long time. I don't want to start anymore family crises."

She smiled. "I think I have to go to work, too, and learn about newspapers."

"Because you're going to own Hayman Newspapers Incorporated, one day. That is one hell of a big thought."

He sat on the bed, and she made herself go and sit beside him. "Yes," she said. "It'll take two of us to handle it."

He gazed at her. "Di," he said, "if . . . if you want an annulment, I'll just fold up my tent and steal away into the night, you know."

"Because you don't think it'll work, Robert?"

"Hell, no. But . . . well . . ."

"You don't know if you can do it, anymore? With me?"

His smile was twisted. "Maybe with anyone."

"I know." She held his arm, kissed him on the cheek. "But I married you because I fell in love with you. And you know what? I think I'm still in love with you. You sure aren't running off anywhere until I know for sure. And there's only one way to do that."

"You mean you *want* to, here and now?" His eyes were suddenly dancing.

"No," she said seriously. "I don't want to, actually. But I sure as hell *mean* to, here and now. I'm going to worry about the wanting, afterward."

"Just about the sweetest setup in all the world," Allen Dulles said sadly. "And you blew it."

"I went to Russia for only one thing, Mr. Dulles, and you knew that," John said.

"Oh, sure. It just seems kind of sad . . . God knows what we're going to do with you now. It's going to be kind of difficult keeping up the advertising-executive image. But maybe it'll work. 'Advertising Executive Invades Russia to Rescue Niece.'

Good press, that. You're all set to be a national hero. As for Gregory . . ."

"He was the real hero, for getting us out of there," John said.

"Agreed. And he's being treated like one, too. In fact, as everyone is assuming that *he* is the secret agent, we may well have to give him a job. I don't know what your family feels about the situation . . ."

"My family is prepared to accept *any* situation, right this minute," John told him. "They're just happy we're all alive."

"Yeah. Well, that's great. Because sure as hell they're going to have to accept a marriage between those two. Like it or not . . . Well, now, it's all happened, after all. I guess we just have to wait and see."

"Any news?"

"Nothing concrete. Beria was not at Stalin's funeral, though. Officially stated as being unwell. That *could* be concrete. Ivan Nej was there. He's been made Commander of the KGB. You think that's a good thing?"

"No," John said. "But it was him or Anna, and he's the lesser of two evils."

"Let's hope you're right. Your father was on the rostrum too, so I guess he's made the transition okay. Maybe he can keep his brother in check."

"The point is, Mr. Dulles, they're both getting on. They'll have to bow out fairly soon. Anna is still young enough to be a threat for years. Any news of her?"

"Also absent from the funeral. But she has never made a habit of attending state occasions in the past, so it's difficult to assess just how important that is. As far as we can make out, Malenkov is the most likely choice for successor, but our people estimate there is going to be a good deal of jockeying for power for some time. Which is all to the good. Now tell me, do you think there's any chance that this Anna, being a little upset by your departure, may blow the whistle on you as one of our people?"

"We'll have to wait and see," John said. "Anna may not be in a position to blow the whistle on anyone."

Ivan Nej closed the observation window looking down on cell number forty-seven. He looked vaguely ill. "What have you done to her?" he asked. It was the first time in nine months that he had come to see his prisoner.

"There is not a mark on her body, comrade commissar," Maria Kalinova protested.

"I asked, what have you done to her?" Ivan's voice could still rasp.

Maria Kalinova instinctively stood at attention. "I used the water jet, comrade commissar."

"Your specialty," Ivan observed.

"I perfected it, sir," Maria agreed, with some pride. "It is very effective. It destroys people, and leaves no outward mark."

"And you never obtained a confession?"

Maria sighed. "No, comrade commissar. She would only curse me. And you. But does it matter? Comrade Beria confessed."

"No," Ivan said. "It does not matter."

He went down the steps, Maria at his back, followed by the head warden and four of her girls. He opened the door and gazed at the woman. The woman, he wondered? The old hag, crumpled on the floor. Anna's face had collapsed, and her hair, which he had never seen without that splendid sheen, that immaculate parting, was a tangled mat. Her skin was grayish. Yet she had not broken, not confessed. She had only cursed her tormentor, and himself. Because he had taught her to do only that.

"She must be clothed," he snapped.

"Of course, comrade commissar," Maria agreed, and summoned the waiting guards. They released Anna's wrists, pulled her away from the wall, and began to thrust clothes on to her.

Anna blinked at them without, apparently, comprehending what they were doing, and then located Ivan, and recognized him. "You have come to release me," she muttered. "You need me after all, Ivan. Russia needs me."

Ivan gazed at her. He had taken her from an orphanage when she was sixteen years old. She had known no other man but him, then. He had made her into an extension of himself, had discovered too late that she was even more ruthless, even more deadly than himself. But where had it got her? He was in command now, and she had destroyed herself. He could afford to be generous. "Yes, Anna," he said. "I have come to release you."

Anna sighed. "I am not well, Ivan. I have pain. . . . My belly hurts all the time, Ivan. Sometimes I weep with the pain. Me, weeping—would you believe it? I will soon be well again. But right now I would like a warm bath. I would like that more than anything else in the world. And some of my own clothes. And then I would like to rest for a while." Her gaze flickered past him, found Maria, and her face seemed to close, for just a second.

Ivan watched her in fascination. He had given her to this girl, Maria Kalinova, trained by Anna herself. And Maria had used her hose. What did she call it, the big prick? He could not imagine what Anna must have suffered, what her guts must indeed feel like, after Maria had had possession of her. And yet she could live, in her mind, and hope, and believe in the future, her future. That was the difference between her and Maria, a creature mindless in her viciousness.

He smiled at Anna. "You are going to rest for a very long time, Anna," he said. "You will enjoy your rest."

She was fully dressed, in the uniform of a colonel in the KGB. "Where do you wish me to go first?" she asked.

"These young ladies will show you," Ivan said. "You will go with them."

Anna nodded, and stepped toward the doorway.

Maria Kalinova smiled at Ivan. "I will confess, comrade commissar," she said, "that I will be much happier when it is done. With Anna Ragosina, one never knows if there *is* an end."

"There is an end," Ivan Nej said. "Even for Anna Ragosina. But I think it is time to make an end of all her creatures, as well." He snapped his fingers, and the other two women stepped next to Maria.

Her jaw dropped. "I do not understand," she said. "Comrade commissar, you promised . . ."

"I promised that you could interrogate Anna Ragosina," Ivan said. "You have enjoyed that privilege."

"But . . . I am a loyal servant of the state," Maria shouted. "I have been a loyal follower of you, comrade commissar!"

"That is true," Ivan said thoughtfully. "But you can never replace Anna Ragosina, Maria. And yet you would *try* to do so. That is the problem. You would try."

He walked out the door.

The senior warden had entered the cell. "Tie their wrists behind their backs," she commanded.

Anna gazed at her, uncomprehending.

"You cannot do this," Maria spat at her. "You cannot. I am—"

The warden stepped toward her and hit her, several times, on the face and on the body. Maria gasped, and doubled with pain, and nearly fell; the other girls grasped her shoulders to hold her up. Anna looked on with polite interest.

"You are fortunate, Maria Kalinova," the warden said, "that it is to be now. I would have enjoyed having *you* in here, for a few days. Even a few hours. You are fortunate."

The door was open, and now there were men waiting for them.

"You are to come with us, Comrade Ragosina," the captain said.

Anna made to move, and seemed to realize for the first time that her wrists were bound behind her back. Then she stepped forward.

Maria Kalinova burst into tears. "You cannot," she moaned. "You cannot."

Another door was waiting for them, to give admission into a courtyard. It was again winter, a December morning, and very cold; snow was falling. But the courtyard seemed crowded with armed men, and another prisoner was approaching from another doorway, his wrists also bound behind his back, his great bald head blue in the chill, his body trembling.

Anna looked at him. "You failed me, Lavrenti Pavlovich," she said.

"You failed *me,* you bitch," Beria snarled.

Anna shrugged, and turned away. Two of the guards showed her where to stand, and one produced a blindfold.

"That is not really necessary," Anna said. "I am not going to *die*."

The guard blinked at her, then gave his superior a hasty glance. The captain shook his head, stepped up to Beria in turn, and removed the pince-nez.

"Do not break them," Beria said. "Without them, I cannot see."

The captain nodded, and the blindfold was set in place.

"Please," Maria Kalinova begged. "There has been a dreadful mistake. *Please!*" Tears continued to dribble from beneath the blindfold, and her entire body shook.

Anna looked at the soldiers facing her, rifles at the ready, and then above them, at the window overlooking the courtyard, where Ivan stood.

"Silly girl," she said. "We are not going to *die*. We are on our way straight to hell. I am sure they will make me welcome there. But you . . . I am going to roast *you,* Maria Feodorovna, for all eternity." She looked up again at Ivan, and raised her voice. "I will wait for you, too, Ivan," she called. "I will *send* for you, as soon as I am there."

She saw the captain's arm move, and made her face smile, and was hit by a million hammers, all at once.

Catherine Nej poured Ivan a glass of vodka. She did not like the little man, but he was her brother-in-law, and tonight even Michael seemed glad to see him. In fact, the two brothers had worked very closely together over the past nine months. They, along with Molotov, had been the old guard, carefully admitting the new guard to executive power. She had been worried; she had indeed been terrified. But Michael had explained that these new men, Malenkov and Khrushchev and Bulganin, *needed* people like Ivan and himself to complete the transition to power in an orderly fashion. And as usual, Michael had been proved right.

And now it was done. The last of the trials was ended, and the last of those traitors who would have subverted the state were dead. She stood behind the two men as they relaxed with their vodka, and watched the evening news. "Now at last," the newscaster said, "the ringleaders of the plot have been brought to justice. This afternoon, in the courtyard of Lubianka Prison, Lavrenti Pavlovich Beria, erstwhile commander of the KGB"—Beria's photograph was flashed on the screen, his face large and urbane, his pince-nez firmly on his nose—"his accomplice, Anna Petrovna Ragosina, a traitor whose crimes are legendary"—Anna's madonna face appeared, staring innocently at them—"together with their principal female assistant, Maria Feodorovna Kalinova"—there was no photo of Maria—"were executed by firing squad. Thus perish all who would oppose the will of the Soviet people, the Soviet state."

Michael leaned forward and switched off the television set.

His glass was empty, and Catherine hastily refilled it.

"I am sorry they showed her photograph," Ivan said.

"It must have been taken some years ago," Michael observed.

"Of course. But it makes you remember what a beautiful woman she was."

Michael studied him. "Were you ever in love with her, Ivan Nikolaievich?"

Ivan started, and flushed. "No. No, of course not. But I could appreciate her beauty." He sighed. "You know, I feel as if an entire era has come to an end."

"It has," Michael agreed. "The Stalinist era did not end with the death of Stalin. It could only end with the elimination of the last of those who thrived under his rule."

Ivan's head turned somewhat sharply.

Michael smiled. "Oh, I include you and me in that, Ivan. But we are old men. Our time will soon come. I am only sorry that Gregory and John turned out so badly. It would have been so good to have them here now."

"Bah," Ivan said. "Hayman was never anything more than Anna's creature. And Gregory . . ." He sighed. "The Americans obviously got at him. We are better off without them, Michael Nikolaievich."

"Perhaps," Michael acknowledged. "But I still think it is a pity. On the other hand, it has been a good life, on the whole, wouldn't you say? Who would have thought, when you cleaned the boots and I polished the silver in Port Arthur or at Starogan, that we would be able to sit here like this, nearly fifty years later, and be able to remember so much? When I think—"

"Of the Japanese shells, bursting over Port Arthur," Ivan said. "Do you remember sheltering in the cellar, with the old Countess Borodina, and Ilona and Tatiana? How afraid they all were?"

"*We* all were," Michael corrected. "But do you remember Moscow, in 1907? The secret meetings? No, you were not there. That was where I first saw Lenin. We thought then that the revolution was about to start."

"Tattie's birthday party, in 1914," Ivan said thoughtfully. "Both the Stein girls were there, and then the Princess Irina, Peter's wife, came home and threw them out. I could have hit her. But you were already hiding in Switzerland, Michael."

"With Lenin," Michael reminded him.

"I remember marching off to war," Ivan said darkly. "I remember the German machine guns, and the shells, and my wooden rifle." He chuckled. "But I remember coming home again, too."

"Yes," Michael said. He did not wish to reminisce about the massacre at Starogan.

"And then the war against the Whites," Ivan said. "We fought shoulder to shoulder then, Michael, against Denikin and Borodin."

Again, Michael merely nodded, because by then the revolution had already been going wrong. He knew this; he had known it then. However, he had supported Lenin and then Stalin with all the loyalty that was innate in him. His family had always served; his father had been born a serf. But he had served the very highest, and accompanied them to the heights, even if one step behind. Russian noblemen or Bolshevik revolutionaries, they had all been capable of terrible things, things he had recognized at the time to be terrible; but he had still served. As he had served Stalin, even during the years when Stalin's policies had meant employing people like Anna Ragosina, and the man sitting beside him, and turning them loose to destroy all who would oppose him. If there was any justice in this world, Ivan would also have stood against that wall this morning. And perhaps he himself should also have been there. He was an accessory, at the very least.

But that was bourgeois thinking. They had survived because not only had they learned early the art of survival, but because they were important. More important than Anna Ragosina or Lavrenti Beria.

"Great days," Ivan mused. "But there are a few of them left. Do you know, all my life I have dreamed of commanding the KGB. All of my life Stalin promised me that, one day. And he never honored that promise."

Because he knew you for what you are, Michael thought, thinking of the frightened little man he had gone to find in Tomsk. He wondered if Anna Ragosina would not have been better off to be left in Tomsk, with her black-marketeers and her subversives?

"But now it is mine," Ivan said, his eyes gleaming behind his spectacles. "Did not someone once say, everything comes to him who waits?"

"Yes," Michael said. "I think it may even have been the Bible."

Ivan laughed. "So perhaps there is a God. But He is a God of the strong, eh, Michael? Do you know, I have a suspicion that Anna Ragosina believed in God, or a devil. Catherine, some more vodka. I will tell you, I wish to celebrate. I wish to get drunk. I will admit that as long as Anna lived and breathed, even in a cell in Lubianka, I could not rid my mind of the fear that she would somehow rise up and strike me down, yet again. Even when I saw the bullets hitting her, watched the blood spurting from her body. I went down into the courtyard and stood above her for several minutes, waiting for her to start breathing again, and get up, and smile that smile of hers, and say to me, 'Well, Ivan, what are you going to try next?'" He shivered, and Catherine refilled his glass.

"Her last words," Ivan continued, "were that she would never die. She was merely being translated to another life, in hell. And that she would send for me to join her there. What a monster."

"You will make yourself ill," Michael said. "She *is* dead. She cannot harm you now. That is one fact about the dead. They are gone forever." But in view of the conversation, even he sat up with a start, the hairs on his neck seeming to bristle, when a knock sounded on the door.

Ivan was also sitting up. "Who can that be?" His voice trembled.

Michael forced a smile, slapped his brother on the shoulder. "At least you know that it cannot be Anna Ragosina, Ivan Nikolaievich." He got up, waved Catherine back, and went to the door, aware that his heart was pounding. He opened the door and frowned at the man who stood there. The stranger was middle-aged, short, somewhat overweight, and wore horn-rimmed spectacles. His clothes were threadbare and dirty, as were his fingernails. His unkempt air was increased by the fact that he was either drunk or under the influence of some enormous emotion.

"Yes?" Michael asked.

"Will you not let me in, Uncle Michael?"

Michael's frown deepened, yet he was slowly recognizing the face. "Nikolai?" he asked. "Nikolai Ivanovich? My God! Come in, my dear fellow. Come in." He stood back, turned to look at Ivan. "Ivan, Nikolai is here."

"Nikolai?" Ivan rose to his feet and gaped at his eldest living son. "Nikolai? What are you doing here?"

"I came to see you, Father," Nikolai said. "I went to your apartment, and they told me you were here. So I came. I wished to see you, too, Uncle." He glanced at Michael.

"Well, sit down, my dear fellow," Michael said. "Catherine, some vodka for Nikolai Ivanovich. You have never met my wife, Nikolai. Catherine, this is Ivan's son, Nikolai."

"Nikolai," Ivan muttered, clearly confused. "But . . . after all these years, have you come to see me? What about?"

"I have come to kill you, Father," Nikolai explained very quietly, and drew the revolver from his inside pocket.

"To—" Ivan's voice rose into a scream.

Michael turned toward the younger man, and was checked by the barrel moving in his direction.

"For Anna," Nikolai said, and squeezed the trigger twice. The bullets smashed into Ivan Nej's breast and sent him tumbling backward across the sofa and onto the floor.

"We were lovers," Nikolai said, and turned the gun on Michael. "And you killed her."

Michael put up his hands, as if he could catch the bullet, was suddenly breathless, and discovered he was lying on the floor.

Catherine screamed, as shouting came from outside. Nikolai looked at the woman for several seconds, then said, "Goodbye, Comrade Nej." He placed the revolver muzzle to his own ear and squeezed the trigger.

Catherine stood absolutely still, while the door burst open, and men and women stared at the scene with their mouths open. Then she knelt beside her husband. "Michael," she said. "Oh, Michael."

Michael's smile was twisted. "From beyond the grave," he whispered. "She sent someone to fetch us." And then he died.

Sunday lunch at Cold Spring Harbor. The largest Sunday lunch they had had for some time, and the happiest, even with Nona Nej sitting next to Ilona. Or perhaps because of Nona Nej.

What did she feel about her father's death? How much had she always known about her father's life, and that of his brother? A great deal, George suspected, and thus she must have known that those who rule by force almost always die by force, in the end. She had wept, but not excessively. Perhaps because she had already made up her mind never to return to Russia.

Her mother would know the truth, of course, because the story, as released by the Soviet news agency, Tass, was too absurd to be believed by anyone. According to Tass, Ivan and Michael Nej, together with Ivan's son Nikolai, had been drinking, had got drunk, had quarreled, and somehow managed to shoot each other so that all three had died. The news agency had suggested that this was a fitting end for three members of the old guard.

Which meant, George knew, that their deaths might even have been an execution. But somehow he did not think so. Yet they had died on the day Anna Ragosina and Lavrenti Beria were shot. Could that have been coincidence?

He wondered if Catherine would mourn her husband and her brother-in-law. If so, she and Nona would be the only ones. He looked at John, sitting next to his Natasha, with Alex and Olga playing around them. John had merely looked him in the eye, and made no comment when the news had arrived. His face had been sad, but there had been no real grief. John had respected his father, but had never loved him. And to John, what had happened was inevitable, and had been for a long time.

He looked at Gregory, sitting next to Felicity, a laughing, smiling Felicity, such as they had not seen in a very long while, had indeed despaired of ever seeing again. To see Felicity like that made up for a great deal. Hers was an absurd love, even, in some states, an illegal one. But was not love too profound an emotion to be criticized in such terms?

And what did Gregory think of *his* father's death? There had certainly been no regret there. Was that unnatural? George did not think so, in the special circumstances that applied to Gregory. He counted the boy as a third son, now. He was content with his three sons.

He looked at George junior and Elizabeth. There was happiness! But there was something more, too, because they had had too easy a life, up to now. It was not something he would say to any member of his family, but he knew it was true. George junior had been born to millions, and Elizabeth Dodge had been born to beauty and talent, and had come to the millions early enough. They might have lived their entire lives as two of those elevated people for whom the traumas which ordinary folk had to suffer and survive had no meaning. Then tragedy had reached out and stroked them with its icy fingers, before relenting. Yet the touch had been enough, and they would both be better people for it.

And Diana? The same thing could be said for her, casually. But it would never have been true, he thought. Unlike her parents, she had been aware from the beginning how empty the life of an heiress can be, and she had sought her salvation down some unlikely and even dingy pathways, before being overtaken by a descent into hell itself. He looked at her, sitting next to her Robert, still both as contented with each other as if they were newlyweds. Physically, she had aged prematurely, but had lost nothing in beauty for that, while the premature aging of her mind had *created* beauty. Of them all, even John, Diana had looked the most pensive when the news of Anna Ragosina's death had been announced. "She deserved to die," she had said. "I wonder what she thought at the end?"

No one would ever know, George reflected, what had happened between Diana and Anna in that prison cell. And no one deserved to know.

And lastly, he looked down the table at Ilona. As always, whatever had happened to individual members of this family had happened to her as well. In the beginning, she had abandoned her home and position to flee to her lover. Then, returning to be reconciled, she had been caught up in the horror of the war and the revolution, and had again come face to face with the man who had fathered her eldest son. After the war, Ivan's grim talons had reached out to pluck her back, unsuccessfully. Her role during the Second World War had been more muted, but following that had come the trauma of Gregory and Felicity, now so happily resolved.

And now Michael was dead by violence. As was her brother Peter, shot down by her own son. But like John, had she not always known that such an end was inevitable, for them both? She had said that no Borodin had ever died in bed since 1905. That was true. But she was going to die in her bed, in the fullness of her years. He would see to that.

As if she read his thoughts, she caught his gaze, and held it down the length of the table, and blew him a kiss. Fifty years, and they were all together at the end. Those who had survived.